The Basker Twins in the 31st Century

Danger at the Clone Academy

by

APRIL 2016

Kristi Wright

Dear Parinita :
I had such a grand time writing
a story with you and your class!
Happy Reading ☺

Kristi Wright

"The Basker Twins in the 31ˢᵗ Century: Danger at the Clone Academy," by Kristi Wright. ISBN 978-1-60264-045-0.

Library of Congress Control Number: 2007933258.

Published 2007 by Virtualbookworm.com Publishing Inc., P.O. Box 9949, College Station, TX 77842, US. ©2007, Kristi Wright. All rights reserved. No part of this publication may be reproduced, stored in a retrieval system, or transmitted in any form or by any means, electronic, mechanical, recording or otherwise, without the prior written permission of Kristi Wright.

Manufactured in the United States of America.

For Sarah, because you are so very precious to me. Thank you for believing in me and this story, which was written for you. Special thanks to Aunt Theresa for making my dream possible. I miss you. Deep gratitude to my parents, Liz and Cliff, and my wonderful husband, Dan—thanks so much for your unwavering love and support. I love you!

And finally, here's to you Matt. In my future, Friedreich's ataxia is a thing of the past.

PROLOGUE
Dastardly Mr. Snickers

Life was quite civilized in the year 3002 E.C. (Earth Calendar). War had been outlawed in the Milky Way Galaxy for two hundred years. Violent crime was nearly non-existent; so were homelessness, excessive poverty, and religious intolerance. No species had gone extinct in one hundred and forty-four years. Disease was all but eradicated. And only historians knew the meaning of the word smog.

Best of all, in 2897 humankind rediscovered the secret to creating a no-calorie chocolate that satisfied all but the most persnickety of tastes.

Life was sweet.

For five years in a row, Earth had been voted the second best planet in the galaxy to raise a family, and all the nations of Earth were excessively proud of that title. They were determined to dethrone Glagcha, the current Milky Way Galaxy champion, through a planet-wide campaign labeled "Gotcha Glagcha." Someday, who knew, they might even be able to place strongly in the inter-galactic survey. If only the Xlexuri Galaxy, which held spots one through sixty-two, would get sucked into a black hole.

But there were still lower members of the human species who remained greedy for more. It wasn't enough to be healthy and to have the promise of a long, productive life. It wasn't enough to live in a world of peace, a sphere of beauty. Even no-cal chocolate couldn't make these individuals happy.

Some people didn't want to just live in such a paradise; they wanted to own it. For some, power was still prized above all. And virtual currency was power. The more you had, the more you owned.

At times, officers in the Cyborg Police Squad were forced to step in and reprimand the worst of these offenders. For greed could not be tolerated on this world. Not if Earth was going to be voted best planet in the Galaxy any time in this millennium.

On the morning of April 12, 3002, Cyborg Officer Lilituck paid a visit to just such a culprit.

"Sir, it is my grave duty to inform you that your time travel days are over." The officer folded her arms and narrowed her eyes in displeasure. Half human, half processor, she was perpetually tapped into the Galactic Knowledge Bank and knew down to the virtual penny how much profit this perpetrator had gained through his illegal activities. He had zero chance of escaping her. All of her reflexes had been enhanced and her muscle magnified by a power of ten. No one messed with a cyborg officer of law.

"Is this some kind of Slarmi joke?" asked the troublemaker. The Slarmians were known throughout the universe for their practical jokes. "What about my research?"

Officer Lilituck laughed humorlessly. "Research, pah! You're nothing but a petty cheat, tampering with the past with no thought to the consequences. How dare you take so lightly the heavy responsibility of time travel? How dare you abuse your privilege? Don't you realize that your actions could cause the Galactic Council to rethink time travel exploration? Because of you, whole fields of study could be abolished. Worse, this world could lose its status as second best planet in the galaxy. *You irresponsible fool.*"

She stepped closer, raised her silver hand, pulled back his shirt, and pressed her palm against his bare shoulder. He gasped. Standing back, she watched a colorless, glutinous substance seep into his pores until it disappeared altogether.

"You are now tagged. We will know where and when you go. You cannot escape us," she flasered him with her sternest look, "so don't even try. Your plastic scavenging days are over. If I hear so much as a hint of even one unexplained mint condition Barbie showing up on the collectors' grid, I'll be on you like slime on a bogdog from Sleztar."

Backing up even further, she let her gaze drift to the far wall as she spoke to her distant partner, "Officer Gelarg, please remove me and the confiscated time travel vehicle from this vlem's presence."

Over four hundred years ago, the Vlemutz humanoid species had unsuccessfully attempted to wipe out all of mankind on Earth. The seventy-five year war had been followed by a two-hundred year long Age of Darkness and Despair, and only in the last two hundred years had Earth managed to flourish again. There were no worse insults in the English language than "vlem" or "vlemutz."

Without another glance at the man, she and an ancient gray beat-up 1988 Honda Civic that had been converted to a state-of-the-art time travel machine were transported to Cyborg Police headquarters. She only wished she had been granted the authority to take the criminal in, but this was his first proven offense, and the people of Earth prided themselves on being both tolerant and compassionate.

She, however, would be watching him.

Left behind to contemplate his crime, the man in question craned his neck to look at the spot where the cyborg had inserted her tag, then stared thoughtfully at the priceless tapestry hanging on his office wall. He drummed his fingers on the one-of-a-kind, carved wood throne-room chair. Over fifteen hundred years old, the item was still in mint condition. Since wood was protected on planet Earth in the year 3002, wood furniture could no longer be replicated. One was forced to go to the source. And that source was the past.

He'd been lucky up until now, but that luck had dried up.

Now he would have to rely on wit alone. He grinned, revealing a perfect set of pearly white teeth, none of which were those he'd grown as a boy. He'd had them regenerated ten years ago.

The power, prestige, and virtual currency he would derive from his next foray into crime would be that much sweeter now that the stakes had been heightened. He selected and bit into a no-cal chocolate to celebrate, but it wasn't quite as satisfying as a candy bar, or even better, a dark chocolate truffle from the twenty-first century. For him, it wasn't because caloric chocolate tasted better—it was just so much more satisfying to eat something forbidden. He should have smuggled more of the real thing in on his last trip to the past.

"System, please locate Mr. Kisses for me. Tell him Mr. Snickers is anxious for a little chat." He wasn't worried about the police overhearing his conversation. His crime hadn't been grave enough for them to be given the authority to violate his privacy to that extent. Cyborg police had an enhanced sense of honor, which could be used to their disadvantage.

On his desk under a soft spotlight, a miniature man suddenly appeared sitting in a tiny nanofiber chair. Mr. Snickers derived much pleasure from configuring Mr. Kisses as small as possible.

It gave him such a lovely sense of power. On the slim chance that a cyborg officer of law would one day confiscate Mr. Snickers' log, the man wore a ceremonial Pallaccii mask to protect his identity. The Pallaccii lived three galaxies away and were known for their extravagant parties. This man was no Pallaccii.

"You rang, Mr. Snickers?"

Mr. Snickers knew that as an extra safety precaution, the voice was disguised as well, as was his.

"I did indeed. Mr. Kisses, it appears that my traveling days are temporarily on hold."

The man settled more comfortably into his chair, resting the ankle of one leg across the bent knee of the other. "You must be devastated."

"That I am." The man, who called himself Mr. Snickers, cracked the knuckles of his left hand, then his right. "I have a list of no fewer than sixty clients anxious to transfer vast sums of virtual currency to me for a rare and whimsical plastic from the twenty-first century. I would be delighted to share my wealth with the right partner. You come highly recommended by our mutual friend, who is unfortunately unable at this time to lend me aid on this particular project."

"I've shown myself to be made of the right stuff in the past." The man who was known as Mr. Kisses picked up a water vial sitting on the miniature table next to him and sipped. "Of course, since I will be taking all the risks, I'll expect a generous portion of the profits."

"I'm a reasonable man," Mr. Snickers replied, dipping his head. "You may have twenty percent."

"Fifty-fifty is more what I had in mind."

Mr. Snickers laughed heartily, then his eyes narrowed to dangerous slits. "Thirty percent for you, and you'll be grateful for it."

"You strike a hard bargain," Mr. Kisses said amiably, apparently unfazed by the underlying threat in Mr. Snickers' words, "but I accept your terms. So which Barbie do they want now?"

Mr. Snickers shook his head. "Barbies are rather hot at present. I have something else in mind—something equally rare, equally plastic, and equally desirable. I think your situation will lend itself beautifully to our endeavor."

Mr. Kisses leaned back with his hands clasped behind his head. "I'm all ears."

As Mr. Snickers filled him in, Mr. Kisses began to laugh softly. "Nothing could be simpler."

"I need the items no later than two weeks from now."

"No problem, Mr. Snickers, no problem at all."

"There better be no problem. Understand me well. I make a very good friend, Mr. Kisses. But you don't want me as an enemy."

CHAPTER 1
The Basker Twins' Very Bad Day

Moods were particularly cranky in the Basker family's Utility Hover Vehicle on the morning of the parents' "Secret Mission", as twelve-year-old Elsie chose to call it with rolled eyes and fingers curling quote marks in the air.

"Mom and Dad are going on a..." drawn-out pause, "Secret Mission," she had told her friends. "So we have to go to Uncle Fredrick's boarding school for clones."

The moans and screeches had been deafening.

Her twin brother, Everest, refused to say a single word about the changes that were being thrust upon them, but Elsie knew he was as unhappy as she was.

It wasn't that they had anything against clones, but flasers, they didn't want to leave their friends and live with their rule-obsessed, fusty uncle who smelled like rotting vegetables. And they didn't exactly like the idea of everyone assuming they, too, had been birthed from a single cell in some sterile vial. It was already weird enough to share the same brown skin and hair, the same almond-shaped blue eyes, the same height, even the same nose. Being twins was bad enough; being labeled clones would be social suicide.

But the absolute worst thing about their parents' "secret mission" was suddenly being parent-less. Sure Mom and Dad were the most cerebrum-heavy geeks in the galaxy, and Elsie and Everest wouldn't have been normal kids if they hadn't done their best to ignore their very existence. But that didn't give them the right to just pick up and leave!

"Mom," Elsie moaned from the back of the UHV, "how many days did you say this mission is going to take?"

"Deng," Everest muttered, finally joining the conversation, "you've asked her four thousand three hundred and fifty-two times, yocto-brain. She already told you they'd be gone at least six months."

Elsie glared and jabbed him in the side. "Shut down, twenty-first-century throwback!"

"Elsie, don't tell your brother to shut down," their mother, Justine Basker, snapped, her patience stretched to the breaking point. "If you must, use 'power down.' It's more polite."

Everest snickered and mouthed, "yocto-brain."

As if she had eyes in the back of her head, their mother added, "Both of you can stop your name-calling this instant or, so help me, I'll eject you from this vehicle."

Since they were whizzing along the hoverway at 300 kilometers per hour using the commuter height, which was twenty meters above the single occupant vehicles, neither Elsie nor Everest took her threat seriously, but they did return to sullen silence.

Elsie heard her parents swivel their chairs around, but she kept her eyes down and pretended intense fascination with the blur of see-through vehicles as they bumped, weaved, stretched, and shrunk. She clutched the scruff of Pooker, her pet bobcat, who also stared unblinkingly at the traffic below, equally disgruntled. As domesticated as bobcats had become over the past five hundred years, they still preferred open spaces.

"You know," their mom said after a few minutes of silence, "there was a time when it was dangerous for vehicles to bump into each other while in transit."

"We *know*, mom," Elsie responded. "We read all about it in ancient history." Now she concentrated on the pretty moss lanes underneath the flying vehicles. Planned rain must have fallen last night. The moss was a particularly rich shade of green, and the never-ending lines of yellow glow sparkled.

"Then I suppose you can tell me why on-world travel is so safe today?"

Elsie groaned. "Because hover vehicles are designed for safety."

"Yes, but *how* do we have the technology necessary to design such safe vehicles?"

"Flasers, who cares?"

"Everest, would you like to help Elsie with the answer?" asked their dad.

Everest shrugged and mumbled, "Because someone invented it."

"Exactly. You're alive and well today because of the hard work and sacrifice of generations of scientists that culminated in the invention and application of jellach."

Elsie desperately wished her parents would shut down. She was already miserable enough without having to deal with a lecture on history.

"Science matters," their mom said. "The research your father and I are doing matters."

"Sure, Mom." Maybe if they agreed with her, she'd stop droning on.

"We hate to leave you, but our work is important... to our world and to others. The hardest thing we've ever had to do is leave you behind. We love you so much."

Their mom placed one hand over Elsie's and the other over Everest's, then their dad placed his larger calloused hands on top. Elsie peeked at her brother and was slightly cheered by the fact that he was obviously embarrassed by their parents' display of affection.

"Let's not forget that Baskers can handle anything." Their dad chuckled halfheartedly. "At least we didn't send you to boarding school on Mars."

Elsie rolled her eyes. "You so don't get it! If we'd been sent to an off-world boarding school, our friends would have thought we were zeller. Instead, they pity us."

"Your uncle's school isn't so bad. From an educational perspective, you couldn't ask for better."

"Like that's a selling point," Everest mumbled. School was just the time he had to endure between sports.

"We have a gift for each of you—for good luck."

Elsie perked up slightly and exchanged glances with her brother, who also had straightened from his habitual slump.

"Sorry, Everest, our gift may be kind of a letdown for you." Their mom reached into an inner pocket. "Hold out your hands."

Elsie shot out hers, but Everest was reluctant. When he finally offered his hand, their mom dropped something warm to the touch on both of their palms.

"Mom!" Elsie gasped at the exact same moment that Everest groaned with disgust.

"Jewelry?" he moaned. "You've got to be kidding."

"Not exactly jewelry," their dad said.

"Mom, Dad," Elsie said, "don't listen to him. They're beautiful. Besides," she wiggled her eyebrows, "Everest looks great in jewelry." She cracked up as he jabbed her with his elbow. Guys wore just as much jewelry as girls did in 3002, but

Everest didn't like to wear anything that wasn't directly related to sports. Plus, the necklaces were a little too pretty for his taste.

"Don't tease your brother. As your father said, they are not exactly jewelry."

They were disks, 2.3 centimeters wide and a purplish-silver in color. In the middle of each disk there was something like an ancient keyhole. An intricate pattern of interweaving lines had been etched along the outer rim of each disk. The charms hung from sturdy silver chains.

"These are special," their mother added hesitantly, "made out of a very rare alloy. Keep them with you as much as possible. Wear them if you can, but keep them hidden under your shirts. It's important that you don't lose them, and it's best if they stay secret. There may come a day when a Dr. Stephen Yee shows up, wanting to talk to you about these disks. You can trust him." She didn't add that if Dr. Yee arrived, that meant *they* were presumed dead. "Do I have your promises that you will keep these safe?"

"Of course," Elsie said clearly, whereas Everest's "Yeah" was barely audible and filled with disgust. They both slid the disks over their heads, but while Elsie continued to admire hers, Everest shoved his underneath his shirt.

"Your father is right. We Baskers can handle anything, even living apart."

Something about their mother's tone brought Elsie's attention back to her parents. Even though they both wore reassuring smiles, Elsie sensed that their mom, at least, was close to tears.

"We'll be fine." Elsie forced a smile. "It'll be an adventure."

CHAPTER 2
A Painful Goodbye

Fredrick Lester-Hauffer, Justine Basker's much older half-brother, was both founder and chief administrator of the *Academy of Superior Learning*. For over sixty years he had presided over the school, which catered particularly and almost exclusively to "children of the clone persuasion," as he liked to refer to them. Due to strict laws and astronomically high costs, cloning remained quite rare. The use of clone technology required no less than approval from the United Nations of Earth, and prohibitive royalty payments to the original were mandated. In the year 3002 EC, less than one thousandth of one percent of the population was cloned. And a good number of that group had done time behind the walls of this academy.

Elsie's first impression of her uncle's boarding school was better than she had anticipated. It was a large estate surrounded by an ancient tevta wall, a smooth as glass lavender substance that she vaguely remembered had been popular right before the first Vlemutz invasion almost five hundred years ago. The gate into the academy was engraved tevta depicting a herd of running horses, their manes flying in an invisible wind. What must it have been like when herds of horses had roamed free?

How had this place survived the Vlemutz attacks? In history last year, she'd learned that at least eighty percent of all the buildings in the Northern California Bay Area had been leveled by that monstrous race. It had taken hundreds of years for Earth to recover from that invasion and regain a level of sophistication.

The extensive gardens were meticulously groomed, and a combination of April sunshine and regularly scheduled nighttime rain had them bursting with new growth and vibrant with color. Fragrant flowers made the place smell pretty too. In the middle of the property, a large tevta building loomed, a simple rectangle with two identical towers, the mirror-like walls perfectly smooth, reflecting the day's beauty and the garden's charms. Other smaller buildings dotted the landscape, but the towers drew the eye.

In silence, the Baskers walked up a jewel-toned gravel path, Elsie and Everest exchanging nervous glances. For reassurance, Elsie kept her hand on Pooker's silky head.

The few times Uncle Fredrick had chosen to visit them, he had shown an avid desire to, well, groom them. Specks of dust had been brushed off their shoulders; smudges had been bluntly pointed out. Last time, he'd gone so far as to request that Elsie do something with her hair before joining them for dinner. Then he had lectured them on the virtues of cleanliness and tidiness. For an hour! Living with Uncle Fredrick would be about as much fun as growing teeth replacements—over and over again.

Since this was a Wednesday during school hours, they didn't have to deal immediately with the other students. Elsie had never met a clone before. She didn't think Everest had either. Once, a scientist had come to their school and lectured then on the topic of yocto physics. Afterward, the hot rumor had been that he was a clone of a famous physicist from the twenty-ninth century. She had never been sure whether the story was true or not.

They reached the massive front door, another intricate example of engraved tevta and, sensing their presence and identity, the door dissolved to allow their entry. On the other side, a hologram of their uncle stood in greeting, his lips turned up slightly in a stiff smile. He had the same excessive height and hunched shoulders, the same pinched nose, sunken cheekbones and narrow, dirty brown eyes. He even managed to give off a slight but nasty odor. But the shimmery quality around his edges clued them in to him being a hologram. Plus, he looked a little handsomer than Elsie remembered her uncle being, as if he'd been enhanced, though not nearly enough.

His eyes widened when he saw the bobcat. "Welcome, please come with me to the second floor."

Since Elsie didn't know whether the hologram merely emulated her uncle or provided him with a steady stream of information, she suppressed the desire to grimace at Everest.

The entrance hall was spacious, with distinctive light murals on the two side walls. On the far end was an impressive staircase. The floors were tevta, too, with a thin slip-proof jellach coating. The hologram led them across the room and up the main staircase to the first landing. He escorted them down a long corridor, pointing out the staff room and library in a mini tour. When he reached Uncle Fredrick's office, he requested admittance, then as the door rearranged its atoms for entry, he disappeared with a slight bow.

Behind the door were Uncle Fredrick and two other adults, a woman of indeterminate age with curly black hair and a rather large nose, wearing a silver pantsuit, and a young very handsome man in blue vlatex who could have been mistaken for a student. He had milk chocolate skin, high cheekbones and auburn hair. Elsie found herself staring. When he smiled at her, her cheeks got hot, which really was embarrassing. She hoped Everest hadn't noticed. The last thing she needed was to give him something new to tease her about.

"Welcome, welcome." Uncle Fredrick rubbed his hands together as he crossed the room. "Let me take a look at my young niece and nephew. So grown up since I last saw you."

Elsie felt as if he studied her under a quarkscope, and it was all she could do not to stick out her tongue and cross her eyes. Instead, she sucked in her breath in defense against his strong smell and focused behind him on tevta shelves that held an extensive collection of perfectly lined-up Vlemutz invasion miniatures. No question about it, the hologram's appearance had been zetta-enhanced. Why in the universe were they stuck with this suzo-shrimp as their guardian? Wasn't there anybody else?

"Elsinor," he said, waggling his finger, "posture, posture..." He leaned forward and flicked something off her shoulder.

She flasered him with her eyes, but he had already turned his attention to her brother.

"And Everest, my good man, I hear you will be an excellent addition to the Academy's skyball team. Most impressive height." He bobbed his head to punctuate his words.

What about her? Elsie thought. She was her brother's equal in any sport.

Everest mumbled an indecipherable response, his expression pained.

With relief, Elsie realized that Uncle Fredrick had switched his attention over to their parents.

"Justine and George, as robust as ever, I see," he said. "Let me assure you, Elsinor and Everest will be well taken care of while they are under my academy's roof."

"We do appreciate that, Fredrick."

Elsie's jaw dropped at her mother's relieved and even grateful response. What was it with adults? Why didn't her parents see what she and Everest had seen immediately? Their uncle was a freakazoid alien.

Uncle Fredrick motioned over the other two people in the room. "Justine, George, do let me introduce you to a couple of my staff members. Instructor Sura," he pointed to the large-nosed woman, "is my right hand in charge of students and staff. The efficient day-to-day running of this academy is largely due to her competence. And this," he gestured again, "is Instructor Gerard. He is responsible for our enrichment programs—sports, field trips, dances, theatricals. Since he's come on board we've become quite well-known for such programs. The rest of the staff is with the children right now, but they come with the highest of credentials and recommendations."

"We're pleased to make your acquaintance," Elsie's father said mildly, leading them all to shake hands and exchange light pleasantries.

Once the conversation had dried up, there was an awkward pause. Then Uncle Fredrick added, "I take it your research has gone well?"

Elsie thought her parents looked a little startled. Finally, her father said, "We're cautiously optimistic about our progress."

"Excellent. If you need a safe haven to store your backup notes while you are gone, look no further. We have exceptional security. You could do no better."

"We appreciate the offer," Elsie's mom said, "but we've already made arrangements."

For some reason, her mother's response seemed to irritate her uncle. It was odd how someone's eyes could harden and cool. Elsie couldn't wait to discuss his reaction later with Everest.

"I see," Uncle Fredrick replied. "Perhaps you should tell me these arrangements, in the unlucky event that something untoward happens."

Elsie's hands fisted. How dare he even think such a thing, let alone say it? Why didn't her dad get angry? She could have screamed when he just smiled and answered that safety precautions already had been taken.

Uncle Fredrick took a while to respond, and when he did, he simply said, "Excellent," again, his thin nose pinched. He glanced down at Pooker, then back at Elsie's mom. "And what arrangements have you made for your animal?"

Elsie clutched Pooker's scruff and sought her mother's eye, panic doing an odd sort of stomp in her belly. She felt rather than saw Everest draw near. Sensing her distress, Pooker gave a very low growl.

Her mother replied evenly, "We had assumed that Pooker would remain here with Elsie and Everest. She's suited up with the latest pico-trainer, which makes her extraordinarily well-behaved."

Their uncle shook his head emphatically, conjuring a mournful expression. "I'm sorry, that is out of the question. Pets are forbidden."

"I'm not leaving Pooker!" Elsie shouted. She swung to her parents. "You can't make me. If Pooker goes, I go."

Uncle Fredrick's tone changed immediately. "Now, now, let's not get carried away. Elsie, do calm down. I realize you are attached, but how will it look to the other students if I let my own niece have a pet while forbidding my other boarders the same pleasure? Surely, you don't wish me to show favoritism?"

"I'm not staying here without Pooker." They were asking too much. First, the loss of her parents and friends, then the loss of her pet? She told her bobcat all of her deepest secrets, things she had never told another human soul, not even her twin. She swallowed back tears, determined not to cry.

Her mother sighed. "I'm sorry, Fredrick, we should have anticipated this. We'll just have to rethink our plans, delay our assignment for a couple of days until we can find another situation that is more flexible on the issue of animals."

"Let's not be hasty," Instructor Gerard inserted smoothly. "Perhaps we can contrive a suitable arrangement."

Uncle Fredrick's lips barely moved as he asked, "What do you have in mind, Gerard?"

"What if we include the bobcat as an enrichment program? Make it the B12 pet? We could settle it somewhere in the garden. I suspect the children would be thrilled to learn about one of our more unusual domesticated beasts."

His gleaming smile directed full-force at Elsie made her forget to be annoyed by his use of the word "it" in reference to Pooker, as if she were an inanimate object.

Instead, she responded weakly, "Pooker sleeps with me. She always has. She'll be miserable sleeping outside."

"You'll see the creature every day," Gerard replied cajolingly.

"What do you mean by B12 pet?" Elsie asked.

The instructor looked a little taken aback, then he chuckled pleasantly. "I'm sorry; we're so used to our terminology here at the academy, we forget when we use a word that is not widely known. Since we board children from the time they are born, we have our own way of classifying them for their learning programs. A0 through A6 include newborns through six-year-olds, B7 through B12 comprise our middle years, which consist of seven-year-olds through twelve-year-olds, and then there are the senior children, classified as C13 through C18. You and Everest will, of course, be included in our B12 program. And therefore, the bobcat will be the B12 pet."

"Elsie," her mom interjected, her eyes pleading, "what do you think? Could you make this compromise work? We don't want you to be miserable."

It was her parents' duty to go on this assignment. She would feel horrible if she made their mission even more difficult.

"I guess so," she agreed reluctantly.

"Excellent notion, Instructor Gerard," Uncle Fredrick said, but something in his tone and the way his eyelids flickered made Elsie think he wasn't actually thrilled by the suggestion.

At her side, her brother was even more quiet than usual.

Too soon, it was time for them to say goodbye to their parents. Now Elsie couldn't stop her tears from flowing, but it didn't seem to matter. Her mom's eyes were all watery, and her brother cleared his throat over and over.

At least Uncle Fredrick had the sensitivity to leave them alone. He excused himself and his associates from his office, informing Elsie and Everest that he would be back for them in ten minutes.

Their mother offered them a reassuring smile. "I admit your uncle isn't the easiest person to warm up to, but I can promise he will take good care of you while we are gone. He takes his responsibilities very seriously."

Elsie hunched her shoulders. "I don't want to be someone's responsibility!"

Her mother's hand gently trailed over her hair. "He doesn't really know you. We haven't stayed in touch as much as we should have over the years. I'm sure you'll all be the best of friends by the time we return."

"But when will that be?" Elsie cried.

Her dad laid a hand on her shoulder. "Longer than we would like," he said cryptically. "We'll do our best to send you periodic transmissions, but it won't always be possible."

Elsie stared with horror. "But if you're sending us transmissions instead of holocomms, that means you're not even in our galaxy."

Their parents exchanged helpless looks. After a few seconds her mom said, "You're a little too smart for your own good. That should work to your advantage here. You'll be able to hold your own with the clones. Remember, they are humans too, so don't treat them like oddities. They'll have special skills, that's all. You'll need to work hard to keep up, but it'll do you good to be challenged."

Elsie rubbed her new and very unusual pendant, trying to find solace in its warmth. Wasn't it enough of a challenge just to live without their parents for who knew how long?

CHAPTER 3
The Basker Twins Meet the Clones

Slumped in chairs made of slick nanofiber, Elsie and Everest faced each other in the B12 recreation room. Instructor Gerard had explained that B7 through B12 students were housed in the North tower, and C13 through C18 were housed in the South. Because the twelve-year-olds were the oldest on this side of the building, they lived on the top floor. A0 through A6 students were housed in separate cottages in the gardens, and were for the most part engaged in separate activities.

The instructor had also run through the more basic rules. Unless they had special dispensation, by 19:00 students had to be inside the building, and by 21:00 they had to be in their dorm rooms. Lights out was at 22:00. He gave them a litany of other regulations, but the only one that made them sit up and take notice was that neither holoputers nor Virtual Entertainment Devices, better known as VEDs, were allowed in the dorm rooms, and usage in specially designated locations was limited to a few hours on the weekend. Everest felt bad about all the hologames he would miss, but he felt even worse for Elsie. She lived for her friendships, and even before this move, she'd spent hours holocommunicating with her friends. He might tease her about her constant talking and h-comming, but he'd never wish this on her. The VED restriction wasn't as big of a deal, since their parents had already been limiting their weekday access.

After laying down the law and indicating that he would send up some students to show them their rooms, the instructor had swept off to organize quarters for Pooker with the promise that Elsie would see her pet soon.

"Maybe it won't be so bad," Everest finally managed to mumble.

"No holocomms? I'm going to die," Elsie moaned. "Our lives couldn't possibly get any worse."

The softest of noises brought their attention to the door as it dissolved. Five bodies clothed in gray vlatex entered and ranged themselves in an intimidating wall.

Everest groaned. It could always get worse.

The middle student stepped forward. She was tall—as tall as they were—and flasers, was she muscled. Her hair was scraped back in a tight ponytail, and she had jammed a sports cap on her head so that her face was shadowed. With arms crossed over her chest, she glared at them as if they were suzo-shrimp from Suzorq. And her nose was wrinkled as if they smelled that bad too.

"If it isn't the little niece and nephew, slumming at their uncle's home for freakazoids," she said.

"Is that what this is?" Everest asked mildly. "I thought it was a boarding school."

He had the feeling he'd heard her speak before. He might even recognize her if she took off her cap. Or at least he'd recognize who she'd been cloned from, assuming she was a clone.

When he realized that Elsie had leaped up and was on the verge of doing something rash—no surprise there—he hastily rose and grabbed her wrist.

16

"We know what you ute-babies think of us dupes," the girl snarled.

"Ute-babies?" Elsie asked. "Dupes? What in asteroids are you talking about?"

The tall girl snorted. "Ute—uterus—get it? A natural baby? Dupe—duplicate—a clone? I guess it's true that brains are few and far between for you utes."

"Maybe our brains just aren't as prejudiced as yours," Elsie responded tartly. "We don't label people."

"Sure you do," the girl replied. "We've been called clones all our lives by people like you."

"You don't know us. You can't possibly know what we're like."

Everest shot a warning look at his sister. Their parents would not be happy if they got in trouble their first day at boarding school. He reluctantly joined the conversation. "You don't want us here, and we don't want to be here. But we're not looking for trouble, so just leave us alone, and we'll stay out of your way."

The girl laughed, exchanging wide grins with her gang. "Oooh, the itsy bitsy ute-baby wants to be left alone. He must be scaredy."

Their shouts of laughter had Everest gritting his teeth, and he had to react quickly when Elsie tried to yank free from his grip, her own hands fisted. He wasn't much stronger than Elsie, and she could be tricky.

"We're not scared," he said, pushing down anger. "We just don't see a reason to fight."

"You being here gives us all the reason we need," said the shorter, wiry boy standing to the left of the leader.

"Course, it won't be much of a fight," the lead girl drawled. "Let's face it, ute-babies are soft. They've got their parents to take care of them."

17

"Not these ute-babies," Elsie yelled. "We'll kick your behinds to the next galaxy."

"We'd love to see you try." The girl in the cap jerked her chin toward the far door. "Fight room's through there. Let's see what you're made out of, little ute-twins."

Without a word Everest and Elsie pivoted and marched across the room toward the indicated door. From the age of two, every child on Earth practiced the fighting arts daily. For the past two hundred years, ever since the end of the Age of Darkness and Despair that had followed the defeat of the Vlemutz, Earth had managed to avoid war and had almost abolished violent crime by getting aggression out on a daily basis through controlled confrontation and attack.

Everest was plenty happy to show these clones a thing or two. He and Elsie were top of their class in both singles and doubles when it came to fights.

Sensing them, the door dissolved, and he stepped inside in tandem with Elsie. His initial impression of the room was good. This was first class fight space, with a ten-meter ceiling that left plenty of room for jumping. Strong ropes hung from the ceiling, hooks climbed the padded walls, and a thick pad covered the floor. Top rate.

Light-weight jellach bodysuits hung on hooks. As they walked past, Everest and Elsie grabbed a couple, then dragged them on. When they reached the center of the room, Everest turned around and bowed to the five teens who had followed them in. "So what's it to be? Two on two? We're happy to take the five of you on if you're too chicken for a fair match." He grinned at the leader's scowl.

"I don't need a partner," she replied. "I'll take the two of you solo and eat you for lunch." She sneered at their feet. "And it won't do you any good to be wearing those fancy skyboots."

Everest hadn't even noticed till then that the clones' athletic boots were outdated and lacking in the latest pico-spring technology and ankle support. Their older models didn't even shoot off sparks. "We don't take unfair advantage," he said. "You want to fight, you find yourself a second, and we'll go barefoot." He yanked off his ultra-thin, super springy athletic boots, and Elsie quickly followed suit.

Without taking her eyes off him, Dar said, "Fine. Vlas, let's have some fun." As she spoke, she toed off her footgear too.

After he got rid of his boots, the wiry boy stepped forward, and the other kids drew back behind the see-through pad that protected spectators from the action.

"Referee," he called, and a short, bald, black and white striped Clegl humanoid appeared in the room, his edges shimmering ever so slightly, the only sign that he was actually a holographic projection, an avatar that embodied a particular system--in this case, the fight room's extensive rules and regulations.

Everest was impressed that their referee avatar was a Clegl. Since Clegls had eyes in the back of their heads, they made the best officials for fight matches, but they were much more expensive.

The girl who had challenged them ripped off her cap and flung it through the door. When he got his first good look at her without her cap, Everest struggled to breathe as if she'd already managed to kick him in his solar plexus. She was the most beautiful girl he'd ever seen, with skin a soft shade of gold, huge green eyes, and hair a perfect match for her skin. Even scraped back it looked thick and shiny. Her face was sculpted like some ancient statue of a forgotten goddess. He gulped, feeling his face heat up. Why did he feel so weird? She was just a girl.

"Shadara!" Elsie whispered, her tone awed.

No one alive could not know who Shadara was. The most famous beauty in the past ten decades, her music had made people weep, and her tragic death had been mourned by seven galaxies.

"Don't-ever-call-me-that," the girl spit out. "My name is Dar. Call me anything else and I'll take you out." With blinding speed she shot out her foot at Elsie's gut.

CHAPTER 4
The Fight Competition

Only her years of training and split-second reflexes had Elsie lunging back enough to soften the worst of the blow.

"Foul," screeched the Clegl referee, madly waving his hands over his head.

"Declined," Elsie yelled as she threw herself into a series of back handsprings to put some distance between herself and her opponent. These clones would call her a wimp if she hid behind some technicality, like the match not officially having been started.

"Fight on," the little man yelped, the eyes in the back of his head blinking as Elsie shot past.

Since Dar dogged her heels, Elsie switched to the offensive, executing a well-placed blow with her foot, followed by two chops with her hands. Then she sprang over Dar's head and caught one of the hanging ropes. From rope to rope, she swung until at the far end of the room she scrambled to the ceiling to survey the battle below.

Everest was holding his own with Vlas, but they were surprisingly well-matched. She'd rarely seen anyone in the same age range put up a decent fight against her brother.

Instead of following her, Dar had decided to double team Everest. Flasers, the girl was clever! Dar knew perfectly well that Elsie wouldn't leave her brother to fight alone.

She shimmied down a couple of meters, then swung hand over hand to Everest, who was now using every defensive move he'd ever learned to shake the two clones. The three spectators cheered on Dar and Vlas while jeering at Everest.

With a warrior's cry, Elsie dropped down and caught Dar around her neck. The force of Elsie's body knocked them both to the springy padding. They wrestled, grappling and rolling, each struggling for dominance. Both held rigidly to the rule against attacks to the face. Elsie gave Dar credit for her fair play, but that didn't stop her from feinting to the right, then scissoring her legs and flipping Dar onto her back. She sprang backward, landing on her feet, and Dar did the same. Slowly circling each other, they searched for any weakness. They controlled their breathing by bringing air through their noses then releasing short puffs through their mouths.

From the corner of her eye, she saw the striped referee hopping on first one leg then the other. He had his back to her, so she saw eyes, but no nose or mouth.

"You had enough, ute?" Dar asked with a sneer.

"Not even," Elsie replied.

From across the room, she caught Everest's almost imperceptible sign. The clones might think the advantage was theirs, but she suspected they hadn't fought twins before. And the Baskers had a few slick tricks up their vlatex sleeves. With another battle shout, she shot into a cartwheel round off in her brother's direction, followed by a forward handspring. When she met up with him, he bent at the waist and with his hands guided her in a roll across his back. Coming out of the roll, she dived straight into a somersault and shot her feet into Vlas's stomach.

Caught off guard, he landed hard on his rear. Meanwhile, Everest flung himself at Dar and scissored her feet right out from under her.

The audience let out a collective gasp as their leader landed flat on the mat. In a heartbeat, Everest had pounced and pinned her.

Elsie took advantage of Vlas being distracted by Dar's defeat. As he stood up, she kicked his legs out from under him so that he landed face first. She rammed her knee into his back and imprisoned his arms behind him.

The Clegl referee screeched "Match" in seven or possibly even eight alien languages, and hopped with so much excitement and energy that he tumbled on his back and rolled around for awhile before righting himself. The kids' heavy breathing, somewhat muffled on Vlas's part was the only other noise in the room. There was stunned silence on the part of the spectators.

"If I let you go, will you abide by the rules?" Everest asked mildly.

The winner of a fight competition could not be challenged for one month, and the loser was expected to treat him or her with respect during that time, which meant no insults or aggressive behavior. In addition, the loser was expected to protect the winner from other challenges.

"I'm no cheat," Dar said through gritted teeth.

"And your little buddy?" Everest asked.

Vlas growled in the back of his throat and glared from his smashed position on the floor.

"He'll abide by the rules."

Everest rolled off her and flopped onto his back, expelling his breath slowly. Elsie released Vlas and also rested on the pad. This was the toughest match she'd ever fought, and it easily could have gone the other way. They'd been lucky.

"You fight well," Everest told Dar.

"Not well enough," she replied bitterly, springing lightly to her feet, her expression grim. She began to peel off the jellach bodysuit that had protected her from injury.

Elsie fought back a smile. She could relate to a girl who didn't like to lose. Following Dar's example, she stripped off her suit.

The little referee rushed over. "Where do I register the final score?" he asked excitedly.

"This was not an official match," Dar said.

"Your beginning move was highly irregular," he responded with a censorious frown. "This time you get a warning. Next time, I'll be forced to speak to your instructors."

Dar rolled her eyes. "*Please* forgive me."

"Humph."

"Clear Ref," Dar said in a slightly raised voice to no one in particular, and the Clegl hologram immediately vanished. Dar turned to Vlas. "Did you have to call in that particular referee?"

Vlas shrugged. "Don't look at me. The system randomly picked him."

After making a face, Dar wiped her sweaty palms down her front and stretched out an arm to Everest.

Not convinced Everest should trust her, Elsie watched as her brother tentatively clasped Dar's hand, but the girl merely pulled him to his feet. Elsie moved over to stand shoulder to shoulder with her twin.

And Vlas shifted to Dar's side.

After a long and silent pause, Dar dipped into a slight bow, and Vlas followed suit. Everest and Elsie returned the courtesy in the manner they'd been taught since their toddler days.

"Next time, we'll win," Dar said.

Everest shrugged. "Maybe."

Dar addressed Elsie. "Well roommate, do you need help moving in?"

Elsie's jaw dropped. "We're sharing?"

Dar raised an eyebrow, and her mouth formed a wicked grin. "Didn't you know? My room's the only one with a spare bed. My roommate left school a couple months back. The government needed her assistance with some yocto-physics research."

Elsie swallowed a groan. Could life get any worse? Rooming with someone who hated her? Bleck.

"I left my bags in the rec room," she said resignedly.

"Well then, let's retrieve them and get you settled." Dar swung around, scooped up her worn-out skyboots and sauntered toward the door, replacing the jellach gear as she passed the hooks. It hadn't taken her long to regain her cocky attitude. Elsie doubted anyone would get that Dar had just lost a match and been humiliated in the process.

When Dar realized that Elsie wasn't following her, she looked over her shoulder. "Don't worry," she drawled. "I don't eat utes for breakfast." She paused, then added, "Just lunch."

Everest stepped forward. "No name calling, remember?"

Dar widened her eyes. "I'm sorry, what should we call you?"

When Everest didn't immediately answer, Elsie took in his slack-jawed expression with something akin to horror. Bleck...he looked like a major freakazoid. She kicked him in the shin and had to bite back a screech. She'd forgotten she was barefoot.

"Flasers!" Everest exclaimed. Then as if he'd woken up from a bad dream, he mumbled, "Everest and Elsie."

Dar shrugged. "Vlas, why don't you escort *Everest* to his room? Elsie, you come with me. Oh," again she paused, "welcome to the academy."

With that, she crossed the threshold, found Elsie's bags, and strode off.

Some welcome, Elsie thought as she grabbed her skyboots and ran after the girl.

The dorm room was at the end of a long corridor to the left of the rec room. Elsie gathered that the boys lived to the right. The walls on the way to Dar's room were covered with light murals that bled one color into another, first fast then slow, so that a person might imagine a song kept tempo.

Dar's side of the chamber was covered floor to ceiling with sports memorabilia—holographic replays of famous moments in skyball, extreme hover boarding, fight competitions, and other popular sports. A skyball hoop hung in the corner. The area above the bed was a sea of gold medals and flashing ribbons.

An athlete herself, Elsie was drawn to Dar's collection. Too bad the girl was such a first-rate vlem. Elsie was doing her best not to be impressed by Dar's fighting skills. The last thing she wanted was to actually admire the girl. To keep herself busy, she reached for her first bag and opened it.

Dar flung herself onto her bright turquoise bed and sighed as the jellach conformed around her for comfort. Elsie's bed was neon purple. "Touch the wall over there to enter your storage area." Dar waved her hand in the general direction. "There are shelves for clothes and some rods for any fancy gear you might have. We passed the communal showers and toilets on the way here." She flicked her thumb toward the wall behind the end of her bed. "You'll find plenty of no-cal snacks in my closet. For this month, eat what you like. In thirty days when Vlas and I kick your twin rears to Xlexuri, you can buy the no-cals. Keep in mind that I'm partial to Blackholes."

Dar's generous albeit caustic offer was a little hard for Elsie to swallow. And she didn't know what to think about the fact that they both loved the same candy. Her favorite no-cal was also the Blackhole—a super dense, super strong chocolate ball that heated up when it touched the tongue and ended in a small explosion of intense flavor.

Dar reached under her bed and pulled out a smaller, lighter version of a skyball. She aimed the shiny silver orb, flicked her wrist and sent it swishing through the hoop, causing the target to burst into dazzling white light. Since there wasn't a chorus of whistles, Elsie figured the hoop was muted. Because Dar made the shot, the skyball careened back to her. She caught it one-handed and tossed it up again for another perfect shot and more bright lights.

"So, why'd your parents dump you at the Academy? They get tired of you?"

"No!" Elsie responded angrily. "They're scientists. They were forced to leave because of their research."

"Why couldn't they take you with them?"

"I don't know," Elsie admitted. "It wasn't something they could discuss."

Dar glanced her way, a curious gleam in her expression. "Secret, huh? Maybe my sponsor can find out something."

"Your sponsor?"

Dar rolled her eyes as she aimed and flicked her wrist for another shot and another dazzling light show. "The poor sap who paid to have me created. He was totally besotted by Shadara. He visits sometimes, brings me gifts. Adriatic Mink is his name, and he's some big cheese in the United Nations, otherwise no one would have approved the cloning of someone as worthless as my original. By the Light, the woman was idolized for her beauty and her voice. Talk about stupid reasons for existing."

Elsie frowned. Shadara was more an icon of her parents' generation, but Elsie was still a fan. "The woman wasn't just a singer; she had the best voice in a hundred years." She paused in organizing her mostly vlatex wardrobe and considered Dar, who was shooting the skyball over and over, making sparkling white rays of light shoot out to each corner of the room.

"Don't you sing?" she asked.

Dar snorted. "Not if you put a flaser to my forehead."

"But you're a clone. You must have the same genetic gifts."

"No one can force me to be a Shadara copy. No way will I ever dress up in frilly low-cut gear so that a bunch of old men can slobber all over me. I refuse to sing a bunch of silly songs about love and romance—bleck!"

She scrunched up her face and crossed her eyes, and suddenly Elsie was laughing so hard her sides hurt.

She gasped for breath. "You've got a point, Dar, but I don't think anyone who's been in your presence for more than five minutes could possibly confuse you for a Shadara copy."

Dar grinned back. "You know what, Elsie? Give us a millennium or two and I might find myself actually liking you."

CHAPTER 5
Dinner with the Clones

Meals were served in a great, high-ceilinged hall on the main floor that reminded Everest of a huge cavern. It was so loud. How was a person supposed to think straight? He'd read somewhere that at one time people had created brightly colored wall hangings made of dense yarns to both enhance the beauty of the tevta rooms and dampen the noise. Nowadays, light murals were popular, and there were a number in the hall. The way one color blended into the next was zeller, but the artwork didn't help one bit to shut down the noise.

A quick scan of the room turned up Elsie at a table along the far wall, sitting to his dismay next to Dar. None of the guys from the boys' side of the dormitory had bothered to let him know when supper was served. Vlas had disappeared as soon as he'd dumped Everest in his room. Not that he blamed him. It wasn't much fun to lose a fight competition. Despite everything, he found himself grinning. It was much more fun to win. Alone in his dorm room, unpacking and arranging his stuff, Everest would have missed the meal altogether if his stomach hadn't started to rumble. As it was, it looked as if he might be the last person to arrive.

The room was jam-packed with children of all ages wearing the same uniform, thin gray vlatex that clung to the skin like a layer of fine fur. The students clustered at tables, the smaller kids closest to the entrance with the adolescents and older teens at various tables along the back wall. There had to be close to three hundred people there, and as far as he knew, all of them were clones, except him and his sister.

As he neared the table, Elsie spotted him and raised her hand in greeting, her smile lit with relief.

"Everest!" she exclaimed. "I was beginning to worry about you."

Dar's raised eyebrow spoke volumes. He could just imagine what she was thinking about Elsie worrying over her helpless twin brother who couldn't find his way to dinner.

"I lost track of time," he said shortly.

Elsie slid over to make room for him on the bench. The idea of being sandwiched that close to Dar made him frown. He might as well be having dinner with a giant exoctopus from Mitzorian, or *be* dinner for that matter.

"Who are you rooming with?" Elsie asked.

"No one. They had an empty room."

"Oh." Her envious expression made him feel a little better.

All of a sudden, no one was talking at the table. Instead they were staring. At him. He hated being the center of attention, especially when the natives weren't particularly friendly.

"I'd better get some food." He left abruptly. When he was at the counter, he snagged a tray and checked out the selection. Healthy was about all that could be said. Good thing he wasn't picky.

After loading up on vegetables and protein, he dragged his feet back to the B12 table. It was weird the way everyone watched him. Even kids from other age levels. Was ute-baby stamped on his forehead?

As he settled onto the bench, he nudged Dar sideways to give himself enough room. No surprise, she pushed back, her leg muscles tense. He just barely suppressed a grin when he thought about the surly look she had to be throwing his way. For a moment, he envisioned how she would react if he reminded her of her duties as loser of their fight competition.

Deciding to play it safe, he began to shovel in his meal, plain fare, but no worse than his old school's cafeteria food.

"Everest," Elsie said, "you've already met Vlas and Dar."

He lifted his head, still chewing on a chunk of soy protein. "Yeah."

"Across from you are Lelita and Borneo."

He recognized two of the kids who had watched the fight earlier. The girl had dark brown hair, big brown eyes, and a round face. The boy was tall and thin as a blade of grass, with very white skin and messy white hair. His eyes were light pink. Everest nodded in greeting, struggling to suppress the grin fighting for release. He'd been preoccupied earlier, but this time, he recognized Borneo immediately. He couldn't believe it had taken him this long. In his school, the term "borneo" stood for a zetta-geek. "You're related to that Astrophysicist—Borneo Lankersten."

Borneo went red. "Yeah, I was duped from him."

Duped. They seemed to use that word or just "dupe" a lot when talking about themselves. Was that a term clones reserved for themselves? What would happen if he were to use it? He hadn't expected clones to be so sensitive about their births. But then, it wasn't something he'd ever given much thought.

Dar leaned forward, her expression grim. "No one uses 'Borneo' as anything other than a name around here, so you can wipe that smirk off your face."

Everest frowned. Couldn't she give him any credit? It had to have been obvious that he was doing his best not to smile.

Quickly, Dar rattled off the names of the other kids at the table, but he doubted he'd remember—red-haired kid, Flanners; brown-skinned blond-haired boy, Pelio; petite black-haired, almond-eyed girl, Yoshira. The rest were a blur. The only thing he took away clearly from the introductions was that not one of them smiled at him. Just a couple dozen stone-faced clones who hated him and his sister. Welcome to the academy.

"What? Do I have dirt on my nose?" he asked the table at large. Everyone shook their heads. *"Then stop staring."*

"They can't help themselves," Dar said, her tone that of a spitting bobcat. "No twelve-year-old has ever beaten me before in a fight competition. Basker, you're a celebrity."

Flasers! That was all he needed. Dar was their leader, and he and Elsie had humiliated her by winning. Should they have thrown the match?

Too late to think about that.

His mouth twisted as he made a weak attempt to change the subject. "So what's this place like?"

No one answered. Instead, they all looked to Dar for guidance on how or whether to respond. She shrugged, her expression blank. "It's okay."

He gave up on conversation and concentrated on shoveling down his meal, and thinking about the day his parents would come home and their lives would return to normal. Till then he could handle the silent treatment. He felt sorry for Elsie, though. She cared a lot more about having friends.

"What exactly do you mean by okay?" Elsie asked, her chin jutted out. "Do you mean the teachers are okay? The facilities are okay? The food? The sports? The students?"

Everest wasn't surprised that she continued the awkward conversation, but he kicked her in an attempt to make her stop. She glared and kicked him back.

Dar snorted. "You know something, Basker? You and your brother give me a real pain. What makes you think we would ever spill out our guts to you? Being ute-babies is bad enough, but you're also old Lester-Hauffer's niece and nephew. You're the enemy."

Titters erupted around the table.

"For your information," Elsie replied huffily, "we've only met our uncle a handful of times, and none of the experiences were anything to talk about."

"Those of us with no family," Dar said, "have had it jammed down our throats that families stick together." She jabbed her finger at Elsie. "You and Lester-Hauffer are family."

Everest stared down at his now-cold vegetables. He'd forgotten that clones had no parents. His food suddenly tasted like dirt. His parents had only been gone for a matter of hours, and already he really missed them. What if something happened to them? What if he never saw them again? He rubbed the charm hidden behind thin vlatex. He didn't want to be like these clones, parentless and alone in the world.

He wished his parents would come home now.

CHAPTER 6
Elsie's Bobcat

"I need to check on Pooker," Elsie mumbled as she stood up from the table. She had the horrible feeling she might cry if she didn't escape, if only for a few minutes.

"Who's Pooker?" Lelita asked.

It was the first time any of the clones other than Dar or Vlas had spoken to Elsie. She wasn't surprised when Lelita shifted her eyes nervously toward Dar. The supreme leader of the bunch, Elsie thought with a little curl of her lip.

Because she was desperate for even the pretense of friendship, she answered Lelita's question. "Pooker's my pet bobcat. Because pets aren't allowed here, she's been caged outside." She shook her head. "You can't imagine how much she hates being enclosed in confined spaces. Plus she's not used to being separated from me."

Lelita's round eyes grew even rounder. "A bobcat? Wow! I've never even seen a kitten in person, let alone a bobcat." There was no mistaking the longing in Lelita's voice and eyes.

Elsie leaned forward, her palms flat on the table. "Would you like to come with me to visit her?"

"Would I?" Lelita said breathlessly.

Elsie smiled. Maybe this clone wasn't as bad as the rest. Maybe she could be a friend. "Come on."

Lelita clambered off the bench. Dar slid out as well. "I'll join you," she said, looking bored.

"I don't remember inviting you," Elsie responded shortly.

"Too bad. Since you won the fight, it's my job to protect you. You've never been on the grounds before, so it's my duty to escort you." She gave a little bow of fake respect.

"Thanks a heap. I ought to warn you that Pooker is very sensitive to emotions. If she senses you don't like me, *she's* not going to like you, and she's got very big and very sharp teeth."

"I'm sure I can pretend to like you for a small period of time," Dar responded, suddenly cheerful. Rather than scaring the girl off, Elsie had managed to stir her competitive nature.

Elsie wanted to dislike everything about Dar, but she couldn't shake a grudging respect for the girl. She showed honor in a fight, and she was determined, brave, and smart. Too bad she was such a pain.

"I don't know where Pooker is. How would I get a hold of Instructor Gerard to find out where he took her?"

"Oh, he's long gone by now," said Dar blithely. "We only ever have two jailers during the night, and that painful duty is rotated. Instructor Gerard's night duty was last week, so he won't be back until tomorrow morning."

"What about Uncle Fre—I mean Director Lester-Hauffer?" Elsie asked. She just had to find Pooker!

Dar snorted rudely. "Your precious uncle never takes night duty—unless you count his holograms. He rockets out of here every day precisely at 17:00. Instructor Sura and Instructor Legnarchi have duty tonight. If we can't find your kitty, we'll go to Sura, but I expect they settled your pet near the garage."

Elsie turned to Everest. "Are you coming?"

The pained expression on his face warned her she was about to be ditched.

Shrugging his shoulders, he confirmed her hunch by saying, "Nah, I think I'll make it an early night."

Elsie glared, but he refused to make eye contact. She hated the way Dar smirked, as if to say that Everest was a total suzo-shrimp. Furious with her brother for abandoning her, Elsie marched off, Lelita running along at her side. Dar sauntered behind, her footsteps quietly following them down the long corridor. They came to the end of a hallway, and Elsie turned left.

At the sound of someone clearing her throat, she paused and looked around. Lelita and Dar stood at the junction. *"What?"*

Pointing her finger just slightly in the opposite direction, Dar said, "Outside is that way." She didn't smile, but Elsie knew the girl was laughing at her.

"Maybe you should lead," she said stiffly.

"If you can handle it," Dar responded.

"Oh, I can handle it." Following Dar would make it that much easier to kick her in the rear.

It turned out they didn't need Instructor Sura's help to locate Pooker. Dar's guess about the bobcat's whereabouts had been annoyingly accurate.

"Ooh!" Lelita gasped. "They used dancing sensors."

To the left of a large building that Dar assured Elsie was the garage, fingers of pink, blue, and white light danced along a square perimeter. Each finger of light pulsed to silent music. Some vertical strands were tall, others short, but they all had the pulsing beat in common. The display was prettier than it should have been, given that it was responsible for caging her poor bobcat within an eight-by-eight meter square.

A beautiful rosewillow tree grew directly opposite the pen, a curtain of delicate leaves and rose-like flowers rippling in the gentle breeze.

In one corner of the cage were food and water dispensers. The opposite corner had a waterproof canopy about one and a half meters high, with a pile of old blankets that must have been intended for sleeping. Pooker would never use the space. The bobcat had a bad case of claustrophobia. Even now, Pooker was giving that corner a wide berth as she slowly paced back and forth, miserable in her prison.

When she saw Elsie, she let out a cough-bark and sprang toward the dancing lights. But the lights turned black and zapped her, making her lunge backward with a pained howl.

"Pooker!" Elsie cried. She couldn't bear it that Pooker was being frightened and hurt in this monstrous cage.

Dar drawled, "Some kitty."

"What do I do?" she wailed.

"Stop the dramatics, Basker," Dar ordered. "She's not permanently damaged by the lights. They're just warning her not to try to leave. See that thin stake next to the square? All you have to do is press the blue button on top to give yourself an opening. I doubt your little kitty will try to escape too many times now that she knows what will happen if she does."

Elsie ran to the button and followed Dar's directions so that enough of the dancing light fingers disappeared to let her through. She quickly slid inside and found herself nose to nose with her baby.

Now she really fought tears. The idea of Pooker sleeping out here alone was unthinkable—caged and frightened. Pooker had never had to sleep by herself. "Are they treating you all right?"

Pooker stared at her with soulful yellow eyes.

She buried her forehead in her bobcat's scruff and breathed in the musky scent. Finally, she straightened, wiped her eyes, and turned to Dar and Lelita. "This is Pooker." She slanted a stern look at her pet bobcat. "Pooker, this is Dar and Lelita. Despite anything you might sense to the contrary, you should treat them as friends." She rubbed the tip of Pooker's nose affectionately. "Do either of you want to touch her?"

Lelita nervously shook her head and stepped back a pace.

"What about you, Dar?"

If Dar had hesitated for even a second, Elsie would have known, but there was no hesitation in her response. "Sure," she said nonchalantly. "What's the etiquette?"

Elsie shrugged. "Just come over and put out your hand. Pooker will sniff you then make up her own mind what to do about you."

"How reassuring." Dar moved inside the sensored area. She placed her hand near Pooker's watchful face. "Pleased to meet you." Her voice surprised Elsie with its gentleness.

After a moment, Pooker sniffed her then butted her head against Dar's fingers. "She's soft!"

"Yeah," Elsie found it hard to maintain her irritation with Dar, given the girl's warm response.

"I've never touched anything like her."

"Hmm," Elsie responded, "Pooker must be a worse judge of character than I thought."

"Funny, Basker. Very funny," Dar replied. "Pretty stinky, isn't she?"

"She is not!" As far as Elsie was concerned, Pooker smelled wonderful.

"If you say so," Dar said with a half-grin.

Lelita pushed forward, less afraid now that Dar had taken the plunge. "Can I touch her now too?"

"Sure." Elsie moved to the side to make room.

Following Dar's lead, Lelita raised her arm. Again, Pooker butted up against the proffered hand. She made a satisfied noise in her throat and licked Lelita's fingers.

Startled, Lelita jumped back, laughing nervously. "It's rough and ticklish." With an embarrassed glance at Elsie, she said, "We've never had an animal on the compound. This is the first time I've touched one."

"Really?" Elsie couldn't imagine her life without animal friendship. She didn't know what to say. "But what about stray cats?"

"The director gets rid of any uninvited guests," Dar said.

"No!"

Dar shrugged. "We've got curfew pretty soon. We'd better go back inside." She grabbed Lelita's arm and pulled her beyond the dancing lights.

Elsie stared blindly at Pooker. How in the universe was she going to get through the night? Not only would she be without her parents, but, also, she would be without Pooker curled up at her side. They had slept together for as long as she could remember. Tonight was the worst night of her life.

"I'm not going," Elsie finally croaked. "I'll just sleep out here with Pooker."

"Don't be ridiculous. There are rules here, you know. If you're caught outside after curfew without an instructor's permission on record, you've got detention for weeks. If you're caught outside after lights are out, you've got detention for months, maybe life. It ain't pretty, Basker."

Elsie swallowed hard. "I can't bear it."

"You aren't crying, are you?" Dar sounded angry.

"Of course not." Elsie clenched her hands into tight fists. It would be so humiliating to be caught blubbering.

"Stop it," Dar said tightly.

"Oh, why don't you just dive into a black hole? Pooker's *never* been by herself at night. For all I know there's a planned rainfall coming. She'll be frightened, wet, and miserable."

"She's a bobcat. She's supposed to be outdoors."

"She's my pet!" Elsie yelled. "And has been since she was eight weeks old. Besides, she may be meant for outdoors, but that doesn't mean she was meant to be caged." She waved her hand angrily in Dar's direction. "Just forget it. Let's go."

She pushed out of the sensored space and briskly secured the area by pressing on the blue light again, then stormed down the walkway, not caring if anyone followed.

"Wait a sec," Dar called out.

Elsie swiveled around, tired and angry, furious with herself, with Dar, with blecky Uncle Fredrick. Dar remained standing next to Pooker's prison.

"What?"

"I'll help you sneak her in at night."

Elsie goggled at her. "You'll what?"

"You heard me. I'll help you under two conditions."

"Two conditions?"

"You don't tell anyone that I helped you."

Elsie slowly nodded. "And?"

"You owe me—and I can call in your debt any time I want."

Elsie was just desperate enough to accept her terms. "Deal."

They shook hands gravely. Dar then looked over at Lelita. "No telling tales—not even to Jillian."

Lelita nodded vigorously. "No way, I promise."

Elsie vaguely remembered Jillian as Lelita's roommate, a girl with long auburn hair and a faraway expression.

"So what do we do?" she asked.

"Right now, nothing," Dar responded. "Be ready by 22:00. Wear your darkest clothes. I should be back by then."

"Where will you be?"

"That, Basker, is none of your business."

Elsie reminded herself that she and Dar didn't have to be friends. All she needed was the girl's help.

Her hands shoved into the pockets of her jacket, she walked back to the smooth lavender facility that was almost lost in the gloom of the evening and tried not to think about the favor she would owe Dar.

To be exercised at the girl's whim.

Now that was a scary thought.

CHAPTER 7
The Girls' Adventure

Dar was late for their 22:00 appointment, blast her. Could this be her idea of a mean joke? Maybe Dar never had intended to help.

And what was the deal on the broken curfew? How could Dar be out and about when the rules required they be in their dorm room with lights out?

Elsie flopped back on her bed and stared angrily at the ceiling, not that she could see much of anything since *she* had followed the rules and the room was pitch black.

At 22:30 with no sign of Dar, Elsie felt like a zetta yocto-brain. The only good news was that her eyes had finally acclimated to the dark. She shoved off her bed. How was she supposed to save Pooker now? Her frustration mounting, she grabbed a skyball and with one flying leap, slammed it into the corner hoop. Sparkling lights flashed and sizzled making her flinch.

At the exact same instant, the door dissolved.

Elsie swung around and glared at Dar who leaned against the doorjamb, looking unconcerned as if she hadn't just kept Elsie waiting for thirty minutes. She held a brightee for light. Because Elsie had stopped paying attention to the skyball, it managed to glance off the side of her head as it boomeranged back, knocking her sideways.

She screeched, and Dar burst out laughing.

"What black hole did you get sucked into?" Elsie furiously asked as she rubbed her ear.

"Keep your aura on, Basker. I'm here now. And where I was is none of your business."

"What about curfew?"

"Don't worry, ute-baby, I've got permission to be out past curfew. Anyway, I'm not the one lighting up the room with a skyball fireworks show."

Elsie had the unexpected urge to punch her roommate, then immediately felt bad. Violence outside of a fight competition was strictly prohibited. Where had that impulse come from? She took a deep breath. When she was more in control of her emotions, she asked, "Are we going or not?"

"Yeah, we're going." Dar moved further into the room and put her hand to the wall. It erased to reveal clothing behind. "Give me a few minutes to change," she said as she disappeared into the closet.

Soon she wore the strangest jumpsuit Elsie had ever seen. It wasn't the style that was weird, but the material. Thinner than vlatex, fluid as water, it was neither black nor gray, but something in between. If forced to label the color, Elsie would have named it 'shadow.' The outfit had a hood that covered Dar's bright hair. But strangest of all was the shadowy veil that hung down over Dar's face and attached to the collar. Dar couldn't be a stranger to nighttime jaunts. This outfit had been custom-made for secrecy.

"What kind of material is that?" Elsie asked, trying not to sound too impressed.

"Vlatex II. Not yet released. I read about it and asked my sponsor for a sample in this color. Poor sap, he probably thinks

I'm making la-di-da dress-up clothes." She rubbed her hands together and grinned. "Time for the great Pooker escape."

She rummaged around in her bedstand drawer and pulled out a small vial. Tipping it slightly, she extracted a couple of tiny patches, one of which she handed to Elsie. "Put in this earpatch. Don't worry, it's a picobot and will cling to your skin. You'll be able to hear me even at a whisper, and if you whisper back, I'll hear you." She reached under her veil and hood and inserted the tiny communication device.

"Oh, I've already put in nighteyes drops. You'd better do the same. Catch!" She tossed a small dropper bottle toward Elsie.

Elsie caught. She'd used nighteyes once before on a school camp-out, so she quickly plopped two drops in each eye. There was a metal taste in the back of her throat, and her eyes felt as if they were expanding. The room became so visible that she doubted she needed the brightee to see. Now her vision would be as good as Pooker's in the dark.

Next, Dar got down on hands and knees and pulled out a box from under her bed. Inside were strange gloves and funny looking light-weight boots. "We'll put these on when we're ready."

"What are they?" Elsie asked.

"Spider gear, so we can crawl along the side of the building."

"Are you nuts? Why don't we just sneak out the back door?"

"The sensors are too sophisticated. Plus, Lester-Hauffer has his holograms watching the exits." She caught Elsie's horrified expression, and her grin grew. "Don't tell me the itsy ute-baby's afraid of heights?"

Elsie frowned. "Of course not, it's just so extreme."

"You're the one who wants the poor scaredy bobcat to sleep inside away from the cold. If you're ready to give up, just say so."

And be labeled a suzo-shrimp forever? Uh-uh. "So how come if Uncle Fredrick has such tight security, he hasn't thought of the windows?"

Dar groaned. "Stop calling him that. Mostly he has, but there's one skylight he's overlooked—the one in the exercise room."

"Aren't you forgetting something?" Elsie asked sweetly. "Pooker's a bobcat, not a stuffed doll. We can't exactly throw her over our shoulders and haul her back up the side of the building, and I don't think she's up to wearing spider gear."

Dar rolled her eyes. "What do you take me for? A yocto-brain? I've got it covered." She strode back to the closet and disappeared inside. When she reappeared, she carried a small backpack also made out of Vlatex II, which she slung over her shoulder. "Let's jam."

"What's in that?" Elsie asked.

"If we get caught, it'll be better for you not to know."

When they emerged into the dark corridor, Dar nearly disappeared from view. Even with her nighteyes drops at full strength, only the faintest of shadows showed Elsie Dar's location. She, on the other hand, was a flashing beacon even in black. If anyone was going to get them caught, it would be her. And she had the horrible feeling that Dar would be the one to pay because of whatever was in that sack.

"Stay in the middle of the corridor so you don't cause any doors to open." It was as if Dar floated down the hall, her feet barely touching the ground.

Though she attempted to copy the girl's light-footed gait, Elsie might as well have been a lumbering elephant in contrast. Because her eyes were already accustomed to the dark, Elsie immediately identified the thousands of almost invisible-to-the-eye brownies who were busily cleaning walls, floors and ceilings.

The picotechnology creatures banded together at night to disinfect and clean. The huge quantities of brownies that swarmed around Elsie, sometimes scratching her skin with their abrasive coating, made her feel as if she were in the middle of some strange shower. At home, they had a hundred brownies at most. The technology wasn't cheap.

"I've never seen so many brownies in one place," she said quietly to Dar.

"Really?" Dar whispered back. "The director's a total alien about cleanliness. In another hour or so, they'll move into the dorm rooms. These are new models, only a couple of months old. Fortunately, they're only programmed to clean, not to spy. Lucky for us, the director was a little too cheap for those models. You should see the ones my sponsor bought. He sent me specs on them. They combine housekeeping with state of the art security."

All of a sudden, Dar came to a crashing halt. "Okay—this is it—the fight room."

"Don't we have to enter through the rec room?" Elsie asked.

Dar shook her head. "We aren't going in through a door. Now shut down and do what I tell you to do."

"How are we going to get in?" Elsie asked despite Dar's order to stay quiet.

Instead of responding, Dar pulled out a small gadget and punched in a code. A couple of meters before the entrance, she ran the device in a large square pattern over the tevta wall. Then she brushed off the surface just in case there were brownies. Stepping back, she aimed the device at the wall and pressed a button. In slow motion, the atoms rearranged themselves, leaving a gaping hole.

Elsie gasped and anxiously looked around. Now they'd done it.

Dar must have read her mind, because she whispered, "Don't alien on me, Elsie, it's only temporary."

"What is that?" Elsie pointed to the device Dar was busy stuffing back into her bag.

"A portable matter-mover. My sponsor gave it to me three years ago. It's an older model so it only works on walls that are less than ten centimeters thick. That's why we couldn't just leave from our room. The outer walls are way too thick for this baby." When she finished hiding away the device, she turned to Elsie. "The hole stays until we return, so we better be quick. Don't let your feet touch the ground because the mat is sensored too. Follow my lead." Dar stepped up onto the thin ledge of the new opening, bent her knees, swung her arms and sprung to the nearest rope. Within seconds she had shinnied up to the ceiling. "Light speed, Basker. We haven't got all night."

"We haven't got all night," Elsie mimicked under her breath as she clambered onto the temporary ledge.

"Heard that," Dar said in her ear.

Even though she'd been hearing Dar in surround sound ever since they'd started their little mission, Elsie had forgotten about her picobot earpatch. She made a face. At least Dar couldn't *see* that with her back to her. Elsie leapt and caught the rope next to Dar's, then ascended hand over hand.

When they were once again face to face, the girl pointed to the skylight a few meters away. "There it is."

"Now what?" Elsie asked.

"Now we become spiders."

CHAPTER 8
The Rescue

Elsie cautiously accepted the funny-looking boots and gloves that Dar thrust at her. They smelled like glue, but they didn't feel particularly sticky. What if they didn't work?

"Cover your skyboots and legs first," Dar said. "Just shove your foot inside, and the boot will handle the rest. You'll need to grip the rope with your legs, so you can free up your hands to put on the gloves." Dar managed to be graceful as she slipped on the spider boots, which proceeded to crawl up her legs till they conformed to her skin right up to her thighs. With her legs tightly wrapped around the rope, Dar smoothly fitted the special gloves over her hands. Then, as if she really were a spider and the rope her thread, she fluidly transferred to the ceiling.

No way would Elsie exhibit equal grace.

Dar quickly crawled upside down to the skylight, whispering "Hurry up, slowpoke."

Elsie had only just barely managed to poke one shod foot into the first boot. Fortunately, the boot took over and fitted itself to her leg. It was kind of creepy the way the boot worked its way up her calf and over the knee. Ticklish too. As quickly as possible she got her other boot on, then slipped on her gloves. When she pressed her hands against the ceiling, she both heard and felt the suction attaching her to the tevta. Weird. Taking a shaky breath, she let go of the rope with her legs and slowly raised her knees. Her stomach tight, she curled up and kicked her knees and feet to the ceiling. Blood rushed to her head. She couldn't believe she was upside down ten meters in the air. She didn't even want to think what her parents would say if they ever got wind of this adventure. Her first crawl forward was miserable. Her legs and arms felt impossibly heavy.

"Light speed," Dar urged as she opened the skylight and maneuvered herself through.

Elsie fought her way to the skylight then hoisted herself through the opening. On the other side, they paused for a moment. It was a sparkling night with a sliver of a moon and an infinite number of blazing stars, some of which were really spacecraft. Hover vehicles were bigger balls of light, moving at high speed and bumping into each other with regularity. There was a crisp smell in the air. "I forgot to check whether rain was scheduled for tonight."

"No rain, unfortunately," Dar said. "We could have used the extra cover." She stood on the edge of the building and slipped on a pair of binoc-glasses to scan the property. "All's quiet. To be safe, we'll go down the West side. It's nearer to Pooker's cage and isn't as closely monitored as the front." She pocketed the glasses. "Go down head or feet first—your choice."

Elsie chose feet first and fell far behind Dar, who scrambled down like a baby jamming across the room for a favorite toy. When Elsie arrived at the foot of the building, she found Dar once again bristling with impatience. She had already removed the gear and was slapping the gloves impatiently against her thigh.

"Spider gear doesn't work on grass, so you can step down before removing it. Be quick about handing it over. We really need to rocket."

"Look, I've never used spider gear before," Elsie hissed, "so stop yelling at me." Flasers, she was only twelve. It wasn't as if there was any reason for her to be some kind of expert at covert missions.

"I'm not yelling," Dar responded, "but I will if you go all whiny on me. We don't have time for this."

In stony silence, Elsie peeled off the boots and gloves then handed them to Dar. She reminded herself that earlier today *she* had been the best and smartest when she'd whipped Dar's rear-end in the fight competition.

Once Dar had stowed away the gear, they crept toward the garage, using garden trees and hedges for cover. It was crisp out, but not cold. The jewel-toned gravel sparkled dimly in the moonlight. Elsie smelled the strong citrus scent of a nearby Limonino tree, native to Bandogiar, a planet from Xlexuri. Its bright pink fruit was more sour than any other substance in the universe. She knew because Zulu had one in her yard. As they approached Pooker's pen, she made out the droopy lines of the rosewillow tree directly opposite.

When Pooker smelled Elsie, she started to make funny little sounds in the back of her throat. Again Elsie had to fight back tears. Dar would be merciless if she caught her sniveling.

"Here's the deal," the girl said from behind. "We're going to rig this place with a mini-transport system. That way we'll be able to easily transport your kitty to and from our room on a nightly basis. Where should we put the device? We don't want her peeing on it."

"How in the universe did you get a transport system?" Elsie couldn't believe it.

Dar shrugged, but before she could say anything, Elsie signaled with her hand that she didn't want to hear what Dar had to say. "Don't tell me, I can guess. Adriatic Mink gave it to you."

Making a face, Dar said, "A rich sponsor is all I've got. I might as well take advantage of it."

Elsie rolled her eyes before surveying the square allocated to Pooker. "I guess I'd hide it under the canopy."

"I don't think she should be sleeping on the equipment either."

"Pooker hates confined spaces. Believe me, she won't go in there unless I take her in myself."

Dar pursed her lips. "Okay, but when you transport down you'll have to crouch. Otherwise, you'll have a Zylorg headache."

Elsie cringed at the thought. Zylorgs had two heads, and they were very prone to monster headaches. "I can handle it," she said grimly.

"The transport system should be safe here as long as you're the only one who cleans up after your bobcat."

"I'm sure I can get Uncle Fredrick to agree to that."

Dar gave a prolonged sigh. "Stop saying that."

"What?"

"You know: 'Uncle Fredrick…' Imagining him as an uncle gives me the creeps." She visibly shivered.

"I'm sorry, I keep forgetting."

"For the sake of my churning stomach, call him 'Director.'" She pushed the blue button to deactivate a portion of the dancing lights perimeter and motioned for Elsie to precede her into the pen. "Come on, we don't have all night. Keep your bobcat busy while I settle the transport equipment."

Elsie sank down and rubbed her face against Pooker's. "We're breaking you out of here," she whispered, curling her fingers into her bobcat's scruff and continuing to rub her cheek against the soft fur. She breathed in Pooker's comforting scent.

After a few minutes she heard Dar's whisper. "Come take a look."

She left her bobcat and crawled underneath the canopy.

"This may be small," Dar said, showing Elsie where the transport device was hidden underneath the blankets, "but it's top of the line. All you have to do is touch it and Pooker at the same time, and it'll pick up both of you." On hands and knees, she backed out of the shelter then stood up and brushed dirt off her Vlatex II clothing. "Stay down here with your kitty, and I'll return to the room and bring you both up."

Dar made to leave, but Elsie grabbed her hand. "I can never repay you for this." Why would Dar take such a risk for her when they weren't even friends?

The veil covering her face didn't hide Dar's discomfort. "No big," she mumbled. "Just stay out of sight until I get back to the room. I'll let you know when I've arrived." She rummaged in her sack. A few seconds later, she pulled out a large square of fabric.

Elsie recognized it as more Vlatex II.

Dar handed it to her. "Use this to cover yourself if someone comes by. With a little luck, you'll blend into the shadows and won't be caught.

With that she slipped out of Pooker's cage and melted into the night. Elsie wondered how hard it would be to track down Vlatex II material for her own outfit. It could come in handy to be able to become mostly invisible. Settling into the old blankets, she softly called to Pooker. Despite her hatred of confined spaces, the bobcat crawled in and curled up across Elsie's lap. Comforted for the first time since she'd arrived in this alien and less than welcoming place, Elsie let herself be lulled into a near sleep.

CHAPTER 9
Everest's Adventure

Everest restlessly shifted from side to side on his narrow bed. In having his own room he'd gotten off luckier than Elsie, but he still felt suffocated by the long row of dorm units packed with boys. If there was one thing he hated, it was crowds. Just because he didn't have to see them didn't mean he couldn't feel the other boys' unfriendly presence.

Staring up at the ceiling, he was sure he'd alien if he had to lie there all night. Where was a pick-up game of skyball when you needed one? Something that would wear him out so that he'd be too tired to think. His brain was too full right now—full of people, full of loneliness. It didn't make sense. All he knew was that he was totally messed up. He jerked upright. He had to get out of here, take a walk or something. Get some fresh air. Somehow escape this feeling of being caged. Maybe while he was at it, he would track down Pooker. They had a lot in common right now.

Instructor Gerard had communicated a strict curfew, but Everest figured if he got caught, he could plead ignorance or confusion or just plain stupidity. Everyone here thought he was a yocto-brain anyway. His mind made up, he quickly changed into dark clothing.

He set off down the boys' hallway, keeping a wary eye out for other nighttime wanderers. The dim lighting made it difficult to tell, but he was pretty sure there were a lot more pico-brownies hard at work than he was used to. He was itchy all over, as if he was being pricked by a million of the little suckers.

When he reached the stairs, he took a deep breath, then began to sneak down, his heart racing. The children's dorm rooms started on the fifth floor, and the B12s lived on the tenth at the top of this particular tower. So he had nine flights of stairs to cover if he wanted to escape the building. The nanovator would have rocketed him down in a blink of the eye, but being an older model, it generated a nasty high-pitched hum and a pretty extreme vibration. Someone was bound to realize it was being used and decide to investigate.

On the fifth floor, a stair crackled and snapped as the ancient tevta reacted to Everest's weight. He froze, but eventually, when no one came, he continued. Maybe this wasn't such a crazy idea after all. Maybe he *would* gain some temporary freedom.

As he neared the ground floor, he heard someone singing in a deep voice. He recognized the words as Italian, because his dad was nuts over the language and had insisted it be included in their pre-birth education. Everest dived down the last few stairs, flattened himself against the wall in the shadow of the staircase, and leaned out slightly to find the singer. The guy's gooey love song was turning his stomach.

He was in the enormous entrance hall. On the far side to the right of the door, someone paced back and forth in front of a large front desk, singing ancient opera and emphasizing the words with wild arm gestures. The faintest shimmery glow surrounding the singer tipped off Everest that the performer was in fact a hologram, and something about the way the singer stood, his excessive height and rounded shoulders, alerted Everest that the hologram was Uncle Fredrick's.

Everest's shoulders slumped. Flasers. Now what? He chewed his lower lip. A Basker never quit. Therefore, he just had to figure out how to get around the holograph.

In his experience holograms were pretty predictable, and they weren't exactly cerebrum-heavy either. Maybe if he figured out this one's pattern, he could find a way to slip past. Caught up in the game of outwitting the image, he crouched with his back to the wall and observed. As Everest expected, the hologram performed a series of tasks over and over again.

For about five minutes, he would pace back and forth in front of the door, singing and gesturing. Then he would take a slow walk around the room, humming softly, hands loose at his sides. Halfway around the room, he would arrive at a door. Everest didn't know what was behind it, but the hologram never failed to dissolve the door and enter the chamber behind. He would disappear for about thirty seconds, then return to finish his loop around the hall. He would finish by standing in front of the desk and staring out into the hall's darkness in case someone dared to intrude.

Everest decided to streak across the hall and dive behind the desk the moment the hologram entered the other room. Then while the hologram was singing, he could attempt to slip out the front. Holograms weren't known for having good hearing. He suspected that was why Uncle Fredrick's image was singing so loudly. Surely ancient Italian opera sung at full blast would drown out the airy sound of atoms rearranging themselves as the front door erased, and then refreshed itself. Everest reminded himself to act like a total yocto-brain if he was caught. After all, it was only his first day. How was he supposed to remember the rules?

The hologram went from singing to humming and started off on his long trek around the hall. As he passed the staircase, Everest held his breath. Lucky for him, holograms didn't have much of a sense of smell either. He was drenched in sweat, as if he'd played skyball for three hours straight. When the image disappeared into the side room, Everest sprinted across the hall and ducked behind the front desk. He grinned. Adrenalin pumped through him, as thick as blood and as swift as a river. This was the first fun he'd had since he'd arrived at this clone-home. Okay, maybe that wasn't exactly true. It had been fun to kick clone butt earlier today. Zetta fun. Then he looked up and saw himself reflected in the mirror-like tevta wall. Flasers! Not so fun after all! If he'd been sweating before, it was nothing to the moisture pouring from him now.

All of a sudden, footsteps sounded on the staircase, and moments later Instructor Sura strode briskly into the room. Double flasers! Only a few seconds earlier and she would have caught him in the act as he ran across the room. Now, with one good look at the wall, she would see him. He held his breath again as if somehow that would make him invisible.

"FLH1?" she called.

The hologram stuck his head back into the great hall. "Yes, Instructor Sura?"

"Anything to report?"

"No, Instructor."

She marched to the front desk. Luckily, her back was to the wall where his reflection gave him away, but this time he was dealing with a living, breathing human who had full use of all five senses.

"My goodness, FLH1. Are you storing a pile of dirty socks in one of these drawers?" She waved the air. "You might want to track down some air freshener."

56

"I'm sorry Instructor. I don't know what could have happened."

"Oh, forget it," she grumbled in disgust. "I'll be turning in now. Make sure that between you and FLH2 you make rounds throughout the building—both towers, mind."

"Of course, Instructor Sura."

"In case you have need of him, I believe Instructor Legnarchi is holed up in his office playing hologames." She sniffed loudly, then briskly left the room.

Everest breathed a deep sigh of relief.

The hologram immediately began to sing again, this time in a language that Everest couldn't identify. Had to be off-planet, but which galaxy was anyone's guess. The hologram's pattern had been broken by Instructor Sura's interruption.

Everest couldn't believe his luck when FLH1 left the great hall again. He jumped up from his hiding place, rubbed his damp palms down his pants and headed for the door.

Stepping into its sensor range, he whispered "Open, please," and watched it dissolve into nothingness. He quickly crossed over the threshold. On the other side, he paused for a second. Once he passed the door's sensors, it would become solid again. Odds were good it was locked to entry from the outside. Maybe he wouldn't be able to sneak back in. With a shrug, he moved past the sensor range. Staying out all night wouldn't be so bad.

As he heard the airy swish of atoms rearranging themselves into a solid state, he breathed deeply. Freedom. Grinning up at the billions of winking stars, the distant spaceships, and the spinning, bumping, and blinking jellach vehicles, he felt like the only person in the universe.

Then a siren pierced the sky, so high-pitched and sharp it hurt his eardrums.

CHAPTER 10
Everest's Narrow Escape

Everest bolted down the porch stairs. Without thought, he turned to the left, running at full tilt, his heart pounding, his mind blank to everything but one desperate need—escape. He shot around the corner of the building.

Everywhere lights blazed on, turning the garden from night to day. Light even streamed from the building windows. Only the dorm rooms remained dark.

Flasers, he was in trouble. But he couldn't just give up. Legs and arms pumping, he raced down the path, his chest feeling as if it was going to explode. Raised voices could be heard in the distance, and the siren continued to blast its angry warning into every nook of the property. The place was an alien world.

As he turned the next corner, something dropped from the sky directly into his path.

He yelled, then went bright red when he realized it was Dar.

"Yocto-brain!" the girl hissed. "Put these on." She shoved something into his hands.

He had no idea what she had given to him.

"On your feet and your hands. *Light speed!* They're going to catch us any second.

That was when he realized he held long boots and gloves. He started to follow Dar's directions.

As soon as he managed to slip on one of the boots, he figured out that it was spider gear. The boot crawled up his leg to mid-thigh. He quickly turned to boot number two and then the strange gloves. He'd heard of spider gear, but never actually seen it in action.

"Follow me," Dar said, then really confused him by whispering urgently, "Stay where you are. I repeat, stay where you are." She pulled something out of her ear and stuffed it into a pocket, then attached herself to the wall and began crawling up like a spider. She ordered over her shoulder, "Climb."

Without further thought he complied.

Dar was fast. It took everything in him to stay within a couple of meters of her. Course, she had the advantage of knowing how to use the gear. It was as if she were a real spider scurrying up its web. And what in galaxies was she wearing? The fabric almost made her disappear, despite the blazing lights. He had the feeling it wasn't the kind of material you could buy on the galactic store grid.

Through the pandemonium, he heard Dar say, "We're almost there." She pulled herself onto the roof and dragged off her boots and gloves at a hopping run. He did likewise.

"It's going to be close. Odds are good they'll start checking beds for missing students. Give me that stuff." She yanked the gear out of his hands and shoved it into her sack. "We can only hope they waste time in the garden first."

With what looked like long practice, she popped open a skylight and lowered herself through. "Don't touch the floor— there're sensors all over it. Swing yourself to a rope and do what I do."

She disappeared, and he followed her through the hole. In the dark, he recognized the fight room. Dar was swinging from rope to rope toward a gaping hole in the wall. When she was in line with the opening, she pumped her legs and swung until she could touch it with her toes. On her second trip, she let go and shot through, landing with a thud on the other side.

"Come on!" She stuck her head through the opening and motioned vigorously.

He threw himself at a rope, caught it, and started swinging after her. When he was close enough to attempt the leap, he leaned forward, then arched back to get his rope really moving. Using his body, he managed to swing closer and closer to the hole. When he judged the distance near enough, he let go and crashed through. The next thing he knew, he was on his back with Dar frowning over him.

He groaned. When he had snuck downstairs all the corridors had only been minimally lit, but now the hallway was aglow.

"Get up, yocto-brain, and jam to your dorm room. Throw on pajamas, dive under the covers, and pretend to be fast asleep when they come to your room. Whatever you do, don't confess to anything. You'll wish you were dead if you get me in trouble. Now blast off." She shoved him toward the boys' wing. As he ran, he looked over his shoulder at Dar. Instead of jamming, she turned around and pointed a small silver device at the opening in the wall. He paused to watch the atoms rearrange themselves back into solid tevta.

When she saw that he still stood there, anger clouded her face into a sudden storm. "Run," she said again in a harsh whisper, then took off like a flaser beam in the other direction.

This time he ran—straight into a hoard of pico-brownies that couldn't seem to move quickly enough to get out of his way. He itched everywhere from their abrasive, nearly invisible surfaces.

It was hard to feel grateful to Dar when she went out of her way to make him feel so brainless. No one had asked for her help. If he'd been caught, he would have taken his punishment without complaint.

A part of him contrarily felt like letting himself be caught rather than being in Dar's debt, but he knew that would upset Elsie. Plus, if his parents heard about it, he didn't know what they would do. If he thought that getting into trouble might bring them home for good, he'd be sorely tempted, but their research was too important for that to be the outcome. Instead, they would just be disappointed and worried from very far away. Or worse, they'd rush all the way back just to have to leave again. So he continued to race to his room.

Luckily, he made it there without incident. With all the sirens going off, he was surprised no kids milled around in the corridor. They couldn't possibly have slept through all the racket. After changing quickly and tossing his dark clothing into the back of his closet, he threw himself onto the bed, asked it for a blanket, and closed his eyes. His heartbeat pounded in his ears, and he was drenched in sweat. Luckily, mlenler blankets were naturally absorbent, so he didn't expect there to be any tell-tale signs. That had been way too close.

With his own safety assured, he had time to wonder why Dar had been roaming around outside in suspicious clothing with equipment a professional thief might envy. Clearly she'd been up to no good. And Elsie was her roommate. If Dar was up to mischief, then Elsie could be involved.

Dar had better hope not. Because if she got Elsie in trouble, she'd wish she'd never been cloned.

CHAPTER 11
Elsie's Narrow Escape

When the siren went off and the lights illuminated the gardens, Elsie knew she was in big trouble. Had someone caught Dar? She shivered as she imagined the consequences of the academy authorities finding her in the pen with Pooker. There were voices in the distance, and they were definitely nearing.

When she heard Dar whisper directions to someone else and then urgently command that she stay put, she didn't know whether to be relieved or terrified. Who was Dar talking to? She wasn't yet caught, but wasn't it just a matter of time?

On her belly, Elsie crawled backward further into the shelter and lay down flat, her head cradled in her arms. She covered herself with the Vlatex II material. When Pooker tried to curl up next to her, she shoved the bobcat forward.

"You have to pretend to be alone," she whispered, not really expecting the bobcat to understand. "They have to be able to see you."

Amazingly, Pooker did move beyond the canopy out into the middle of the square, where she began to restlessly pace. Thank goodness the cat didn't like enclosed spaces.

With no more communications from Dar, Elsie felt very much alone. Dar must have removed her earpatch.

Who had the girl run into? Judging from her name-calling, it had to be another student, and not one Dar liked any more than she liked the Baskers. Dar should have been back in their room by now. Could she have been caught along the way? Just as Elsie went into a full-blown panic, Dar's voice sounded in her ear. She had never felt more relieved.

"Okay," came the brisk whisper. "I'm in our room. Have they checked the pen yet?"

"No, not yet. Wait!" she whispered frantically. "The voices arc really close now."

"Then shut down. After they've checked out your bobcat's cage and moved on, I'll transport you back—*by yourself*—so you can be here for the bed check that's bound to happen shortly. You'll have to wait a little longer to bring up Pooker."

"Okay." Elsie spoke the word so quietly that she almost didn't hear it herself. Burrowing more deeply into her bobcat's bedding, she tried to quiet her breathing. Fear made her heartbeat sound like a booming drum in her ear.

"I know someone is out here." It was Instructor Sura's sharp voice.

"Maybe it was a faulty sensor," said a man who Elsie didn't recognize.

Instructor Sura snorted.

"Well if someone's hiding out here, he's doing a good job," the man added.

"I would not be surprised if the culprit were a *she*," the instructor responded tartly. "And I would give anything to catch *that* girl red-handed!"

Suddenly a powerful beam nailed Pooker's jail, causing the dancing fingers of light to jump and jolt frantically. The bobcat shifted and made an unhappy noise in her throat.

"Turn off that beam; it's bothering the cat," the man said. He didn't sound half as bad as the woman.

"What is this confounded racket?" A third voice joined the fray. There was something about it that made Elsie shiver. It was deep and dark, filled with threat and anger. She wished she could see who owned the dreadful voice, but she couldn't without raising her Vlatex II cover, and there was no question of that.

"Dr. Wei," Instructor Sura gasped. "We apologize for the commotion." The woman's voice shook. "I hope it didn't wake you."

"I assure you, Instructor, I rarely sleep. I was in the middle of an important experiment, which now will have to be redone from scratch due to this ridiculous interruption. I am most displeased."

"Oh, sir." Instructor Sura sounded desperate. "We are terribly sorry. Is there anything I can do to make amends? Anything at all?"

"I'm afraid the damage is done."

There was a miserable silence, then Instructor Sura said, "We will check the dorm rooms for missing children. When we find the culprit, he or she will receive detention for a month. Come, Legnarchi."

"The punishment is hardly relevant, since it cannot undo the irrevocable harm this disturbance has caused me," was Dr. Wei's parting shot.

Elsie listened to the rapidly retreating footsteps. Finally, she braved a peek out from under the Vlatex II and was horrified to find the tall, intimidating figure of a dark stranger staring into the pen from the vantage point of the rosewillow tree.

Dr. Wei? She ducked back under the material and listened to her racing heartbeat. Had he seen her? Finally, she heard him clear his throat then move away. His footsteps crunched as they disturbed the path's gravel.

When she judged that the man was well and truly gone, she whispered. "Sura's on her way to the dormitory."

"Okay, prepare to be transported," Dar responded.

Elsie firmly told Pooker to stay. She put her hand on the mini transporter and whispered, "Ready."

Suddenly, the enormity of what she was doing hit her. She had only ever been transported by experts, and then only a handful of times. Now she was trusting Dar's home equipment? What if it scrambled her molecules so badly that she could never be put back together again? She closed her eyes tightly and tried not to think about all the millions of things that could go wrong. Baskers could handle anything, couldn't they?

There was a strong tug, and she tensed a split second before she felt nothing at all. It was as if she were in the midst of a black void, with no sense of space, no feeling of time, no smell, no touch, no sound. She couldn't open her eyes because she had no eyes. She couldn't feel her fingers because they had vanished without trace.

Just when she was sure she would never be solid again, she landed with a thud in her pitch-black closet.

"No time to lose, change into your pajamas," Dar said urgently. "We're cutting it really close."

Elsie stripped off her black outfit and quickly replaced it with a loose top and some vlatex sweats. She dived onto her bed and whispered, "Blanket, please." A thin mlenler blanket shot out to wrap her in its aromatic and soothing warmth. She wanted to ask Dar about the sinister Dr. Wei, but there wasn't time. Even as the jellach bed molded itself to her frame and started its gentle massage, without warning, their door erased, and the light from the hall spilled into their room.

A very angry Instructor Sura strode over the threshold.

CHAPTER 12
An Unconventional Avatar

"Lights on," the instructor commanded, and the room was flooded with bright violet-tinted light.

"Ow!" Elsie screeched, blinking. Panic tied her stomach in knots when she realized that her nighteyes drops hadn't worn off. Would it be obvious to Instructor Sura? To be safe, she kept her eyes slit as if she were fighting free from a deep sleep.

Dar made a show of slowly waking, stretching her arms and squinting through eyes that were also just barely open. "What's going on?" she asked, yawning. "Why the sirens? Is there a fire?"

"No fire." Instructor Sura gave them both sharp looks. "Someone's been wandering around outside, most likely a student. Any ideas?"

Dar yawned again. "Sorry, Instructor Sura, I've been asleep, and as far as I know, Elsie here has been sleeping too. Elsie?"

Elsie stretched her mouth in a wide yawn and patted it with the back of her hand. "Out like a light," she croaked. "Anyway, I only know a few of the students, so I can't be much help."

"Humph." Instructor Sura stared at them so long, Elsie was afraid her cheeks would catch fire with guilt. She concentrated on keeping her breathing even and centering herself for inner calm.

Finally, Instructor Sura snapped, "Avatar, show yourself."

Elsie gasped as an incredible creature appeared from nowhere, draping herself across Dar's desk chair. She might have been mistaken for a beautiful human if her skin hadn't shimmered with gold and her forehead hadn't displayed a pure gold unicorn horn that twisted to a delicate point. She had a regal nose and impossibly high and defined cheekbones, and she wore a gown of rich gold. Strangest of all, the room was haunted by the smell of sweet liligilds, the tiny gold-tinged blossoms from Blumflor that drenched gardens with the fragrance of spring.

Instructor Sura pivoted sharply to face Dar. "Who is this?"

Dar took her time answering, then spoke distinctly as if to a young child. "This is Melista, the room's avatar."

"I find her highly inappropriate for an adolescent's room. You're far too old for fairy-tales."

"Melista has been my avatar for as long as I can remember. I believe loyalty is always appropriate."

"Humph." Instructor Sura turned back to the avatar and spoke sharply. "Report your charges' activities over the course of the evening."

Elsie choked as she swallowed another gasp, and Instructor Sura shot her another narrow-eyed glare.

Melista shifted slightly, assuming an even more relaxed pose, apparently unaffected by the tension in the room. "20:00: Ms. Basker entered for the night. 21:58: lights out. 22:30: Dar entered. 22:33: Ms. Basker fell asleep. Dar took a few minutes more. 23:28: Instructor Sura entered room for spot check." Her voice was low and melodic, like a warm tropical rain.

Instructor Sura glared at Dar. "Everyone is supposed to be in their dorm room by 21:00 with lights out by 22:00."

"Lights were out before 22:00," said Dar, "and I have special permission from Instructor Esqualti to be out after curfew—for the good of the academy. I thought you were aware of my dispensation."

The woman's nose flared with displeasure. "Now that you mention it, I am aware of your unique circumstances. I will check with Esqualti to verify your whereabouts earlier this evening." She turned back to Melista. "No one left the room after Dar entered at 22:30?"

"No, Ma'am," Melista replied softly. Her head turned slightly so that she showed Instructor Sura her profile and was able to give Elsie a slow wink.

It took everything in Elsie to keep her face expressionless. She couldn't believe it. Melista had lied! She'd never seen a room avatar be anything but truthful. How had Dar achieved such reprogramming? Wasn't a room avatar's sole purpose the monitoring and controlling of the room, including its occupants? If anyone found out, Dar would be in serious hot water.

"Humph," the instructor said again, then pivoted with the precision of a soldier and marched to the door, which quickly erased itself so she could pass. Once she was through, atoms rearranged back to their solid state so that Sura disappeared from view.

Dar put a forefinger to her lips to keep Elsie quiet. They hadn't heard the sound of receding footsteps outside. Instructor Sura had to be standing on the other side of their door, waiting and listening.

"Thank you, Melista," Dar said. "Don't forget our 6:00 a.m. wakeup call."

The golden creature dipped her head. "Of course."

Dar grinned. "You're excused."

The human-unicorn offered them a graceful smile and slowly disappeared.

"Lights out please," Dar requested, keeping the same sleepy cadence in her voice. The room plunged back into darkness.

"Wonder who set off the sirens?" Elsie asked around an exaggerated yawn.

"Who cares?" Dar's tone was deliberately cranky. "Let's get some shut-eye."

Elsie was lying in bed, her eyes wide open, her thoughts on what Dar had been up to this evening. Why did she have special permission from an academy instructor to break curfew? Sura seemed pretty steamed about the arrangement.

Finally, the instructor's footsteps sounded in the hallway and slowly melted away into the distance. Elsie let out a breath of relief as she rolled out of bed, her thoughts immediately returning to Pooker.

"Can I go now?" she whispered.

"Wait a sec," Dar said. "Melista?"

Melista reappeared, this time lounging at the foot of Elsie's bed. The floral scent had returned with her.

"Can you touch base with Folgar and make sure he keeps his trap shut?"

"Done," Melista said, smiling.

"Excellent," said Dar. "How I love your light speed communication skills."

"Always aiming to please."

"Thanks, Melista, this time you really are excused."

The human-unicorn again shimmered away to nothingness.

Dar returned her attention to Elsie. "*Now* you can go pick up Pooker." She shoved a thumb toward the wall. "Into the closet."

"Who's Folgar?"

Dar shrugged. "Another avatar."

Like that told Elsie anything. She would have pursued the subject, but her desire for Pooker overrode her natural curiosity.

She wanted to ask about Dr. Wei too. Who was he, and why had he seemed so sinister? But that would have to wait till a less fraught time.

She was more prepared for the transport process, and arrived in Pooker's enclosure feeling like a pro. Her bobcat was less accommodating, but ultimately, Elsie managed to cajole her into the corner structure where the transport lay hidden.

She whispered to Dar that she was ready and once again lost all sensation while she and Pooker were transferred to the dorm room. Pooker came out of the transport with her fur standing on end and a low growl deep in her throat, as if she felt threatened by some unknown danger.

Kneeling at her side, Elsie wrapped her arms around Pooker's neck and murmured reassurance. The transport process would become easier over time for the bobcat, just as it was getting easier for her.

"Basker, give me your earpatch." Dar had the little vial out again.

Elsie quickly picked the picobot out of her ear and dropped it in the solution. She crawled back into bed, then patted the portion of jellach next to her to entice Pooker. The bobcat leapt onto the bed and circled two times before curling up next to Elsie.

"I've never seen an avatar lie," she commented. "What gives?"

"Melista and I have a deal," Dar responded. There was laughter in her voice.

Elsie grinned despite her worry, and despite the fact that once again Dar had avoided giving her a straight answer. The girl sure was a mystery. She had to admit that some of this adventure had been fun. Then she remembered the enormity of what Dar had risked for her. "Thanks Dar, I owe you."

"Yeah, don't worry, I'll find a way for you to pay me back."

Elsie heard Dar settle more deeply into her mattress, the jellach conforming to her body.

"So, how come the sirens went off?" she asked. "Who'd you run into?"

"Surprised you didn't figure that one out for yourself. Your yocto-brained brother decided to take a night-time stroll, and I had to save his sorry keister."

Elsie groaned. Everest? Why in galaxies had he been wandering around outside at night? A guilty voice inside her head whispered that she'd been doing the exact same thing. She hugged Pooker and reminded herself that she'd had the best of reasons to break the rules. But she still couldn't figure out Dar. Why had the girl put herself to so much trouble on their behalf?

Elsie found herself whispering the question aloud.

After a slight pause, Dar answered, "You and your brother beat me fair and square in our fight today. That makes me your protector. It's a matter of honor. Now will you please power down and go to sleep?"

The girl's voice was as sharp as ever, yet Elsie had a feeling she wasn't as tough as she liked to make out. Dar could blame her actions on the fact that she had lost the competition earlier today, but that didn't fully explain why she had opted to sneak Pooker inside for Elsie. Dar had demonstrated a real generosity of spirit that had nothing to do with who had won the fight competition. Elsie vowed then and there that no matter how rude Dar acted, she would do everything on her part to be her friend. It would be her first step in paying Dar back.

She sighed, her thoughts turning to her parents. It was hard to believe they had been gone for less than one day. Were they already in some other galaxy? With one arm wrapped around Pooker, Elsie clutched at her new necklace with her other hand, finding a small measure of comfort in the warmth of the pendant made from alien metal. Missing her parents made her stomach hurt.

And then she had the horrible thought that clones had no parents at all.

What would it be like to live your whole life without a mother or a father?

CHAPTER 13

Morning at the Clone Academy

"Wake up, ladies," sounded Melista's low, melodic voice, the smell of spring back in the air.

Groggy, Elsie rolled onto her side and moaned into her pillow. Pooker made a funny grumbling sound and extended her claws, inadvertently poking Elsie in her side.

"Ow!" she screeched.

"Would you shut down?" Dar mumbled grumpily. "Melista, are you sure it's 6:00?"

"Quite positive, my dear." There was laughter in the avatar's voice. "On another note, when are you planning to officially introduce me to your new roommate? It's not like you to be so impolite." It was weird hearing Melista rebuke Dar.

"*Sorry,* but I had other things on my mind last night." Dar waved her hand from Elsie to Melista and back again. "Elsie, Melista...Melista, Elsie."

Elsie flipped onto her back. "Pleased to meet you, Melista," she said shyly. "Thanks for covering for us last night."

"Just one of my many services." Melista's speech continued to hold laughter barely in check. "It's a pleasure to meet you as well. I've never met a child conceived the old-fashioned way."

Elsie smiled, and Pooker chose that moment to run her rough tongue over her cheek and mouth.

73

"Bleck!" Dar said. "Do you have to let her do that?"

"She's my baby." Elsie kissed Pooker on her nose, and got another lick in return.

"That is so gross. Do you know where that tongue's been?" Dar rolled out of bed. "Let's get her back to her pen before anyone discovers she's missing and before she licks you again."

"Oh, Pooker," Elsie said soulfully. "I'm sorry I have to do this to you."

"Light speed," Dar commanded, holding out the earpatch vial. "We'll need to wear the patches so you can let me know when you're ready to come back. And don't spend all day down there. You never know when someone might decide to check on you or your bobcat."

The transport process was easier this time. Pooker still growled as she came out of it, but she didn't seem as afraid as the first time. Elsie remained hopeful that soon her bobcat would be used to the twice-daily event. Pooker settled resignedly into her pen.

"You'll sleep with me again tonight," Elsie whispered, "and I'll visit every chance I get today."

"She's a bobcat, not an A-level," she heard Dar say in her ear, reminding her that at the academy the under seven-year-olds were categorized as A-levels.

"Eavesdroppers aren't allowed to comment," she hissed back. She bent over and gave Pooker a sloppy kiss on the nose, then returned to the transport device. "Okay, I'm ready when you are."

"Serving up scrambled Elsie for breakfast," Dar teased a split second before Elsie was being transported.

She landed on her rear in the closet. "Funny, very funny."

"That's me, everyone's favorite comedian." Dar crossed her eyes.

"Yeah, you're a real allen." A few decades back, the Academy of Entertainment Arts and Sciences had conducted a study and determined that 'Allen' was by far the most common name—last or first—for successful humorists. After that, it had become a popular term in the English language.

"How exactly did you manage to con a transport device out of your sponsor?" Elsie asked.

Dar shrugged. "Every year on the anniversary of the first day of my existence, he gives me one gift of my choosing. I figured a transport system would come in handy."

Elsie suspected it was just one of many handy items Dar owned. "It must cost a fortune."

"He's one of the richest humanoids in the universe," Dar said matter-of-factly, "which is the only reason I exist." She pulled on basic gray vlatex exercise pants and a matching sleeveless shirt. Without brushing her hair, she scraped it back into a tight ponytail and shoved a cap over it.

It was weird. Dar was so beautiful that it was almost hard to look at her. With her golden hair, she was the spitting image of Shadara even without the layers of makeup the original had favored. Yet Dar did everything she could not to capitalize on her looks. Clones were hard to figure. Course, she was having trouble getting a handle on anything at the moment. Thinking about how confused she was made her remember one of her burning questions from last night.

"Dar?"

"Hmm?"

"Who's Dr. Wei?"

The girl sent Elsie a sharp look. "You sure are the queen of questions. Why do you ask?"

"He was in the garden last night. The ruckus made him really angry. Sura sounded scared of him."

"*Everyone's* scared of Dr. Wei. He's not someone you want to mess with. The man's a genius, a scientist who specializes in clone research, and he makes his home here on the grounds. You might call him our granddaddy. Pretty much every clone at the academy has him to thank for their existence."

"Huh." Elsie didn't know how to respond. The world of clones was so different from what she was used to. She knew one thing, though. She was keeping her distance from the man. He had given her the creeps.

"Did Director Lester-Hauffer issue you uniforms yet?" Dar asked in an abrupt change of subject.

Elsie shook her head, happy to get off the topic of the sinister Dr. Wei. Why did she constantly feel the need to ask questions? It wasn't as if answers always reassured her.

Dar tossed her a matching exercise outfit. "Use my spare for now."

Elsie slipped on the gray garb. She and Dar were basically the same height, but Dar was well ahead of her in the figure department. The borrowed clothes hung loosely.

"Come on," said Dar. "Let's track down Instructor Legnarchi. He's in charge of uniforms. He was on duty last night, so he should be around."

"Can we pick up my brother? He needs a uniform too."

Dar sighed. "Do we have to?"

Elsie made a face, which Dar threw right back at her. They both ended up laughing.

It was still early enough that the halls were nearly empty. When they reached Everest's room, Dar spoke to the door. "Dar and Elsie here."

"How come our door opened to Instructor Sura without her introducing herself or us giving her permission?"

"Teachers have unlimited and automatic access to all the students' rooms, but we're only given automatic access to our own dorms and the shared rooms."

The door dissolved to reveal Everest standing ill at ease on the other side.

"Thanks," he mumbled to Dar without actually looking at her.

"Just doing my duty as your protector," she said with arched eyebrows. "Don't sweat it."

"What possessed you to go outside last night?" Elsie asked, her fists on her hips.

He frowned at her tone. "I just wanted some air, that's all. No big deal. Don't know why this place is sealed up like a cyborg prison."

"Maybe because it is one," Dar said.

Since Elsie and Everest just gaped at her, she continued. "Look, utes, clones are expensive. Not only is the technology and the funding of ongoing research zetta VC, but the huge royalties that have to be paid to the originals and their estates makes us an exorbitant proposition. The United Nations of Earth expects to get its money's worth. We're not allowed to just make up our own minds about where and when we want to be. Why else do you think there are so many restrictions here? Did you know we're not even supposed to use the Grid except on the weekends?"

"Instructor Gerard said that was to keep us focused on our studies."

Dar snorted. "And I've got a lovely resort location to sell you in the Cassiopeia system."

Elsie gaped. "But...it's not fair. You shouldn't be treated differently just because you're a clone."

Dar rolled her eyes. "Are utes always this naive?" She started to turn, but Everest grabbed her wrist.

"Was that why there weren't any kids in the hallway last night after the alarms went off? Are they all that afraid of breaking the rules?"

Dar broke his grip, and her lip curled into a sneer. "No one's afraid. I break plenty of rules."

"But you're the only one."

"One day at the academy doesn't make you a clone expert, ute-boy. We may be picky about which rules we break and when, but at least when we do break a rule, *we* don't get caught—unlike certain yocto-brains." She turned on her heel and motioned for them to follow. "Can we make light speed? I get cranky when I miss a meal."

Everest didn't budge. "I thought we agreed there was going to be no name calling."

"Think of ute as a term of affection."

Everest snorted and held his ground. "And yocto-brain?"

Dar swung around. "Definitely a term of affection. I'm sure your sister's called you that before."

Elsie laughed. "She's got a point."

Even Everest's mouth twitched at the corners. "I can come up with some terms of affection too, *Shadara*."

Her cheeks went pink. "I'll knock your head sideways if you call me that one more time."

"And here I thought you were our protector... *Shadara*," Everest replied. He stepped sideways as she lunged forward and had to continue to dance out of her way as she lunged again. "As long as you call us names, we'll respond in kind. You want to be called Dar, don't label us yocto-brains or utes." He stopped dodging her and held out his hand. "Do we have a deal?"

Dar reluctantly accepted his handshake. "Deal."

Their grips tightened, each fighting for dominance. Gritting their teeth, their arms shaking under the strain, they pushed and pulled trying to throw each other off balance, but they were an even match.

Elsie sighed. "Will you two knock it off? You're both yocto-brains."

Dar grinned, suddenly full of good humor. "You're probably right. We'd better jam if we want to get your gear before breakfast. I'm starved."

She strode down the hallway, leaving Elsie and Everest to trail behind. Everest caught Elsie's eye and twirled his finger in the galactic sign for crazy.

Elsie frowned. She owed Dar. Too bad she couldn't explain to Everest just how much. It felt wrong to keep secrets from her twin, but she'd promised not to tell anyone.

They took the nanovator, and as it had the day before, the older model made Elsie a little woozy. Plus, her cheeks rippled and tickled from the vibration. She wondered why their uncle didn't upgrade to something more modern.

On the ground floor, they took a corner too quickly and careened into a boy a couple of years older than them, who was both taller and broader. He had high cheekbones and a square jaw, and his eyes were muddy. His face looked as if it had been frozen years ago into a perpetual sneer.

"Well, if it isn't little Miss Beauty Queen," he said to Dar in a nasty sort of voice.

CHAPTER 14
Bad and Good Meetings

"At least I don't have to worry about the walls cracking when I walk by," Dar said, her tone quiet but dangerous. She pointed to their reflections in the mirror-like walls.

"Weak, Shadara. Very weak." The boy's sneer grew more pronounced. "Of course, that's all anyone could expect from a dupe of a ditzy performer." He laughed. "Better luck with the comebacks next time, fluff-brain."

In growing horror, Elsie watched Dar's fists clench and tighten so that her knuckles turned white. Surely, the girl wasn't going to do battle in the corridor? At Elsie's old school that was cause for a suspension. All physical confrontations had to be resolved through refereed fight competitions.

It was weird seeing someone harass Dar. She was so self-assured and in charge, Elsie had kind of figured that she led the whole student body.

After a slight pause, the boy continued, "What? Has your tongue been sucked into a black hole?"

"You're so pathetic, you aren't worth talking to," Dar replied as she tried to shoulder past him.

He shoved her back, his expression mean. "Step aside, Shadara. I've got the right of way here."

"Hey," Everest said, "leave her alone."

"Stay out of it, ute-boy," the bully sneered.

Did everyone in the school know who they were?

The boy turned back to Dar. "Hiding behind utes now? Heard they beat you in a fight. Talk about pathetic." He scanned the group. "Hard to say which is worse, hanging with utes or hanging with clone rejects like your loser sidekicks." He paused then added, "Or have you finally dumped Lelita and Vlas?"

Dar's jaw clenched. "Keep it up and you'll need a new growth of teeth in the very near future."

"Oooh, I'm shaking." He left no doubt that Dar's words hadn't fazed him a bit.

Dar flat-handed Everest's chest to stop him from stepping into the boy's path. She glared at the boy for a long time, then slowly shifted sideways to give him room to pass, sweeping her hand out to indicate a clear path. "Don't let us keep you."

He laughed and stomped down the passage. They could hear him cackling as he disappeared around the corner.

Dar watched him go, her hands fisted at her side, the knuckles stark white. After a moment, she eased her fingers wide and took a slow breath. "Sorry for not introducing you. That was Kindu, a B14, cloned from a famous statesman in the twenty-fourth century. He's a bit of a vlemutz."

She rubbed the back of her neck and rolled her shoulders to release tension. "If I were you, I'd keep my distance from him and his crowd. If you think I have a problem with utes, you haven't seen anything yet."

Elsie didn't need another warning, but she shot a worried look at Everest as they continued down the hallway with Dar setting an extremely brisk pace. Elsie had a feeling her brother was wishing he could take on the boy in a fight competition. Everest was good, but Kindu had a couple of years and more than a few centimeters on him, and she couldn't shake the notion that he wouldn't act as honorably as Dar had in a fight.

Dar stopped so suddenly that Elsie barreled into her.

"Oomph," she gasped.

The girl's expression was grim as she pivoted around to face them. "I'd appreciate it if you'd keep to yourselves what Kindu said about Lelita and Vlas. Vlas could care less—he'd just think it was a big joke—but Lelita's sensitive and even knowing what a vlem Kindu is, it would still hurt."

They quickly promised. Elsie wished she had the guts to ask what Kindu had meant when he'd called them clone rejects, but the expression on Dar's face kept her silent.

Dar swiveled around and strode down the hallway at top speed, forcing them to walk even faster to keep up.

Instructor Legnarchi's office was on the third floor. He was a friendly sort, with the belly of someone who had a real fondness for food that could not be satisfied by no-calorie snacks. His warm brown eyes crinkled as if he smiled all the time, and his skin was olive-toned. When he spoke, Elsie recognized him as the man who had been outside with Instructor Sura last night. Her heart beat a little faster, and her palms got clammy, but after a few minutes of conversation, she calmed down. He clearly didn't suspect a thing. Instead, he acted delighted to be in the presence of non-clones. It turned out he hadn't met many in his life.

When Elsie asked him where he'd been before coming to the academy, Legnarchi explained that for most of his life he'd participated in a special off-world study regarding the cloning of various humanoid forms from multiple galaxies. This was his first year at the academy.

"What do you teach?" Elsie asked politely.

"Literature and the spoken word—most common languages. I was cloned from a famous linguist. Unfortunately, I was a disappointment to my sponsors—never quite reached the level of my famous forbearer who could speak as many languages as were known in the universe, but I manage quite well with the couple dozen or so premier languages, and I like to teach. I was useful during the study because I could communicate with all the clones who participated." He rubbed his nose. "Which languages do you study?"

"We learned English, Italian, Zylanderin, and Chinese in the womb," Elsie said. "And we've been studying Spanish, French, Japanese, and Quorr."

"And sign language," added Everest.

"Excellent, signing is such a handy thing to know, especially when it comes to Tenorians who don't have ears. Have you ever met a Tenorian?"

Elsie and Everest shook their heads.

"Delightful creatures—highly intelligent with an acute sense of smell. Never wear perfume around them. They can't stop sneezing once they start. Their noses are rather impressive. I hear the academy does an exchange once a year with either a Tenorian or a Pellaccii school. Now there's another fascinating humanoid race."

As he spoke, he rummaged around in various bins.

Elsie shot her brother a nervous glance. As usual, he was being awfully quiet.

"Quorr's another excellent choice," Instructor Legnarchi continued, his voice muffled because his head was now inside a bin. "As Glagcha's most important language, it will come in handy. Now that's one amazing planet. I attended a seminar there once. The most beautiful place I've ever seen. Course, I've been told that the Xlexuri Galaxy has even more incredible planets, but I find that hard to believe. Glagcha isn't number one in the Milky Way for nothing. Have you ever been?"

"No," Elsie responded, "but my best friend is half Glagchian."

"Really? How delightful." With an excited yelp, the instructor pulled out a set of gray vlatex sweats and shoved them into Everest's arms. "I believe these will fit you, young man. And I don't think I need to offer you any skyboots. Yours are much more state-of-the-art than anything we can offer."

Turning his attention to Elsie, he shook his head in dismay. "My dear girl, that uniform positively swims on you."

"It's Dar's."

"And it's not exactly swimming." Dar sounded irritated. "It's just a little loose."

He beamed at the girl. "Good of you to lend her something, but we can do better." After a few moments, he tossed Elsie an exercise uniform that was a much better fit. Next were the dress clothes. "The director is quite adamant that uniforms should last a full year, but I'm equally strong-willed, and above all else, I believe that uniforms should fit properly. At twelve years old, you're all going to be sprouting like saplings, so you come to me if your uniform gets too short at the ankle or too tight at the waist, and I'll work something out. Just make sure you bring your old uniforms with you."

"Thank you, Instructor," Elsie and Everest said in unison.

The Instructor shoved the dress uniforms at them, then shooed them off with his expressive hands. "Run along now. I believe we're going on a history field trip today, which doesn't leave you much time for breakfast."

"Flasers!" Dar hissed. "I totally forgot about the field trip." She shoved Elsie toward the nanovator. "Drop off your clothes at your rooms and meet me in the cafeteria. Don't worry about changing. We'll be dressing in period costume for the history lesson anyway. I'll grab us some food—okay?"

Both Elsie and Everest nodded their heads. *Period costumes?*

"Hurry." Dar was already jamming down the corridor to the cafeteria as Elsie and Everest ran for the nanovator.

When they met up again in the cafeteria, Dar was half way through her protein smoothie, more commonly known as a fruicey because of a famous chain of stores from the twenty-ninth century. Two more fruiceys sat side by side in front of her. The straws were wiggling and dancing, turning one color after another. Elsie's straw started to whistle, but she grabbed the drink and quickly sucked on the straw to shut it down. The same group of twelve-year-olds sat together, chattering excitedly. Most had already finished their meals.

At a table to their left, Elsie spotted the vlem who had harassed them earlier. When he caught her staring, he pulled a ghoulish face. Looking away, she tried to put the nasty boy out of her mind. Everest didn't appear to notice Kindu. He had already slid onto the bench and was slurping his fruicey as if he hadn't a care in the world. Elsie never could understand how her brother managed to tune out everything and everyone when food was available.

The drink was good—a mixture of kiwi, strawberries and pink zikwik berries with protein, vitamins, and agri-nutrients added. Between slurps she asked, "Why is everyone so excited about the field trip?"

"Yeah—weird. It's just history," Everest said, yawning. "What's so exciting about going to some moldy old museum?"

Dar's smile felt a little wicked to Elsie.

"I think this field trip will be a bit better than the ones you're used to." Her grin grew broader. "Trust me."

A few students giggled at Dar's words.

Bemused, Elsie searched the faces of the kids at their table. "Come on—give. What's the secret?"

"Don't worry," Dar said. "It won't be too painful."

"Don't listen to her." Lelita tugged gently on Elsie's sleeve. "It's totally zeller. You're going to love it."

At that moment, Elsie was distracted by Uncle Fredrick's hologram entering the cafeteria. Once again, she had to remind herself to think of him as Director Lester-Hauffer.

He cleared his throat, then said in an amplified but tinny voice, "B12s, please come to the History Center. Don't dawdle."

There were a few jeers from the older tables, especially from Kindu. The hologram glared sternly before pivoting around and leaving the room.

Ignoring the rude cat-calls, Lelita leaned over to Elsie and said, "Director Lester-Hauffer loves his holograms." She rolled her eyes and giggled. "He uses them for everything."

Vlas added, "Yeah, we call them his hall-i-gram monitors. Since he got his second one, I don't think we've seen him in person once."

"You're talking about Elsie and Everest's uncle," Dar reminded the group.

"I told you, we hardly know him," Elsie said. "I don't mind whatever you say about him. We're not snitches."

"He smells like rotting vegetables," Everest said in such a low voice it took the other kids a few seconds to digest his words. Then the whole table burst into laughter. A half-grin played at his lips even as his cheeks turned bright red.

Vlas leaned over conspiratorially. "Did you notice that his holograms are better looking than he is? I heard he had them enhanced!"

Elsie grinned. "I noticed that right away!"

"Come on, B12s," Dar interrupted in a commanding voice. "We'd better blast off or they'll cancel the trip."

That got the kids pushing and shoving to be first in line. Elsie and Everest found themselves scrambling with the rest of them, and they didn't even know why.

No surprise, Dar took the lead, and the rest of the B12s filed in behind her. They left the building and followed the same path Elsie had used the night before to see Pooker. In the morning breeze, the flowers scented the pathway, enticing noisy bees and silent butterflies, and the sun shattered the jewel-toned gravel into prisms of light and color. The beauty of the gardens did nothing to cheer up Pooker, who sprawled morosely in the pen, managing to appear both bored and mesmerized by the dancing lights. Elsie's stomach dipped in response to her bobcat's misery.

They passed the big garage and stopped in front of an even larger building. It had a huge light mural in front that flashed "Lester-Hauffer History Center" in brilliant colors. As with all the structures on the property, the building itself was constructed of tevta. In the shape of a giant rectangle, it looked like an overgrown storage shed.

Vlas leaned over to Elsie, "Your uncle named the building a couple of years ago. I guess he thought it had a nice ring to it."

"Huh." She couldn't think of a thing to say. The sign was very large and bright, not something anyone would miss.

The children entered slowly, their excited speech now moderated to animated whispers. Elsie looked around with avid curiosity. The building was crammed with vehicles from every imaginable time period—ancient stage coaches and chariots, sailing vessels and trains, cars and SUVs, planes, flyers, and hover vehicles. It smelled musty and felt slightly damp.

"Wow!" she said under her breath.

Instructor Gerard was already there, motioning the B12s to the rows of metallic benches they bumped into almost immediately when they entered. Elsie was pretty sure he was dressed up in some sort of historical costume. Either that or he was a zetta freakazoid, but that hadn't been her original impression. She didn't recognize the time period.

Elsie ended up squashed between Lelita and Everest. On the other side of her brother was Dar. She could tell Dar still made Everest uncomfortable because of the amount of squirming he was doing in his seat. He might have defended her against the local bully, but that didn't mean they were suddenly buddies.

Instructor Gerard moved to stand in front of the benches. He rubbed his hands, excitement bringing color to his cheeks and a sparkle to his eyes. His broad smile encompassed all twenty-four students. "This is a very special outing," he began. "A trip back in time, where we will see first hand the amazing world of the early twenty-first century."

CHAPTER 15
Prepping for the Time Travel Field Trip

Elsie suspected that her mouth gaped as if she were trying to catch a grandoso fly from Spindora.

A time travel trip? Zetta zeller! Weren't those trips reserved for University students? Even then, she was pretty sure you had to be studying special subjects like history or sociology. She remembered her parents discussing how expensive the technology was.

Pretty quasar, she thought with a grin. Not a bad first day at the clone academy. Wait till she told her best friend, Zulu. She'd go orange with jealousy. Zulu was half Glagcha, which gave her skin a tinge of apricot until her emotions ran high and she went bright orange. Taking a deep breath, Elsie forced herself to listen to Instructor Gerard's excited lecture.

"Some of you have heard this time period that straddles the turn of the millennium referred to as the 'Silicon Revolution'," he was saying, "a time when computers were still in their infancy, yet computer companies already had a stranglehold on the world. A period when there were still royal families, though they were slowly dying out. For countries where royalty was already extinct, actors and actresses, not to mention sports figures, were the equivalent of royalty—perhaps not much different from today." His glance slid to Dar, who scowled back and shoved her cap down lower on her head.

He cleared his throat. "If you can imagine, this was a time when the majority of Earth's population believed theirs was the only planet in the universe with intelligent life. Of course, there was a benefit to this ignorance. Humans didn't have to deal with Glagcha beating their planet in all things, and they didn't even have to dream that a Xlexuri Galaxy existed. Despite Earthlings' primitive understanding of the universe, it was a period of amazing technological innovation and one of extravagant wealth—for entertainers and sports figures, for corporate executives and politicians. Countless people had more money than they could spend in a lifetime—especially when that lifetime spanned on average less than seventy-five years." He paused as the students gasped.

Elsie had a hard time imagining life over so quickly.

"Death came in a variety of ways," he continued. "In one year alone, car crashes accounted for over one hundred thousand deaths in the United States, and let's not forget about all the disease. You cannot imagine how many people died just because their hearts stopped functioning correctly. And cancer was a particularly troublesome plague on the earth, destroying lives by the thousands. Then there was AIDs and Alzeimer's, not to mention the common cold and flu.

"If illness or accidents didn't get you, murder, war, natural disasters or terrorism did. This was a violent, polluted, unhealthy period of history." Again he paused, his expression now serious and a trifle sad. Then he smiled. "It also gave us some of the greatest music of any millennium, delightful literature, and it was *the* golden age for two-dimensional movies. All in all, I think you'll really get a kick out of this trip." He cleared his throat. "And of course, you'll learn a lot too."

He rearranged his features into stern lines, which appeared to be something of an effort given his upbeat friendly nature. "However, more than ever, it is critical that you abide by all timed field trip rules. I cannot impress upon you enough how dangerous this period in history was. They were poised on the brink of the Age of Terror."

When a couple of students gasped, Instructor Gerard held up his hands to calm them. "Of course, we've done our homework and determined that nothing bad happened on this particular day in history, but we still must stick together, and we must not under any circumstances interact more than superficially with the natives." He cleared his throat for the second time. "All of you will be writing essays on what you learned when we return, so I expect you to make copious voice entries in your jellach diaries. I may even request that you submit your JEDs for my review."

The students' collective groans echoed in the cavernous building.

"Any questions?"

A B12 with bushy brown hair and a prominent chin who Elsie couldn't quite place raised his hand, and when Instructor Gerard nodded at him, he stood up. "What country will we be visiting?"

Instructor Gerard smiled broadly again. "For this trip we are staying close to home. In fact, we'll be within spitting distance of this very location. A thousand years ago, this property was populated by single-family residences, a religious convent, and a few small businesses. Nothing particularly noteworthy. Therefore, we won't visit this exact site, but we'll be close by as we tour the heart of Silicon Valley."

"Zeller!" Lelita whispered. She raised her hand excitedly.

"Yes, Lelita?"

"Will we be allowed to do any shopping?"

"I'm afraid on this trip we won't be able to satisfy your prodigious capacity for purchasing frivolous items." His audience laughed, and Lelita blushed. "I shouldn't have to remind you that it's against Galactic rules to bring back items from a time travel trip. As usual, Lelita, your memory leaves something to be desired." The girl went pink at his insulting reprimand. "I will bring a small amount of coins and bills to pay for meals, tours and any other incidentals. Otherwise, we will stick to a rigid agenda designed to satisfy our educational needs rather than our mercenary ones."

Still burning with embarrassment, Lelita turned and whispered, "It's not fair. They had real shopping centers, not like our galactic shopping grid. Why can't we at least visit one? I don't have to purchase anything."

With a pointed glare at Lelita, as if he'd heard and disapproved of her comment, Gerard clapped his hands together to regain the students' attention. "Time to get this show on the road. Most of you know the drill. Dar and Vlas, help Elsie and Everest find suitable clothing in the costume room. Be back in your chairs and in appropriate attire in nine minutes flat. Anyone who's late or who hasn't changed will have to remain behind. Oh, and don't forget to take off all jewelry and leave it here." He shooed them with his hands. "Blast-off!"

Before she could even think to yell, Elsie was yanked out of her seat and dragged by Dar toward the far left corner of the room, weaving past other students at breakneck speed.

"Deng, Dar, where's the fire?" Elsie asked as she raced to keep up.

"Instructor Gerard's not kidding about leaving students behind. Besides, if we're at the end of the line, we'll be stuck with totally blubber costumes."

"We dress up like we're kids from the twenty-first century?"

"You're so bright I'm afraid I'll go blind." Dar shoved Elsie through an archway where they were confronted by row after row of wild clothing in an amazing array of styles.

Along the perimeter of the room, adolescent holograms strutted their stuff, wearing bizarre outfits that Elsie hoped were *not* twenty-first-century garb. "Ignore them," Dar said when she saw Elsie gaping at a model wearing a top that ended above her belly button and low slung pants made of very strange material. "I've already researched this period. What we need is jeans."

At Elsie's blank look, Dar continued to drag her forward but added, "Stiff pants made out of cotton, often dark blue." We'll try the boys' section first since we're both a bit taller than your average twenty-first-century girl. Once we find the pants, we'll need tennis shoes and t-shirts and scrunchies for our hair. We won't be fashion queens, but we won't feel like blubbers either." She tipped her head and studied Elsie. "I guess we just need the scrunchies for *your* hair since I can probably get away with my cap. It's already pretty retro."

Elsie's head was spinning with all of Dar's directions. Soon a pile of clothes were being thrust into her arms.

"We'll change over there."

Elsie looked where Dar pointed and saw a series of dressing rooms.

"Come on, before they're all taken." Again Dar dragged Elsie across the room.

There were shouts of laughter as kids dressed in clothes from ancient times—clothes that were stiffer, thicker and baggier than their normal gear.

"Stars, what a bunch of suzo-shrimp geekoids we are," Dar said, but she was laughing like crazy. Elsie had to laugh too.

Lelita found them as they left their changing rooms. She wore bright pink jeans that hung low on her hips and a white top that stopped a couple of inches above her belly button. It had a pink star embossed on the shoulder. In her brown hair were a half a dozen pink scrunchies so that pieces of her hair stuck up in all directions. She giggled when she saw them and twirled to show off her new look.

'How'd you do all that so quickly?" Elsie asked, goggling.

"Trust me," Dar said, "it's a gift. Anyway, it's easier for her. Being such a shorty, she can actually find something that fits in the girls' section. Not that I'd want to dress up like that. Flasers, Lelita, you're so girlie."

"I like it. You're just jealous."

Dar snorted. "As if."

Lelita just continued to smile. "Your costumes are great too. Zetta zeller."

Dar's jeans were ripped in countless places and were a whitish blue, whereas Elsie's were dark blue and straight-legged. They both wore t-shirts. Elsie had been thrilled to find a Mickey Mouse t-shirt in the pile Dar had grabbed. To her, Mickey Mouse was *the* symbol of that time period. She even had an antique Mickey plastic figurine that her parents had given her a couple of years ago on her birthday. It was a prized possession.

Dar's shirt had a picture of a humpback whale with the words "Save the Whales" emblazoned on the front.

"With all the animals that *have* gone extinct over the last millennium, it's too bad I can't tell the people from the twenty-first century that the humpbacks actually survived," she said.

"Hey, Elsie," Lelita said nervously. "Are you wearing a necklace? You need to put it in the safety box over there. You can pick it up when you return."

Elsie had been worrying about her pendant ever since Instructor Gerard had laid down the law. "I can't leave it. I promised my mom."

"Well, your uncle will have a fit if he finds out that you took it with you," Dar said.

Making a quick decision, Elsie unclasped the necklace and stuffed it deep into her jeans pocket. It would be safest there.

A high-pitched bell sounded.

"That's the one minute warning. Let's go!" Dar grabbed Elsie's wrist. The students surged forward, intent on regaining their benches before it was too late.

No one wanted to be left behind.

CHAPTER 16
Time Travel in a Mustang

Everest hated wearing dress-up clothes. He might as well have "borneo" flasered on his forehead. The thought immediately curled guilt deep in his belly. He really had to stop himself from using that term, even in his head.

How weird was it to be cloned from a famous person with such a geekoid reputation? He sought out Borneo in the group and found him one bench back, looking hopelessly "borneo-like" in checkered pants and a striped shirt. Catching his stare, Borneo turned bright red. Everest tried to make up for his thoughts with a sheepish grin. After a moment, the boy returned the smile before they both looked away.

Everest's costume was simple, with stiff pants labeled Levis on the back pocket, sports shoes that made him feel as if two extreme bowling balls were attached to his ankles and a cotton shirt depicting someone riding the waves on an ancient surfboard. He liked the twenty-first-century shirt, but how anyone managed to do anything active wearing the stiff pants and shoes was beyond him. What was the point of these boulders weighing down his feet? Footwear for sports was supposed to be ultra light and fit like another layer of skin. Still, he'd have worn an Aginoza breathing apparatus to go on this outing. Just wait till he told his friends that he'd traveled through time. They'd be as green as street moss.

Catching Elsie's eye, he grinned broadly, and she smiled back, signing "Z" for "zeller". This was going to be one amazing adventure.

Instructor Gerard firmly clapped his hands to quiet the excited chatter. While they had been changing into their costumes, three teachers had arrived. One was Legnarchi, but Everest had never seen the other two.

He turned to Vlas sitting next to him. "Who are the female teachers?"

"Instructor Bebe and Instructor Tchakevska—history and geography," Vlas whispered.

Instructor Bebe was petite, even shorter than Lelita, and she wore her soft silver hair quite short. In color, her eyes were an exact match to her hair. It was almost impossible to determine how old she was because her skin was smooth and her body toned, but Everest sensed that she had a few more years of seasoning than did Instructor Gerard. From the serene light in her silver eyes, he suspected she was a meditation master, possibly an aura adept. Instructor Tchakevska was the tallest of the chaperones, impossibly thin with a narrow face and tightly muscled arms. There was something in her eyes that made him uncomfortable. She couldn't be fully human.

Instructor Gerard clapped his hands again, even more loudly, and this time everyone powered down. "We'll use four automobiles, or cars as they were more commonly referred to, so everyone divide up into groups of six. It will be a tight squeeze."

Kids rushed to group themselves. Within seconds, Everest and Elsie looked around and saw that they were the only ones not in a group.

Dar grimaced as she made eye contact. "You better come with us," she said reluctantly. "Jillian and Karn, you go in the group over there." Karn was the boy who earlier had asked where they were going in the twenty-first century. He shot Everest and Elsie a dirty look before moving to the other group.

"Hmm," Gerard said as he took in the groups. "Legnarchi, you take Hura and gang."

Everest felt zetta envious. Good-natured Legnarchi had to be better than any of the other chaperones. Next, Gerard matched up Tchakevska and Bebe.

Deng, they were stuck with Gerard. No matter how much Elsie oohed and aahed over him, Everest couldn't shake the feeling that the teacher wasn't as perfect as he seemed. Maybe he just didn't like the way Elsie went all moony over the guy, as if he were some blast-music star. Zetta bleck.

Everest, Elsie, Dar, Vlas, Lelita and Borneo lined up beside Instructor Gerard, who said in a pleasant voice, "I promised Director Lester-Hauffer that I would take special care of his niece and nephew on their first timed field trip. Don't worry kids," he said directly to Elsie and Everest, "this'll be a glide in the park."

Everest swallowed a groan when he caught Dar's smirk. Where was a black hole when you needed to be sucked into one? They'd be hearing about Instructor Gerard's coddling forever.

The man then turned to Dar and Vlas. "Just as well I've got you two in my vehicle. You always deserve a little special attention. Maybe the director's niece and nephew will exert a good influence over you both."

Perfect, thought Everest. Now they were being held up as role models. How to become social outcasts in one easy step.

When Instructor Gerard swiveled around to lead their party, Everest caught Dar rolling her eyes at Vlas and vigorously rubbing the top of her nose. No surprise that those two were pegged as the B12 troublemakers.

Course, if he'd been caught outside last night, he'd have been labeled a troublemaker himself. He should be thanking his lucky stars that Dar was enough of a rebel to be out after curfew and able to save his sorry behind. Then again, it might have been better to have been caught. At least then he wouldn't be labeled a suzo-shrimp goody two-shoes.

Why had Dar been outside anyway? Somehow, she'd managed to distract him from asking this morning.

Instructor Gerard stopped in front of a beat-up car.

"This little baby is what they call a convertible. It can be driven with a closed top or an open one."

Despite being dented and rusted with cracked and faded upholstery, it was still a real beauty. Everest circled the car, pausing to view the trunk, which read Ford and displayed a small metal picture of a running horse. He appreciated the safety of today's jellach HVs but, flasers, the ancient metal cars were zeller.

"You expect six of us to sit in this pico-chip of a car? Seven counting you?" Vlas asked incredulously, staring at the bucket seats in the front and the cramped back seat.

"Does it expand?" Elsie asked. Jellach cars stretched and shrunk depending on the number of passengers.

"Deng, Elsie, we're going back a thousand years, not yesterday," Dar muttered, and received a rather severe look from the instructor.

"We'll fit," Instructor Gerard said in an even more optimistic tone than usual. "Elsie can sit on her brother's lap, and Lelita can sit on Borneo's."

"No way!" Elsie screeched at the same time that Lelita gasped and went bright pink.

Gerard's sparkling smile disappeared. "I'm afraid the only other choice is for two of you to miss the field trip. Is that your preference?"

Elsie shot a nasty look in Everest's direction but erased it before she made eye contact with Gerard. "No, Instructor, I'll sit on my brother's lap."

Both Lelita and Borneo still looked horrified.

"Don't worry, Lelita," Dar said, "You can sit on my lap."

Lelita seemed to be on the verge of bursting out in tears of relief.

"Hey," Instructor Gerard added, "it'll only take a minute." He hopped into the driver's seat and waited expectantly.

They all groused and moaned as they clambered in.

Instructor Gerard held up his hands. "I mean it. You're all welcome to stay home."

"We didn't say we didn't want to go," Dar said. "Come on, everyone, light speed."

Everest and Elsie took the front, while the others crammed into the back. It helped that the convertible top was down.

"What are these belts for?" Lelita asked, holding up a thick nylon strap.

"They're seat belts—to protect passengers in case of an accident. Remember, travel was a dangerous business back then."

"But how does belting a seat protect anyone?" Elsie asked.

"They belted *in* the passenger, yocto-brain."

"Don't call me yocto-brain!" Elsie yelled at her brother.

Gerard held up his hands again. "We aren't even going to drive the cars, so the seat belts are irrelevant. The vehicles are just portals back to the twenty-first century. Once we're there, we'll walk or take a bus—"

"Stop," called a deep and dark voice from the building's entrance. For some reason, a chill ran down Everest's spine.

Even weirder, he could have sworn that Instructor Gerard shuddered, and his hands suddenly clenched the wheel.

Everest craned his neck to see who had spoken. In the dim light of the building, all he could make out was a silhouette of a tall, thin man wearing black and sporting, of all things, a trim, pointy beard. Talk about a freakazoid alien. No one wore beards in the thirty-first century. Most men chose not to grow facial hair. Since nervous whispers swelled around him, Everest figured he wasn't the only student staring.

Instructor Gerard slowly relaxed his hands. He climbed out of the automobile and turned to face the new arrival.

"Hello, Dr. Wei. What brings you out of your laboratory on this fine day?"

"You have, of course."

"I?"

The man nodded from across the room. "Yes. You and this field trip. I've decided to join you."

Everything from groans to moans to gasps greeted this statement. Elsie giggled nervously. Everest poked her in the side to try to shut her down, but she jabbed back with her elbow.

Gerard moved toward the doctor. "This is indeed an honor." He paused. "But, as you can see, we are terribly cramped. There is no room for another traveler, even one as exalted as you."

The man walked further into the room, bringing his features into sharp focus. Besides his unusual beard and ultra-thin mustache, a long, thin scar sliced his cheek and his eyes were a piercing blue. His cheekbones were sharply defined, his nose was long with a prominent bump, and he had very thin lips. His hair was limp and black and hung straight to his shoulders.

Everest had the distinct impression that Dr. Wei was amused by Gerard.

"Lack of room can easily be fixed. I'll just take your place."

Two red blotches colored Gerard's cheeks. "I am in charge of enrichment for this academy. Director Lester-Hauffer would be very displeased if I shirked my duty."

Dr. Wei shrugged. "And the director would be even more displeased if you were unable to accommodate me."

Instructor Gerard looked around helplessly. Finally, his gaze zeroed in on the serenely smiling Instructor Bebe. "I'm sorry, instructor, but would you be willing to give up your spot to the good doctor?"

She dipped her head slightly. "Of course. I would be happy to help in any way." She gracefully exited the large vehicle in her charge, and with a sweep of her hand motioned Dr. Wei to the car.

He bowed slightly and smiled thinly. "You are too kind."

Gerard ran his hand through his hair. "This is quite unfortunate. Instructor Bebe is our historian."

Everest figured that Gerard picked Bebe because she was least likely to kick up a fuss. Then again, he couldn't imagine any of these teachers actually wanting to play chaperone, even on a timed field trip. Why in galaxies did Dr. Wei want to go?

"I'm sure we'll muddle through," Dr. Wei responded after a slow, measuring look.

Instructor Gerard pivoted around and returned to the car. His face was red, his breathing hitched, and his jaw clenched. Everest hoped Elsie would have the sense not to ask him questions.

There was dead silence for a space of time while Instructor Gerard breathed in and out and strangled the wheel with his hands.

"How does time travel work?" Elsie asked in a small voice, breaking the tense silence.

Everest rolled his eyes and swallowed a groan. Leave it to his sister.

Instructor Gerard twisted around, and at first, it appeared that he would lash out in fury, but then he seemed to get a hold of himself. He even made a feeble attempt at a smile. "Sorry, I should have done a quick explanation for our new students. It's quite simple, really. All we need are vehicles that existed in the period we are visiting."

He signaled a slight delay to the other chaperones, then continued, "We pinpoint precisely *when* the items were created then calculate the exact time difference between their creation and when we want to visit. The tricky part is the where. You need to know without a shadow of a doubt where an item was located at some moment in its useful life. We use that as a coordinate, then calculate the distance between it and our target destination. Depending on how an item was found, we may know this information without needing any additional testing. However, if the coordinate is unknown, we can send the vehicle back in time with a probe that will return with the necessary data. As part of your C17 curriculum, you'll do calculations for our field trips. May the Light be with us."

Everest wondered if anything else could be used to go back in time besides a vehicle. He thought about the skyball his dad had bought him from the 2992 galactic playoffs. Could he use it as a portal? It would be so zeller to see the game first hand.

"Once you calculate the coordinates, do they stay intact?" Dar asked from the back seat. "I mean, once you come back from the trip, would you go the same place again if you didn't do a recalculation?"

Instructor Gerard was busy keying in a series of numbers into a small black device attached to the dashboard. "I suppose so," he said absently. Suddenly, he paused and glared into the rear view mirror. "But you'd need the key." He pulled a car key out of a small pocket in the jacket he wore. Everest noted that the jacket material exactly matched his own pants.

Instructor Gerard signaled to the other adults that they were ready. Despite his growing excitement, Everest couldn't help but notice that their vehicle was by far the smallest. Not used to being closed in, he felt smothered with Elsie sitting on his lap in such cramped quarters. His palms were a little clammy as Instructor Gerard inserted the key.

"Here we go," the instructor yelled. There was a muffled poof, an intense jerk, and the room disappeared.

CHAPTER 17
A Smooth Landing in 2002

Everest spun faster and faster in ever-tightening concentric circles. His head pounded from the pressure, his cheeks rippled from some unseen force, and his teeth chattered uncontrollably. At least, he thought they did. He couldn't actually hear them. He couldn't hear anything. He only knew that he should be hearing rushing wind. He couldn't see anything, yet he felt as if he were surrounded by a kaleidoscope of neon colors. He couldn't taste anything, unless it was the taste of fear on his tongue.

Was his body going to explode into a million jagged pieces and become a microscopic meteor shower? And what about Elsie? She had vanished despite his ginger hold of her when Instructor Gerard had put the car in motion. He couldn't feel her, couldn't smell her. She was gone.

He was afraid he might be screaming, the kind of scream you'd make on a virtual reality flying coaster ride.

After countless heartbeats, the spinning ceased, and all went calm and black. There was an endless moment of this nothingness, then a flash, and he really and truly heard again, the rapid thump of his heart...once, twice. And though he still couldn't see, he felt Elsie's weight on his knees and heard her gasping for breath. He heard his own ragged breathing. Finally, as if a light sensor were triggered, sight flooded back with a brightness of color that nearly blinded him. He blinked, feeling like a Dangor genetically-altered miner mole squinting up at a never-before seen sun.

Lelita whooped with excitement. "I always love that spinning—the faster the better." She leaned forward toward Elsie and Everest. "You should feel what it's like to go back 2000 years. Deng, that's a ride."

Everest's stomach churned so badly he was afraid he would make a fool of himself by getting sick. He didn't even want to think what a longer trip would do to his innards. When Elsie clamped her hands over her mouth, he guessed she wasn't feeling so good either.

"Oops," Dar said cheerfully from behind. "We forgot to mention time travel sickness. Next time you can pop a pill."

"Thanks a lot," Everest grumbled.

For the other kids, this wasn't a new experience. Only Everest and Elsie were new to the sensation of spinning through time. Just as being utes separated them from the group, once again they were the odd ones out, and the feeling of being different colored this experience.

But nothing could completely ruin the excitement of his very first time travel. He wouldn't let it.

They were still crammed into the car, but the tevta building had vanished. Instead, they sat in the middle of a sea of parked cars. And whereas before the trip their automobile had been rusty, chipped, and banged up, it was now in pristine condition— cherry red, bright, and cheerful, with perfect supple upholstery and no tape in sight.

"Zeller," Everest gasped. He'd thought the car quasar before, but now it was amazing—the most beautiful vehicle he'd ever seen.

Instructor Gerard pulled the key out of the ignition and dropped it back into his little pocket. "Excellent landing."

He waved his hand, and Everest saw that the other vehicles had arrived as well. Dr. Wei was already standing slightly off to the side, a very intimidating figure. Who was this doctor, anyway? It almost seemed as if Gerard was afraid of him.

"Let's get moving," Gerard continued. "We've a very full schedule. We can gather around on the steps over there." He pointed at the mostly glass building in the middle of the car lot. A sign read "Ernie's Used Cars—We're the Lowest."

Beyond the lot was a busy street where vehicles rumbled past at a slow and jerky pace.

"The sky's empty," Elsie whispered in amazement. "I've never seen an empty sky."

Everest nodded absently as he took it all in. It was totally alien seeing all the traffic rolling along on the ground with almost nothing up above. The only manmade objects he spotted overhead were few and far between, little more than specks playing a hide-out game in the clouds.

A loud screeching brought his attention back to the alien streets. Lights were flashing red, green, and yellow while cars stopped or started in some intricate dance. The noise of the motors alone was alien. In addition, pounding music, honking, and screeching filled the air. One long-nosed, low-to-the-ground car boomed by with thumping, ear-splitting music pulsing out of its open windows. The air carried the pungent smell of burnt chemicals.

With her hands over her ears and her nose wrinkled, Lelita yelled over the din, "How do they stand this? Why is the past always so noisy?"

"People from this time period are used to the noise and the smell of exhaust," Gerard explained. "They just don't notice."

"How come the sky's so gray?" asked Borneo. "Is it going to rain later?"

Everest had been wondering the same thing. The whole world was gray—the sky, the ground, even the buildings.

"That," said Instructor Tchakevska, "is the color of this time period's air pollution, better known as 'smog.' It isn't so bad today. You can still make out the mountains in the distance."

"But," Lelita faltered, "if we're in the same *where*, those mountains are really close. It shouldn't be so hard to see them."

"Bleck!" Elsie said in a totally disgusted voice. "No wonder so many animals went extinct."

"We're not going to get some weird ancient disease breathing this junk, are we?" a boy in a bold floral shirt and khaki shorts asked, his hand covering his mouth and nose. Everest thought his name was Zike.

"You'll survive," Instructor Tchakevska said briskly.

Somehow, Everest wasn't reassured.

"Of course we'll *all* survive," Legnarchi boomed. "Some of you might feel a little shortness of breath, but that will disappear as soon as we are home. We would never take you anywhere unsafe."

Everest wasn't convinced, but he forced himself to smile slightly in a show of nonchalance. Dar would be bound to notice if he acted even a tiny bit afraid. Then she'd make him the butt of another joke.

"There's no street moss," Elsie suddenly commented, as if she'd only just now noticed the hard gray ground surface.

Everest barely refrained from whispering *yocto-brain*.

Instructor Tchakevska smiled thinly. "Wheels were not designed to roll on moss. We weren't able to rid ourselves of all the concrete until vehicles could hover."

"Yes," Instructor Legnarchi said, "but on many streets you'll notice beautiful, tall trees. Our ancestors didn't have to deal with the tree height restrictions we have due to hover travel."

"Okay, troops," Instructor Gerard interrupted, "listen up! It's exactly 8:00, and we are in the heart of what was then Santa Clara County, better known as Silicon Valley in the State of California. Instructor Tchakevska, please give the students a quick rundown on the geographical changes over the millennium."

The instructor cleared her throat. "As all of you should know from your studies, counties were done away with seven hundred years ago. However, the city names remain intact. The only cities from this area that you won't find in 2002 are Googleopolus, Packard City and Cisco Ville. They didn't come into being until the end of the twenty-first century, when San Jose finally outgrew itself."

She wrapped her thin, strong arms across her chest. "There are some terrain differences as well. A dangerous global warming trend affected both the coastline and the mountain ranges in Northern California, as did this area's propensity for earthquakes. Believe it or not, until 2152, our ancestors were unable to properly control earthquakes. And it wasn't till we replaced fossil fuels with sunergy that we saw our climate stabilize."

Everest winced at the thought of a world at the mercy of earthquakes and rising ocean levels.

"Later today, you'll have the opportunity to participate in a simulation of an earthquake of large magnitude. I'm sure you'll all find it enlightening." Tchakevska turned to Gerard and motioned for him to take over.

He read off his JED. "Here's our agenda. First we'll sample a traditional twenty-first-century breakfast at a popular early morning restaurant. After that we'll take a bus to San Jose's Tech

109

Museum, which will give you an excellent understanding of what people found innovative in this era. We'll buy picnic lunches at Hasty Hawley's, arguably the most important fast-food restaurant chain from the mid twenty-first century up until the Vlemutz Wars in the twenty-sixth century. In 2002 Hasty Hawley's had only been in existence for a handful of years, so you'll be eating there before its phenomenal commercial success. In the afternoon, we'll visit a video game center in a nearby shopping mall to give you a sense of how children your age played." He waved back to Tchakevska. "Instructor Tchakevska will go over the rules in more detail before we begin. Instructor?"

She stepped forward. "It is absolutely imperative that you *not* disturb the natives." She eyed them all as if they were liable to set off flaser showers at any moment. "You will not speak to anyone from this century other than to say 'hello,' 'thank you,' or 'excuse me.' If someone asks, 'How are you?,' you may simply respond, 'Fine, thanks.' For some reason, in this time period Americans found it necessary to ask complete strangers just such bizarre questions, but I can guarantee they are not really interested in your answer. If necessary, in order to explain any anomalies Silicon Valley-ites may perceive in our dress or speech, we will say we are visitors from Beverly Hills, California—a city known far and wide for its unusual population." She crossed her arms sternly. "You will not speak any language that would be considered gibberish in this time period—no Zylanderin, no Quorr, nor any other off-world lingo you may have learned in the womb. You may quietly talk amongst yourselves *in English*. However, you may not mention cloning, which is a terrifying and controversial concept in this era; skyball, since it doesn't yet exist; anything to do with flasers, or any other items that might cause today's humans to take a second look at our little group. In other words, *be discrete.*"

Dar raised her hand. When Instructor Tchakevska acknowledged her with a nod, she said, "Instructor, I understand that in this era, twelve-year-old children were not nearly as tall as we are. Do you think it would be a good idea for us to suggest that we are members of a basketball team?"

Everest stared at Dar. What in galaxies was basketball? It had to be some sort of sport, despite its wimpy name.

"My dear girl," Tchakevska replied. "I hardly think that will be credible, since in this day and age, boys and girls rarely played together on the same team."

Exclamations of surprise and disgust rippled through the crowd of students. Everest couldn't imagine being separated from his sister in sports. They were so used to working as a team, whether in fight competitions or in skyball.

Instructor Tchakevska held up her hand for silence. "In all fairness, women and men did vary much more in size and muscle than in our present day. That, coupled with a lingering and highly inappropriate sense of male superiority—a hold over from centuries of abominable behavior—caused this bizarre tradition." Her voice had risen, and her color had heightened. She looked as if she were working herself into some kind of fit.

Instructor Gerard cleared his throat and motioned for her to wrap things up, which caused her to speak faster. "Finally, you will not under any circumstances wander off, and you will refrain from any rude exclamations or comments about the natives, their attire, their actions, or their speech. Am I understood?"

The students nodded their heads vigorously and chorused, "Yes, Instructor Tchakevska."

"Excellent. This should be an intriguing and enlightening day." She said it as if she were about to take a particularly vile agri-nutrient.

Everest rolled his eyes at Elsie, who looked as if she were fighting a bad case of the giggles.

Intriguing and enlightening? Huh! They could do better than that.

CHAPTER 18

The Baskers in the 21st Century

Tchakevska turned to face Gerard. "Shall we?"

"Excuse me," Dr. Wei inserted, once again stopping everyone with his deep, dark voice.

Gerard looked at him with open dislike. "Yes?"

"When will you be back?"

Now the instructor looked completely flummoxed. "Back? Aren't you coming with us?"

"Good galaxies, no." There was amusement in Dr. Wei's voice. "I have important research to do today."

"But you're leaving me one chaperone short." Gerard tugged on his pants as if they were shrinking in size by the second. "Director Lester-Hauffer will hear of this, I assure you."

"I have no doubt. A time, please?"

"Be back no later than 15:30."

Dr. Wei dipped his head, then strode off down the busy street, his black lab coat flapping with each step.

Everest heard Instructor Gerard mumble "Good riddance" under his breath. Then the instructor motioned for the students to rise. "Follow me."

They marched through the rows of cars until they reached a cement walkway for pedestrians. He turned right and continued down the congested street.

113

Everest had mixed feelings about this ancient world. The noise made his head ache, something he'd rarely experienced before, and the smells were disgusting. One huge truck barreled by, puffing a stream of black smoke into their faces which threw Everest into a choking fit and made his eyes water. Despite all that, he still thought many of the vehicles were zetta zeller with their sleek lines and spinning silver disks, their bright colors, their lights and unexpected whistles. This time period was altogether more exciting, more dangerous, and more interesting.

When they reached a cross street, Instructor Gerard stretched out his arm to stop their forward motion. He pointed to the light. "It's red."

Elsie asked, "So what?"

"You can only cross the street when the light is green."

Elsie rolled her eyes at Everest. In their time period, hover vehicles traveled above pedestrians, so the idea of lights controlling their every movement was pretty barbaric.

But Everest quickly decided there was probably a good reason for the rule. The vehicles did not hover, they rolled, and though they didn't go as fast as hover vehicles, they were heavy and solid. An accident in one of these would hurt. And if one ran into someone, it wouldn't be pretty. He had no idea if this time's medics would be able to put people back together again with as much success as those of his period.

When the light turned green, Everest grabbed his sister's wrist and checked both ways to make sure no vehicles were bearing down on them.

"Is the ute-baby fraidy of the big bad twenty-first-century cars?" Dar whispered with a wicked grin as she stepped past him and sauntered across the street. So much for her promise not to call them names.

Elsie's expression was fierce as she yanked herself free from his grip.

Everest felt like a blubber for having displayed so much caution, but he also felt righteous. So what if he was afraid? Wasn't his fear justified? It wasn't as if he'd been on a timed field trip before—not like some people.

At the restaurant, they had to split into smaller groups to be seated. Since it wasn't too crowded, the tables were close. Everest, Elsie, Vlas, and Dar quickly filled up one of the booths before an instructor could join them. Borneo and Lelita joined Lelita's roommate at the next booth over along with a B12 Everest didn't know. A server handed out menus. Everest couldn't stop staring at the woman. He'd never seen anyone wear so much goop on her face. Her eyelids were bright blue.

They heard Instructor Gerard telling the woman attending them that the entire party would like three buttermilk pancakes each with glasses of water all around. After a quick headcount, the lady walked away to place their order.

Everest ran his fingers over the plastic menu. In the thirty-first century, plastic was a rare substance. Some forms were still made but when petroleum had been exhausted as a resource in the twenty-second century, most production of plastic had dried up as well. In their world, mint-condition petroleum-based plastic was worth a fortune.

"I'm glad Instructor Gerard ordered for us," Elsie said. "I haven't the slightest idea what any of this is."

The woman returned with a couple of men who carried large trays of water glasses that they began to distribute as she collected the menus.

"Excuse me," Elsie said, "Can you tell me what bacon is?"

The woman serving them sighed. "Listen, kid, I don't have time for jokes."

Everest nudged Elsie, trying to get her to power down. Didn't she remember they weren't supposed to be talking with the natives?

"No, really," she continued, shoving him back, "I've never heard of it."

"Never heard of it? What planet are you from?"

Elsie sucked in her breath and shot Everest a nervous glance.

It was a little late to stop ignoring him, he thought grumpily, but he still jumped in to help. "Actually, we're from Beverly Hills."

The woman barked with laughter. "Guess that's as close to outer space as anyone I know will get."

He attempted a smile. Elsie zetta owed him.

"Poor kids," she continued, "you probably live on tofu and sprouts. Tell you what, the next time you see your parents, you ask *them* what bacon is." She walked away, shaking her head.

Everest caught Instructor Tchakevska glaring at their table and pinched Elsie hard for drawing attention their way.

She yelped and pinched him back.

"Knock it off, you two." Dar leaned forward, staring hard at Elsie. "Didn't you hear a word Tchakevska said? Like when she told us not to converse with the natives? For your information, bacon is pig fat."

"Pig fat?" Elsie snorted. "That's a good one."

Dar rested back against the shiny cushion. "It's the truth. I've been researching this time period."

"You are such an allen, you're going to make my sides hurt from laughing too hard."

Dar shrugged and pulled out her JED. In a low tone she began to describe the restaurant, pointedly ignoring Elsie.

Vlas murmured, "Odds are good she's right. She drives the rest of us crazy with her constant studying. Her misbehavior would have gotten her kicked out of this school a long time ago, only she's by far the best student they've ever had. Plus, it doesn't hurt that she has such an influential sponsor."

"Shut down, Vlas," Dar said without missing a beat as she continued to speak into her JED.

Everest wondered how a girl cloned from the most beautiful woman in the universe—a woman who had sung for her living—ended up being more brilliant than a pile of kids who had been cloned from bona fide geniuses.

Just then, Dar looked up and caught Everest's stare. "If you know what's good for you, ute-boy, you'll look at something or someone else."

"Don't make us regret your presence today, Shadara," Instructor Gerard said, barely a meter away.

Everest flinched, but Dar hardly registered the instructor's surprise attack. A look of mild resignation flitted across her face. "Absolutely not, Instructor Gerard."

"Did you encourage Elsie to talk to that woman?" he asked in a low voice.

"She had nothing to do with that," Elsie said quickly. "In fact, she reminded me afterward not to speak to the natives."

His expression was unusually hard. "No need to jump to her defense. Shadara is quite capable of taking care of herself. Your uncle was not pleased when he realized you would be required to share a room with the girl. We even discussed reshuffling room assignments. We can still do that, if necessary. Shadara has always had a disruptive influence on the students."

Elsie blinked. "But it really was my fault. I was curious and forgot the rules."

"I see." He pursed his lips. "In that case, please do adhere to them from now on. We're very proud of our innovative and progressive timed field trip program. We would be displeased indeed to have it stripped from us because our students didn't know how to follow simple directions."

"I'm very sorry," she repeated.

"Yes, yes, well, we'll put this behind us. But Shadara," he stared sternly, "do remember that, as well as being completely inappropriate for this time period, 'ute-boy' is a term to which we always take exception."

Everest was amazed that Dar let the instructor get away with using the longer version of her name. Surely he knew how she felt about it?

As soon as Instructor Gerard turned his back on them, Vlas snickered, causing the instructor to swing around, his eyes blazing. It took everything in Everest not to flinch again. Ever since Dr. Wei had joined them, Gerard had acted like a freakazoid alien.

After a few seconds, though, the instructor visibly relaxed, and his expression calmed to a pleasant smile, "I do hope I can count on the four of you to be model students on our little outing. I would hate to have to exclude you from the next one." His smile widening, he waited a full thirty seconds before he pivoted on his heel and returned to his booth.

When he was beyond earshot, Dar leaned toward Vlas, and Everest heard her whisper, "jerk!"

Everest choked on suppressed laughter. He recognized the word as being an old-fashioned term for "vlem."

Then Dar grinned slyly and added in a more carrying voice, "Now *that* is a twenty-first-century term."

CHAPTER 19
Pancakes, Bicycles and Buses

The pancakes arrived, soft disks stacked three high. The server also slammed down a couple of small metal pitchers in the middle of the table.

At a loss, the four of them stared at the food. Should they pick up the disks with their fingers? Everest checked out the teachers' table and watched them cut the pancakes into bite-sized pieces. Starting with Tchakevska, each instructor picked up a pitcher and poured a gooey brown substance on top of his or her pile of food. Then they ate. Instructor Legnarchi, in particular, shoveled in the pancakes with gusto.

After cutting a few pieces himself, Everest picked up one of the pitchers and sniffed. The goop inside smelled like candy, and the pitcher itself was sticky. Grimacing, he poured some on his pancakes then offered the thick brown substance to his sister, which she nervously took and followed suit. When he placed the first piece in his mouth, he was shocked by how sweet it was. Not only did it smell like candy, it tasted like candy. In texture it was like eating a soft, thick piece of bread, or maybe an old-fashioned cake.

He hoped it wasn't real sugar, or he was going to need a heap of protein for balance, and judging from this example of food in the twenty-first century, he couldn't be sure how readily available soy protein would be. Pancakes tasted fine, but he had a feeling they were going to sit like mud in his belly.

"They ate this for breakfast?" Elsie whispered, wide-eyed, with a quick glance at the teachers' table. "Someone's got to be pulling a Slarmi joke."

"I like it," Vlas said, shoveling in more.

Dar just toyed with her food. Everest wondered if she'd been upset by Instructor Gerard's reprimand. She hadn't acted upset, but now she seemed distracted.

Still watching her, he took a sip of water. "Bleck," he sputtered, making a face at the clear liquid.

Vlas burst out laughing, and suddenly Dar woke up. When she realized what Everest had done, she laughed too.

"I guess drinking the water's out." Vlas dug out a blue gel-tablet from his pocket. "Here's a hydration pill. I always bring extras. You never know what we're going to be expected to drink. Usually one of us has to volunteer to be the test case. It was zeller of you to sacrifice yourself."

Nice of them to warn him. Everest accepted the pill with a grimace. Though it would help his body retain fluids so he wouldn't have to drink anything for a while, he knew his parents wouldn't be pleased. Despite being scientists, or maybe because of it, they harbored a healthy distrust of thirty-first-century medicine, since it relied so heavily on picotechnology. All pills nowadays were strictly regulated picobots, which would have been reassuring if there hadn't been a couple of well-publicized cases of picobots running amuck over the last few years. "Do you have one for Elsie?"

"She can have one of mine." Dar dropped one next to Elsie's plate, once again surprising Everest with her generosity.

"Thanks," Elsie murmured, then asked, "Why don't they offer something drinkable?"

Vlas shrugged. "Probably the natives have no problem with this water. Their taste buds would be used to it. Besides, maybe nothing is worth drinking in this day and age. I read somewhere that people used to drink various forms of sugar water. Maybe Instructor Gerard was trying to offer us a healthy option." He wriggled his eyebrows. "I kind of doubt it, given the pancakes. The most likely reason we've been given water is because it's cheap in the twenty-first century. If there's one thing Instructor Gerard hates, it's to waste money."

After breakfast, they were reminded that they would be taking a bus to the Tech Museum. They had to cross the street again to be on the same side as the bus that would eventually take them. Once at the bus stop, they watched avidly as the vehicles stopped and started in the busy thoroughfare. It was so herky-jerky, so different from the smooth flow of air traffic in their present day. Course, there wasn't any bumping going on either. Since someone could actually get hurt in a car accident, it appeared that people paid more attention while navigating than they did in the thirty-first century.

Besides automobiles, there were also people-powered machines, sleek and precarious on two wheels with pedals that pushed the machines forward. Most of the riders wore painful-looking helmets.

"Those are bicycles," Dar said, noticing Everest's curiosity, "a popular form of exercise in the twenty-first century."

Everest had read about bicycles in ancient books, but had never seen one. He'd pictured something a little different, more like a jellach peddle pusher, which was nothing more than a human-operated hover vehicle. "I've heard of them. They look pretty dangerous."

Dar shrugged. "People didn't seem to be as concerned about safety back then, or maybe they just didn't have the technology to play it safe."

Borneo added, "A bicycle was considered a more environmentally correct vehicle because it was human rather than gasoline-powered. In certain parts of the world, bicycles were the primary form of transportation. Remember, this time period had very primitive forms of energy, hence the smog-filled valley."

Everest suppressed a grin. Borneo sounded like a fifty-year-old instructor.

"What's that?" Elsie asked, pointing to a vehicle that was two-wheeled like a bicycle but engine-powered.

"That's a motorcycle," Borneo said reverently. "Zeller, huh?"

Lelita stood on tiptoes to see over her taller friends. "Bicycles and motorcycles look fun, but most of these automobiles give me the creeps. The people are all closed in like cages. I liked the one we came in because it doesn't have a top, but those other ones! I can't imagine being cooped up in such a small dark space for any length of time."

"Well, I think they're zetta zeller," Borneo said. "Our jellach vehicles all look exactly the same. There's no thrill, no danger. These cars have character."

"Why, Borneo," Vlas said, wiggling his eyebrows. "I had no idea you were such a daredevil."

Borneo's face went as pink as his eyes. "Not really," he mumbled.

Vlas clapped him on the shoulder, grinning. "I like it." If possible Borneo went even pinker, but now he looked pleased.

"As far as I'm concerned, all they are is smelly," Yoshira said, coming up from behind, her nose clamped between her thumb and forefinger. "How did people live with this filth?"

"It's no worse than our last trip," Dar said. "Pollution was just a part of everyday life for most ancient civilizations."

A dirt-encrusted man ambled up and slumped onto the bench. He carried a grimy old gray pack on his back, which he slid off and dropped at his feet. With all the hair on his face, he almost could have been mistaken for a wild animal. Before Dr. Wei had shown up today with his very trim beard, Everest had never seen hair on a man's face except in two-dimensional images. Most men opted for genetic tweaking to stop facial hair from even growing. He raised his eyebrows at Vlas, who was also staring, and they both grinned. There was no comparison between this guy's shaggy mane and Dr. Wei's perfectly groomed triangle of hair. It was as if the grizzled man wasn't human at all, but some kind of lower life form.

Then he raised his head and stared at them with bleak, desperate eyes, looking all too human, but miserable and alone, and Everest felt awful for secretly laughing at the man. His stomach dipped.

"Got a dollar?" the man asked gruffly.

Everest shook his head and backed up a few steps.

"You?" the man barked at Vlas.

"No, sir," the boy croaked, not at all his normal cocky self.

They both looked around guiltily for the instructors' whereabouts and found all three of them staring with dismay at the boys' interaction with the native.

Everest shoved his hands into his pant pockets and stared fixedly at the automobiles roaring by, trying to get the desperate look in the man's eyes out of his mind.

As he concentrated on the colorful cars, he found himself agreeing with Borneo. Sure hover vehicles in the thirty-first century were practical, comfortable, and safe, but they were *boring*. Jellach for vehicles was required by law to be perfectly clear for 360-degree visibility. It also had to be molded into bubble-shells to shield passengers from injury in the event of an accident. Noise regulations demanded near silence by the vehicles, which meant that anything beyond a slight swishing was absolutely forbidden.

There was something to be said for the sleek, bright, and dangerous lines of the twenty-first-century cars. Too bad they dumped so much pollution into the air. Powered by a never-ending supply of Sunergy, hover vehicles added virtually no pollution to the skies.

Maybe he would research this time period and build a model automobile for fun. He wasn't sure if any of the parts or ingredients still existed—he'd have to do a lot of research.

"What's the matter?" Elsie whispered at his left shoulder.

"Nothing," he mumbled.

She snorted. "Yeah, right."

"I'll tell you later," he said.

He glanced at the bench, but the worn-out man had departed and now shuffled down the street, the bag slung over his shoulder, which was hunched from more than just the bag's weight.

Elsie followed his gaze. "Did you see all his hair?"

"Yeah, I saw it," Everest answered shortly.

A huge bus covered with advertisements screeched to a stop in front of them, and the street smell grew nearly intolerable because of its potent exhaust. Everest coughed, his throat stinging, and heard Elsie coughing at his side. In fact, most of the B12s were choking on the fumes. The teachers had prepared better and were covering their noses and mouths with hands and scarves.

Metal doors opened jerkily, and the students filed up metal stairs into the bus. There was a sweaty stink inside.

Waving his hand in front of his face, Vlas said, "Whew, this reeks worse than a bogdog from Sleztar."

After a scowl at Vlas, Instructor Gerard yelled through his scarf, "Take your seats now." He pushed his way up to the front and held a low conversation with the driver. Money exchanged hands.

Everest slid in next to Elsie.

"Well, Dorothy," he said, "welcome to Oz." He figured the instructors couldn't take exception to a reference to a 2D movie from the twentieth century. A couple of years ago, they'd seen it in school. He remembered now that someone had ridden a bicycle in it—Dorothy maybe.

Elsie nervously laughed. "I don't think a click of our heels is going to send us back home any time soon."

"Guess we'd better just enjoy the ride." He punched Elsie's shoulder in a brotherly attempt to reassure her, then sank further into his seat and immersed himself in the unusual herky-jerky feel of the moving bus.

CHAPTER 20
The 2002 Tech Museum

The building that housed the Tech Museum wasn't at all what Elsie had expected. Mainly because she had never seen anything so big be such a bright orange and blue. It brought to mind old-fashioned children's building blocks, which made the place kind of appealing despite the garish colors.

The dome on one side was interesting-looking, and the building was lined by pretty matching tables with blue umbrellas for shade. The museum was so different from the traditional and somewhat colorless buildings that surrounded it.

Downtown San Jose was even noisier and smellier than the area where Ernie's used car lot was located. There were bright yellow automobiles that Instructor Gerard identified as taxis, and a form of transportation ran noisily on tracks nearby. The automobiles in this area often sounded like angry geese. Elsie had read enough historical novels to identify the noise as the honking of car horns.

When the bus came to a halt directly in front of the museum, there was a long high-pitched squeal, then a sucking sound that accompanied the doors opening out. The B12s clambered down the bus stairs, and the instructors herded them toward the museum as if they were Aginoza bandits about to be jettisoned off-world.

Elsie couldn't see enough of this dirty but fascinating ancient ancestor to the place they called home. It was exotic and different and exciting. She had a google of questions. How did people live in such filth? How did they survive even a lifespan of seventy-five years with all the toxins they consumed just by inhaling?

But it was colorful and noisy and fun, like a Pallaccii carnival. People wore all sorts of outfits, from jeans to formal wear. And there were dogs everywhere attached to their owners by long ropes. This puzzled Elsie. Were the owners afraid the dogs would be hurt by the chaotic traffic? The animals seemed to be straining against the ropes, so Elsie couldn't imagine that they actually enjoyed their confinement. Yet they seemed happy, too, just like dogs in 3002, though she'd never seen any tied up before. Was it possible there wasn't anything like a pico-trainer in the twenty-first century?

Elsie was also fascinated by how people *looked* in this time period. Many were shorter and wider, like Instructor Legnarchi, who had anything but your average thirty-first-century body. They seemed softer, too, less muscled, as if exercise wasn't a priority. And there was such variety—in features, coloring and clothing. It was as if they represented the whole spectrum of the rainbow, in contrast to 3002 when it felt as if the colors had been swirled together to create a group of people who were impossible to classify.

She had read somewhere that the average thirty-first-century human was a melting pot of no less than a dozen nationalities, and many like her friend Zulu had off-planet genes as well. But in 2002 most people still identified themselves with one distinct race. Elsie was a bit fuzzy on her own background, but she was pretty sure she was a relatively equal mix of Asian, African, and Western European ancestry.

In her "Accepting Alien Diversity" courses, she'd been astonished to hear that a thousand years ago, humans on Earth had shown the same level of prejudice toward each other that some now showed toward certain humanoid species on other planets. This was the era when the great martyr, Martin Luther King, Jr., sacrificed his life in his peaceful crusade to stop such hatred. It was weird to think that he had been assassinated less than forty years before this moment in time.

As they shuffled into the museum, whispering and pointing, Elsie tried to look everywhere at once, which caused her to trip in the process. She stumbled into Dar, who fell into Lelita, who looked around startled and began to giggle when she realized Dar was hanging onto her arm. Dar righted herself and glared at Elsie.

"Watch where you're going," she grumbled.

"*Sorry,*" Elsie said, making a face at Dar's back when the girl turned away. It wasn't as if she'd lost her footing on purpose. Dar was such a crank.

While Instructor Gerard joined the ticket line, the rest of them hung back, watching people swarm around them. Humans in 2002 spoke a slightly different version of English, and many surprised Elsie by speaking with thick accents. Since English was a required womb language, she'd only ever heard it spoken fluently. Granted, in 3002 some spoke with an American accent while others chose British, but even toddlers had an extensive knowledge of vocabulary and grammar. Here that wasn't so.

Lelita leaned near. "This is a lot easier to understand than the English we heard when we visited 16th century England. We needed translators for that trip. I guess because womb learning has been in place for most of the millennium, the languages are much more stable."

"Don't you find all the accents hard to understand?"

Lelita shrugged. "Believe me, it could be a lot worse."

128

In addition to English, Elsie heard people speaking Spanish, various dialects from India, Japanese, and at least one Chinese dialect. Many of the words used had been antiquated for centuries, but it was amazing how similar the spoken word was despite the thousand-year gap in time.

Judging by the groups of children wearing matching t-shirts and huddled together in the lobby waiting for tickets, they weren't the only school here on a field trip. But Elsie was pretty sure they *were* the only students visiting from a different time. Were they too conspicuous? Should they have worn some kind of uniform to blend in more? There was nothing they could do about their height. Kids grew taller in the thirty-first century. She just hoped no one thought their group was too alien-looking. She couldn't shake the feeling that everyone was staring. She surprised herself by giggling out loud. Had she ever been this paranoid?

Lelita had been standing quietly at her side, but suddenly she nudged Elsie. "I like the walls."

Elsie wrinkled her nose. "They're very bright." People in this day and age sure did like vibrant hues. The museum walls were painted such a bright shade of blue they were nearly royal purple. They couldn't be more different than the academy's lavender tevta. To be fair, in the 31st century, light murals were the craze, and those could be pretty wild too.

"What do you think 'will call' means?" Elsie whispered. Instructor Gerard stood in front of that sign chatting with one of the attendants.

On her other side, Everest shrugged, but Dar, who had been standing nearby, answered, "That's when you've already bought tickets. The C14s came here last week, so Instructor Gerard must have purchased our tickets then. Tomorrow is the C13s' turn."

"What's a ticket?" Elsie asked.

"A piece of paper that says you've paid for the right to visit the establishment."

"Weird," Everest murmured.

"Talk about expensive," Elsie added.

Borneo nodded. "Can you imagine how much it would cost in our time to print out the tickets? More than the price of admission for sure."

"I guess paper was pretty easy to come by in this time period," Elsie said, though it was hard to fathom.

In the thirty-first century, all information was stored in the Galactic Knowledge Bank. When people attended an event or purchased something, that transaction happened within the GKB, with people uniquely identified by their auras. Over the course of a thousand years, souls and their associated auras had proven to be the only identifier that couldn't be duplicated. Of course, humanoid species boasting multiple souls had posed something of a challenge for the GKB. And returning, or reincarnated, souls had been a nightmare to figure out, especially since only a handful of returning souls wanted to be linked to their previous lives. Eventually the GKB had been fine-tuned to handle these special cases. Much more difficult had been the species that wished to be treated like humanoids but were soul-less, such as the Vlemutz and certain extremely advanced, artificially intelligent beings. It had taken decades to perfect an artificial aura, and unfortunately, the artificial ones did not provide the added benefit of changing color to reflect emotions. Many a guilty member of society had been apprehended through aura analysis.

Instructor Gerard returned to the group, his boyish grin expansive as he handed out the tickets, which turned out to be stiff rectangular pieces of paper with printed information. "We have an 11:00 a.m. showing at the iMAX," he said, pointing to the theater entrance. "That gives us a couple hours to wander around."

Elsie couldn't get over her amazement at visiting the museum with kids who had died nearly a thousand years before she was born. Time travel technology was mature—otherwise students wouldn't be allowed to take field trips—but it had so many regulations and it was so outrageously expensive that most people didn't ever get the chance to take such a trip.

She was pretty sure her parents had traveled backward before they'd had children—scientists were the most likely candidates for this type of outing—but she doubted that they had ever traveled this far back.

A full millennium!

Was it possible that somewhere in this valley lived ancient ancestors of the Baskers? Not that it would be an easy matter to track them down. A lot had changed over the course of the millennium.

The Vlemutz invasion had hit this area hard, which made artifacts from this time period extremely difficult to come by and ultra expensive.

"Check it out," Everest whispered, interrupting her thoughts. She glanced around hastily, but hadn't the slightest idea what he was referring to.

In answer to her quizzical look he added, pointing, "That thing. It's a computer. Might as well be from the first dark ages."

They both burst out laughing. It was a monstrosity. Huge and heavy, with what appeared to be a text-based screen, it was a far cry from the floating minuscule holoputers of their world that gave three-dimensional holographic access to people, places and things, and the malleable jellach journals and portable JEDs that gave instantaneous access to googols of stored information.

"Imagine carting one of those around to classes."

Everest snorted. "Sure would make your daily conversations with Zulu a pain in the—back."

Elsie smiled weakly. She couldn't find it in her to laugh at her brother's teasing. For the past three years, she hadn't gone a day without a chat session with Zulu. With the academy's strict rules, she would have to wait until the weekend for a heart-to-heart with her best friend. Did Zulu miss her even half as much as she missed Zulu?

"Primitive holoputers weren't invented until the twenty-third century," Dar hissed from behind. "There was too much destruction before then. Hard to be technologically advanced when you're stuck in the throes of *The Age of Terror*. Keep your auras on, you two. You look as if you've never seen a computer before, and even in these ancient times that would be considered very odd."

Dar swept past and led them to the Life Tech section of the museum, which Elsie found positively barbaric. An MRI machine was displayed as the height of technology instead of someone's idea of an ancient torture chamber. Zetta thin and fat mice ran or slept in glass cages as genetic test cases, and there was a table set up with various scientific props. Most were common A4 lab activities in modern day 3002. Descriptions of ancient remedies for common illnesses made Elsie cringe. Then she found herself nervously giggling when she read the cards on early genetic research.

She sobered immediately. All of the diseases highlighted in this section of the museum had been eradicated through gene manipulation over eight hundred years ago, but the people surrounding her today were still plagued by those horrible blights. There was so much suffering in this age. What kind of lives could they have led under the threat of such death warrants?

Yet for the most part they seemed happy—the children laughing and the adults smiling.

When they reached a card that addressed the clone controversy, Elsie leaned over to Lelita. "Instructor Tchakevska wasn't kidding when she said that these guys were afraid of cloning."

"Shh!" Lelita looked around nervously. "Don't even say that word. I don't want to get into trouble."

Elsie sighed. Lelita was nice, but she worried way too much. Dar could be a pill, but, at least, she could take a joke. On the other hand, Lelita *was* the only clone who had offered her friendship from the start. She deserved Elsie's support in return.

"Don't worry, Lelita," she said softly. "No one's going to get into trouble."

"Easy for you to say. You're not like the rest of us. What if someone figures out what we are? Maybe in this time period they send people to jail for being the 'C' word."

"No one in this time period would have the technology to tell the difference. I'm not even sure if people in our time know how to identify a clone."

"The newest auralizers do," Lelita said glumly. "I read about them in the *Galaxy News*."

It had never crossed Elsie's mind that the girl's status as a clone could actually put her in danger. Though she didn't believe this for a minute, now she understood why Lelita was acting so strange.

Draping her arm along Lelita's shoulders, she whispered, "Don't worry, no one's going to find out, and even if they did, they'd never believe it. Didn't you read the card? They've only just cloned a sheep successfully. Human clones are still hundreds of years away."

"I'll prove it to you, Lelita," Vlas said, sidling up to them from the right. "I'll go up to the first native we see and tell that person you're a clone. They'll think we're nutters, but you won't get carted away."

"Shut down, yocto-brain," Elsie said in a ferocious whisper. "You're upsetting Lelita." She patted the girl awkwardly.

"I'm not really going to do it," he responded, his lip curled. "I was just joking."

"Yeah, real funny."

To distract Lelita from her worry over being a clone in such a hostile environment, Elsie dragged her over to an exhibit that promised a virtual roller coaster ride. They had fun designing a primitive roller coaster, then enjoying an even more primitive simulation.

Afterward, they all trooped over to the earthquake demonstration. Elsie was terrified by the force of the San Francisco Earthquake of 1906. She could tell Lelita was scared too. The girl grabbed her hand and gripped it so hard that Elsie almost yelped with pain. What would it be like living in an environment where you couldn't predict and divert an earthquake of such magnitude? How had people lived with the threat of this type of destruction hanging over their heads? They must have been very brave.

The iMAX theater was fun in a low-tech sort of way. Elsie was used to interacting more with her entertainment, but it was kind of relaxing letting it just wash over her.

The 2D movie was about ancient Egypt, and Elsie was fascinated by the idea that she had landed a thousand years in the past to watch that culture explain another culture that was even more ancient. She had studied Egypt herself as part of her "Ancient Cultures" course of study. This movie was pretty accurate, but it was missing some important information that hadn't come to light until the late 2400s, when the Plantarvareians had returned to Earth and revealed their part in the building of the pyramids and their roles as models for the Egyptian gods and goddesses.

After the iMAX movie, the instructors herded them outside. "Places to go, things to see," Instructor Gerard said cheerfully. "Instructor Legnarchi left earlier to arrange our picnic lunch. We'll meet him at the park. I should warn you that the food will be very rich by our standards, so eat slowly. We wouldn't want any stomachaches."

Elsie left the museum reluctantly. The day was flying by much too fast. She never wanted it to end.

CHAPTER 21
A Twenty-First-Century Picnic

The bus ride to their picnic spot was uneventful, but painfully slow, with the vehicle stopping and starting so many times Elsie figured they could have walked faster. The buses sure were alien the way they were plastered with funky advertisements, most of which Elsie didn't understand. This was an odd period in time. There were even large boards on the streets that advertised all sorts of seemingly unimportant things.

At one point as they chugged along, she thought she recognized the used car lot. Moments later, they passed the breakfast restaurant. After what felt like a millennium, Instructor Gerard tugged on the thin wire that ran the length of the bus to signal that they would like to disembark.

Elsie's stomach grumbled as she descended from the bus, and she anxiously searched the street for signs of Instructor Legnarchi. When she didn't see him, she gave a resigned sigh and trudged after the other kids, who were all whinging about their empty stomachs. If they'd known there'd be delays in eating, they would have brought some protein pills to help them get by.

Despite her hunger, she perked up when they reached their destination. Memorial Park was adorable with its rolling hills and pools of water filled with ducks. She almost thought they'd been transported forward to their time. Only, the park was bigger than those in 3002. Hover vehicles may have enabled a better environment by eliminating the need for gray highways and streets, but 3002 had a much larger population to shelter, so park space was in short supply. Fortunately, kids could play on the moss lanes without fear of injury, since all the traffic was in the sky.

"You all go play while we organize the lunches," Instructor Gerard said, then called out to someone, "No, no, Instructor, I'll get that." He rushed across the grass. Much relieved by the promise of food, Elsie swiveled her head to watch his progress.

Instructor Legnarchi *had* beaten them to the park, and he stood by a picnic table loaded with heavily patterned white bags. Instructor Gerard and Instructor Tchakevska had joined him, and they all were engaged in a heated conversation. They were too far away to hear, and Elsie couldn't read anyone's lips from this distance. Legnarchi nodded his head so frequently that he looked like an antique bobble-head toy, and Tchakevska had a pinched, disapproving look on her face.

Hunger drove Elsie to fixate on the bags as Pooker might stare at a rodent after a few days of starvation. She had the sudden thought that the bags might actually be paper, which was unheard of in 3002 because trees were protected above all things due to their ecological importance. In the twenty-second century, Earth had almost self-destructed because people had allowed it to turn into a wasteland.

In 3002, dwarf trees lined all of their moss hoverways, a good ten meters shorter than hover height, and even the tiniest parks of the thirty-first century boasted tree groves, each spot specializing in a different tree type. Forests were sacred places, designated for limited recreational use and more importantly, as havens for endangered species. Cut wood was only made available to artists and then only after a lengthy application process.

She snuck closer for a better view of the lunch set-up. At that moment, Instructor Gerard looked up and caught Elsie's riveted attention. For a heartbeat, a frown darkened his face, making Elsie take an involuntary step backward. It had been so unexpected, like earlier today at breakfast. Then he smiled and looked so kindly that she wondered if she had imagined his darker expression.

"Miss Basker," he called across the field, "lunch will be served shortly."

"Can I help?" she asked, desperately curious.

"No, no," he responded jovially. "I do appreciate the offer, but we wish for lunch to be a surprise." He motioned with his fingers for her to follow the other students, and reluctantly, she complied.

He said something to Instructor Tchakevska, and she departed as well, carrying a few large brown bags.

After what to her stomach felt like forever but was probably only ten minutes, the B12s were called over to the picnic tables and informed they were eating organic cheeseburgers and fresh cut French fries.

"Wow!" Elsie heard Borneo exclaim. "These tables are wood!" Elsie felt a similar thrill. Picnic tables in 3002 were made out of steelorq, or sometimes even jellach, but they were never made out of precious wood.

She sat at the end of one picnic table across from Dar and Lelita. Next to her sat Lelita's roommate, Jillian. Earlier, Lelita had told her that Jillian was cloned from a twenty-sixth century political poet. Elsie had a vague memory of a famous piece she'd been forced to memorize at the age of seven, a sad tale of the Vlemutz annihilation of a small gambling town on the border of

California and Nevada. The girl was tall—almost as tall as Dar and Elsie—with rich auburn hair that curled down her back, mocha skin and brown eyes.

She talked even less than Everest, which was almost not at all, but Elsie had a feeling more went on inside the girl's head than she could ever imagine. Was Jillian so caught up in crafting poems that she couldn't stay engaged in the chatter swirling around her?

Sighing, Elsie concentrated on her lunch. The paper bag was soft and smooth, and she couldn't stop running her hands over it. Finally, she pulled out the wrapped cheeseburger, the bag of golden sticks that were called French fries, paper napkins, tiny plastic pouches of ketchup, and even tinier paper envelopes of salt. She had a hard time fathoming the use of paper and plastic in 2002 for the most trivial of items. After setting the food on the picnic table, she carefully folded the paper bag into a small, smooth square to save as a very special souvenir. With a quick look at the instructors to make sure their attention was elsewhere, she pocketed the zeller paper memento. It was such a small thing. Surely one little piece of paper wouldn't matter.

The food's odor was different from anything she'd ever smelled before—not bad but very strong, much more intense than any burger she'd ever eaten in the thirty-first century. She sniffed it again, then nibbled on one edge. It was definitely made out of a protein substance but not one she could identify. She chewed slowly. It was good—much better than the flatcakes this morning—but saltier than she was used to.

"How do you think they make the cheeseburger?" she asked Lelita and Dar. Lelita was eating as carefully as she was, but Dar just picked at the French fries, dabbing them experimentally in the ketchup.

"I don't know." Lelita's forehead was scrunched as if she was puzzled. "I like it, but it's saltier than our burgers, and tastier." Her thoughts mirrored Elsie's.

Elsie leaned forward and asked Dar again. "What do you think?"

When she finally looked up, Dar wore a funny expression on her face, kind of confused and unsure, not Dar-like at all.

"Come on, give." For certain Dar was hiding something.

"You don't want to know," the girl said seriously.

"Oh yes we do," Elsie responded.

Dar sighed and stopped even pretending to eat. Leaning forward to ensure she would only be heard by Lelita and Elsie, she whispered, "It's meat."

"What?" Lelita asked, confusion still painted across her features.

"Cow meat," Dar said a little louder.

Elsie dropped the cheeseburger. "No way! But this is California!"

"Shh!" Dar glanced around nervously. A couple of heads had popped up. "Almost everyone ate meat in the twenty-first century. It's just what they did. We should eat it too, only I can't bring myself to. And Hasty Hawley's is one of the best fast food restaurants in the twenty-first century because of its organic-only policy. When we went back two thousand years, we packed our own lunches so we wouldn't have to attempt their food. But it's silly not to eat. After all, there are still plenty of meat eaters around the world, even in our time. Just because California's a no-eat-meat zone in 3002 doesn't make eating meat wrong. The cow's already been dead for a thousand years. It doesn't do it any good for us to starve ourselves. Besides, from everything I've read, meat does taste good."

"Bleck!" Elsie said, loud enough to catch the attention of more kids. She hunched in an attempt to make herself invisible.

"Deng, Elsie, you'll cause a riot," Lelita whispered. She had stopped eating too.

"What's the matter?" Everest asked from the table next to them. Having just taken a big bite of his cheeseburger, he swiped his napkin across his mouth to catch the ketchup dribbling down his chin.

"Nothing." Elsie struggled to erase the horror on her face as she watched her brother chew a cow. She stared down at her own cheeseburger, her appetite gone.

"The French fries are okay," Dar said. "They're just potatoes."

"I'm not hungry," Elsie replied. "I doubt I'll ever be hungry again. How could the teachers serve us meat? How can they eat it themselves?"

"Maybe that's why they were arguing a few minutes ago," Dar suggested.

Lelita eyed her food sorrowfully. "I don't want to eat the burger, but how will I survive the rest of today without lunch? *I'm starving.*"

Elsie pushed her French fries over to Lelita. "Maybe two sets of fries will hold you."

"Are you sure?"

Jillian was so far into her own little world that she missed the whole exchange. Instead, she stared dreamily at the smog-drenched mountains, barely touching her food, not out of distaste but because she didn't appear to know she had food in front of her.

"I'm positive." Elsie really envied Jillian right now for being so oblivious. No way was she eating cow. Even the thought made her feel guilty, as if she'd eaten her bobcat. Wrapping the cheeseburger carefully, she pushed off the bench. "I think I'll check out the park."

After only a few steps, Instructor Tchakevska blocked her way. "Ms. Basker, no B12s should be wandering around without supervision. Surely you haven't finished your lunch?"

"I'm not hungry," Elsie said. "All those flatcakes for breakfast really filled me up." She patted her stomach, which betrayed her by rumbling.

Instructor Tchakevska speared her with a sharp look but didn't pursue the issue. "Those were *pancakes*, and if you really are too full to eat, then you can sit under that tree until the rest of the children are finished. We mustn't lose each other. After lunch, we leave to visit the video arcade. It would be quite distressing if you didn't make it onto the bus.

Elsie glanced around the tables where all the students, besides Dar and Lelita, were enjoying their meals. One of her mother's favorite obscure sayings came to mind—'ignorance is bliss.' She wished she'd been smart enough *not* to ask Dar about the burger. It had tasted so good, and she was so hungry.

"Where's Instructor Gerard?" She hadn't noticed until now that he had disappeared.

"He had a quick errand. He'll meet us at the video arcades."

Elsie sighed. If only she could have joined him on his errand rather than sit here and wait for her classmates to finish eating a meal her grumbling stomach couldn't stomach.

Odd that he had an errand in the twenty-first century. What could it be?

CHAPTER 22
The Baskers at the Video Arcade

Everest noticed that his sister didn't eat her lunch. Because they sat at different tables, he couldn't ask her why. For Elsie to miss a meal, something had to be very wrong, especially since this was the best cheeseburger and fries he'd ever eaten.

Now they were on the way to the video arcade, and they were still separated. He'd ended up next to a boy named Sago, who was something of an experiment since he was an h-clone or a hybrid. Somehow in the time it took to travel to the arcade, the boy managed to tell his life story. Cloned from both a famous physicist and an extremely successful inventor, Sago's progress was being monitored very closely by the Scientific Institute of Clone Research, better known as SICR.

"If I meet or exceed their expectations," he told Everest, "they'll fund more h-clones." Confidentially, he let Everest know that some of the hybrid experiments in the past had been failures. "The majority view is that cloning enhanced by genetic manipulation or even cyborg technology is generally more successful than h-cloning."

This was more information than Everest needed to know about Sago on that short bus ride to the video arcade. The kid was a bit too serious for his tastes. It was a safe bet that Sago wasn't a big skyball fan. Maybe any person who had been treated his entire life as a risky experiment would find it hard to act like a normal kid.

The video arcade was located in a huge shopping center called a "mall" that had Lelita gasping in longing.

"Why don't *we* have real shopping centers?" she moaned. "The Galactic Store Grid is so boring."

"Maybe we should just ship off a third of our population to another planet to make space for a mall," Dar suggested.

"Do you think we could?"

"Deng, Lelita, I was joking."

The arcade was as loud as a Bobebol game room, both dark and bright, with lights flashing, sirens pulsing, music pounding and children screeching. Everest didn't like it. He preferred to play his hologames in the privacy and quiet of his own room. Still, he was drawn to the race cars and couldn't resist taking his turn at steering one through a fast-paced course. The graphics were hokey, but there was an element of skill involved.

Instructor Legnarchi had rationed out fifteen tokens for each B12 and then given them a time limit, after which they were to gather at the main entrance. He'd also given them strict instructions not to turn in their tickets for twenty-first-century prizes, since they weren't going to be allowed to take them home.

On Everest's third attempt at driving a zeller silver and gold car that appeared to have been built for speed, he noticed out of the corner of his eye that Instructor Gerard had entered the facility. Even from this distance, Everest could tell the man was beaming as usual.

He rolled his eyes. He didn't care what Elsie thought, that guy was a total alien. Where was an auralizer when you needed one? An aurascan would probably be pretty illuminating. And where exactly had the guy been? For that matter, what in galaxies was Dr. Wei up to in the twenty-first century?

Deciding it wasn't any of his business, Everest returned his attention to the racing game. Once he had the hang of it, he easily won a free turn.

Before pressing the start button, he scanned the place for his sister and found her in a corner, laughing hysterically with Lelita over a game that consisted of a large claw that could be positioned to pick up one or more plastic toys.

Leave it to Elsie to be shopping for souvenirs even at an arcade. It wouldn't be a bad idea if Instructor Legnarchi hadn't expressly forbidden it. Anything plastic would be worth plenty of VC in 3002. Sure enough, Gerard was marching toward the girls, his customary smile absent.

Everest pressed the start button, then the pedal with his foot, and accelerated to another victory.

After handing over his second free ride to Borneo, who hadn't quite gotten the hang of these old-fashioned games, he went in search of Elsie. He found her watching some kids execute an intricate dance as they followed the lead of a big screen.

"You going to try?" he yelled over the noise.

Elsie's smile was pretty carefree, so Gerard couldn't have come down too hard on her. Whatever had been bothering her at lunch must be in the past too. "I think I'll just watch. I won 300 tickets at the Wheel of Fortune a few seconds ago."

"But you can't do anything with the tickets."

She made a face. "*I know.* I gave the tickets to a little twenty-first-century girl. She was really excited."

He leaned closer so he wouldn't have to shout. "What was the matter earlier?"

She shrugged. "I'll tell you later." She pointed toward a stationary motorcycle where a number of B12s stood waiting their turn. "I think I'll stand in line to ride that."

145

Everest decided it had to be some blecky girl thing. Making a face, he fell in step with his sister to ride the motorcycle. He sure wished it was a real one. Now that would be zetta zeller.

They walked toward the bike, and Elsie dug deep into her pocket for the last of her coins. "Jeans sure are difficult to maneuver in. Everything's so constricted, even the pockets. With a final wrench, she dragged out her last tokens, flipping the pocket inside out in the process. One flew in the air. There was so much noise in the arcade, they didn't even hear it land.

"Deng," she said, exasperated. "My last token."

She scoured the ground, but too many people were walking by and despite all the flashing lights, it was dark in the room.

Everest figured the token could have rolled anywhere.

"Don't worry about it," he yelled over the noise. "You can have one of mine. I've won a few free games. I still have enough for a motorcycle ride for both of us."

"Did some alien take over your soul?" She punched him in the upper arm. "You're being way too nice."

He shook his head. "Pity does strange things to a person. Besides, if I don't replace your token, you'll just moan and whinge so that I'm forced to crawl all over the floor until we find the missing one."

She laughed. "You've got that right." She pulled a token out of her other pocket. "Hey look, I must have miscounted."

It was weird. Without their parents here, he didn't have the heart to really lay into Elsie. In fact, he had a freakish desire to protect her. It wasn't exactly a feeling he appreciated.

Too soon, it was time to meet the instructors at the main entrance. After Gerard took a headcount, they all made their way back to the used car lot where their time travel machines were parked. This time they were close enough to walk.

Everest grinned. This sure had been a zeller day.

As they neared the used-car lot, however, they discovered that there was one more Zanbardi pit to leap over before they could return to their time. The place was not only open, but it appeared that Ernie was on a roll. In fact, he and his victim were hovering over the same bright red Mustang that Instructor Gerard had used as a portal to the past earlier this morning.

And it looked as if they were making a deal.

CHAPTER 23
The Used Car Salesman

Everest and Elsie stared at each other in horror. Ernie was selling their time-travel vehicle?

The salesman was quite large, at least half again as wide as anyone in the thirty-first century—Legnarchi included—and he sported a very red face. Even from this distance, Everest could see moisture collecting on the man's upper lip. He was gesticulating wildly with his arms and talking a kilometer a minute.

When Elsie clutched Everest's forearm, he tried to give her a reassuring smile, but he couldn't shake the feeling that he was doing a bad imitation of a flapping-mouthed Flurry fish from Fluth.

He checked to make sure the other cars weren't already sold out from under them and let out a big sigh of relief when he found the other three safe and sound. Worst case, they could take two trips to shuttle everyone safely home. But how were they going to leave with twenty-first-century witnesses hunkered down at the lot?

"Stop catching flies, ute-boy," Dar hissed from his other side. "I'm sure the instructor's got it under control. There's always a back-up plan."

"What did we tell you, Shadara, about using inappropriate language?" Instructor Tchakevska had moved as quietly as a hologram and now stood directly behind them. "For that little slip, you'll write an extra report on the twenty-first century—you pick the subject—due one week from today."

Dar froze like a marblon statue, but there was a hint of pink on her cheeks that hadn't been there before.

"Did I make myself clear, Shadara?"

"Yes, Instructor," she responded, her jaw clenched.

"Excellent."

A part of him wanted to gloat over Dar being caught and punished, but mostly he felt bad. He didn't know why. Maybe it was because the punishment seemed overly harsh for the crime. It wasn't as if she had called him a name in front of actual natives.

"Sorry, Dar," he muttered, scuffing his shoe against the hard cement.

"Nothing to be sorry about," she replied curtly. "If I'm enough of a yocto-brain to be caught, then I deserve the punishment. Now shut down. I want to watch the show."

He decided to play it safe and not remind her that "yocto-brain" was also a thirty-first-century term.

Gerard took a couple steps forward, then paused and turned back. "Instructor Tchakevska, please keep the children together and absolutely silent."

Just as the woman nodded her assent, a deep voice spoke in little more than a harsh whisper from behind. "Having problems, Instructor?" It was Dr. Wei. Despite the low tone, he sounded authoritative, intimidating, and even dangerous.

"Nothing I can't handle," Gerard said through clenched teeth.

Everest pivoted so that he could see both adults. Instructor Gerard looked as if he might pop.

"Just to be safe, why don't I handle this instead?" Dr. Wei asked, his face expressionless.

Gerard went a bright shade of purple. "Now see here—"

"No." Dr. Wei effectively silenced Gerard with that one word. "You see here. Because of your bungling of the logistics surrounding this field trip, we are in serious danger of being exposed, and that is something I will not tolerate." He brushed past. "Do attempt to keep yourself and the children quiet."

Instructor Gerard glared furiously.

Everest couldn't believe Dr. Wei had slammed Instructor Gerard in front of everyone. He stood there gaping until he realized that the rest of the B12s were scrambling for a spot to watch the doctor in action. He quickly moved to do likewise.

Crouching behind a short hedge, he watched as if a play were unfolding on a theater stage. Dr. Wei had planted himself in front of the two men who were holding an animated conversation about the Mustang.

From a distance, it looked as if he flashed them some kind of badge. "Inspector Wei, Department of Transportation," he said in his most intimidating and carrying tone. He pinned the salesman with a steely glare. "Might you be Ernie?"

"Yes, sir," the man responded in like volume. Everest wasn't surprised that Ernie, the huge-waisted used car salesman, had a booming voice.

"I've heard disturbing reports about you, which I've finally decided to investigate." Dr. Wei made it sound as if Ernie were a miniscule gnat that barely deserved his attention. He flicked a speck of dust off one black sleeve.

"Reports? What reports?" Ernie was sweating even more profusely than before.

The doctor chose not to answer the man's question directly. "This Mustang—you have the proper papers for it?"

"Course I do."

"Excellent, then you wouldn't mind showing them to me?"

"Can't you see I'm busy? We're coming to terms."

"Makes our conversation that much more timely."

After huffing and puffing for a while, Ernie finally gave in and marched over to the glass building.

Dr. Wei spoke in undertones to the man who had been contemplating the car purchase. Everest couldn't make out the words, but it was obvious they upset the buyer, who turned on his heel and stormed out of the lot.

From what they could see of Ernie through the glass windows, it looked as if he were ripping apart the office searching for papers he couldn't possibly own. Everest grinned. Pretty slick move on Dr. Wei's part.

After a while, the doctor marched to the building and up the stairs. He entered and began an animated conversation with the used car salesman.

Everest found himself creeping forward with the rest of the students so as not to miss a thing.

Dr. Wei pulled out a pad of paper from a sack he carried, wrote rapidly, then ripped off the piece of paper and handed it to Ernie.

How had Dr. Wei come by the paper? Everest wondered. He had to have bought it here in the twenty-first century. Wasn't that illegal?

More arguing ensued. Suddenly, the man threw up his hands, grabbed a briefcase, and stormed out of the building. Dr. Wei followed more slowly. When they both were out, Ernie used a large circle of keys to lock up. In a huff, he crossed over to a light blue Chevrolet, wrenched the door open, stuffed his large frame inside, and peeled out of the parking lot.

No sign of satisfaction, or any emotion for that matter, crossed Dr. Wei's face as he watched the man drive away. Once the prospective buyer had disappeared from sight, he curtly motioned the group to him.

"That was amazing," Vlas exclaimed as they neared. "What did you do to make him leave?"

"That is none of your business."

Vlas looked crestfallen.

Dr. Wei sucked in his breath. "Very well. I said that I was writing him up for trying to sell a car without a pink slip, and I suggested that his selling was over for the day. Now, can we please go?"

"What's a pink slip?" Elsie asked.

Everest had been wondering the same thing, but he wasn't about to ask with Dr. Wei so eager to depart. Leave it to Elsie.

Dr. Wei stared down his nose, then marched to his vehicle without another word.

Instructor Tchakevska cleared her throat. "It's an ownership certificate. In this day and age, if you don't have a pink slip, you don't have proof that you legally purchased a vehicle. I believe it may be against the law to sell an automobile without the pink slip."

Still looking decidedly peeved, Instructor Gerard said, "We'd better jam in case Ernie decides to call the Department of Transportation to check Inspector Wei's identity. His story was very weak. My approach would have been far superior. However, through sheer luck, Dr. Wei's forceful personality appears to have prevailed."

"What if Ernie had already sold one of the cars while we were gone?" Borneo asked nervously.

"None of the automobiles have fully functional motors, so no one would have been able to drive away in them. The man was a yocto-brain for even contemplating selling one."

Everest wished he had the guts to point out that 'yocto-brain' was a thirty-first-century term and, therefore, off-limits while they were in this time. If Dar had said it, she would have been punished again.

"Besides," Gerard continued, "there's a tracking device on each car. They wouldn't have gotten far without me finding them."

"Instructor!" Dr. Wei roared. "Don't you have the slightest ability to influence your charges? It's well past time for us to leave!"

Instructor Gerard went purple again and seemed to be on the verge of going on the attack, but instead he swallowed hard and curtly nodded his head. "Everyone back to your vehicles—light speed!"

Everest's stomach rolled over just thinking about the return trip. He stepped reluctantly toward the Mustang.

"Hey, Basker," Dar said from behind.

He turned and saw that her hand was out with two purple tablets resting in her palm.

"Take one; it'll keep all that Hasty Hawley's food settled where it should be. Give the other to Elsie."

His sister was already at the door of the convertible.

He hesitated then took the pills. "Thanks."

Dar shrugged. "I don't want to have to clean up after you. It's one thing for you and Elsie to get sick in the past, but we don't need you messing up our time period."

He didn't know whether to grin or grimace. Instead, he stuck one of the pills on his tongue, where it immediately dissolved, leaving behind a slight hint of sweetness. He had a feeling Dar would never admit to doing something nice for someone else, especially him. She was like the cooligrars on Elxsir, the scrappy fox-like creatures who couldn't stop biting and scratching at each other, all day and all night. They finally had gone extinct except for the few who lived separate and lonely lives in zoos.

Everest shook his head and followed her to the car. She wasn't going to bother him. If there was one thing he was good at, it was tuning out other people when necessary. Otherwise, Elsie would have driven him crazy years ago.

It would be no problem to tune out Dar too.

CHAPTER 24
Elsie's Big Mistake

When they arrived back in their time, Dr. Wei immediately stomped off. Elsie caught Instructor Gerard making a face at his retreating back, and she had to bite her lip to keep from giggling. She wasn't sure what to think about Instructor Gerard. He wasn't as nice as she'd thought. The Hasty Hawley meat cheeseburgers made her zetta mad. She sighed. But he was cute.

She barely heard Instructor Tchakevska order the children to quickly change back to their uniforms and to assemble outside, but she had no problem feeling Dar shove her toward the costume room.

With the rest of the B12s, Elsie scrambled out of her incredibly stiff twenty-first-century outfit and back into her much more comfortable exercise gear. Her legs were only slightly wobbly from the wild spinning, and the little purple tablet had saved her from an upset stomach.

She couldn't wait until the weekend, when she'd be able to holocomm with Zulu about her zeller timed field trip. It almost made up for Elsie not being able to communicate with her friend on a daily basis now that she was stuck in this clone academy.

She was one of the first to change back into her uniform. As she blasted out of the huge History Center, she had the sensation that the Earth of 3002 was almost too vivid. The bright green

155

ground and the amazing blue sky nearly blinded her in comparison to the gray of 2002. Then there were the brilliant, soaring mountains that she could almost reach out and touch, and the beautiful jewel-toned gravel at her feet.

The tevta buildings mirrored the extraordinary colors, making the world seem broader and brighter than even it was. If only she could somehow reach past all the bumping, weaving, stretching, and shrinking hover vehicles. She'd never really noticed how cluttered the sky was in her time period. Course, it was a lot less chaotic than the autos screeching around on the ground in the twenty-first century. Those were totally alien.

And 3002 smelled so much prettier than the smog-filled twenty-first century. She couldn't really describe it with words, but the air smelled fresh in comparison to a millennium ago. On top of that, Elsie breathed in the amazing scent of the little liligild flower that now made her think of Melista, and she caught the slightest whiff of tart limonino blended with sweet rosewillow. Faced with the sparkling reality of the thirty-first century, the field trip was beginning to feel like a far-off dream.

Following the lead of the students who had arrived before her, she sank to the ground and crossed her legs, waiting patiently for the instructors to excuse them.

Everest plopped down beside her. "Wait till Mom and Dad hear *when* we went!"

"Yeah, I guess they're not the only Baskers having adventures—" She gaped at Everest. Mom! Her necklace! In the twenty-first-century jeans pocket. "I forgot Mom's necklace! I'll be right back."

She raced back to the History Center, then down the aisle to the costume room, passing children going in the opposite direction who were talking excitedly about the field trip. A smattering of B12s still waited for changing rooms. The jeans she

156

had worn were folded neatly on a bench to the right, exactly where she'd left them. Digging into the left pocket, she searched for her pendant, but the pocket was empty. She tried the right-hand pocket next. Empty. Then the back pockets. Then the left one again. She went back and forth from pocket to pocket. Finally, she sank to the floor and stared with growing panic at the space below the bench. Surely the necklace was here somewhere. She even tried searching other jeans in case she'd been mistaken about which were hers, but she knew she hadn't been.

Around her the noise decreased as more students left the building. She was unable to move and perilously close to tears.

"Elsie?" Dar's voice was softer than Elsie had ever heard it, more melodious, as if it were Shadara's voice come to life again. "What's the matter?"

Elsie applied pressure with the heel of her hand into the bridge of her nose. How could she have been so irresponsible? Such a yocto-brain? She should have kept her necklace on, even though it was against the rules. Or she should have left it here despite her mother making her promise always to keep it close.

"I lost something," she said in a shaky voice.

"What did you lose?" Dar asked as she crouched down to Elsie's level.

Since Elsie had expected sarcasm, Dar's gentle question brought a first tear trickling down her cheek.

"Right before she left," Elsie said quietly with a nervous glance at the few remaining students in the changing room, "my mom gave me a zetta special piece of jewelry and made me promise to take care of it. Remember when Lelita noticed I was wearing a necklace and I decided to stuff it into my jeans pocket rather than leave it behind? It's not there any more, and I have an awful feeling I lost it at the video arcade. Something fell out of my pocket, but I thought it was a token. I forgot about the pendant." Elsie scrubbed at her face. "How could I have forgotten about it?"

She pushed up from the floor and brushed off her exercise pants. "I'll have to tell Instructor Gerard. Maybe there's something he can do. Only I promised my mom I wouldn't tell anyone about the necklace. Now I've told you, and I've got to tell him. Mom's going to be so angry."

"I don't think it's a good idea to tell Instructor Gerard," Dar whispered in response. "He'll never agree to take you back."

"But what else can I do?" Elsie had never felt so miserable in her entire life. If only a black hole would suck her up and put her out of her misery.

"First, you can stop feeling sorry for yourself," Dar said, her more caustic nature kicking back into action. "This crybaby act is really grating on my nerves."

"Thanks for the sympathy." Elsie glared. "Why don't you just blast off?"

Dar heaved an exasperated sigh, then lowered her voice. "Sympathy isn't going to retrieve your necklace. If we're going to sneak back to the past, break into the video arcade, and find your mama's little present, we've got our work cut out for us. This is no time for you to fall apart."

Elsie stared at Dar in disbelief. "Are you serious?"

Dar didn't look as if she were teasing. If anything she looked excited, energized, as if the idea of doing something this outrageous actually appealed to her.

Elsie folded her arms. "Wait a sec, you *are* serious, *and* you can't wait."

Dar grinned. "I've been dying to get my hands on one of those time travel vehicles. Now, I can do it with a good conscience."

"But...we'd be breaking every rule in the school's holoputer!"

This time Dar laughed. "Pretty zeller, huh?" She grabbed Elsie's arm. "Come on, we're the last ones still in here. We'd better hurry before we're punished for being late. We don't have time for that if we're going to pull off our after-hours caper."

Elsie raced alongside Dar, her thoughts a jumble. How could the girl be so confidant? So happy over the prospect of not only breaking school rules, but most likely a half dozen Earth rules too? A million things could go wrong. What if her parents found out? Or Uncle Fredrick? What if they made it backward in time but never made it forward? What if they ended up in a totally different *when*? Or for that matter, a totally different *where*?

How had life gotten so complicated? Just two days ago, everything had been so simple. Her parents had taken care of them, shielding them from all dangers and complications. The biggest adventure they'd ever had was a trip to a Chalux resort on the other side of the Milky Way. Every day, they'd been fed, clothed, reminded to do their homework, to pick up after themselves, and not to ruin their appetites with the no-cal junk food. Now everything was their responsibility. And Elsie wished desperately for her parents to come home and start taking care of them again. Twelve years old felt too young to have to make all the decisions and take all the consequences.

Yet Dar and Vlas and possibly all the clones at the academy were not only used to making their own decisions, but they looked for opportunities to do so. Didn't the students here ever wish they had someone else they could turn to?

Maybe in a way that someone was Dar, at least for the B12s. But didn't she ever get tired of having to be in charge?

CHAPTER 25
The Baskers Reveal a Secret

When Elsie and Dar exited the History Center, Instructor Tchakevska was waiting for them, her nose pinched with disapproval. The other students had already been excused.

"Ah. Elsinor and Shadara. Might I inquire what took you so long?"

"Sorry, Instructor," Dar said in a surprisingly humble voice. "I couldn't find my exercise pants. With all the mad rush, someone must have picked them up by mistake. I found them on the other side of the room under a bench." Elsie enthusiastically nodded her head to show her agreement with Dar's story. "Elsie helped me find them."

"Hmm." The instructor sucked in her narrow cheeks, and her thin nose flared slightly. "Very well. You are excused."

Dar and Elsie nodded again and murmured their thanks as they brushed past the instructor.

When they were about ten meters away, the woman called out, "Dar!"

Dar glanced over her shoulder.

"Do remember your special report is due in one week."

Elsie was impressed by Dar's angelic smile.

"I'm looking forward to it," the girl replied, her tone as sweet as her expression.

Elsie had the weirdest impression that there was a glimmer of humor in the instructor's eyes, but she had to be imagining things. Instructor Tchakevska didn't appear to have a sense of humor.

Dar tugged on Elsie's sleeve, and they both ran off down the path toward their dorm.

When they reached the B12 rec room, they found Everest, Vlas, Borneo and Lelita collapsed on nanofiber couches in one corner, anxiously awaiting them.

"Why were you so late?" Vlas asked. "Did Instructor Tchakevska give you another detention assignment?"

Dar stretched out in one of the chairs. "No. Guess she figured one was enough."

Elsie flopped down next to her brother, feeling exhausted. The night's plans loomed large and zetta dangerous.

"Everest thought you were upset about something," Lelita said to her.

"Everything okay now?" Everest asked.

Elsie couldn't meet her brother's eyes. "Not exactly."

"What does that mean?" he asked. "You did find it, didn't you?"

She shook her head.

"Did find what?" asked Vlas.

"Nothing," said Elsie. "It's no big deal."

Everest rounded on her. "*No big deal?* Mom's going to flaser you. I'm going to flaser you—"

"Shut down, Everest. It's under control."

His eyes narrowed. "What're you up to?"

"If you'll mute for a second, we'll tell you." Dar glanced pointedly around the room, and Elsie became aware of the other B12s lounging around, who were exhibiting plenty of interest in the heated exchange.

"Let's go into the fight room," Lelita suggested. "I think it's empty."

Fortunately, the room did give them the privacy they needed. After toeing off their skyboots, they dropped to the mats.

"Okay, give," Everest commanded.

Dar addressed the group. "Elsie's mom gave her a special pendant, which she managed to lose at the video arcade."

Everest let out an exasperated snort.

"Tonight, we're going back to find it," Dar added.

"Why can't we just buy Elsie a new one?" Lelita asked hesitantly.

"It's not replaceable, and she was under strict orders not to lose it."

Lying back on the mat, Elsie covered her eyes and groaned.

To let off steam, Everest jumped up and executed a series of back flips. "I can't believe you did this—" he started in on Elsie, but Dar quickly cut him off.

"Leave her alone. Can't you tell she feels bad enough?"

"She's my sister. It's my job to give her a hard time."

"Not around me, ute-boy. I don't have the energy to deal with sibling tantrums. Elsie says you have one of these necklaces too. We need to see it, so we know what to look for."

Everest turned bright red. "It's not a necklace," he mumbled. "Besides, I'm not supposed to show anyone." He turned on Elsie. "You were supposed to keep this a secret, galaxy-mouth."

She moaned and refused to uncover her eyes.

"So when do we go?" Vlas asked, ignoring Everest's grumbling.

Dar grinned. "You in?"

"Does a cat on Meldoon have two heads?" Vlas was grinning too.

"Hey, this is a Basker problem," Everest said. "We'll take care of it. Baskers can handle anything—*without your help.*"

"Well this Basker," Dar pointed to Elsie, "*wants* my help, and I'm giving it to her."

Elsie found the strength to sit up. "I'm sorry, Everest. I know I'm a total blubber for doing something so stupid, but we need Dar's help. She knows stuff we don't know. If anyone can get us back in time, it's her."

Everest ran a hand through his already messed-up hair. "I don't like this. You've lost the pendant, and now we've told everyone about it when it was supposed to be a secret. Mom made it sound as if it was a matter of life or death. Why'd you have to take it off in the first place?"

"They said we had to leave jewelry behind."

"It's not jewelry."

"You mean you just left yours on?" Elsie asked.

"Course I did," Everest said, his tone dripping with disgust. "You are such a yocto-brain."

"Everest, leave her alone." Dar crossed her arms and took on an intimidating stance. "Now show us what we have to find."

"No way." Everest backed up, frowning.

"Everyone here can keep a secret." Dar looked around at the other B12s.

"Sure we can," they chorused.

"You don't even like us," Everest protested.

Dar shrugged. "What does that have to do with us being able to keep a secret? Since you beat me in a fight competition, I'm required to take care of you, and judging from your first couple of days at the academy, you need a lot of care."

Vlas stepped forward. "We'll take an oath never to reveal to anyone the details of either necklace."

"They're not necklaces," Everest protested again, a pained expression twisting his face.

Dar rolled her eyes then placed her hand over her heart. "I solemnly swear never to reveal to anyone outside the present company the existence or the particulars of either Everest or Elsie's secret necklaces."

"They aren't necklaces!"

Ignoring Everest, Vlas, Lelita, and Borneo placed their hands over their hearts and murmured the same vow.

After a long pause and with great reluctance, Everest revealed his pendant.

Dar gasped. "1010511!" Her tone was reverent, awed. She studied the item as if it were a precious piece of art. "Do you know how impossible it is to purchase anything made out of 1010511? Believe me, I know. I asked my sponsor for some last year, but even he couldn't find a source when the purpose was frivolous. Your parents must have some serious connections."

Leave it to Dar to know more about the pieces than they did.

Everest shrugged. "They're scientists."

"Whatever they're doing must be really important."

"Maybe." He rubbed his neck, at a complete loss.

"Can I touch it?" Dar asked longingly.

"Deng, Dar, keep your aura on," he responded, but he shoved the pendant toward her.

She ran her forefinger across it, drawing back slightly from the surprising warmth. Her eyes met Everest's. "It's amazing." Then she stepped back and clapped her hands together. "To business." She pointed at Lelita and Borneo. "We'll need you to stay behind in case something goes wrong. In that event, you'll need to get in touch with my sponsor. He'll know what to do. If any instructors discover us gone, stall them for as long as you can. For now, the first order of business is food, then rest.

Everybody come back to our room at 22:00. Dress for comfort and for stealth—exercise clothes will do. Vlas, bring your gear."

She grinned broadly and rubbed her hands together. "This is going to be fun."

CHAPTER 26
The Mission

When Everest arrived early at the girls' dorm room, he found a restless Elsie flopped on her bed. Since it was after lights-out, the room was dark, but Elsie had squeezed on a brightee for a dim glow.

"What is it with Dar?" she asked. "She disappears right after dinner and doesn't show up again until late at night. She did it yesterday, and I just know she'll be late again tonight. She makes me crazy. What in galaxies is she doing?"

"Just doing my job, Basker." Dar leaned against the edge of the dissolved door, a mischievous grin on her face.

"Where have you been?" Elsie asked angrily. "Why do you have special permission to be out after curfew?"

"That's none of your business and nothing to do with tonight's little adventure."

Vlas strode up behind her and was quickly followed by Lelita and Borneo. Borneo was out of breath, and he wore his exercise top inside out. In the dark hallway, his white hair glowed.

"Sorry," he blurted out. "I fell asleep."

"That's okay," Dar said, patting Borneo's shoulder reassuringly. "We've all just arrived. Everyone inside." After the door was solid behind them, she flopped onto her bed and sent a skyball through the corner hoop. Lights sparkled and flashed, and the ball careened back.

"Knock it off, Dar," Elsie said, "Someone's going to investigate."

"I doubt it," she replied, but caught the skyball one-handed and didn't take another shot. Instead, she addressed the group. "We all know the mission—go back in time and retrieve Elsie's bauble without getting caught on either end of the time continuum. Fortunately, yesterday, Elsie and I already paved the way for this excursion."

Elsie brightened considerably and shot up from where she'd been sitting on her bed. "The transporter!"

Dar laughed. "Yeah." She addressed the rest of the group. "We placed a mini-transport system in the bobcat's pen last night so Elsie could bring her pet up each night to sleep in our dorm room."

Everest gaped at Dar. That was why Dar had been roaming around after hours? She had done that for Elsie? Why hadn't Elsie told him? Guilt seeped through him for every bad thought he'd had about the girl, and then he was mad because no one had set him straight.

Dar burst into laughter. "The look on your face, Basker! Don't worry, I'm no angel of mercy. I helped Elsie so I wouldn't have to hear her crying into her pillow all night. Nothing I hate more than whinging and sniveling. Besides, she owes me. And after tonight, she's going to owe me even more.

"Transporting to Pooker's pen is the easy part of tonight's adventure. It's the History Center that's going to cause us grief. It has the tightest security on the property. Any ideas, Vlas?"

"I kind of figured getting past the security would be my problem, so I spent the last couple of hours modifying some of my favorite toys." He patted a bag slung across his hip. "I've got it covered."

"Zeller. I've read up on time travel, so I'll take responsibility for getting us back to the past. We'll time it for the night hours of the same day. We'll need the matter-mover," she rummaged through her black pack, "and stunners." She pursed her lips. "I'll bring the spider gear just in case. Anything else you can think of?" she asked Vlas.

Everest felt useless. How come twelve-year-olds had all this gear more suited to spies or thieves? What could he add to the party?

"Everyone should use nighteyes drops and bring brightees," Vlas responded. "Maybe we should take a few foggers in case we need a diversion."

"And some smellers," Borneo suggested.

"Bleck," Lelita said with her nose pinched. "That's just for practical jokes."

"No," Dar said, shaking her head. "They could be useful. Good idea, Borneo. I think we can get by with wearing our exercise clothes. They're not that different in style from 2002 exercise gear, just made from a material that didn't exist. We'll take our chances with thirty-first-century footwear. None of us needs to be dealing with the extra weight of those clunky twenty-first-century sports shoes. Oh, and we need our earpatches. Vlas, did you bring yours?"

"Yeah," he responded, holding out a matching vial to Dar's.

"Excellent. Lelita, here's an earpatch for you. You transport us down, okay? Then wait here for our return. Borneo, you're with Lelita. If something goes wrong, we're counting on you to troubleshoot. Everyone, make sure you're on hands and knees to transport. Our destination has a very low ceiling. Ute-twins, as soon as you arrive, get off the device because we'll be right on your heels."

The two transports, first of Everest and Elsie, then of Dar and Vlas, went smoothly with Pooker only emitting the slightest growl to indicate her displeasure at having her space invaded.

Everest barely had time to worry about how they were going to get past all the dancing lights that surrounded them before Dar strode over to an impossibly thin stake with a blue button on top. She pressed it, and the dancing lights in a narrow section immediately vanished. He quickly followed her out of the sensored area.

"Pick it up to light speed, Elsie," Everest muttered when he saw his sister hugging her bobcat instead of jamming with the rest of the group.

Once they were all outside of the pen, Dar pressed the matching button to keep Pooker from following.

They ran in groups of two, taking advantage of their nighteyes in the pitch black. The stars were shrouded due to the fast approaching planned rainfall, and the jellach cars were twirling shadows.

"If we time it right, we might be able to miss the rain altogether," Vlas said to no one in particular.

"Timing is everything," Dar responded.

Her tone gave Everest the impression she was smiling. This nighttime excursion didn't appear to be making her stomach churn the way his was. In fact, he had a feeling she was enjoying herself. The idea that she was getting a kick out of their mission didn't sit well with him. It wasn't that he didn't like adventures, but he couldn't stop thinking of the millions of things that could go wrong. His problem was that he thought too much. Just as Elsie's was that she *talked* too much.

When they reached the History Center, Vlas extracted a flat black triangle from his back pocket.

"What's that?" Elsie asked.

"It's a scrambler—my design. These three points send out pico frequencies which jumble the security currents." He palmed the triangle against the tevta wall. As soon as it touched the surface, it began to glow a bright blue.

Everest smelled a strong chemical substance. Elsie immediately pinched her nose.

"Sorry," Vlas said to no one in particular. "I could fix that stink, but I'd need a real lab."

After a minute, the color began to change, a gradual shift from blue to purple to red to pink, then to a pearly fluorescent white. "That should do it."

He snapped off the triangle and pocketed it, then requested permission to enter. The door dissolved to utter silence.

"Excellent," Dar said as she led the way into the oversized building.

Vlas grinned. He took a few seconds to reverse the process so that the building was once again secure.

"You're a genius, Vlas," Elsie said.

Instead of appreciating the compliment, he frowned. "You better not spread that around."

"Why not?"

"If *they* find out I can do more than play skyball and compete in fight challenges, I'll be stuck in some lab till the Vlemutz return and take over the world. No thank you. I've got more to do with my life than be chained to some geekoid tower for the next millennium. As long as they think I'm a clone reject, they'll leave me alone."

Everest and Elsie exchanged befuddled looks. Clone reject was the term Kindu had used. It had to mean someone who wasn't living up to his or her clone potential. Only in this case, Vlas was a genius but nobody knew. Kindu had called Lelita a clone reject, too. Was she having difficulty living up to her original's reputation, or was she hiding her talents like Vlas?

As Everest jogged between carriages, automobiles, and chariots, he thought how weird it was that Vlas would want to hide his brilliance. For as long as he could remember, Everest had been taught that it was his sacred duty to make a difference in the world. His parents were determined to invent something that would be the next big leap in science. It was more important to them than anything, even their children.

He shook his head. No, that wasn't fair. If his parents thought either he or Elsie truly needed them, they'd drop everything without a moment's thought. It was just that they were willing to make tough choices for the sake of their research.

So if Vlas had been cloned solely because of his inventor's brain, why would he want to keep his inventions hidden? It didn't make much sense.

He would never understand these clones.

When they arrived at the rusty, dented Mustang, Dar vaulted over the front door and slid into the driver's seat, then started messing with the keypad. Vlas landed in the bucket seat next to her.

"Be careful," Elsie hissed as she clambered into the back. "We don't want to end up in Medieval Europe."

"Keep your aura on, Elsie, I've got it covered. I tapped into the Time Travel Scientific Institute earlier this evening and did some research."

"Is that legal?"

Dar shrugged. "Let's call it a gray area."

"But we're not even supposed to have holoputer access, except on the weekends."

Dar gave Elsie a funny look. "Using a holoputer is the least of our worries. If we get caught tonight, I don't care who your uncle is, you'll probably be expelled, and they'll do a lot worse to us clones."

Everest closed his eyes. He was getting a headache the size of a spaceship from Kalkulla.

"Okay, I think I've got it—just enough hours after we left the twenty-first century for the shopping center to be shut down for the night." Dar reached deep into one of her pockets and pulled out a handful of purple tablets. Handing two of them to the back, she said, "Baskers, take these. Someone might notice if you mess up the backseat."

"Thanks," Elsie said weakly as she took one of the tablets. Everest had never seen her look so worried.

He accepted the pill and dissolved it on his tongue without saying a word.

After a short pause, Elsie asked, "What about the key?"

Dar grinned into the rear view mirror. "No problem." Out of another pocket, she retrieved a gooey, dirty gray ball. Pressing it flat on the keyhole, she murmured, "Unlock it."

The ball began to shift and bump, stretching itself and taking form, wriggling up, thinning out, and developing edges along one side.

"What's that?" Everest asked as he watched the blob turn into a key likeness, then harden into an unbendable form.

Dar shrugged. "Another gray area."

"Your sponsor?" Elsie asked.

Dar nodded. "My birthday a few years ago—called an 'object cloner.' Mink saw it as a bit of a joke."

"Don't you find his choice of gift odd?" Elsie asked. Everest had been thinking the same thing.

"A little eccentric, but I'm not complaining."

172

Everest had a feeling the guy was zetta more than just a little eccentric.

"Okay, I think that'll do it," Dar murmured. "Let's shake this Millennium." She turned the switch.

Chapter 27
The Break-In

The spinning was the same, the pressure in Elsie's head, her rippling cheeks, and chattering teeth. But this time, the feeling that she was about to explode somehow reassured her. Surely the time travel was working?

Despite the purple pill she'd taken, her stomach dipped and churned, but she suspected it had more to do with her fear and anxiety than with motion sickness. She'd like to travel someday under less stressful circumstances. She might actually get used to the sensation. Maybe even start to like it as Lelita did. If nothing else, a trip back in time was exciting.

They arrived in the middle of a rain shower. Luckily, vlatex was waterproof, but it was weird feeling all the water pour down. Usually they were asleep when it rained. Everyone rushed to pull up their hoods as water streamed into the little convertible. Raindrops blurred Elsie's vision, but she still recognized Ernie's Used Car Lot. She breathed a huge sigh of relief.

It wasn't that she'd doubted Dar's ability to get them here— Elsie had a feeling she could do anything—but so much could have gone wrong.

"Light speed, Elsie," Everest urged. The others were already out of the car. She clambered out of the backseat.

"Vlas," Dar was saying, "how many earpatches do you have?"

He held up a couple of fingers. "Two."

Dar shook her head as she handed Elsie one of the small devices. "Mine's a set of four, but I gave one to Lelita. I should have thought to use Vlas's set to communicate with her."

"We'll manage," he replied. "Give me your fourth one, and I'll give Everest the match to mine. I can handle two conversations. It's not like ute-boy over here," he thumbed at Everest, "talks all that much. With the possible exception of Elsie, who can't seem to shut down, I doubt any of us will be doing much talking."

Elsie grimaced and opened her mouth to protest, but for once, Everest beat her to the spoken word.

"She can stay quiet when it's important." He squeezed her arm. "Right, Elsie?"

Flasers, these clones were irritating. "It's not like I don't know how to power down."

Her brother betrayed her by snorting with laughter.

"How bout you both shut down now so we can get moving?" Dar grumbled as she inserted a picobot in her ear. "We'll jog to the mall. The sooner we get this over with, the better."

"What if this is the wrong night?" Elsie asked.

"It's not the wrong night," Dar asserted.

"How do you know?"

"I just do. Now, can you please shut down? We're wasting time. We need to jam." Dar jogged through the parking lot and vaulted over the chain that crossed the entrance driveway.

"Probably have no idea if it's the right day," Elsie muttered, tired of Dar's know-it-all attitude. Just because it was nighttime didn't make it the right nighttime.

"If it would make you feel better, I'd be happy to ask the first person we run into what the date is," Dar hissed back. "I'll leave it to you to explain why we're out jogging at 10:00 p.m. on a school night."

Elsie made a face at Dar's back as they ran.

"What if someone has already found the pendant? What if they've already analyzed it and found out it's a new metal alloy? What if somehow it changes the course of history?"

"Deng, Elsie, keep your aura on," Dar advised. "Spinning into outer space isn't going to help any of us. Whatever happens, we'll deal with it."

Elsie took a shaky breath, ashamed of her outburst.

Vlas' laughter sounded in her ear. "Flasers, if I'd known you two were going to bicker so much I'd have asked Everest to wear the two earpatches."

That made Elsie power down.

Four near-silent shadows, they went unnoticed on their jog to the nearby mall. At this time of night, there was less traffic, but the streets were still noisy and jarring with the flashing lights and an occasional screech of tires. The ground was harder than any surface they were used to, and even with the cleansing rain, the air was stale and unappealing with not a hover vehicle in sight, though something very high up blinked by. It was such an odd time period in history.

The covered parking lot was empty. Elsie was grateful to have shelter from the pounding rain. It wasn't that she was all that wet. Her vlatex outfit's built-in water-repelling system had done its job, but she did have a harder time seeing through the rain, and her hands and face were frozen. Fortunately, her clothes had heated up in reaction to her cold body temperature, and the warmth felt wonderful.

When they reached the building, Vlas and Dar went into a huddle in front of the glass entrance doors. Elsie pressed her face up to the glass to stare at the back side of the escalators. Beyond them was the arcade, with its bright neon sign off for the night. A few recessed lights gave the blackened room a dim yellow glow. A floor to ceiling metal structure served as barrier to the arcade.

"What do you think? Motion sensors?" Dar asked Vlas in a low voice. Elsie heard the quiet question through her earpatch.

Vlas shook his head. "I don't think so. There isn't enough to steal here. Who's going to walk off with one of these video games? Can you imagine how many kilos they weigh? I'm betting whoever's in charge just secures the doors, then adds video cameras. You know," he added at their blank looks, "old-fashioned devices for two-dimensional moving pictures. The site might have security guards monitoring it too."

"Security guards?" Elsie asked.

"Humans who watch for security breaches."

"Weird."

There was a moment of silence, then Dar whispered, "Vlas, your assessment sounds reasonable." She made a sweeping gesture with her arm. "Go for it."

He considered the setup. "I don't think I need the scrambler. This is your basic twenty-first-century electrical alarm system, complete with backup nickel batteries. My jammer'll be enough."

He pulled out a slim little tube and squeezed. A thin light shot out of the tip. He winked at Elsie. "I made it for a B9 science project, then somehow forgot to turn it in." He ran the tube along the edge of the door, paying careful attention to the bottom and top.

"That should do it," he said as he squeezed once more to turn off the jammer. He replaced it in his inner pocket. "Shall we go for the matter-mover, or can I pick the lock?"

"Pick the lock?" To Elsie, that sounded like something from an ancient two-dimensional movie. She had a hard time following Vlas's conversation. How could he forget to turn in a science project? And earlier he'd sworn them to secrecy about his genius qualities. He sure was one strange clone.

"Yeah, I've been researching the history of locks," he replied. "Just a side interest. I think I can spring this one."

"And you're just dying to try," Dar said, rolling her eyes. "Wouldn't the object cloner be a simpler option?"

"Yeah, yeah, but where's your sense of adventure?" Vlas's mischievous grin was infectious.

"All right," Dar said with a deep sigh. She turned to the other B12s. "We'd better let him have his fun, or there'll be no living with him. Just be quick about it." She directed the last statement at Vlas.

Still grinning, he pulled out a small rolled-up cloth and unrolled it to reveal a number of slim tools.

Elsie watched in fascination as Vlas selected one of the devices and inserted it into a lock three-quarters of the way up the door. With a delicate touch, he wiggled the tool up and down, then left and right, and Elsie heard the slightest snick. Then Vlas inserted another narrow instrument into a lock at the bottom of the door. When that one clicked as well, he tested the door, and it swung forward. They all paused on the threshold waiting for a siren to blare, but nothing happened.

"Excellent," Dar exclaimed in an undertone.

She and Vlas quickly distributed brightees, foggers, smellers, and stunners from their packs.

"What's our plan if a security guard finds us?" Elsie asked.

"That's what stunners are for," Dar said shortly, as if Elsie were a yocto-brain for asking. But Elsie felt stunned herself that anyone would expect her to actually stun another human being.

"To be safe," Dar continued, ignoring Elsie's obvious signs of distress, "we should knock out the cameras. Any ideas, Vlas?"

"Actually, I brought PicoBoy along with already downloaded video equipment knowledge from this time period for exactly that reason. He'll fix those cameras."

With that, he pulled out a small object no bigger than a pinkie fingernail. It was a dull smooth gray. Speaking in a low murmur, Vlas admonished the object to find and disengage the cameras. He held out his slightly cupped hand with PicoBoy resting on his palm and quietly commanded, "Go."

Immediately, the object lifted up from his hand, twirled a few times then rose at breakneck speed. He rammed straight into a video camera directly above them and attached himself to it. After a few seconds, they heard a small click, then PicoBoy left that camera and careened toward the opposite corner. Five times the little techno-creature searched out a video camera and went to work.

Vlas said quietly, "He's pausing each camera so that it freezes on the last frame taken. The security guards should be fooled into thinking all is quiet."

Finally, PicoBoy zoomed back and crashed onto Vlas's sleeve. "Good boy, Pico." He slid the little gray techno-creature into his pocket.

"Why didn't you program PicoBoy to open the door for you or to cut off the alarm?" Elsie asked dazedly.

Vlas snickered. "That's not nearly as much fun. Haven't you ever heard that the one with the most equipment wins? I like to win."

Dar cleared her throat. "I hate to break up Vlas's little fun fest, but we'd better jam. Keep your eyes open for security guards." They filed through the entrance.

Elsie had a hard time believing this place was the same as the one they'd visited earlier today. The whole shopping center was powered down, dark and eerily silent with only the softest glow relieving the darkness. With the lights off, the escalators stilled, the crowds missing, and the arcade itself shut down, Elsie was reminded of a holo-adventure right before the show started. What a difference from their earlier experience, with the pulsing and flashing lights, screaming children, and whistling and clanging games.

"Hmm." Dar strode up to the security gate, pulling out her matter-mover and pressing a series of numbers. It took less than thirty seconds for her to make a meter-by-meter square opening to provide access into the arcade. She motioned to Everest to go first, and the rest of the team quickly followed.

"Where do you think you lost the necklace?" Dar whispered. The girl was already many meters ahead of Elsie with her strong stride eating up the floor.

"I was watching a dance game—"

"No, we were heading toward the motorcycles," Everest interrupted, close enough to hear her without the benefit of an earpatch. "I was going to lend you a token because you thought your last one had flipped out of your pocket. If only we'd realized then what really had happened."

"Stop interrupting me. I was already going to say all that." Elsie frowned at her brother.

"Who cares who said it first?" Dar asked, exasperated. "Let's just go look."

Elsie had the oddest sensation that they were being watched. She even imagined she saw something flutter in the distance, like material dancing in the breeze or near invisible pico-brownies caught in the light. She screeched to an abrupt halt and carefully scanned the arcade. Had those been footsteps retreating? She silently told herself to stop imagining things. Besides, how would someone else have gotten in? The place had been locked and was being monitored with hidden cameras. Plus, there was a floor to ceiling gate. If someone was there, the security guards would know. Taking a deep breath, she stepped forward, her thoughts centered on the task at hand.

"This is it," she said, pointing down to a spot on the worn, industrial-strength carpet. "I was standing in this general area."

"Okay, we'll spread out and see what we can find." Dar lowered herself to the ground and, squeezing on her brightee wand, started a methodical survey of the floor. The others did likewise.

After fifteen minutes of intense searching, Elsie pulled herself to a sitting position. So far, they'd found nothing. Not even a token. Elsie rubbed the back of her neck. "I think someone got here first. Not a cleaning service—there's too much grime. But someone else. In a place like this, it doesn't make sense for there to be no lost tokens. Whatever could be found of value has already been taken. But who took it?"

"That would be me," said a strange, disembodied voice.

Chapter 28
The Boy From 2002

Elsie whipped around at the unfamiliar twenty-first-century voice. It sounded awfully young and male. But that was crazy. Why would a kid be hanging out here after hours? And how had he snuck in?

"Show yourself," she commanded, holding up the stunner she'd been given and doing her best to keep the nervousness out of her voice.

Dar leapt onto the nearest video machine and, raising her brightee, peered into the gloom, while Vlas and Everest took on their fighting stances.

Elsie made eye contact with Dar, who shifted a little and almost imperceptibly shook her head to indicate that she hadn't yet found their unexpected visitor's location.

"How stupid do you think I am?" the voice asked.

"We mean you no harm," Everest said slowly, straightening from his fight position and stretching out his hands, palms out.

The hidden person laughed. "Mean me no harm? Who are you? Star Trek dudes? Well, mebbe I mean you no harm back. Mebbe I can even help you."

"How?" Dar asked.

"You're looking for something. Me? I'm good at finding things. Who knows? Mebbe I've already found what you're looking for."

"Do you work for a cleaning service?" Vlas asked.

"Naw. Me and the manager have a deal. When it's wet, he gives me a roof."

Elsie stepped in the direction of the voice. Because he sounded young like them, she couldn't think of him as a threat. "I lost a necklace—a gift from my mother. It meant a lot to me."

"Aw...you're making me cry," he said, sniffing loudly. "Supposing I have this necklace or know where to find it, how much is it worth to you?"

"I...I," she cleared her throat, "I don't have any virtual currency."

He laughed like a crazy person. "Virtual currency? Girl, I want cash."

Elsie was confused. What had she said that was so funny? What was cash?

Dar saved her by jumping off the video game and calling out, "She doesn't have cash."

"No cash, no necklace," the voice responded.

Blast him, Elsie thought. He knew where her pendant was. She raised the stunner again in what she hoped was his direction. "Give me back my necklace."

"I don't think so. I ain't making no deal with you toting that gun."

She immediately lowered it. From the corner of her eye, she saw that Vlas and Everest were inching in the general direction of their invisible speaker. She hoped their nighteyes gave them an advantage over the boy. Surely the people of these ancient times didn't have such technology for seeing in the dark.

In Elsie's ear, Dar whispered in Pallaccii, "Keep him talking and distracted so Vlas and Everest can find him."

Of course, as soon as Dar asked her to keep him talking, her mind went completely blank. A first for her. "Uh, I don't want to hurt you, I just want my necklace back. What will it take for me to be able to claim it? My brother has one just like it, so I can prove it's mine."

The voice laughed again. "Your brother has a necklace that matches yours? That's a good one. In that case, the one I found is too girly to be the one you want."

"Tell me about it," muttered Everest, loud enough to be heard without the aid of an earpatch.

That drew the speaker's attention.

"Hey, you better freeze," he said. "Crowding me ain't going to get you what you want."

Both Vlas and Everest froze.

"Look, I got no reason to be unfriendly. All you got to do is ante up some dough, and you can have your girly jewelry."

Again Elsie was puzzled. Dough? Now he wanted bread in exchange? Was bread terribly expensive in this day and age? She shot Dar another confused look.

Surprisingly, Dar grinned in return and whispered into her ear, "Elsie, you are such a yocto-brain." Then she raised her voice for the benefit of the hidden boy. "I already told you, she has no money."

"Tell me you're joking."

"No joke," Dar responded firmly.

The boy said a word Elsie had never heard before, but she suspected from his tone that it was inappropriate in the twenty-first century.

At that moment, footsteps clattered outside the arcade and everyone dove to the ground. In unison, they shut off their brightees. Elsie thought the movement came from the escalators. She still hadn't pinpointed the twenty-first-century boy's location.

Suddenly, two big shadows loomed forbiddingly in the lobby, first peering at the mall entrance then turning around to stare at the arcade. A bright beam of light arced eerily into the gloom, hurting Elsie's already dilated eyes.

"The door's been jimmied and the alarm turned off," a voice said in raspy undertones. "There's going to be hell to pay."

"Do you think they're still here?" asked a second voice nervously. "No way they'd be able to get into any of the shops."

"We better call the police. Got to be professionals to turn off the security."

Elsie's palms dampened and a rush of nerves hit her stomach. What should they do?

"Abort," hissed Dar in her ear. She heard Vlas relay the message to Everest.

"But he's still got the pendant," Elsie whispered back.

"We mustn't be caught by the authorities." Dar was speaking so quietly Elsie barely heard her through the earpatch. "Everyone, foggers ready. On the count of three we'll make a run for it. If necessary, don't hesitate to use your stunners. Vlas, you and Everest release your foggers as we charge. Elsie, release yours when you reach the escalators. Everyone got it?" Again Vlas relayed the directions to Everest.

Dar continued, "Don't stop running—not for a picosecond, not until we've reached Ernie's."

"Hey," one of the guards yelled to the other, "look at this!"

They had found the matter-mover hole that led to the arcade. The other guard said something Elsie didn't understand and began punching buttons into an old-fashioned communication device. She remembered that it was called a phone.

"Who's out there?" the first security guard called. He stood at the hole in the gate. "Whoever you are, slowly show yourself with your hands behind your head."

"Don't be a hero, Frank. Let the police handle it." The security guard began to talk urgently into his phone, communicating their location and high-level details of the break-in.

"Ready?" Dar whispered. "Go."

Released foggers immediately caused a thick white cloud to obscure the arcade. The children charged forward, stunners ready and aimed at the guards. The first one went down with a tremendous thud.

"Frank's been shot," the other guard yelled into the phone. He turned heel and ran for cover.

Dar beat Elsie to the hole, but boosted her through first.

"Keep on running," Dar whispered as she followed. When they reached the escalators, they both released their foggers.

Elsie caught a glimpse of Vlas behind them, but she couldn't see her brother. "Where's Everest?"

She started back, but Dar grabbed her arm. "Don't alien on me. We've got to get out of here. Everest will find us. Vlas, locate him."

Elsie heard Vlas whispering frantically for Everest.

"He's on his way," Vlas said in her ear. "He says to keep running, and he'll catch up. He's already outside the arcade."

"Then go." Dar pushed Elsie toward the entrance, and the three of them shot into the parking lot in a mad dash toward Ernie's Car Lot.

"Vlas, keep in contact with Everest," Dar commanded.

Elsie heard Vlas checking in. Everest seemed to think he was fifteen meters behind them, but Vlas reported that for some reason he was having a hard time catching his breath.

"What's the matter with him?" Elsie asked. He was the fastest runner she'd ever known. No matter how hard she tried, she'd never beaten him in a race, which really irked her.

Vlas whispered to Everest to pick up the pace. After a pause while he listened, he said, "Everest is carrying something heavy that's slowing him down."

"We need to help him." Elsie spun around as she spoke. She thought she saw him, but he looked bulkier.

Sirens blared in the distance, but they were rapidly closing in.

"No!" Vlas yelled. "Everest wants us to keep on running—to get the car ready so we can leave right away. The police are going to be here any second."

At top speed, it took them about three minutes to return to the used car lot and hurdle the chain.

Dar hopped into the Mustang and started to press the series of buttons that would send them forward to their time. Vlas and Elsie hovered near the entrance of the lot, anxiously waiting for Everest. Through the downpour he took shape, and the reason for his slower pace soon became apparent.

A body was slung over his shoulder.

When he reached them he was out of breath, and Elsie had never seen him so upset.

"What have you done?" she asked frantically.

"I stunned him." He sounded stunned himself.

Elsie stared at her brother in horror. "Who is he?"

"The boy who has your necklace."

"He is?" Elsie squeaked. Stunned the boy? Kidnapped him? Everest could go to cyberjail forever! And they'd go right with him as accomplices.

"I saw him a few seconds before Vlas let go of his fogger. He was trying to crawl away toward one of the side entrances. I didn't think; I just stunned him. I'm pretty sure he's younger than us—he's smaller, at least." Everest shook his head. "I don't know why I did it. I guess I panicked."

The sirens in the background were growing louder.

"Deng," Vlas said under his breath. "You didn't flaser him, you stunned him. You don't see me crying all over because I stunned someone. Ute-babies!" He reached out and took the boy from Everest, then slung him over his shoulder.

"Come on, folks, get in the car," Dar ordered. "All of you. Bring the boy."

"We can't bring him," Elsie wailed.

"We have no choice. We'll just have to return him later."

They all jammed to the car. After Elsie and Everest jumped into the back—getting soaked in the process since the rain had poured all over the seats of the topless car—Vlas dumped the unconscious boy onto their laps. He leapt into the front as Dar turned the key.

The last thing they saw before they were jerked into the wild ride forward to the thirty-first century was a police car screeching to a halt in front of the driveway of Ernie's Used Car Lot.

CHAPTER 29
An Unexpected Visitor

Oddly, the ride forward seemed to happen in a blink and take forever. Everest was still sweating from his weighed-down sprint to the time-travel Mustang. Not that he actually felt the sweat dripping down his face. He just kind of knew it was there. He was dizzier and more nauseated than any of the previous times. A mix of fatigue, adrenalin, and fear churned up his stomach, and there'd been no opportunity to take a time travel pill.

Their return was abrupt, and in contrast to the last time, he was both freezing cold and boiling hot. He shook uncontrollably, and his teeth chattered.

When the Mustang landed, no one moved or said a word.

Just a few seconds before, the car had been full of water, but now it was bone dry. However, their exposed skin was still wet from all that twenty-first-century rain. Water dripped into Everest's eyes. Fortunately, his water-proof clothing had protected most of his body.

Finally, Dar spoke. "All right, everyone to the costume room. We need to decide what to do with our guest. And, Everest, if you even think about losing your dinner, you'll regret it."

As if he could help having an upset stomach.

189

Dar focused on the inert boy from the twenty-first century, then glanced back at Everest and cocked an eyebrow. He looked away.

"You Baskers sure do know how to liven up a joint. I don't think we've had this much adventure in our entire lives—and all in the space of two days."

He swallowed hard, determined not to humiliate himself further by getting sick in front of her. "This is pretty unusual for us," he said weakly.

"Ute-boy, let's hope so."

Everest didn't have the energy to complain about the name calling.

Suddenly, Dar got a funny far-away look on her face. Then she said, "Lelita, we're back, but there are a few complications. Nothing to worry about, but we're kind of busy. I'm going to take out the earpatch for now. Okay?"

Everest had forgotten about Lelita and Borneo. All his concentration was on the boy he had stunned. How could he ever make it up to the kid?

After removing and pocketing her earpatch, Dar motioned to Elsie and Vlas to do likewise. "If we get separated or are otherwise unable to communicate, put them back in. For now, I don't want to upset Lelita and Borneo with references to our new friend. Lelita doesn't like to bend rules. Smashing them into tiny pieces will cause her to totally alien." She shot another look at the motionless body sprawled across Elsie and Everest.

"Do you think he's okay?" Elsie asked anxiously.

"He's fine. He'll have one Zylorg headache, but otherwise being stunned is the least of his problems. And ours." She turned to Vlas, who had jumped out of the Mustang and was leaning against the door, looking, in Everest's opinion, a little too thrilled over the adventure.

"Vlas," Dar commanded. "Carry the boy to the costume room. I don't think ute-baby here," she pointed to Everest, "is up to any more physical activity tonight. He's looking stunned himself, and he's still a nasty color of green."

"I'm fine," Everest said brusquely.

"No you're not," Elsie responded.

Everest frowned. Even his sister was against him.

"No really," she said. "You can't be. We've zetta done it this time. I can't imagine what Mom and Dad are going to say."

"You're not seriously thinking of telling them?"

Dar's look of utter disbelief shook Everest. They'd never kept secrets from their parents before. Then again, they'd never found themselves in this much hot water before.

"Well," Elsie said hesitantly, "they are our parents."

"Haven't you learned by now that adults can't be trusted?" Dar persisted.

"Of course they can be trusted," Elsie said. "At least, our parents can be."

"*Ute-babies!*" She sounded totally disgusted. "You better hope you never tell them, or I never find out you did. Now let's blast."

Everest helped Vlas to drag the boy out of the car. Then he clambered out of the back seat himself, feeling as if he'd just run twenty kilometers instead of a little less than one. He really hated to admit it, even to himself, but Dar was right, deng her. He was wiped out.

He slowly followed Dar and Vlas as they made their way across the building to the room that housed the various period costumes. Elsie walked next to him, concern written all over her face. She wouldn't stop looking at him.

"I'm okay," he grumbled. If Elsie didn't stop hovering, Dar'd be all over them for being "itsy-bitsy ute-babies."

When they reached the other room, Dar pulled some nanofiber cushions off nearby benches onto the floor. Then she motioned for Vlas to prop the boy against the cushions.

As much as he didn't want to, Everest looked to Dar for guidance. He didn't have any bright ideas himself. He'd made such a mess of things.

"Don't look so flasered," Dar said, surprising him with her support. "Things happen for a reason. If I didn't believe *that*, it would be impossible for me to put up with you attending this academy. Besides, it does no good to second-guess things. What's done is done."

He made a face. If that was her best attempt at cheering him up, it was pretty pathetic.

Flashing him a grin as if she knew his thoughts and found them hilarious, she nudged the boy with her foot. "He should wake up pretty soon. Not that I've ever stunned anyone before. I wasn't even sure the guns worked. Thanks for testing one out for me, Basker. You, too, Vlas."

"Anytime," Vlas said, matching her grin.

Everest kept his mouth shut.

"Shouldn't we try to take him back before he wakes up?" Elsie asked nervously.

"I don't think so," Dar answered. "We all need to rest up before we attempt any more time jumps. Experts recommend a few hours between trips. Besides, we still don't know where your pendant is, and I'm reluctant to search him while he's unconscious."

"But we can't let him know he's in a different time period. It could change the course of history."

Dar shrugged. "We'll just have to do our best not to give away that little tidbit."

Dar made Everest feel like an alien. No way could she be as calm as she was acting. He'd stunned another human being. That was huge. He'd stolen someone from the past. That was zetta huge! Vlas was even worse than Dar. He didn't seem to care in the slightest that he had stunned that security guard, and he appeared to have no qualms about dragging someone forward in time.

The twenty-first-century boy groaned and shifted slightly. They all stared down at his collapsed body, and for the first time, Everest really focused on him. His skin tone was only a slightly richer shade of chocolate than Everest and Elsie's, but his hair was shiny black and curly instead of glossy brown, and his eyes were rounder in comparison to their own almond shape. He was at least ten centimeters shorter than Vlas, which put him at maybe one hundred and sixty centimeters. Since Vlas was considerably shorter than him, Everest felt like a giant next to *this* kid.

What had the boy been doing in the arcade in the middle of the night? Where was his family?

The boy groaned again and blinked his eyes a couple of times. Then he shot up to a sitting position, looking wildly around.

"Where am I? What'd you do to me?" He scrambled to his feet, pressing his hand to his forehead and making Everest feel even more guilty for stunning him.

"You had a little accident," Dar said.

"An accident?" the boy yelled. He pointed at Everest. "He shot me!"

"I did not," Everest retorted. "I stunned you."

The boy's hands fisted. "I know when I've been shot."

"You don't know anything."

Dar raised her hands. "Gentlemen, nothing is going to be resolved by bickering." She addressed the twenty-first-century boy. "All we want is the necklace. You give it to us, and we'll let you go."

"Yeah, right." The boy took a good look at his surroundings. "Where are we?"

"Just a nearby garage," Dar asserted at the same time that Vlas said, "a warehouse."

Both sucked in their breath as they pivoted to face each other. Dar glared while Vlas sheepishly grinned.

Everest didn't think this was such a big goof. A garage and a warehouse were pretty much the same thing, weren't they?

On a deep sigh, Dar swung back to the boy. "Where is irrelevant. All that matters is that you do what we ask. No one wants to hurt you. We didn't even search you while you were out cold. We could have, but we didn't. So let's make a deal. We don't ask questions, you don't ask questions. Just give us the necklace, and we'll return you safe and sound to the arcade."

"Thanks for nothing. That place is swarming with police by now. You bring me back, and I end up in juvie."

"Juvie?" Elsie asked.

Everest kicked her. Just once, couldn't she refrain from asking one of her burning questions? She jabbed him with her elbow.

The boy snorted. "Where are you from? Another planet?"

Dar shot him a dark look, which sobered him abruptly. "If you don't want to be deposited at the mall, then where do you want to go?"

"Just let me walk out of this room now, and I'll find my way."

"That's going to be difficult."

The boy's eyes narrowed. "You're not going to let me go, are you? You're going to kill me, aren't you?"

Everest gaped. How could he possibly have such a thought? Instructor Gerard had said that the twenty-first century was a violent time in history, but murder? Even to joke about it was wrong.

"Don't be ridiculous," Dar said, mirroring Everest's thoughts. "We don't do stuff like that. Now, can we just get down to business? Give her the necklace, and we'll bring you wherever you want."

Everest figured that someone would have to stun the boy again to bring him back. But it wouldn't be him. He didn't ever want to touch one of those stunners again.

The boy stared at Dar for a long time. At least, he seemed to. The room was pretty dark, so Everest didn't think the kid could really see Dar's features. Nighteyes hadn't been invented in the twenty-first century, had they? Then again, by now, his eyes could have grown accustomed to the dark.

Finally, the boy said, "I ain't big on trust. Why should I trust you?"

"Because you have no choice?" Dar smiled slightly.

"Like that's a good reason." Amazingly, the boy grinned too.

With a whoosh, Everest let out his breath, and it was only then that he realized he'd been holding it.

"You sure she doesn't have any dough?" the boy asked, thumbing at Elsie.

Dar's smile widened as she shook her head. "This just isn't your lucky day."

"You promise I'm going to live through this?"

"I promise."

Everest didn't think he'd ever heard Dar sound so gentle. For a moment, she sounded a lot more like Shadara than Dar, not that he would ever tell her that. He didn't think that particular observation would go over well.

"Okay, turn your backs," the boy ordered.

"We can't do that," Dar said.

"No one sees my secret hiding place." He crossed his arms, his face fixed in a very stubborn frown.

Dar gestured her acceptance of his terms with her hands. "Fine. But don't mess with us." She twirled her forefinger at the group to indicate that they should turn around.

When Everest faced the tevta wall, he had to swallow a snort of laughter. Tevta's mirror-like qualities gave him a perfect view of the twenty-first-century kid.

The boy sat down on the floor and untied one of his clunky white shoes. Everest recognized them as being similar to the ones he had worn earlier today. Vlas had explained that people in the twenty-first century wore them for sports and exercise. Amazing, but true. The boy pulled off the left one and dug inside with his fingers. A second later, he pulled out the plain silver chain with its unusual pendant.

After the boy shoved his shoe back on and scrambled to his feet, he called, "All clear. You can turn around now." From his hand dangled Elsie's necklace. "Have to say, this is one weird pretty piece...never knew metal could carry so much heat."

Elsie pressed her knuckles to her mouth, but still a sob of relief escaped. Everest's ears heated with embarrassment. Why'd she have to pick now to become a crybaby? She'd never been one before.

"Take it before I change my mind," the boy said, thrusting his arm out.

Elsie stepped forward and retrieved her necklace. "Thank you," she said in a strangled whisper.

"No big." The boy shrugged.

They all contemplated each other.

"Now, I'm going to walk out that door," he pointed, "and find my own way home."

"There's just one little problem," Dar said.

"Hey, you promised."

"I promised you would live through this and you will, but we can't just let you go. It wouldn't be safe. We have to escort you to wherever you want to be."

"Don't mess with me," he warned.

She lifted her nose in the air. "We wouldn't dream of it."

A muffled noise from the outer room made everyone freeze.

"Will the fun never end?" Dar murmured. She moved silently to the boy's side and whispered, "This would not be a good time to take off." Turning to the others, she motioned with her hands that everyone should get down. She mouthed, "Hide."

As quietly as possible, they all tiptoed to different parts of the room and slid beneath clothes, under benches, inside changing rooms. Everest crawled under a bench against the wall closest to the building's main room.

From the other side of the wall, he heard a steady drone, as if one person were engaged in conversation with another. But who were they?

He couldn't tell if the speaker was a man or a woman, young or old.

Hadn't they had enough adventure for one night? Flasers, they'd had enough adventure for the twenty-first and the thirty-first century combined.

Apparently, it wasn't over yet.

CHAPTER 30
The Dangerous Mr. Kisses

Nearly smothered under a pile of ancient clothing, Elsie wished she could just go to sleep and pretend this was all a bad dream. The worst part was that it was her fault they were here and about to be caught. Her fault they had broken curfew. Her fault her brother had stunned someone.

Could they be up on criminal charges? It had to be illegal to stun and then transport a citizen of the past into the future. At minimum, this would be grounds for throwing them all out of the academy. What would happen to Dar and Vlas? They had no family, nowhere to go. And what about the twenty-first-century boy? Who knew what would happen to him? He had to be terrified despite his iced act.

Elsie closed her eyes and barely stifled a groan. Please don't let the cyborg police come after them, she thought. If they did, she would have to make sure that all the blame fell squarely on her shoulders, not her brother's and not the clones.

Her life would be ruined.

In the distance, the unidentified voice droned on.

Was everyone else as scared as she was? She wished they weren't all scattered around the room. It would have been more comforting to hide together.

Then she remembered the earpatch. Dar had told them to replace the patches in an emergency, and this had to qualify. Digging into her tiny pocket, she retrieved the glutinous picobot and inserted it into her ear.

"Lelita," Dar was saying so quietly that Elsie almost didn't hear her.

"Dar, what's the matter? What's going on?"

Elsie flinched. In stark contrast to Dar's almost inaudible tone, it was as if Lelita screamed in her ear. Surely the person in the next room would hear.

"Calm down, Lelita," Dar whispered when the girl finally took a breath. "We're dealing with a couple of minor hitches. Stay put and we'll be in touch. Okay?"

Minor hitches—ha! What would Dar classify as a real disaster?

From the other room came muffled footsteps and a raised voice.

Dar said in her ear. "We've got to find out who's there and what they're doing. Vlas, ideas?"

"PicoBoy could amplify the sound."

"No, they'll be able to hear the amplification too."

There was a pause. "I think I can get him to synch to both earpatch sets and broadcast to us."

He went quiet, and Elsie assumed he was retrieving his minuscule picobot and programming the task.

Elsie peeked out from under the pile of clothes just in time to see the tiny object fly like a gray ladybug in the direction of the intruders. It slipped under the door.

A moment later, a quiet but distinct voice said in her ear, "Mr. Snickers, you must understand. I am *already* the proud owner of two thirds of the shipment you've been waiting for."

199

The voice was higher-pitched and rounder than any Elsie had heard before. Were there alien teachers at the academy?

"Indeed, I do understand and am quite pleased by your progress," another strange voice responded. "You will have the final third shortly?"

"Very shortly."

"Disguised," Dar whispered in her ear as if she'd read her earlier thoughts, which Elsie was beginning to suspect Dar could do.

That was why the voices sounded so odd. They were system-modified for secrecy. She'd experienced something like that in a holo-adventure once. Thank the Light the twenty-first-century boy couldn't hear the conversation.

"Mr. Kisses, this is marvelous news indeed."

"Indeed." There was a pause, then Mr. Kisses spoke again. "So why not post two thirds of my fee to my account immediately?"

"As I've explained repeatedly, Mr. Kisses, that is out of the question, and I must inform you, your request is growing tedious. It would be foolish for me to post virtual currency without actually *obtaining* the merchandise. I'm a businessman. If you can supply me with an early shipment of these items, I will be happy to pay you the VC you request."

"Unfortunately, I have to retrieve them as a complete set. As you know, they must age properly, and it would be a mistake to waste multiple storage units on a single transaction."

"In that case, we have no choice but to wait until you provide me with all the items. At that time, the VC will be yours."

Mr. Kisses did not immediately respond.

What was this? Disguised voices...fake names...a business deal...virtual currency involved...items that couldn't be retrieved until they had aged properly?

Was something criminal going on at the academy? Wouldn't that be just zeller? Especially if Mr. Kisses and Mr. Snickers found out they had witnesses!

"Dar," she whispered, "I don't like this."

"Join the club," Dar whispered. "Can Pico take pictures?" she asked Vlas.

"I'd need to call him back."

"Leave it then."

Finally, Mr. Kisses spoke. "I'm taking all the risk and yet, will have nothing to show for it until *after* I provide you with your merchandise."

"That is the nature of our agreement. And in return, you will be amply compensated. If you would rather attempt to sell the items yourself, I'll quite understand, but you may find it difficult without access to my extensive network. It would be a shame for us to sever such a mutually beneficial partnership. After all, you can be assured that I will play fair with you. Why would I cheat someone who has such potential to continue to supply me with the collectibles my clients desire? It would not be in my best interest."

There was another long pause, then, "You'll have your merchandise by Sunday." Even with his voice disguised, Mr. Kisses sounded disgruntled but resigned.

"Excellent," Mr. Snickers responded jovially. "As delightful as our chat has been, I believe we should bring it to an end. May good luck be your friend."

There was the slight sound of air molecules rearranging themselves, then silence.

"Yeah, right," Mr. Kisses said. "*You vlemutz.*"

The voice was still oddly disguised but its tone had changed. Now it sounded rough and hard and scary. Not so resigned after all.

"A holocomm," Dar murmured.

They heard a loud thud that sounded as if someone had kicked one of the vehicles in the other room.

"Mr. Snickers, you'd turn your mother over to the authorities if it suited you." There was another loud thud. "And you'd double cross me in a heartbeat."

Suddenly, something crashed. Elsie flinched. That was too loud to be coming from the next room. She peeked out and to her horror saw the twenty-first-century boy wrestling with a pile of falling clothes. He must have stood up and bumped into one of the hanging structures. Now, all the clothes had fallen on his head. And the structure had collapsed to the floor.

Everest rolled out from under his hiding place, grabbed the boy by the arm, and dragged him into the nearest changing room. Not a split second later, the door erased.

Elsie held her breath.

Standing there was a man wearing a heavy black cape that made him look huge and sinister.

"Who's in here?" said the strangely modified voice of Mr. Kisses. He sounded really angry and zetta dangerous.

Cyberjail was beginning to seem like the least of their worries.

"I know you're in here, and I'll find you if I have to tear this place apart."

Deng, her heart beat so wildly he had to be able to hear it drum.

"Lights on," Mr. Kisses commanded, and the room flooded with bright light.

At the same time, Dar whispered, "Foggers." Elsie threw one as hard as she could at Mr. Kisses and saw others explode in the room. Smellers too.

The man cursed and swiped at his cape. One of the smellers had been a direct hit.

"Go," Dar yelled, deepening her voice to protect her identity.

Elsie glimpsed Everest yanking the boy forward. She knew it was Everest because as her twin, even his hand was easily recognizable, but everything else was obscured by thick, white fog. She pelted in the general direction of the door.

Was the villain in their way?

There was another yell and the thud of someone hitting the ground. She prayed it was the bad guy. Someone bulky *was* lying across the doorway. She dived over the body and somersaulted to land on her feet on the other side. Ahead of her were Dar, Vlas, and Everest, with the twenty-first-century boy still in tow. It looked as if he willingly ran alongside Everest.

As soon as Vlas saw her emerge from the fog, he threw another fogger to obscure the main room.

"Come on," Dar cried.

They burst out of the building and raced toward Pooker's cage. The sparkly gravel glistened even more than usual because it was drenched from the planned rainfall, which had already come and gone.

Dar rattled off instructions to Lelita as they ran.

As they entered the cage, Dar said, "Sorry, Elsie, Pooker better stay here tonight. We've got a galaxy of other problems to deal with—let's not add to this mess."

And every problem they had was her fault. Elsie hated leaving Pooker behind, but Dar was right.

"Everest, you go first with the boy." Dar turned to their twenty-first-century visitor. "What's your name?"

He shook his head blankly, as if she spoke in a language he didn't understand. He stared up at the sky, as if he'd never seen such a thing before. "Man, like, there's a gazillion stars. And all those weird objects! Why are they zipping around and bumping into each other? Where are we?" He looked around and flinched when he saw the bobcat. "Jeez, that's a wild animal." He backed up into the dancing lights, then yelped and jumped forward when they surged and zapped him.

"Your name!" Dar said more forcefully, even as she pushed him to the corner where the transport system sat.

"Larry," he managed in shaky tones.

"Well, Larry, welcome to the thirty-first century." She shoved him to Everest who dragged him onto all fours and under the canopy.

"Lelita, two to beam up," Dar said.

Larry gasped as he and Everest shimmered, then disappeared.

Dar insisted that Elsie and Vlas go next.

They heard someone racing toward them, his breathing labored.

"You go," Elsie said. "This is my fault."

"Just hurry up," Dar hissed. "I don't want to try more than two people at a time. Lelita, transport them now."

Elsie was plunged into empty darkness. As soon as they landed in the dormitory room, she scrambled off the transport system. "Hurry, Lelita."

"I know," she responded anxiously.

They quickly set up for another trip, and after a long moment, Dar materialized on hands and knees in front of them.

"That was fun," she commented.

"Did he see you?" Elsie asked breathlessly.

"No, I got lucky. He missed Pooker's prison all together. Ran right past." She pulled off her black cap and released her hair from its tight ponytail. It fell in a beautiful jumble around her face.

Elsie's nighteyes were beginning to wear off, but she could still make out Larry fighting the hold Everest had on his arms. His eyes bulged as he took them all in.

The boy let out a string of incomprehensible words, his expression pained. "*You're freaking aliens.*"

"Look, Larry, we're really sorry you got caught up in this," Dar said soothingly, offering a winning smile which was probably lost on him since he hadn't used nighteyes drops. "This has to be an extraordinary experience for you, terrifying even. But we don't want to hurt you, and we will get you back to your time. Truly, you can count on us."

"Where am I?" he asked.

"Earth." Dar continued to act as spokesperson.

Elsie had to be grateful, because she couldn't manage a single word.

"No way! I gotta be on another planet!"

Dar smiled again. "Sorry, but you aren't. You're just in a different time. We're human too, and the last thing we want to do is hurt you."

He stared at them, his mouth gaping, his limbs slack.

Suddenly he broke into a humongous grin. "Man, this is so cool!"

CHAPTER 31
Everest's New Roommate

Everest stared dumbfounded at Larry. Cool? Hijacked one thousand years into the future?

"Don't you get it?" Dar asked, mirroring Everest's thoughts. It was weird the way she did that almost as often as Elsie did. "You've just traveled forward a thousand years."

"Yeah, sweet," the boy breathed as he pumped his fist in the air.

Hands on her hips, Dar looked speculatively at Larry. "Glad you don't see this as a problem."

"A problem? This is the awesomest thing that's ever happened to me." His voice squeaked with excitement. "How old are all of you?"

"Twelve," Dar said. "We're all twelve." As she spoke, she held out her earpatch vial. "Earpatches, please. Everest, give yours back to Vlas."

The kids lined up to comply.

"They sure grow 'em big in the future. I'm twelve too and pretty average for my age, but I'm not even close to your height." He pointed at Lelita. "'Cept for you. What are you? Five foot two?" He jabbed himself in the chest with his thumb. "I'm five three."

Lelita stared at him blankly, then looked to Dar for help. "I've only got two feet," she said, mystified.

Vlas snorted.

Dar sighed. "I hate to break it to you, Larry, but though it took awhile, metrics were finally adopted worldwide in the 2200s. No one here knows a thing about feet and inches."

Larry's expression was one of astonishment. "No kidding?"

"No kidding."

What in galaxies were Larry and Dar talking about?

Now it was Elsie who put Everest's thought into words. "Will you two please speak English?" she demanded. "The rest of us haven't the slightest idea what you're gabbing about!"

"It's not important." Dar waved her arm as if to sweep away the whole subject then continued, "Everest, Larry's bunking with you tonight." She grinned at Everest's horrified expression. "Seems only fair, since you brought him forward from the past. I have to warn you, Larry, that if anyone catches you here in the future, you'll be in serious trouble. We will be too, but that's not your problem. I think we can get you back to the twenty-first century sometime in the next few days, but until then you've got to keep a low profile in Everest's room. We'll smuggle food to you. Okay?"

"Go back?"

Even with his nighteyes wearing off, Everest could discern a zetta stubborn expression on Larry's face.

"You can forget that," the boy said. "I'm staying!"

Dar contemplated him for a minute. "I'm sorry, but that's out of the question. Moving people from one time to another on a permanent basis is strictly prohibited."

"Man, are you sure you're twelve? You sound more like fifty."

Dar seemed disconcerted. "We learn English in the womb. Our vocabulary is extensive even before birth."

"Girl, that ain't what I'm talking about," Larry retorted with a grin. "I'm talking about you spouting a bunch of rules at me." He said something else that Everest couldn't quite make out.

"Uh, Larry, speaking of rules," Dar said carefully, "we don't use that language nowadays."

Once again, Everest wondered what she was talking about. What language had Larry spoken in?

The boy said something else Everest didn't quite catch, but Dar's jaw dropped in response. In a heartbeat, she crossed the couple of meters that separated her from the boy and grabbed him by his shirt.

"Listen, yocto-brain, we don't use those words here. Keep your mouth clean or I'll make you regret it."

"You're kidding, right?" Larry croaked, his eyes bulging.

Dar pulled out her stunner and pointed it between his eyes, shocking Everest. She looked ruthless, hard-edged, and dangerous—not like any twelve-year-old he'd ever known. "Those words were retired from the English language over five hundred years ago," she said, then took a deep breath and gestured with her free hand around the room at the other B12s. "I don't want them corrupted. You cannot imagine how serious it would be if an adult heard them using those terms. Keep it clean, or I'll be forced to wipe out a few of your brain cells." She looked as if she were quite capable of turning Larry into a pretzel.

Vlas snickered. "Didn't they wash out kids' mouths with soap when they used dirty words? That could be fun."

"Jeez, you don't have to freak out," Larry responded, his eyes wide with fear. "It's no big deal. Chill, baby."

Everest had no idea what they were talking about or why Dar had gone alien, but he figured he'd better save the boy with a quick exit. "Okay, Larry, let's jam." He pushed the boy toward the door. "It's time for bed."

Larry turned to Everest. "You gotta be kidding. You expect me to sleep? No way."

"You'll sleep if I have to knock you unconscious," Everest mumbled as he grabbed Larry's arm and dragged him to the door.

The boy's expression of horror made Everest feel guilty. First Dar had threatened to stun him, and now he was threatening to knock the boy unconscious.

"I'm just kidding."

"I knew that." Larry puffed his chest out in a display of bravado.

As they stepped up to the door, it disintegrated, and Everest leaned through just enough to check whether the coast was clear.

"Wicked," Larry gasped. "What kind of trick is that?" Nervously, he stepped across the threshold almost at a run, pulling Everest with him.

Everest snorted. "It's not going solid on you."

"No reason to take any chances."

Vlas and Borneo stepped out with them.

"Wait a second," Elsie cried.

"What?" They chorused as they swung around.

"There was a criminal down in the History Center!"

"Don't alien, Elsie," said Everest, embarrassed by her outburst, despite his similar anxiety.

"What do you suggest we do about it?" Dar asked from behind Elsie, a curious note in her voice.

"We have to tell someone. We have to figure out who Mr. Kisses is."

"Tell who? Your uncle?" Dar shifted her expression to a wide-eyed innocence. "Oh, Director, while we were out *after curfew*, having returned from a quick jaunt *back in time* against school rules and possibly a few galactic ones as well, we ran into a masked man named Mr. Kisses talking on his undoubtedly illegal holoputer to a mysterious man named Mr. Snickers. We think they are dangerous criminals." She fluttered her fingers in the air. "Please do something, sir."

"Okay, bad idea," Elsie responded weakly, "but what *are* we going to do?"

"We're going to sleep on it," Dar replied, "and figure out what to do tomorrow morning when our minds are fresh."

With that, the boys snuck down the darkened hallway.

After a few seconds, Larry screeched, "Ow, something stung me. What are all these bugs? Jeez, this is a freakin' mosquito factory."

"They're not mosquitoes," returned Vlas. "They're brownies. They clean the building at night. You just happened to run into one."

"Brownies? You mean like freakin' elves?"

Everest snorted. "No. They're pico-chip brownies—man-made. They're so small they're almost invisible, but they scrub the walls and remove debris."

"This is a dust-mite free zone," added Vlas.

"Huh." Larry kept swiveling his head as they made for their rooms. He slapped his arm a couple of times.

"Don't do that," said Vlas. "You're smashing perfectly good brownies. They don't come cheap."

When they reached Vlas and Borneo's room, Everest silently waved them off, then continued down the shadowed corridor. He breathed a sigh of relief when they erased his door and stepped inside. This was way more adventure than he needed. Then he remembered he was stuck babysitting a boy who was over a thousand years old. Adventure turned nightmare. He slumped onto his bed and motioned to Larry to take the other one.

The boy stood frozen to the spot.

Everest wished his sister were here. With her aliening about Mr. Kisses, he'd been pretty happy to leave her behind, but now he had to try to communicate with this ancient kid all on his own. He rarely knew what to say to people at the best of times, and this didn't rate as the best of times. Because the boy seemed so scared and Everest's nighteyes had worn off, he risked squeezing on his brightee. A golden glow gave the room subtle illumination.

"Whoa," Larry breathed.

"Sit down," Everest said.

"Is that a bed?"

Everest looked where Larry pointed. "Yeah." Was the boy a yocto-brain?

Larry said something Everest didn't recognize. He figured it had to be another retired word.

"Knock it off. Whatever those words mean, they have no place in the thirty-first century."

"Man, what about my rights to freedom of speech?"

"I doubt a person who doesn't exist in this time period has any rights."

"That's bogus—everyone has rights."

Everest shrugged. "It's your choice, but I will be forced to report back to Dar on your behavior, and I don't think I'll be able to hide your bad language if it goes on for much longer. She can be awfully mean when she wants to be."

"Like I didn't get that."

They both grinned.

"Yeah, you don't mess with Dar. She's scary."

Larry snorted then scanned the room with avid interest. His eyes widened as he took a closer look at the bed. He stepped right up next to it and hesitantly reached out with his right hand.

"It's not going to bite," said Everest.

"What's it made out of?"

Everest took another look. How much could a sleeping device have changed in a thousand years? Judging from Larry's expression, it appeared to have changed quite a bit. "It's made out of jellach. The same substance we use in our hover vehicles, only beds can be different colors, whereas HVs must be clear for perfect visibility. These are old models, so they don't change colors, and sometimes they're slow to answer requests, but they're all right." His was a bright blue and Larry's was the green of street moss.

Larry had a blank look on his face as if everything Everest had said made no sense at all.

"Uh," Everest tried again. "You lie down, and the bed has smarts built into it to make you comfortable. It reads the state of your aura, your body, your emotions, and fine-tunes its response accordingly. Don't you have beds in the twenty-first century?"

"Yeah, but they don't, like, talk to me." Larry poked the jellach with one finger and watched the material indent, then spring back. "Besides, I'm used to sleeping on the floor or a bench—pretty hard surfaces. This looks way too much like jelly for me."

"It's actually very firm once it molds to your body," Everest replied. "These older models provide some limited massage throughout the night. You should see mine at home. It gives deep massage if you ask it to."

"Ask the bed for a massage?" Larry's voice squeaked.

"Sure, all furniture is addressable."

"Oh, man, this is too weird." He cocked his head to the side. "So you're saying there ain't nothing wrong with this bed?"

Everest lay back to prove its safety, and the bed conformed around his body.

"What if you move?"

"The bed moves with you. It's designed to read your body and offer up the most comfort. It will also rock you to sleep if you request it to."

"Cool!" With that Larry leaped face first onto the bed and stuck. "Hey!" His voice was muffled.

Everest laughed as he hauled Larry up with a small sucking sound. "Jumping face first onto jellach is a pretty yocto-brained thing to do. People mostly sleep on their sides and backs, or they ease onto their bellies. The bed won't let you suffocate, but it is a bit disturbing to be sucked in face first."

As soon as Larry's face was unmolded from the mattress, the empty shape popped back to a smooth line. He tried again on his back. "Hey, not bad. Cool the way it makes you a pillow. How does it know how high to make it?"

"Like I said, it reads your body signs so it can tell when you're most comfortable."

"I could get used to this."

"Don't get too used to it," Everest warned. "You're going home as soon as we've got a plan."

Larry shrugged, then changed the subject. "Do I get a blanket or something?"

"Yeah, just ask the bed."

With a skeptical expression, Larry said, "Bed, can I have a blanket?"

A light as air, wafer-thin blanket smoothly came out and molded to Larry's frame.

"Excellent. It's really warm." The boy tugged on it. "What's it made out of?"

"I don't know. It's a mlenler blanket. We import them from Glagcha."

"Huh?"

"Glagcha—another Milky Way planet."

Larry just stared. Finally, he waved his hand. "Whatever."

Everest gave up. He squeezed off his brightee, snapping the room into utter darkness. "Go to sleep."

The boy said something Everest recognized as one of the retired words that he had used earlier.

The kid was going to be trouble.

CHAPTER 32
Introductions

Elsie didn't sleep well that night. With so many things to worry about, it was hard to pick which one to concentrate on. Had Mr. Kisses figured out who they were? For that matter, who was Mr. Kisses? And what criminal activity was he up to at the academy?

What were her parents going to say when they heard about all these adventures? What was her mom going to do when she found out Elsie had not only told people from both this time and from the past about her necklace, but also had come close to permanently losing it—one thousand years ago?

What were they going to do about Larry?

And what about Pooker? How was her bobcat coping all by herself in the cold night air for the very first time?

Deng, her head spun.

It really bugged her that Dar had managed to fall asleep almost immediately after they collapsed on their beds. Didn't any of this bother her?

Suddenly light shimmered on, and Melista appeared at the end of Dar's bed, her legs folded into an aura-yoga position. Her arms were raised to the ceiling as if she called to the sun, and her horn tilted upward as well. In a high-pitched croon, she sang a beautiful morning song. Elsie didn't understand the words, but she felt more refreshed than she would have expected given her sleepless night. The same lovely scent that had permeated the room yesterday was back, making Elsie feel as if she were in the middle of a dewy flower garden.

Dar grunted, then squinted up at her avatar. "Thank all the galaxies that it's Friday," Dar grumbled. "I feel like I just ran a Mormor mile."

"At least you slept," Elsie responded grumpily. "How'd you do that? I couldn't sleep a wink."

Dar opened one eye. "Really? Shadara was a meditation master. They've had me in training since I was hatched."

"Lucky you."

"Lack of sleep sure does interesting things to your personality, ute-baby." Dar rolled out of her bed and started pulling on her exercise gear. "We better blast off. I want to visit our thousand-year-old friend before breakfast."

As she slipped on her ultra-thin exercise boots, she glanced over at Melista. "If anyone comes sniffing around asking questions about last night, Elsie and I were asleep from the time our heads hit our pillows at 22:00 until you woke us up just now. You know nothing, saw nothing. Pass that on to Folgar, too."

"Of course," Melista answered calmly, her wide golden eyes blinking. Her horn shimmered with a tinge of blue this morning.

Two nights ago, Dar also had asked Melista to warn the avatar named Folgar. Elsie figured he had to be Everest's avatar.

"What about everyone else's avatars?"

"Vlas, Borneo and Lelita all know what to do."

Elsie couldn't stop herself from feeling defensive. It was as if Dar were implying that Everest was too much of a yocto-brain to take care of himself. At the same time, she knew the girl was right. Elsie never would have dreamed that a room avatar might actually lie, so Everest wouldn't have considered the possibility either. It made sense for Melista to go directly to Folgar.

She yelped as a skyball caught her on the ear. Lucky for Dar, it was a soft one. Elsie was feeling cranky enough to start a non-regulation fight match.

"Get up, sleepyhead," Dar ordered. "We don't have all day."

"The poor dear is tired," offered Melista.

"Oh well, if the poor dear is tired," Dar said with exaggerated sympathy.

Elsie wished she had her own skyball to bean Dar with. Groaning and moaning, she dragged herself out from under her mlenler blanket and began to dress.

"*Zylander to Elsie*, your shirt's on backward," Dar said with a grin. "You really are out of it, aren't you?"

"I got zero sleep!"

"Ute-baby, cry-baby— must mean the same thing."

Elsie felt like screaming or pulling Dar's hair, but she managed to control herself and with her chin in the air, finish dressing. Afterward, Elsie stalked and Dar strolled down the corridor to the boys' dormitory. Neither said a word.

At Everest's room, they announced themselves and were quickly granted access. Larry was busy first erasing the closet door, then making it solid again by pressing his hand to the wall. While they stood and gaped, he did it over and over.

"How long has this been going on?" Elsie asked her brother.

Everest made a face. "Since he woke up."

Dar cleared her throat. "Good morning, Larry."

Looking over his shoulder, he responded with a grin, "Hey, it's the tall, hot, take-charge babe."

"Excuse me?"

Despite her grumpy mood, Elsie giggled at Dar's expression.

Dar turned on Elsie. "I'm glad to see something has snapped you out of your crankiness this morning." Then she pivoted back toward Larry. "For your information, girls in the thirty-first century find those types of remarks as offensive as they must have found them in your time period. Furthermore, you would do well to remember that we are much better fighters and taller and stronger than you, so if you don't want me to kick your keister to the next galaxy, you'll refrain from such crude discourse."

"Huh? Man, you sound like a school principal. You sure don't look or act like any twelve-year-old I've ever known."

"Times have changed," she replied. "Get used to it."

At that, Elsie and Everest burst out laughing.

"Times have changed," Elsie repeated, bending over and clutching her stomach. "That's a good one."

Larry snickered too, then started laughing for real. "This is so weird."

Dar gave in and laughed too. "Tell me about it."

Larry cocked his head. "So, are you ever going to tell me who you are?"

"Sorry. I'm Dar; this is Elsie Basker. Elsie and Everest are twins. I'm a clone."

Elsie stared in surprise. She wouldn't have expected her to feed Larry so much information so quickly.

"Whoa, wait a minute; you're like a real-life sci-fi clone?"

"That would be me, as are most of the students here at the academy. It's a boarding school."

"What about them?" Larry pointed at Elsie and Everest.

"They're what we affectionately call ute-babies—conceived and born the old-fashioned way."

"Knock it off with ute-baby," Everest muttered.

"*A clone!*" he repeated. "Wicked. Wish I was a clone."

"It's not all Galorian rainbows," said Dar.

After another confused pause, Larry shrugged his shoulders. "Whatever. Couldn't be worse than being stuck with my parents.

Not that I'm stuck with them anymore. Not that I ever was stuck with my loser dad."

"What happened to them?" Elsie asked with wide eyes.

Larry shrugged. "The old guy dumped my ma before I was born, and my ma died a couple of years ago. She was mostly okay 'cept when she wasn't. I'm better off on my own. The guy who runs the arcade is cool. He lets me scrounge for tokens and turn them in for quarters. I do a few odd jobs for him, and when the weather's bad, I bunk there."

"What about the rest of the time?" Elsie asked.

Larry hunched a shoulder. "Lots of places to camp out— parks, parking lots, schools. Plenty of benches around town."

Elsie was shocked by his easy acceptance of his homeless state. Even the non-bandit Aginoza gypsies who occasionally sought refuge on Earth were given real if temporary homes to live in while they found their feet.

"But why aren't you assigned a home?"

"No one's assigning me nothing. They'd stick me in some good-for-nothing foster home, where I'd be beaten or worse." Larry made a horrible face. "No way am I going into the system."

"Surely it's illegal to hurt a child!" she cried.

"Elsie," Everest said, "shut down."

She rounded on him. "There's nothing wrong with me asking questions. The twenty-first century sounds positively barbaric."

"Perhaps," Dar said, "but that's hardly relevant today, and knowing your curiosity meter, we could be here forever—so power down. We have a lot to discuss and no time, what with a full class schedule and the research I need to squeeze in."

"Fine," Elsie said huffily, crossing her arms over her chest, "I won't ask another thing."

"Yeah, right, and tomorrow Earth will leap past Glagcha and all sixty-two Xlexuri planets to win best planet in the universe."

Dar grinned. "No one's asking you to stop all your questions. There's just a time and a place for them, and now's not it."

Everest motioned to Larry with his head. "I don't think it's such a good idea to leave Mr. Twenty-First-Century alone for that long."

"We don't have much choice."

"Not that I need a babysitter or nothing, but doesn't anyone play hooky from school anymore?" asked Larry. "Maybe come down with a dread flu?"

"Flu was eradicated from Earth in 2323," Dar explained. "Children don't get sick anymore, so we never have an excuse to miss school."

"That's gypped."

Larry's pained expression made Elsie forget her annoyance and giggle again.

"I'll be cool on my own," he said. "No prob."

Everest snorted.

Dar stepped up to Larry and stared directly into his eyes, making him squirm under her intense gaze. "You can't imagine how different the thirty-first century is from your time period. I get the impression you're not big on following rules. That's your business. I'm not much of a rule follower myself. But here's the situation: you don't know our period, you don't know our customs, and you have no idea what someone in authority will do if they find you and realize you're from another time. There's no way you can pass yourself off as a thirty-first-century kid. One aurascan would reveal that you don't exist in our time. You seem like a pretty cerebrum-heavy kid to me, so be smart and stay put. We need a plan to get you back in time, and right now I'm fresh out of ideas. However, I'm hoping inspiration will strike soon. One way or another, we'll smuggle you back."

"But I told you I ain't going back." Larry said.

"And I told you that isn't possible."

"Girl, it better be possible, because I ain't budging."

CHAPTER 33
Hologames for Larry

Elsie was having trouble breathing. They were in enough hot water without Larry getting stubborn.

"Changing the course of history is a big no-no in any time period," Dar said.

Larry's eyes went crafty. "Yeah, but what if I was supposed to come to this time? What if it's destiny? How would you like to be responsible for sending me back when there's a possibility that doing so could destroy Earth as we know it? What makes you think I'm supposed to go back?"

Dar looked at him admiringly. "Deng, you're good." She lightly punched him in the shoulder, a friendly gesture which really shocked Elsie. Dar had been surprisingly decent to her, but she was being downright friendly toward Larry.

Dar continued, "I think we can safely assume that you are not the single most important person in the universe."

"It's always dangerous to assume," Larry responded with a grin.

"Will you both knock it off?" Elsie asked, unable to contain herself any longer. "How can you joke at a time like this? In case you've forgotten, we've got a criminal at the academy! For all we know, he's going to kill us in our sleep!"

"She's always had a vivid imagination," Everest said.

Elsie pinched him hard, and he pushed her back, so she stepped on his foot. Whose side was he on?

"I'm pretty sure if Mr. Kisses were going to come after us, he already would have done so last night," Dar said calmly. "He doesn't know who we are."

"But who is *he*?" Elsie asked.

Dar shrugged. "Your guess is as good as mine. The cape he wore hid his shape. I had the impression he was big, but I could have been misled by all that material."

"Could *he* have been a *she*?" Everest asked.

"Maybe. Hard to say."

"So what are we going to do?" Elsie wished more than anything that when she'd awakened this morning, this could all have been a bad dream.

"Not much we can do. We'll keep a low profile, watch the instructors for any suspicious behavior, and figure out how to get Larry back to the twenty-first century without arousing more suspicion."

"No need to waste any energy on me," Larry said.

"Not another word," Dar responded curtly. "You're going back, and that's the end of it. Come on, Baskers, we'd better get moving. One more thing: Larry, do you have a last name?"

"Sure, it's Knight."

"For real?" Dar asked.

He bristled. "Course it's for real—Lawrence Tobias Knight."

"Tobias?" Vlas snickered.

"Yeah, you making something out of it?"

Vlas held up his hands. "Not me."

"Good thing, cuz your name ain't nothing to write home about, brother." He jabbed his finger at Dar. "What's your last name?"

"I don't have one. Clones aren't given last names."

"I didn't know that," Elsie said. "Why?"

Dar turned to her. "A last name shows what family you're from. Clones don't have families."

"Oh." Elsie wished she hadn't asked.

Larry saved her by turning to Everest. "You got any video games I can play while you're off doing the school thing?"

Everest shook his head. "Sorry, if you mean what I think you mean, my uncle confiscated my holoputer. He says we can only use it on weekends."

"Say what? You don't have no games? What am I supposed to do all day? You got TV?"

"Not on weekdays," Dar said. "And it's no longer called TV. It's a Virtual Entertainment Device or a VED."

"Whatever," Larry said. "Jeez, I'll be bored out of my skull." He kicked his foot at the padded floor.

Dar tugged her cap down more tightly on her head and stared at Larry for a long time. "Deng. I'm going to seriously regret this. What I'm about to do goes no further than the people in this room. I'll make any blabbermouth's life miserable if this gets out."

Now it was Larry who held up his hands, looking supremely innocent. "Have faith, babe, have faith."

"Call me babe again and I'll turn you into a twenty-first-century pretzel."

"*Sorry.*" But there was nothing contrite about Larry Knight.

"Yeah, you sound all broken up." Dar turned to Elsie and Everest. "Can I count on you two?"

They both nodded. Elsie figured at this point they all knew so many secrets about each other they couldn't afford to be telling tales. Not that she'd ever been a snitch.

At that Dar addressed the room rather than any one person. "Folgar, we require your assistance, please."

224

Something shimmered in the middle of the room, then an extraordinarily large creature came into view. He looked like a mythical troll from ancient stories, stout, neck-less, with large floppy ears, fleshy lips, and impossibly small eyes. His nose was bulbous and red as were the tips of his ears.

"Holy—"

Dar quickly interrupted Larry. "Don't even think it. You swear in my presence one more time and I'll flaser you."

"What kind of threat is that?" he asked then held up his hand. "Forget I asked. Who the heck is he?"

"He's the room avatar. The room's caretaker. He accepts your commands."

"Sweet," was Larry's response.

Everest and Elsic exchanged glances. This was Everest's avatar?

"How may I help you?" Folgar's voice was rich and deep, like a chocolate stream, and he had a gentle smile.

"Hello Folgar, please invite Melista to join us."

"As you wish." A crease formed between his brows as if he were concentrating really hard.

Almost immediately, Melista shimmered to a near solid state, this time lounging on Everest's blue bed. Her horn dripped with silver morning dew.

"Whoa!" Larry whooped. "Now there's one fine lady! Awesome horn!"

Melista ignored his comment, but a faint smile played at her lips. "You require my assistance?" She addressed her question to Dar.

"Yes, would you give Folgar copies of your entertainment modules?"

Melista smiled at the troll-like creature. "That would be my pleasure."

He managed to turn an even brighter pink. Within a heartbeat, he croaked, "I have them; the transfer is complete."

"Man that was quick!" Larry said.

Dar said, "They're communicating at light speed."

He let out a low whistle.

Dar smiled at Melista. "Thank you for your help. You are excused."

Melista faded, then snapped out like a light, her smile lingering until the last moment and her garden scent remaining behind. Elsie breathed in deeply.

Dar looked tired all of a sudden. "Now you have entertainment. Folgar, can you explain how to play?"

"Yes," he said simply.

In the air above the desk, a number of objects popped up as real as life, but miniature. One was a hairy monster with five heads and three pairs of legs. He emitted a low growl and belched up a slimy purple substance from two of his heads. Another object was a miniature jellach hover vehicle that stretched and shrunk while racing up and down, forward and backward. A third was a spacecraft with stars spinning around it.

"Here are three hologames for your enjoyment—"

"Hold on, Folgar," Dar interrupted. "We're going to be late if we don't leave now. As it is, we'll miss breakfast. Here's the deal, Larry. You can ask Folgar to explain the games and to hang around as your consultant. Most questions he'll be able to answer. If not, he can hook up with Melista. There are more games. Just ask Folgar for other choices. Make yourself at home, but whatever you do, don't leave the room."

"I'm hungry." He looked and sounded pitiful.

Dar played with her cap. "We'll bring you food as soon as we can. Meanwhile," she dug into her pocket, "here's a pill to suppress your hunger so you can hang on until we smuggle in some real food." She handed him a plain brown tablet.

"How do I know you ain't messing with me?"

"Have faith, babe, have faith," Dar mimicked him with a sharp grin. She popped one in her own mouth to demonstrate its safety. "Anyone else? It's going to be a few hours before food."

Elsie and Everest reluctantly held out their hands; their parents wouldn't be pleased.

"You don't have to take the pill," Dar said to Larry, "but if you get hungry, it's an option. We'll see you when we see you."

"What if I have to pee?"

Dar sighed with resignation. "You'll have to sneak to the boys' communal bathroom, which is two doors down on the right. You shouldn't run into any students because they'll all be in class, but come straight back. Sometimes Instructor Sura wanders the halls, and you never know when you'll run into one of Director Lester-Hauffer's holograms. I guarantee you don't want to meet up with either. Your clothes will immediately arouse suspicion."

"Speaking of clothes, how come you all wear those funky socks instead of shoes?"

"These aren't socks. These are exercise boots."

"Pretty dorky, if you ask me."

"No one is asking you. Besides, your shoes are the ones that look ridiculous." She turned to the room avatar. "Folgar, do a quick aurascan of Larry and give him room privileges."

Under Folgar's intense stare, Larry squirmed, his expression miserable. "Why's he looking at me? I don't like being stared at, 'specially by him."

"Sorry, Larry," Dar said gently. "It won't take much longer. He's identifying you so you can leave and return. Otherwise, you'll be stuck on the doorstep until Everest can rescue you."

"Hey, he's boring a hole in my brain." Larry clutched his head.

"Stop being such a suzo-shrimp," Elsie said. "We get aurascans all the time. They don't hurt."

Larry's shoulders straightened, and he glared at Elsie. "I ain't no suzo-shrimp—whatever that is. If I say it hurts, then it hurts. At least, it should hurt."

Elsie rolled her eyes at Everest. Aurascans didn't hurt in the slightest. Everest offered a lopsided grin in return. Elsie could tell he was fighting laughter. She tried to look at it from Larry's perspective. It had to be terrifying, jumping one thousand years into a future of new and alien technology. His time period had been so primitive. That was what he was used to. So why in the galaxy would he want to stay here?

Once the scan was done, Dar shooed everyone except Larry out the door. Looking over her shoulder, she addressed the boy one more time. "Be good, stay out of trouble, and don't be seen by an instructor. Bottom line, stay in this room. Someone will be back at lunchtime with food."

"Yes, Mom," he replied.

Dar ignored him.

When they were in the hallway, she started jogging toward the nanovator.

Elsie ran to catch up. "Are you sure it's wise to leave him there?"

"I can't think of one decision I've made since your arrival that feels wise, but it's the only choice we have, so I guess whether it's wise or not doesn't matter."

"I don't have a good feeling about this," mumbled Everest as he jogged along beside them.

Dar snorted. "I'd be seriously worried if you did."

CHAPTER 34

A Startling Discovery

Dar whisked Elsie and Everest down to the second floor so they could check in with the academy's administration and get their course material loaded onto their JEDs. She dragged them along the corridor, weaving in and out of hoardes of children of all ages as they rushed to their classes.

Someone jabbed Elsie hard in her ribs, knocking her sideways, and she looked up just in time to see Kindu flash by, a ghoulish grin on his face. "Vlem," she muttered under her breath as she hurried to catch up with Dar and Everest.

They turned the corner in unison and ran full tilt into Uncle Fredrick. Swallowing back a groan, Elsie immediately corrected herself in her head. She really had to start thinking of him as Director Lester-Hauffer. He looked particularly stuffy today in dark gray, and smelled disgusting too. Bleck.

"Serendipity at work, I see," His long, thin nose flared slightly. "I hoped to track you down today."

"You did?" she asked nervously, willing herself not to fidget. Her uncle might think she hid something.

Sure enough, the man's narrow eyes narrowed even further into sharp slits. "How are you settling in?"

"Uh, fine," she said. "That is, really well. I mean, we're very settled..." She shot Everest a pleading look. Now would be a good time for him to shut her down.

He reluctantly stepped forward. "Sir, the academy is an excellent facility. We feel very welcome and are settling nicely."

Their uncle caught her brother in an intense stare, one eyebrow raised. "No difficulty sleeping?"

"None at all, sir." Everest remained very still.

"Hmm." His mouth thinned. "I must apologize for the unfortunate incident two nights ago when the facility alarm went off, apparently in error."

"I hardly noticed it," Everest said.

Elsie bit her lip. Everest should have mentioned it. Now he was stuck looking odd for acting as if he'd had two perfect nights of sleep. Her heart raced and her palms were clammy. Everest had to be having a similar reaction, but at least on the outside, he was keeping his aura on.

Director Lester-Hauffer cleared his throat. "How lucky you are not to be bothered by sound. I, however, am extremely sensitive to the slightest noise. I'm very glad I was not in residence that night." He swung back to Elsie. "And you? You, too, were unconcerned by the siren two nights back?"

"I...I...," Elsie cleared her throat. "I woke up but quickly went back to sleep."

"Funny, Instructor Sura said you woke only after she entered your room."

"Yes," Dar cut in, "that's what Elsie meant."

"Yes," Elsie echoed, wishing she could bang her head against the tevta wall.

"I see." He sniffed at Dar, then turned his attention back to his niece and nephew. "And did you enjoy your time travel excursion?"

"Oh yes!" Elsie exclaimed. "It was wonderful."

"We take pride in the unique opportunities we are able to offer our students." He cleared his throat and glanced around at the corridor that had thinned considerably of bodies. "If I'm not mistaken, you are about to be late for your first class."

"You're right, sir," Everest said as he tugged on his sister's sleeve. "We'd better hurry."

"Run along. I offer you my assurances that I will keep a very close watch on your progress."

Was that a threat or reassurance? They pelted down the corridor.

"Deng, Elsie, why not just blurt out everything and be done with it," Everest muttered under his breath.

"Shut down," she responded curtly. "I did the best I could." She was embarrassed by her yocto-brained reaction to her uncle's interrogation, but it had been hard to think. "Besides, you didn't do any better."

"You both need to learn how to lie better," Dar cut in. "Talk about pathetic."

In unison Elsie and Everest rounded on her. "Shut down!"

Dar grinned.

For Elsie, the next few hours were a blur. New course material was transferred to her JED, and after the necessary aurascan, privileges to the academy's extensive library were added as well. She slept through Instructor Legnarchi's language deep learning session and woke up feeling refreshed and with a surprisingly improved Zylanderin accent.

Next was their fight session, which left her both energized and satisfactorily worked out. Then Nano-Physics and an advanced lab made her feel inadequate and hopelessly behind.

Through it all, she let worry gnaw at her the way Pooker might gnaw on an old bone. When she wasn't obsessing over their encounter with Mr. Kisses, she worried about the twenty-first century boy.

What if he refused to go home? Would they have to zap him again with a stun gun? They didn't have a memory eraser, unless Dar had one secreted away in her closet. She wouldn't put it past Dar, but it was highly unlikely. That meant that even if they got Larry home safe and sound, he'd be able to spill the beans on the time travel. Would people believe him? How might it affect history? How deeply would their illegal activities change the world as they knew it?

She hoped the instructors would take her nervousness as first-day jitters rather than delving deeper for the real cause.

The last period before lunch was for research and study, and was held in the library. When Elsie entered the room with Dar, she was amazed by the pristine, dust-free environment filled with a rainbow of thin jellach journals on every subject imaginable. It was much larger than the one at her old school, and zetta cleaner. Pico-brownies had to be working twenty-four hours a day, seven days a week on this place. Dar made a beeline for the far right corner.

"The ancient history section," Dar whispered. "I want to start researching the twenty-first century for my detention report." She slid Elsie a sly grin and added, "Guess what I'm going to do my report on."

Elsie stared back blankly. "I have no idea."

"Hasty Hawley's." She punched Elsie in the arm. Elsie felt ridiculously pleased by the friendly gesture. "Remember, Instructor Gerard said it was pretty new in 2002, but by the mid twenty-first century, it was possibly the most important fast-food restaurant chain in existence. And it lasted all the way up to the Vlemutz Wars! I'll chart its history and then compare and contrast it to other major competitors. Instructor Tchakevska did say I could write my report on any subject."

Elsie shrugged. "Won't she expect something more significant?"

"What could be more significant than food?" Dar asked.

Elsie kind of doubted this was what the instructor had in mind, but the girl was a born rebel. At least it would be an entertaining report.

When they reached the corner, Dar said to the twenty-X century shelves, "Twenty-first-century eating establishments, please."

After a quick aurascan to determine Dar's privileges, three jellach journals slid forward. "Thank you," she murmured as she gathered up the research. She pointed to some nanofiber couches a few feet away. "Let's settle there. Do you need any journals?"

"No, I've got plenty of catching up to do with the course downloads."

"Let me know if you need any help."

"I think I can handle it." Elsie had always been a top student, and that wasn't going to change just because she was in a new academy. But she could tell it would require a lot of work on her part. What in her school had been advanced and optional was just ho-hum for these clones. Still, she wasn't going to admit *that* to Dar.

Dar slumped into an oversized chair and dropped the journals onto a side table. They deflated slightly on impact, then immediately popped back to their smooth shape.

Elsie opened her JED and smoothed it flat. She kept sneaking peeks at Dar, who finally raised her head.

"What?"

"Don't you find it hard to concentrate with everything else that's going on?"

Dar shrugged. "No."

"Aren't you worried? Scared? Anxious? I can't concentrate on anything."

"You really should find time to meditate every day," Dar responded. "You're awfully tense." She glanced over. "Come on, Elsie, keep your aura on. Right now, the only thing that matters is our school work. There's nothing we can do about anything else."

Elsie let out a heartfelt sigh. Easier said than done. She gave up trying to understand Dar and buried her nose in her JED. Whispering "Zylander," she watched the symbols change from English letters to the strange dots that made up the Zylander alphabet. Slowly she found a level of concentration, and was able to settle into verb conjugation.

In the background, Dar murmured various commands to her borrowed journals and a steady stream of notes into her JED. The girl attacked her research with the intensity of a cooligrar, whereas Elsie was sidetracked by everything and anything—a sudden noise as another student slumped into a nearby chair, the whisper of a jellach journal sliding forward for someone to use.

"Well, what do you know?" Dar whispered. Her finger tapped rapidly on the jellach journal she held. She turned to Elsie. "Do you remember yesterday's lunch?"

"How could I forget?" Elsie still felt mildly queasy when she thought of the cow her instructors had expected her to eat.

"Do you remember what the lunches were called?"

"What they were called?" Elsie shook her head. "Hasty something—Hasty Meals?"

"'No, but close. They were Hasty Sacks," Dar said.

"Yeah—that's it. Why?"

"Get this: 'By the mid twenty-first century, Hasty Hawley's was arguably the most popular fast food restaurant in the world. It retained that leadership position until the twenty-sixth century and the onset of the Vlemutz Wars. Much of Hasty Hawley's popularity was derived from its commitment to using only organic ingredients—'"

"Surely everyone used organic?"

"Not back then, and don't interrupt." She took a second to find where she'd left off. "'—as well as its slant on the common practice of offering free figurines with kid meals. Plastic toys from many franchises were widely collected by children and adults alike. However, the Hasty Sack figurines soon enjoyed top popularity due to their environmental themes. The extinct, endangered, and threatened species collections were particular favorites. These rare figurines from Hasty Hawley's early years were manufactured in a plastic derived from petroleum oil. Since Earth's cache of petroleum oil was depleted in 2162, these vintage and extremely hard to come by petroleum-based plastic figurines are collector's items of some note.'"

"Huh," Elsie murmured. "Figures we'd get our Hasty Sacks on a day when they aren't giving out plastic gifts. That would have been a zeller souvenir."

Dar grinned and leaned forward for privacy. *"Zylander to Elsie.* Don't you get it? The toys were originally in the bags, then someone removed them. Someone's smuggling Hasty Sack toys to our time for illegal profit."

Elsie's jaw dropped. Of course. It was the only thing that made sense. "But who?" She thought back to the mysterious man or woman from last night.

Pursing her lips, Dar gave Elsie's question serious thought. After a moment, she said, "Well, it's got to be one of the instructors who came with us, or maybe Dr. Wei. Didn't Instructor Legnarchi buy the lunches?"

Elsie slowly nodded. The idea of Legnarchi as the criminal was horrible. He'd been so kind when they'd gone to him for uniforms. "Instructor Gerard was pretty protective of the lunches," she remembered. "He wouldn't let any of the students come near them while they were being set up." She felt guilty for bringing up Gerard. After all, he'd made it possible for Elsie to keep Pooker at the academy. And he was awfully cute.

"Good point," Dar said. "And he disappeared right after lunch."

"Yeah, but it can't be Instructor Gerard. He's been zetta nice to me."

Dar snorted. "Believe me, he's not that nice."

"Could it be both of them?" Elsie asked, wide-eyed. It was so hard to believe that anyone at the academy could be a bad guy.

Dar shrugged. "Maybe, but not necessarily. It could be just one. Or we're missing something. Maybe it was Instructor Tchakevska or Dr. Wei. It was weird how the doctor decided to come at the last minute. If only I could figure out a way for the villain to be Instructor Sura. Now there's a major freakazoid." She stood up and stretched, then began to neatly fold and stack the jellach journals. She replaced a couple of journals and the others she slipped into her bag. "We should discuss this with the rest of the gang. Let's get lunch and smuggle some up to Larry. He must be climbing the walls by now."

When she was all packed up, she leaned close again and whispered, "I think we'd better remember that we've smuggled something into the thirty-first century that's even more illegal than a few plastic knickknacks."

CHAPTER 35
A Lunch Meeting

Everest juggled two fruiceys and a fistful of protein squares as he entered his dorm room. Slouched at the desk, Larry stared intently at a miniature version of himself, who was busy fighting the five-headed hairy monster. The monster belched up more purple slime, covering the tiny Larry from head to foot.

"Nasty," Larry said with delight. Without taking his eyes off the action, he greeted Everest. "Man, this is wicked awesome. Can you believe it? I'm fighting this monster, I'm kicking his butt, and I don't even have to lift a finger." He wiggled all ten in the air.

"Zeller," Everest said without any real enthusiasm. He didn't have the heart to break it to Larry that the slime was poisonous, and his little double was within seconds of a gruesome death. He couldn't believe how easily distracted Larry was from the more serious issues at hand.

Too bad Everest wasn't so lucky. He'd spent most of the morning looking over his shoulder, waiting to be identified by the mysterious masked man. Who knew what would happen then?

"Loosen up, Ev, my man," Larry said, momentarily taking his eyes and his mind off the holo-fight. "Life is too short to spend it stressing."

Easy for him to say when he was over one thousand years old. "Glad you feel that way," Everest responded, "because your little image is about to be history."

Larry turned back to the game and groaned. His miniature likeness was swaying precariously, with five miniature birds chirping as they flew in a circle around his head. Then all of a sudden, the little double melted into a pool of purple sludge. "I'm melting...arrgh!" Larry cried in a high sinister voice and clutched his throat. "Oh man, that is so sad." He shook his head. "Folgar, I guess that's it for me."

The troll-like Avatar reappeared for a moment to whisk away the damage.

"Thanks, bud," Larry said.

Folgar gave a gruesome grin, then shimmered back to nothingness.

In the next second, Larry bounded out of the chair and swirled to face Everest. "What's for lunch?"

Everest shrugged. "Didn't know what you'd want, so I got you a fruicey."

"A fruicey?"

"Yeah, it's got fruit juice and protein liquid and a bunch of agri-nutrients..."

Larry was looking at him like *he* had five heads. "Uh-huh," he said. "You got anything like a burger and fries?"

Everest shook his head. "Not for lunch, and not anything as good as your Hasty Hawley's."

"Wait a sec. You do have fast food in the thirty-first century, don't you?"

Everest shook his head again. "The Vlemutz Wars wiped out all restaurants and most businesses. It took Earth centuries to recover. We have fast food, but not like anything from your time."

"Man, that is so bogus. I love my burgers and fries." Then Larry brightened. "Guess you got to take the bad with the good. And that bed sure was sweet. I'll deal."

Before Everest could remind Larry that he wasn't staying in the thirty-first century, Dar and Elsie arrived. Their arms were full of fruiceys and nutrition bars too. Elsie burst into laughter when she saw Everest's similar pile of food.

"Oops, I guess we should have planned this better. Hope you're hungry, Larry."

"Not for juice," he said grumpily.

"Well, there are protein bars, and I've got some no-cals in my pack if you prefer," Dar said. "If you're really good and eat all your nutrients, we'll give you a treat afterward."

Everest snorted. She sounded just like his mom had when he and Elsie had been all of four years old.

"Everyone's a comedian," Larry said as he sucked up some of the drink that Everest had brought. "Man, this is the weirdest straw I've ever seen."

Everest contemplated the straw in question. It seemed pretty normal to him. He said as much to Larry.

"You don't see anything weird about a straw that gets fat then thin, changes colors, and moves when you're not sucking on it?"

"That's what straws do," Elsie said.

"Why?"

"For fun, I guess. Kids drink more of their fruiceys with fun straws. We did notice that twenty-first-century straws were more utilitarian."

"Utili—what? Jeez, you sure are a bunch of nerd professors."

"Just because we have an extensive command of the English language doesn't make us suzo-shrimp geekoids," Elsie retorted.

"Suzo-shrimp geekoids," Larry nodded his head. "Not bad. But if that means what I think it does then I'm sorry to say, you all are the biggest suzo-shrimp geekoids I've ever met."

The boy sure had guts. Everest had a sneaking feeling that if he'd landed in a different time and place and been dependent on the goodwill of strangers, he wouldn't have been confident enough to speak his mind.

"So what's with the different accents?" Larry asked in a quick change of subject.

"Huh?" Elsie responded.

"Most of you speak sort of like Americans, but then there's Vlas and Lelita who speak like Brits—you know, posh. If you all learn it in the womb, why not just have everyone speak with the same accent?"

Elsie shrugged. "I don't know. I guess people want to have a choice."

"Most languages provide for at least two accents in the womb," Dar explained. "French is the only language that is limited to only one womb accent, and I can tell you, it's strictly monitored. Sometimes babies learn multiple accents." She switched into a British accent. "I did, for instance."

"Freaky," Larry said.

Just then Vlas and Lelita requested entry from the other side of the door. When it erased, they were revealed with their arms full of more fruiceys. Larry groaned, and added in a squeaky voice, "I'm going to turn into a strawberry."

Vlas and Lelita looked confused, but everyone else laughed. Vlas was the first to see the other protein drinks lined up in a row, and he joined the laughter. It wasn't until Borneo entered with an extra fruicey that Lelita started giggling too.

Dar called for Folgar and asked him to drop the temperature in one corner of the closet so they could store the extra drinks properly. Then they all ranged themselves on the two beds and the desk chairs while they slurped down their lunches.

When Dar finished, she set her cup aside and said, "We've only got twenty minutes or so till classes start up again, so we'd better get down to business." She rose and began a slow pace across the cramped room, her arms crossed over her chest. As usual, she covered her hair with a cap, this time with the bill facing backward. "Since the Baskers joined our academy, we've broken so many rules I'm afraid I may have lost count. We've broken curfew, time-traveled without permission, illegally entered a twenty-first-century building, and kidnapped a minor and brought him forward a thousand years. If all that isn't bad enough, we've embroiled ourselves in some kind of illicit smuggling operation." She paused and scanned the room. "Does that about sum it up?"

Lelita looked ready to burst into tears.

"We've been zetta busy," Vlas said, grinning.

Everest didn't get the feeling that any of this really bothered Vlas. The kid was enjoying himself way too much. Everest, on the other hand, felt sick to his stomach and was wishing he hadn't drunk two fruiceys.

Dar clapped her hands together. "No worries. All we really have to do is figure out who Mr. Kisses is, determine what he's up to, and bring him to the attention of the authorities. Meanwhile, we'll sneak Larry back to his proper century. If all goes well, no one will be the wiser about our adventures." She glared sternly at Everest and Elsie. "And you two can stop dragging us into these daily escapades."

"Hate to burst your bubble, your Darship," Larry said, "but I ain't going home." He crossed his arms. "I like it here."

Everest found himself both snorting over Larry's title for Dar and gasping over the kid's statement that he was staying.

"Don't be ridiculous," Dar replied. "How many times must we tell you that you can't stay?"

"Says who?"

"Says everybody."

"Well, I ain't budging. If you don't like it, you can dump me on your academy leaders, and we'll see how they feel about you kidnapping me." He shrugged. "Not to mention stunning me and dragging me forward in time."

Dar made a noise in her throat that was almost a growl. "Don't mess with us, Larry."

Pulling himself up to his full height, he stared directly into Dar's eyes. "*Don't you mess with me.*"

Dar and Vlas exchanged looks. Vlas shrugged and said in Zylanderin, "We don't need his cooperation. We can just stun him again and bring him back unconscious. I'll look into ways to mess with his short term memory."

Dar nodded.

Larry pointed accusingly at Dar and Vlas. "Don't think I don't know what you're saying. You're going to zap me or something. You try and I'll scream to anyone who will listen about being dragged off by aliens."

"No one will care," said Dar. "They'll put your story into one of those bizarro tabloids and make you a laughingstock. Besides, we'll be long gone."

Larry paled, and slowly his lips turned down into a miserable frown. He ran a shaky hand through his curly black hair. Moisture pooled in his dark brown eyes, making Everest afraid the boy might actually cry. He didn't look tough and confident any more, but pitiful and sad.

"You gotta let me stay," he said miserably.

"Keep your aura on." Everest suspected that Larry was putting on an act to get what he wanted.

Then Larry clutched at his sleeve. "You don't know what it's like. I got no one. *No one.*" He swung around to face the clones. "You all know what it's like not to have parents. Not to have a home of your own. At least you got this place. I got nowhere. Every day I gotta scrounge for food and money and a place to sleep. I sleep in parks, on street corners, under bridges. I got nothing there. I can't even go to school—not even if I wanted to. If I stay in my time, I'm doomed to a life in and out of prison. Do you know what prisons are like in my time?" He shivered. "They ain't pretty."

"Ohhh," Lelita cried. "Can't we let him stay?"

"Honestly, Lelita," Dar said, "you know we can't. How long do you think we'll be able to hide him? He has no identity, no valid aura. Prison now is no better than prison back then."

"You know," Borneo said, "we might be able to tap into the GKB and give him an identity."

They all turned to Borneo in shock. Even Dar's mouth had dropped open. Had an alien taken possession of Borneo's riskless body?

Borneo's extraordinarily white skin flushed a light pink. "Well," he mumbled, "I think we could figure it out. All we need is an aurascan."

"Ain't that what that Folgar dude already did to me?" Larry stared avidly at Everest until he reluctantly nodded his head.

"Borneo, you are the man," Larry said, pumping his fist in the air.

"We could change the course of history by taking him," Dar said weakly.

Vlas shrugged. "I guess it wouldn't hurt to check to see if there's any mention of him in the GKB historical records. If we find some mention after April in 2002, then we have no choice but to send him back. We could do an aura match analysis. It'll take a while, but we'd know for sure whether he's been reincarnated between then and now."

"Fine, Vlas, you hack into the GKB and report back to us." She whipped back to Larry. "No promises, but we'll do some checking."

"Thanks, sister."

"Don't call me 'sister', and don't thank me. It's Lelita, Borneo, and Vlas who hold your fate in their hands."

"You don't know what this means to me."

Everest didn't trust Larry's puppy-dog expression. The boy was an operator. Yet he couldn't help but feel sympathy for the guy. It had to be miserable being all on your own, having to fend for yourself. He could see why the clones were sympathetic. They had a lot in common.

Dar sat down in an empty desk chair and leaned forward, her elbows resting on her knees, her hands loosely clasped. "I think it's time we focus on the criminal in our midst. Who is he? And what are we going to do about him?"

CHAPTER 36

Everest and Larry on Assignment

The last person Elsie wanted to think about was Mr. Kisses. He'd been livid when he'd caught them spying. Who knew what he might do if he ever laid hands on them? Couldn't they just pretend they'd never overheard the man plotting a criminal act? Did it really matter if he smuggled a few plastic toys in from the twenty-first century?

Dar was drumming her fingers on her knee. "Elsie and I figured out what Mr. Kisses is up to."

Elsie waved her hands and mouthed, "No." This was Dar's hypothesis, not hers.

But Dar ignored her, and the other twelve-year-olds clamored for more information. "They're smuggling in Hasty Sack toys from the twenty-first century."

"What are those?" asked Everest, curiosity finally overcoming his aversion to asking questions.

"Back then, with each Hasty Sack, Hasty Hawley's gave out a cheap plastic toy. Those toys are worth a fortune now."

Larry snorted. "Get real. Hasty's isn't all that."

Dar tossed him a grin. "Maybe not in 2002, but it was top dog by 2150. And they made a lot less quantities of those early figurines, so they're worth more to collectors. Besides, nowadays you can't duplicate that kind of plastic because it's petroleum-based, and we ran out of petroleum a long time ago. Even if we were to find another source elsewhere in the galaxy, it's against the law to use it because of the environmental impact. You can make something that approximates that plastic, but it's not the same. Collectors pay a fortune for the originals."

"What a waste of VC," Everest exclaimed.

"I doubt any of us would disagree."

"Then Mr. Kisses has to be one of the teachers who chaperoned our field trip!" said Vlas.

"Better watch out," Dar responded, "your genius is showing."

Vlas snorted. "Why don't you go jump in a black hole?"

Dar laughed.

"Instructor Legnarchi got the lunches," Everest remembered.

Elsie frowned, still unhappy with the idea of Legnarchi as prime suspect. "Let's not forget about Tchakevska."

"Yeah, yeah," Dar said, "Legnarchi, Tchakevska, and Gerard are all possible suspects. And Dr. Wei too! It was zetta weird the way he forced himself on the field trip. We can't rule out some kind of conspiracy. We're talking a lot of virtual currency."

"So what's our plan?" Vlas asked.

"Can't we just ignore it?" Elsie asked in a small voice.

"Tell me you're joking!" Dar's expression was somewhere between appalled and shocked. "We're talking about time travel for *illegal profit*."

"Yeah," Lelita added, "if they get away with this, who knows what they might do? That's why the rules about time travel are so strict."

"Isn't there anyone we can go to for help?" Elsie asked.

Dar shook her head. "Not until we're sure who're the good guys and who're the bad."

Elsie didn't much like Dar's answer, but she knew the girl was right. If her parents were here, it would be a different story; but they were out of reach and she definitely didn't trust her uncle enough to confide in him.

"So," Vlas repeated, "what's our plan? I know you've got one," he said specifically to Dar.

"Well," she wrinkled her nose in concentration, "how hard would it be to find traces of the communication from last night and pinpoint which holoputer it came from?"

Vlas and Borneo exchanged looks.

Borneo spoke up first, but hesitantly. He nervously rubbed his cheek as he spoke. "Maybe we could ping each holoputer and narrow down which ones were used last night and for how long."

"Brilliant," Vlas murmured. "That might be enough."

"With our luck, all of the same instructors were on duty last night."

"We need to check," Everest said.

"It was Instructor Legnarchi and Instructor Tchakevska," said Elsie. "I already checked. They're on tonight too."

Dar gave her an approving look. "Excellent."

Elsie felt so sad. Instructor Legnarchi again. But also Tchakevska, so there was hope that it was someone else.

"I can't believe Instructor Legnarchi's involved," Borneo said, mirroring her feelings. "He's decent."

"I like him, too." Dar rested a comforting hand on Borneo's shoulders. "But we can't ignore such an obvious suspect. Remember, if he is Mr. Kisses, then he's looking for us as much as we're looking for him. And he's probably dangerous."

She raised her eyes to the ceiling. "Melista?"

The beautiful unicorn-human shimmered to solid form. "Yes?"

"Who's chaperoning the thirteen-year-olds today on their field trip?"

"Legnarchi, Gerard, Bebe, and Tchakevska," she answered immediately.

"What about the fourteen-year-old field trip that happened earlier this week?"

"Same four," Melista confirmed.

"Hmm." Dar pursed her lips. "Did Dr. Wei go on any of the other field trips?"

"Just yours."

"Uh, if these plastic toys are worth money, why don't we retrieve them and cash in?" Larry asked.

Everyone glared at him.

"Hey," he responded, "I get it about the time travel rules, but it's not like *we* brought the Hasty Sack toys to the thirty-first century. If someone's going to rake it in, it might as well be us."

"We're not criminals," Dar said. "We might break rules now and again, but that's a lot different from what these folks are up to. They're breaking the fundamental time travel rule to never abuse the technology for personal glory or financial gain. If we take those toys, we're no better than they are."

Dar's passionate response really impressed Elsie. She'd kind of figured Dar saw rules as just waiting to be broken. She was glad the girl had a stronger code of ethics.

"Chill, girl," Larry returned. "I can live with that. It just don't feel like such a big deal. A few lousy toys. But it's cool. We'll be righteous—like superheroes and take those bad guys down." Larry cocked his head. "I still think we should find the hiding place. We can nab the toys and either return them or turn them in to whoever's in charge of this joint."

"Now that, I can agree with," Dar said. "So," she addressed the rest of the group, "any ideas on how we might find Mr. Kisses' hiding place for the stolen toys?"

"We could search some of the instructors' offices," Elsie said. "Maybe find some clues; maybe even find the toys."

"Why Elsie, how daring! Are you volunteering?" asked Dar.

"Uh—" The idea of sneaking into an instructor's office had her sputtering. What if she was caught?

Dar laughed. "The look on your face. A search is a good idea, but I don't think we're likely to find the actual contraband. Last night Mr. Kisses asked for a portion of the VC up front, but was refused because he wouldn't turn over any of the items. He told Mr. Snickers they had to age properly. Clearly he has to store them in a safe spot for a thousand years, and he's storing them as a set. He can't dig up the treasure on this end until after the B13s' field trip."

"But how could he be sure of the spot remaining safe for a full millennium?"

"There are historical maps," Melista suggested, curled up on Dar's bed. "You could study how land usage changed. Find a spot that has never been seriously dug. A garden maybe—but people dig in gardens all the time."

"What about a spot that has always had a building on it?" Elsie asked. "Would someone bury the boxes in a basement?"

"Most sites have enjoyed multiple buildings over the course of the millennium," Melista said.

Despite the element of danger, Elsie was beginning to feel excited about unraveling the puzzle. History was one of her favorite subjects. "We should be able to identify a spot that has never been dug up for plumbing or a foundation. I could research the history of this area, maybe narrow down our search."

"Good idea," said Dar.

Lelita cleared her throat. "I'm not always the best student, but I'd like to try to help Elsie."

"Thanks, Lelita," Dar responded with a smile. She turned to Vlas and Borneo. "While you're pinging the holoputers, can you check on their recent activities? Maybe we'll find someone else who has been up to some interesting research. I know it's a stretch. It feels a lot like we're searching for an uncharted habitable planet in Xlexuri."

Officials from the Xlexuri galaxy were enormously proud of having charted every last centimeter of their galaxy.

"We'll see what we can do," Vlas responded.

Borneo scratched his head. "We'll leave cyber footprints behind. Someone could find *us* if they tried hard enough."

"We'll just have to act quickly enough that it doesn't matter," Dar said.

"What about me?" Larry asked. "I want to do something."

"We've still got a couple of hours before the B13s come back. Everest, why don't you and Larry make a quick search of the instructors' offices?"

Elsie swallowed a giggle at Everest's comical expression. Dar had let her off the hook, but now Everest was stuck. She felt a weird mixture of guilt and relief.

"Excuse me," he finally said, "but don't I have class this afternoon?" He motioned to Larry. "And isn't he supposed to stay hidden?"

"Exactly." Dar grinned. "Everyone else will be in class. You can sneak into the offices, do a quick search, and be out of there without anyone the wiser."

"Cool," breathed Larry.

"I can't just miss class," Everest asserted.

"Actually, you can. It's Instructor Tchakevska's geography course next, and it's bound to be some kind of holoputer self-learning session run by one of her avatars. You'll never be missed."

"If that's the case, why don't you do the detective work yourself?"

Elsie opened her mouth to offer to go with Everest, but Vlas spoke up first.

"Dar, can't you see the ute's scared?" Vlas asked. "Let me go."

"I'm not scared!" Everest yelled. His face had gone bright red. "I just think it's a yocto-brained thing to do." He glared at Elsie, since it had been her idea originally.

Dar contemplated him for a few moments, then turned to Vlas. "Tchakevska may have given her avatar specific instructions about you and me. It would be better if someone with less of a reputation did it."

"Uh," Borneo said, "I c-c-c-ould go."

Dar beamed at him. "Zeller! You're the best, Borneo."

He blushed to the roots of his white hair.

Elsie felt terrible that Borneo was willing to take the risk when this whole mess was her fault. "No, Borneo, you mustn't. I'll go. It's my fault we need to search instructors' offices in the first place."

"I never said I wouldn't go," Everest said grumpily. "It's just too risky to take Larry."

Elsie felt secret relief. Everest going would be as good as her going. He was her twin, wasn't he? He had to be good for something.

Larry contorted his face in a wild grimace. "I'll go freakin' nuts if I have to stay in this room all day. Who knows what I'll do?"

Lelita gasped, and Elsie patted her arm awkwardly in an attempt to reassure her.

"Just take him," Dar said to Everest. "He'll be good, won't you, Larry?"

Larry nodded.

Everest sighed. "I'm telling you, we'll be caught, and when we are, I'll point everyone to you for an explanation. Look at him. There's no way anyone will think he's a modern day clone. Look at his shoes!"

"Obviously, we'll need to get him into more modern clothing," Dar said. "You can lend him some skyboots, and while you're at Legnarchi's you can grab him a uniform that fits."

"You can't be serious."

After a long moment during which they tried to outstare each other, Dar added, "The rest of us should do some hacking while we're in Tchakevska's geography class. See what we can find."

At that moment Melista cleared her throat, making even that mundane noise sound musical. "Your afternoon session is about to begin, my dears."

"Thanks," Dar said.

"Uh, Dar, should someone search Dr. Wei's cottage?" Elsie asked quietly.

Vlas snorted with laughter, spitting out juice, and Everest glared as if she'd purposefully been trying to add more danger to his plate. Elsie glared right back. Dr. Wei was a suspect. Of course she had to ask.

"Sure, Elsie, why don't you take on that job," Dar said with suspicious sweetness.

Lelita gasped. "Dar!"

"I'm kidding," she said to Lelita. "Dr. Wei won't even let in Pico-brownies to clean his mess. Anyone who passes through his doors uninvited will never make it out alive. He's got more booby traps than Xlexuri has stars."

"So, what are we going to do about him?"

"Haven't quite figured that out yet." She turned to Melista. "Can you give Everest and Larry a floor plan of the instructors' offices?"

"It would be my pleasure." She turned her golden eyes on Everest. "Do you have your JED?"

"Sure." He dug into his pack and held it out.

Melista dipped her horn so that it almost touched the JED. "There you go."

When Everest now looked at the screen, he saw the second and third floors with rooms illuminated and labeled with instructors' names.

"Wicked awesome," Larry breathed.

"Thank you, Melista," Everest said more formally.

"You are welcome," she responded in like manner.

Dar stood up and waved toward the door. "Are we ready?"

"Ready to rock and roll," Larry said with a wide grin.

CHAPTER 37
A Dangerous Mission

Feeling zetta grumpy, Everest adjusted one of Dar's earpatches as he led the way to the nanovator. Dar had insisted he and Larry both wear them, so they could remain in contact with her in case of an emergency. Like he wanted her to be able to monitor every yocto-brained thing he did on this stupid mission.

Before the other kids had left for class, he'd borrowed Dar's matter-mover, so he wouldn't have to introduce himself at any office doors. They'd also pocketed some brightees, so they could search the offices without waking up an avatar, who at best would ask difficult questions and at worst would tattle about their visit. Vlas had made a quick run to his room and returned with his exercise clothes, which he had slapped into Larry's arms before dashing off to class. They were loose, but the skyboots had adjusted somewhat to Larry's foot size.

All the way down the corridor, Larry kept jumping and hopping, staring down at his feet. "Weird stuff. Man, can I jump."

"Deng, Larry, of course you can jump in these boots. They aren't like those extreme bowling balls you called shoes in the twenty-first century, but this isn't a game, so stop aliening on me."

The corridors were empty of students and instructors, and Everest prayed they would stay that way. "Dar," he whispered, wishing he'd insisted on Vlas being their contact, "are there hall monitors?"

"Not usually," she responded in a barely audible tone. He had the impression she wasn't moving her lips. "Sometimes Instructor Sura makes the rounds, and then there are the director's holograms. They like to haunt the hallways."

"Great," Everest said with feeling.

"Keep it down," Dar hissed. "Do you want the whole class to hear you? My earpatches are pretty good about not projecting outside the ear canal, but they aren't perfect. Besides, a loud unexpected noise could jerk me right out of my seat, and I'd rather be eaten by a black hole than try to explain." Now her words were muffled as if she'd buried her face in her hands.

Everest decided to save her from having to worry about him speaking too loudly by not speaking at all. He rolled his eyes at Larry, who mouthed "Girls" and made a gruesome face as if he'd swallowed poison.

They took the nanovator down to the second floor, where Instructor Gerard's office was located. If Everest could have predicted the future, he would have taken the stairs. Larry screamed at the top of his lungs the entire way down. Then at the bottom, he was so overcome with excitement, he started to laugh hysterically.

"Shut down," Everest grumbled, "or I'm taking you back to my chamber."

The boy hiccupped, then sobered abruptly.

With the silence, came Dar's muffled voice, "What part of the English language don't you understand? Didn't I just tell you not to yell? I thought my brain was going to explode. I've had to cover my ears, and I'm getting strange looks. Lucky for us an avatar is teaching today rather than Instructor Tchakevska."

"Man, that rocked," Larry said. "Better than any roller coaster, that's for sure."

"Yeah, yeah." Everest took Larry by the arm and dragged him down the corridor. "Can we stick to business?" At Instructor Gerard's office, Everest came to an abrupt halt. He knew the instructor was on the timed field trip, but it was still freaky thinking about breaking in. He took a deep breath then whispered to Larry, "Watch the hallway for a sec."

Dar had given him a lesson on the matter-mover, so it was quick work to make a square opening to the left of the door. He frowned, because he wasn't sure the hole was big enough. Thank the Light Dar could only hear them, not see them.

"Okay, Larry, you first," he whispered. "Say as little as possible once you're in the room. We don't want to alert Gerard's office avatar. Especially be careful not to ask for anything. Some people prefer their avatars to be at their beck and call like personal slaves. That means they could be programmed to do everything, including turn on and off lights."

"No problem." Larry placed his hands on the edge of the opening and pulled himself through, landing with a thud on the other side. Everest did likewise, but found his pack stopping him halfway. He grunted as he struggled to break free.

"Come on," Larry hissed. "Hurry up."

Everest popped back out of the hole, dragged his pack off, tossed it inside, and then heaved himself through. This time he made it with centimeters to spare.

"Larry, squeeze your brightee." Everest put his own words to action, and the room glowed with light, revealing a spotless office space. Instructor Gerard was ruthlessly organized. Clearly labeled jellach journals lined one shelf in alphabetical order.

Against the back wall was an ancient desk. Everest knew it was old because it was made out of the same substance his family's dining table was made out of—a very dark reddish brown wood. It was polished so that it shone, giving the impression it might be as mirror-like as tevta. Desks such as these were zetta rare and zetta expensive. He wondered if the school owned the desk, or whether Gerard had brought it himself.

His heart thumped so loudly Everest was surprised Dar didn't complain about the noise. There was no sign of Gerard's avatar, but that didn't mean it wouldn't show up at any minute.

Larry walked up to the desk and pulled open the top right drawer. "What are all these sticks?" he asked.

"Deng, Larry, I told you not to ask questions. Remember the avatar?"

Larry let loose with a bad word.

"Stop that. I mean it. You're going to get us in big trouble." Everest looked over Larry's shoulder. Lined up by size and color were a number of stylus wands.

"They're for writing." He tried to remember what they used in the old days. Ink and some kind of writing implement. "Like pens," he said, "but without ink."

"Rad. What are they called?"

"We don't have time for this," came a muffled rebuke from Dar. "Larry, if you ask one more question or say one more bad word, I'll wrap you up as a gift and serve you for dinner to Director Lester-Hauffer himself."

"Come on, Larry, her Darship is getting restless." Everest grinned at his use of Larry's coined term. It was such a perfect fit.

"Funny," she said in his ear. "Very funny."

They moved around the room, opening drawers, looking underneath the desk, and under the small round table and chairs.

Instructor Gerard had a fold-out jellach mattress for nights when he was on duty. They carefully unfolded it to make sure nothing was hiding inside. In the end, the only thing they found remotely suspicious was a desk drawer that couldn't be budged. Most likely it was where the instructor kept his holoputer. But if there really was something criminal in Gerard's possession, it would be hidden there too.

"Deng," he muttered to Dar. "We should have brought your object cloner. There's one drawer that's locked."

Larry cracked his knuckles. "Dude, you can forget all your thirty-first-century gadgets. You've got Larry 'Light-Fingers' Knight on the job." He went down on one knee next to the desk. From within his jacket pocket, he pulled out a thin piece of metal.

"You always carry that around?" Everest asked.

"Sure," said Larry. "Now stop asking questions. You never know when an avatar might get interested."

Everest snorted, but remained silent as Larry inserted his thin metal stick and wiggled it around.

There was a faint click, and Larry pulled open the drawer. Flasers, thought Everest, he was even slicker than Vlas. He leaned over Larry's shoulder to see the contents. Sure enough, Gerard's holoputer was there, also a few jellach journals and a holo-image of a beautiful woman. His mother? His girlfriend?

That was it. Nothing remotely suspicious.

"Deng," he muttered.

"Empty?" he heard Dar whisper.

"It might as well be. There's nothing incriminating, that's for sure."

"Then you'd better move on to Legnarchi and Tchakevska," she replied.

"Brilliant suggestion," he muttered back. "Come on, Larry, let's go. Can you lock that desk back up?"

"Piece of cake."

Larry bit his tongue while he worked.

They left as quickly and as quietly as they could, using the matter-mover to rearrange the tevta wall back to smooth, solid lavender. Instructor Legnarchi's office was on the third floor, so they snuck up a flight of stairs.

This time Everest was quicker with the matter-mover, and he made a bigger opening so he didn't have to take off his backpack. Once again they used brightees. As Everest had already seen on his first visit, Instructor Legnarchi's office was much less organized than Instructor Gerard's. The uniforms and skyboots were no doubt sorted properly, but they were heaped in big bins rather than neatly folded. The room was larger than Gerard's office. Probably because Legnarchi was required to store the uniforms. He had a regular jellach bed rather than a fold-out mattress.

Legnarchi had a large collection of jellach journals as well, but his were not alphabetized, and they were stacked in untidy heaps on every surface of the room. Everest had a feeling the pico-brownies didn't visit this room as much as Gerard's. The place smelled a little musty.

As they had in Gerard's room, the boys worked their way from one side to the other, opening drawers and looking under and over every piece of furniture. Everest even searched the bins of clothing. While he was at it, he remembered to grab sweats and skyboots that looked as if they'd be a better fit for Larry. He held them up.

"Psst, Larry."

On the other side of the room, Larry raised his head. Instead of asking a question, Everest just pointed to the sweatshirt then pointed to Larry.

The boy grinned and flashed Everest a thumbs-up.

259

After he had stuffed Larry's new clothes into his backpack, Everest moved to tackle the slick tevta side table that stood next to the instructor's jellach bed. It was tall and thin, with evenly-sized drawers marching up it and a pretty antique porcelain box sitting on top.

It was the last piece of furniture for them to search. Larry reached it first and began pulling open drawers from top to bottom. Suddenly he let out a low whistle.

"Deng, what was that?" Dar asked grumpily. "Can't you keep it down?"

"Sorry," Larry said hastily. "But you won't believe what I just found." He motioned to Everest. "Man, you got to look at this!" He held up something for Everest's inspection.

"What is it?"

"What do you think?"

It was a small object, about the size of the palm of his hand—a beautiful rendition of a giant black and white panda. He touched the object. It was smooth and hard, but it didn't have the density of tevta or the give of jellach. Everest recognized it as plastic.

"Is this what I think it is?" he asked.

"You bet it is!"

"Spill, Larry," Dar whispered impatiently. "I can't see what you two are looking at."

"We've found ourselves a genuine Hasty Sack toy—from the endangered species collection."

Everest stared at the object. "But that means—"

"We've got ourselves our dude," Larry finished. "If this ain't evidence, I don't know what is. We better leave it here. Last thing we want is for the instructor to catch on that we know."

"We better make light speed and get out of here," Everest said urgently. Deng, why did it have to be Legnarchi? He would have had no problem stomaching the idea of Gerard as the bad guy.

"Yeah, time to blow this joint," Larry agreed as he stuffed the toy back into the drawer and ran for the room's temporary opening.

Everest followed Larry out, then sealed the hole with his borrowed matter-mover.

As one, they pounded down the corridor toward the nanovator.

"Don't forget Tchakevska," Dar said.

Everest groaned. "You've got to be kidding."

"They could be working together," she reminded them.

"She's right," Larry said, earning a sour look from Everest. "Where's Tchakevska located?"

Everest glanced down at his JED.

Fortunately, their race to the nanovator had put them closer to Tchakevska on the third floor rather than farther away. They passed the nanovator at a brisk jog and stopped two doors down on the right-hand side.

When they were inside with their brightees on, they found the office to be surprisingly decorative, with rich textiles on the walls and light murals where the tapestries left off. The room glowed with warm pinks and purples. Tchakevska's furniture was modern Zentor vood, the hard glossy black substance that was manufactured throughout the Zentor galaxy. The place was loaded with furniture—a slew of small tables, a couple of desks, a few chairs, a couple of chests. And covering every centimeter of surface were beautiful handmade boxes made out of a myriad of substances from throughout the universe.

"Whoa," Larry breathed, "some kind of place. Like a freaking museum."

"Yeah." Everest felt claustrophobic. "She's definitely into collecting. Be extra careful." His nervousness made him speak sharper than normal.

"Duhhh...what do you take me for? A moron?"

"Deng, there's no reason to get mad. I was just—"

"Stating the obvious?" Larry interrupted. "You be extra careful yourself. If anyone's going to break something, I'll put my money on you."

"Fine, you do that," Everest retorted. "Your money isn't worth a thing in the thirty-first century."

"Boys, will you knock it off?" Dar asked. "You're wasting valuable time and giving me a Zylorg headache."

"Hey, I got all the time in the world to waste," Larry said grumpily. He swung around to start searching the left-hand side of the room and bumped into a small round table. Gasping, he grabbed for it and barely managed to catch it before it and the pretty etched glass box on top crashed to the ground. Everest lunged forward to help. Unfortunately, with Larry already off-balance, Everest's help was exactly what he didn't need. But it was too late. His force made Larry bump forward into the table, and all four of them—Everest, Larry, the table, and the glass box—crashed to the ground.

There was the tinkle of broken glass. Everest moaned.

Trapped under the full force of Everest's weight, Larry cried, "Help," in a high voice.

Everest quickly rolled off him, but once again the damage had already been done.

"What is going on?" said a very deep voice. Larry's cry for help had awakened the room's avatar.

Everest and Larry looked up from their prone positions.

An extremely hairy, long-armed giant towered over them. His arms were like tree trunks, and his head had to be a meter in diameter. His teeth were jagged and stained a yellow brown.

Larry and Everest yelled in unison. Scrambling to his feet, Everest exploded across the room, knocking over more tables and chairs in his haste. Larry was only a few steps behind, but the monster managed to pluck him up as if he were nothing but an annoying flea.

"Calm down," Everest heard in his ear. "Calm down this instant."

"No time," he gasped. "He's got Larry." He turned back and rammed into the giant from behind. For a second, the giant lost his concentration, and Larry fell back to the floor.

"It's an avatar," Dar said. "It can't hurt you. There's no way it *has* Larry. You're letting it scare you into believing in the virtual reality it's projecting. None of it's real."

Easy for her to say. She wasn't being chased by a four-meter-tall, hairy beast. Everest grabbed Larry's wrist and began dragging him to the square opening.

"Stop," the monster yelled. "I demand an aurascan."

Not likely, Everest thought. An aurascan would bust him, and even worse, it would reveal that Larry didn't exist in this time period. He shoved Mr. Twenty-First-Century up to the opening, and the boy flung himself through the hole. Everest came next, diving, tucking, and rolling, and finally landing on his feet. He managed to close the hole with the matter-mover a heartbeat before the avatar could thrust his arm through.

"Come on," Everest yelled, feeling deng grateful that room avatars had to remain within the confines of the rooms under their charge.

They took the nanovator up to the top of the North tower and flew down the corridor to Everest's room.

When they arrived, they flung themselves inside and collapsed on their jellach beds. They were breathing heavily. Course, it was amazing they were breathing at all.

"Deng, that was close," he said.

Dar's voice hissed into his ear, madder than a vlemutz in the midst of battle. "Larry, don't you dare leave that room. Everest, jam to your physics class—now. Talk about yocto-brained."

"Keep your aura on, Dar; we made it back in one piece." He was still out of breath. "That giant wasn't able to aurascan us, so we won't be identified."

"Oh yeah? Melista sent word that she's already been contacted by Tchakevska's room avatar to determine my whereabouts. I suspect Folgar's been communicated with as well. You better hope he kept his mouth shut. I'm taking my earpatch out. All your pathetic ute-baby shrieks have given me a splitting head."

With that, Dar went quiet.

"I hate it when she's right," Everest groused.

"I suspect it's one of those things we just have to get used to." Larry grinned.

"I doubt she has a headache. They were mostly eradicated in 2290 through nano life science technology."

"Too bad! It seems only fair that I give her a pain in the head, since she gives me a pain in my rear."

CHAPTER 38
An Important Discovery

While Everest and Larry were on their mission, the rest of the gang attended Instructor Tchakevska's geography class. A strange and intimidating creature stood at the instructor's desk waving students to their seats. At least a meter taller than Dar and Elsie, who were the tallest students in the room, its skin texture was rough and gnarled like a tree. It had not two legs, but three, and at least seven arms or limbs. Its coloring was a deep and warm brown with a slight tinge of green. Something about the creature was decidedly female.

"Oooh," Lelita gasped, "a Shomaulora."

Elsie had heard about Shomauloras, but she'd believed they were imaginary creatures. Here was one in the flesh.

As Dar steered a gaping Elsie toward the back of the room, she pulled out her earpatch and hissed, "Don't alien, she's not real. I told you Tchakevska would program an avatar to conduct her class. The woman's known for having the most unusual avatars. Who knows what this creature implies about Tchakevska's personality? Supposedly, Shomauloras are quite nurturing until someone crosses them. Then they turn fierce and deadly."

With a wink, Dar slipped her earpatch back in.

Once everyone was seated, the avatar introduced herself as Shlizarcl. Then in a warm and rich voice, she recited instructions for the self-learning geography assignment. Elsie had the amazing sensation of being drenched in silky, soft water. She ached to listen to more wonderful words as they dripped into and over her, but she was supposed to be doing research. She shook her head. It was time to jack into the Global Knowledge Bank and search for possible storage areas for thousand-year-old booty. She was grateful when the avatar stopped speaking, so she could concentrate on her task.

In front of each student, a holoputer hovered. These were older models, disks ten centimeters in diameter. Hers was brilliant amethyst in color. Already, Dar stared fixedly at her sapphire unit, her brow furrowed. She had jacked into the system and now was navigating via her mind within a virtual reality session. Elsie couldn't imagine how Dar was going to find a backdoor out of their prescribed learning areas into the highly protected sections of the GKB, but she'd learned in the last couple of days that Dar could do a lot of things that seemed impossible.

Before she jacked in herself, Elsie remembered that Lelita was supposed to help her with research. She glanced at the girl sitting to her left. Lelita was darting frequent nervous looks at the impressive avatar.

Elsie leaned sideways. "Are you ready to do some research?"

"I guess so," Lelita said weakly.

"What's the matter?"

She took her time responding. "I'm not brave like you and Dar. I don't want to break rules or have adventures. I really don't want to do something that will make Shlizarcl angry. What if Instructor Tchakevska finds out?"

"I'm just as scared as you," Elsie whispered, amazed that it wasn't more obvious to Lelita.

"Really?"

Elsie smiled. "Really."

Lelita looked somewhat relieved.

Elsie had a sudden thought. "Is it a problem that your roommate isn't involved? Are you worried she might tell on you for being out after curfew last night?"

"Jillian?" Lelita laughed. "I'm not sure she even knows I was gone. She isn't the most aware person on the planet. Usually she meditates in the evenings, and once she's asleep, she's dead to the world. An invasion wouldn't wake her."

Despite the reassuring words, Elsie's stomach hurt. She leaned even closer. "I'm sorry for causing so many problems."

The girl's eyes widened. "Don't be silly. It's not your fault that someone in the academy is a criminal." With her chin jutted out, Lelita looked uncharacteristically determined. "It's up to us to stop whoever it is." With a simple neuro-command, she jacked-in.

Elsie quickly followed, sprinkling in a few more commands along the way.

In a heartbeat, they stood in the middle of a square room whose walls were a kaleidoscope of color and shapes. Pounding, throbbing music caused the patterns on the wall to vibrate as they swirled around. Elsie made the neuro request for privacy so that no one else could enter their session.

"Zeller, huh?" she yelled over the noise. "My best friend, Zulu, showed me how to request this background."

"I can't hear myself think!" Lelita yelled back, pressing her hands to her ears.

"No prob." Elsie shrugged. "System: boring white, please."

The walls transformed into pure shiny white, and the noise disappeared. Elsie and Lelita giggled nervously.

"That was scary," Lelita said with a grin.

"There are other backgrounds; some are zetta calm and peaceful."

The girl nodded skeptically. "If you say so. What should we do first?"

"The way I see it," Elsie said, "we need a spot that hasn't been touched in the last one thousand years. I think maybe we should just ask the system to compute which are the most likely spots near the academy and see what comes up."

Lelita worried her lower lip. "Yeah, maybe we'll get lucky."

Elsie nodded and called out, "System?"

A serene, ageless woman, dressed simply in gray, appeared in the corner of the white space, her hands clasped, her expression politely interested. "Ms. Sveltesse at your service," she said.

"Thank you," Elsie and Lelita murmured back.

Elsie had done countless searches for various school projects, and each time the system manifested itself differently. Careful not to alarm Ms. Sveltesse with hints of criminal activity, she explained the problem and asked the woman to review historical data over the last one thousand years to determine likely locations, ones that had remained untouched or hadn't had any major excavations over the millennium.

Ms. Sveltesse pursed her lips. With a delicate wave of her hand, locations began to pop up around them in the white space: a corner of a cemetery with grayish white headstones adorned by bouquets of flowers, a small section of a park with an ancient oak tree holding court, two lots covered in green moss and luminescent yellow lines that identified them as hover vehicle landing spots.

"Hmm." Elsie pressed a finger against her lips as she tried to think of a way to narrow down the search. Locations continued to pop up behind her.

"Hey!" Lelita screeched. "*Look!*"

"What?"

"One of the spots is here."

"Where?"

"Here. At the academy! Look there." She pointed behind Elsie, pushing her to swivel around. "It's the meditational circle right here at the academy."

Elsie took a good long look. It was a charming place, with an arbor of wild roses and a lovely but quite simple marble fountain; plain steelorq benches encircled the area and gnarled trees dotted the nearby landscape.

"Don't you think it's too good to be true?" Elsie asked. "It doesn't look old enough to have existed in 2002."

The lady in gray pointed to an ancient view of the location that revealed an olive tree grove. "In 2002 the property was a nunnery for women of deep spirituality. In 2411, it became a learning center—that was when the current buildings were constructed. However the grove remained intact until 2603, when the meditational circle was built to commemorate the end of the Vlemutz invasion," she said in her low, refined voice.

That explained the simplicity of the fountain and bench design. Still, it was amazing that even this humble tribute had been built during the Age of Darkness and Despair.

Lelita clenched Elsie's hand. "This is so exciting! What if we've found it?"

Elsie addressed Ms. Sveltesse again. "How do we know it was never dug up between 2002 and 2603?"

The woman gave her a superior and knowing look. "If you would like, I can show you pictures year by year of this spot.

Even when olive trees died, the caretakers were very careful in their handling of the sacred life forms. Of course, there was digging to install the fountain, but the locations of the ditches were well-documented."

Lelita squeezed Elsie's hand. "Wait till we tell Dar!"

"I don't think we should leap to any conclusions, but it sure is a coincidence that we shouldn't overlook."

"Please save this information and transfer it to Melista's local knowledge," she requested of their guide. "Save the other locations as well." She wasn't taking any chances. If the meditational circle didn't pan out, she'd review the rest of the sites with Melista when there was more time.

"My pleasure," Ms. Sveltesse said. With a flick of her wrist, the walls returned to their pristine white. At that, the gray lady shimmered, then vanished, leaving Elsie and Lelita quite alone.

"We'd better see what's up in class," Elsie said.

They neuro-exited and found Dar in the middle of a whispered exchange with Everest and Larry. Elsie nudged Dar and asked what was up, but the girl held up her hand for silence.

Finally, she turned to Elsie and Lelita. "They found a Hasty Sack toy hidden in Legnarchi's office, and then they had a little tussle with an angry giant avatar in Tchakevska's office."

Elsie gasped. "Were they caught?"

"Keep your voice down," Dar hissed. Some B12s had glanced around at their excited conversation. Dar glared, and the other kids quickly buried their heads in their study.

Dar turned back to Elsie and Lelita and continued in a low voice. "No, they weren't caught, but they caused a ruckus. Who knows whether Tchakevska has enough clues to lead her back to them? Her avatar immediately contacted all the room avatars in an attempt to track down the culprits. Tchakevska's going to be furious when she returns from the field trip." Dar shoved her cap more firmly on her head and slouched in her chair. "We'll just have to hope for the best."

"If it's any consolation, we have good news," Elsie whispered.

Dar sat upright. "I could use some of that."

"You tell her, Lelita." After all, Lelita had been the one to recognize the place.

Before Lelita could even open her mouth, Dar held up a hand. "You'll have to keep your news until we have more privacy."

Elsie was about to protest when Instructor Sura barged into the room. Without acknowledging Shlizarcl, Sura planted herself in front of the students, searching for someone. Her glare stopped on Dar, paused, and then scooted to Vlas.

Lelita's eyes were huge and her breathing shallow.

Sura whipped around to the Shomaulora.

"Have Dar and Vlas been here throughout class?"

"Of course," Shlizarcl said briskly, her limbs bristling with annoyance.

Dar sat very still as Sura pierced her with another look. It seemed as if Elsie's heart were exploding. What should she do if Sura noticed Everest missing?

After what felt like forever, the instructor broke her uncomfortable stare and stormed out of the room.

By that time, Elsie was shaking like a leaf.

"Keep your aura on, Basker," Dar said coolly. "Sura must have been informed about the damage to Tchakevska's office. She's just checking on her known troublemakers. Maybe we'll get lucky and Kindu will have cut class today. He could take the heat for us. Don't worry, your precious brother's safe—for now at least."

Elsie was grateful Sura had focused her attention on Dar and Vlas. Thank the Light she and Everest were still too new to the academy to be on Sura's radar. If she'd had to deal with Sura, she couldn't imagine what she would have said or done.

Dar smiled slightly. "Once again, you Baskers have really livened up what could have been a dull morning."

CHAPTER 39
Next Steps

Everest's stomach still churned, even though they were back in their dorm room. That had been zetta close. What in galaxies had made him panic and forget that avatars couldn't get physical? It was one thing for Larry to alien, but he knew better. As usual he'd managed to act like a total yocto-brain, with Dar as his witness. Talk about embarrassing.

Larry hadn't really been picked up by the giant. Everest hadn't even plowed into the big guy. They'd both been taken in by a simple mind trick.

But putting that aside, they had a real mess on their hands. What were they supposed to do about Legnarchi? Everest couldn't imagine bringing this tale to Uncle Fredrick. He wasn't the sort of adult who believed a child when it came to farfetched stories. But he *was* someone who would delight in punishing them for breaking the rules.

Everest wished he could reach his parents. They might get mad over the stunts he'd pulled, but they'd believe him, and they'd know what to do. Why did he have to deal with such a zetta problem? All he really wanted to do was play skyball. Deng, he hadn't done that once since he'd arrived at the academy.

While he attended his physics course and then a session on twenty-sixth-century literature, he was forced to leave Larry to his own devices. Who knew what that kid might get up to? He wished he could at least talk things over with Elsie, but there was no way he could whisper across to her during a lecture. He had a feeling that wouldn't go down very well with the instructor. And there were always rules about messaging during class.

It sure was weird how things worked out. Before they'd been dumped at the academy, it would never have crossed his mind to mull over a problem with his sister. Talk about desperate.

The lecture was a monotonous drone about how the Vlemutz invasion had affected the literature of the day, making it somber and bleak. Everest's eyelids grew heavy. He hadn't gotten much sleep since arriving at clone-ville. As his head nodded toward his lap, he noticed a terse JED message from Dar directing them to meet in her room after the class. He jerked upright and looked around nervously. Leave it to her to break the rules once again. Everest didn't respond with an illegal message, but he made eye contact and slowly nodded.

On the way to their rendezvous, he picked up Larry. Everest couldn't believe how accepting the boy was of everything that had gone down. He wasn't afraid at all, just plain fascinated by the fourth millennium and thrilled to be there. Because Larry was still obsessed with his skyboots, he kept hopping into the air and chortling wildly.

"Uh, Larry," Everest said, "if someone sees you hopping along the corridor and laughing like an alien, they might decide to ask you a few questions."

Larry immediately froze, then after a heartbeat began to walk with a distinct swagger instead. "Sorry, man, I'm cool."

Everest prayed they wouldn't run into any B12s. Even Larry at his most calm seemed completely alien.

274

They were the last to arrive at the girls' dorm room. As soon as they entered, Dar broke out her stash of no-cals, which Larry looked at with equal parts distrust and delight.

Everest tossed him a Blackhole. "My favorite."

Larry took a small bite. "Whoa! Awesome." He stuffed the rest of the Blackhole into his mouth, and Everest laughed at the look on his face when the candy exploded.

"These have no calories in them?" Larry asked, his mouth full, making it hard to understand him.

"That's right," said Elsie.

"Wicked." He reached for another one.

Dar cleared her throat. "Perhaps, we all might remember the purpose of this meeting. It is imperative that we stay on track. Our very lives may be at stake."

"Girl, you sure talk smart," Larry replied, shaking his head, "but you need major loosening up."

"As Dar has already explained, we have excellent grammar because we learn English before we're born," Elsie said. "We can't speak as you do because we're conditioned not to. For instance, we don't say 'ain't' because our womb-training explicitly forbids us to."

"Same goes for those bad words of which you are so fond," Dar added.

"*Of which you are so fond*," mimicked Larry in a high voice. "That's a good one. Hey, I haven't sworn once all day. At least, not in your presence."

"Actually, I *was* present because you screamed into my ear the whole time. Now," Dar changed the subject with barely controlled patience, "can we focus on the more important task at hand?" Her raised eyebrows made her look a lot like Instructor Tchakevska.

If he hadn't so recently had to deal with the instructor's nasty giant, Everest might have had a hard time suppressing laughter. He glanced around the room to see how the other B12s were holding up. Lelita looked worried, her big brown eyes shiny with suppressed tears, but Vlas had his same old expression of anticipation. As usual, the boy was treating this like a Pallaccii carnival. He and Larry had to be carved from the same piece of marblon.

Like Lelita, Borneo looked zetta stressed. If he could have been described as being even more white than usual, that's how Everest would have described him. It was as if someone had painted a thin coat of paste all over his body.

"Here's what we know so far," Dar said, her hands folded neatly in her lap. "Legnarchi, Gerard, and Tchakevska are the three instructors who chaperoned all of the field trips to the twenty-first century, but only Legnarchi and Gerard went missing for any significant period of time during our field trip. Legnarchi picked up the food, but Gerard left right after we were served lunch. Both of them could have had access to the plastic toys. Then there's Dr. Wei. It was strange the way he just forced himself onto the field trip. But the B12s' trip was the only one he went on, so that kind of rules him out unless he's an accomplice, which seems unlikely since no one acted as if they wanted him there. Tchakevska hasn't had much opportunity to steal the toys but, like Dr. Wei, she could be part of a smuggling ring. Flasers, they all could be, even Instructor Sura, even the director. When searched, Gerard's office came up clean. However, Legnarchi's office was hiding an actual Hasty Sack toy. We don't know if Tchakevska's office had any suspicious items because Larry and Everest managed to alarm the avatar before they could do a thorough search."

Everest grimaced. She just had to bring that up.

Dar slanted him a look, as if she knew what he was thinking and was secretly laughing. Then she continued, "Oh, and last night Legnarchi and Tchakevska were on duty." She took a breath, then turned to Lelita and Elsie. "I think now would be an appropriate time for you to let us all in on your findings."

Elsie motioned to Lelita. "You tell."

Lelita glowed with pride and excitement. Keeping her voice down, she said, "The academy's meditational circle has been virtually untouched for one thousand years!"

Dar grinned. "Interesting."

"We've got other potential spots, but the circle looks the most promising," Elsie added.

"Dr. Wei's cottage is within spitting distance of the circle," Vlas said.

Dar jammed her cap more firmly on her head. "Good point. We can't rule him out. Oh, one more thing, I found a backdoor to Legnarchi's history file that led me to a couple of intriguing facts."

Everest leaned forward to hear this new information. He wasn't the only one.

Dar continued, "Legnarchi's virtual currency balance is negative by *four hundred thousand units.*"

There was a collective gasp.

"That's a lot of debt," Elsie managed.

"No kidding," said Vlas. "No wonder he's into smuggling."

"That's so sad," wailed Lelita.

Everest grimaced and exchanged a disgusted look with Vlas.

Larry snorted. "Someone owes VC, no reason to get all crybaby over him. He ain't no charity case."

Elsie looked to Dar. "Why does he owe so much?"

"Not sure. Large chunks of VC disappeared over the last two years, but there's no indication why. It all went to the same broker on a planet named Vlorscopia. I couldn't find out much about the place, which makes me zetta suspicious. I need to do more digging."

"Did you find anything unusual about any of the other instructors?"

Dar slumped into her desk chair. "No, they were all squeaky clean. Vlas, what did you and Borneo find out?"

"We pinged every holoputer at the academy," Vlas replied. "None of them were in use during the time in question. That means our smuggler was using an unregistered holoputer."

"And here I thought mine was the only one on campus," Dar said.

Vlas grinned. "Hey, what about mine?"

"Okay, half of the students in this facility have their own unregistered homemade holoputers, so we have to assume that the instructors are equally capable of building them." Dar stretched her hands high above her head and arched her back like Elsie's bobcat. "Here's what we'll do. Lelita, do you mind taking the same role as last night? We need you to transport us back and forth. If you'd rather be closer to the action, I could trade you with someone else."

Lelita shook her head, her relief palpable. "Transport duty is fine!"

"What about me?" Borneo asked nervously. "Shouldn't I be helping her?"

"Actually, Borneo, old pal," Dar threw her arm around Borneo's neck, "we need your help in a different capacity. I'm assigning you to watch Dr. Wei's cottage. Can you do that for me?"

"Uh—D-D-Dr. Wei's cottage?" Borneo's cheeks went pink.

"We really need you to do this," Dar added.

"Are you sure?" he asked weakly.

"Sorry, Borneo, but yes, I'm sure."

"Okay." The word came out kind of strangled and swallowed at the same time.

Everest worried about the guy. He looked as if he might start sniveling—or even faint.

"Zeller," Dar responded warmly, patting him encouragingly on the shoulder. "Next we need Vlas and Everest to figure out a way to monitor Instructor Legnarchi. Maybe PicoBoy can help. It would be ideal if you could work it so you could watch him remotely. If the man leaves the building, we have to know immediately, so we can scram. Everyone besides Borneo, Lelita, and Larry will be required to be at the Meditational Center looking for buried treasure."

Larry thrust his thumb at his chest. "You trying to cut me out again?"

"It's not a good idea for you to roam the property. If someone catches you, we're all in for it. You aren't someone we can easily explain. It was a close call in Tchakevska's office— too close. Everest was right to have misgivings about letting you out of his room."

"Have aliens taken over your body?" Everest asked.

Dar was actually giving him credit for being right?

"My, my, silent boy has a tongue," she retorted.

Larry cleared his throat. "Excuse me. Focus! We're talking about me." He stabbed his thumbs into his chest. "You want me to sit on my butt picking my navel while you have all the fun? That ain't happening." He crossed his arms and went toe to toe with Dar, who also stood. His eyes were level with her chin.

She sighed. "You are such a pain."

"That's what I'm known for. Guess some things don't change with a thousand years. So tell me something I can do *besides* pick my navel."

Vlas snickered. "Let him come with us, Dar. We'll take care of the little guy."

Immediately, Larry's fists shot up into the classic boxer's pose. "Take that little guy thing back, or I'll bust your nose."

Vlas held up his hands. "Hey, keep your aura on. It was a term of affection. Wasn't I offering you a chance to be involved? You should be thanking me."

Larry shrugged, his eyes narrow slits. After a few seconds, he stepped back and eased up his fighting stance. "It's cool. I'll take the deal. But lay off the little guy garbage."

"No problem," Vlas said.

"Okay, Vlas, you've just taken over responsibility from Everest for our thousand-year-old boy," Dar said irritably. "Now, can we get back to business? We need someone to verify that Instructor Gerard has left for the night, and we really should do something about monitoring Tchakevska."

"We can check on Gerard," Vlas offered.

"Maybe Lelita or Elsie should tackle Tchakevska," Dar suggested. "Neither is likely to arouse suspicion."

"How?" Elsie asked. "Do you have another PicoBoy we can leave at her office?"

"Naw—there's only one PicoBoy," Vlas said.

"Besides, Tchakevska's mobile," added Dar. "She makes rounds. We need to plant a tracking device."

"A tracking device!" Lelita and Elsie screeched.

"Where in galaxies are we supposed to get one of those?" Elsie asked.

Dar grinned. "No problem. I've got a few stashed away."

"Let me guess—presents from Adriatic Mink," Everest said. He was a little worried about his sister. Elsie's mouth still hung open in shock.

"Christmas, 3000. He sent me a bunch of disposable ones. All Elsie or Lelita have to do is slap one half of a device on Tchakevska. It will last for about eight hours, then dissolve."

Elsie found her voice. "How are we supposed to slap one on her?"

"You'll think of something."

"Flasers, Dar, why don't you do it?" Elsie asked.

"Sorry, no can do—I'm flat out busy till 22:00." She rummaged around in a drawer by her bed. "I'll give you both a couple trackers. Whichever of you spots her first can do the slap."

"Thanks a lot," Elsie grumbled as Dar handed her a pair of dots that were teeny tiny black and looked a lot like ancient beauty marks.

"Don't worry if you both catch her."

Lelita and Elsie exchanged nervous glances.

"Everyone be back here at 22:00 for last minute details."

"Why can't we start sooner?" Elsie asked. "Why wait until 22:00?" Her expression reminded Everest of storm clouds. What was her problem?

"I'm afraid anything earlier is impossible," Dar said mildly.

Everest read the signs that his sister was about to jump all over Dar. What was her deal? Still, it was important for them to back each other up.

"Wouldn't it be safer to start earlier in the evening?" he asked before Elsie could say something she would regret. "Even now, Legnarchi could be unearthing his illegal goods."

Dar shrugged. "That would be our tough luck. Look, there's too much activity going on until curfew anyway. No one's going to waltz off to the meditational circle to dig it up until everything quiets down for the night. Elsie, you really need to loosen that uptight aura of yours."

She turned to the rest of the gang. "Do we have a plan?"

"Yes," they chorused, though Elsie's response was lukewarm and her expression still stormy.

Everest had a sinking feeling about the night ahead.

CHAPTER 40
Dar's Secret

Immediately after dinner, Dar tried to disappear again.

This time Elsie was ready. Determined to uncover the mystery of why Dar was out past curfew every night, she slipped away a few seconds after the girl, mumbling something about visiting Pooker. Dar's trail led outside. When Elsie reached the garden, she looked left then right, and saw Dar in the distance, striding down the lane.

The garden was full of floral scents and sights—old-growth wisteria climbing a nearby trellis, Cecil Breuner roses cascading along a wall, pretty coral-colored lexlorio dancers bobbing and twirling despite the lack of wind—but Elsie only gave the flowers a cursory glance as she jogged after Dar. She remained far enough back that the girl wouldn't hear or sense her, and hugged the bushes that lined the path so that she was ready to dive into them if Dar decided to glance back. Well away from the main building, charming tevta cottages lined the right-hand side of the path. Dar ducked into the first one.

At that, Elsie broke into a run and quickly covered the distance to the cottage. When she reached the door, she hesitated. If she stepped forward, it might disappear and reveal her to the people on the other side. What if Dar were standing right there? She would just die if that happened. She inched backward.

Taking a closer look at the cottage, she saw a one-story building with lots of airy windows. It was pretty, with its lavender mirror-like walls and finely etched details. She moved to the left until she reached the first window and ducked below it. Slowly, carefully, she raised herself up so she could just barely peek in, and saw a large room with oversized nanofiber chairs, each in a bold primary color such as cherry red, street moss green, sunburst yellow, and deep sky blue. The floor was littered with giggling, howling, and chattering toddlers.

Elsie grinned. They were so funny, some crawling like turtles and others walking unsteadily, a few running full tilt. There was laughter and piercing screeches, and one child bawled in the corner. A couple of adults moved competently from baby to baby, but Dar was nowhere to be seen. Reluctantly, Elsie moved away from the window to try another.

The next chamber was the kitchen, slightly modified to make it suitable for the sheer quantities of little ones. Rows of warming baby formula packets lined one wall. The kitchen was stocked with the most state of the art picotechnology for cooking, cleaning, and refrigeration. She caught the barest whiff of something; maybe warm soy milk or liquid krill. A couple of adults bustled around, cooking and cleaning and organizing.

After one last brief look, Elsie moved on in search of Dar. The next room was nearly empty, an office of some sort with stream-lined tables, slick chairs, and a holoputer device hovering over the middle of the closest desk. A woman lounged in one of the chairs, looking like a fairy godmother from an old tale with spun gold hair, wide brown eyes, and sweetly formed lips that couldn't have frowned a day in her life. She wore a slightly wrinkled gown of diaphanous silver vlatex. Her gaze flickered up to catch Elsie peering in through the window. For a long time she contemplated Elsie in silence before casually glancing away.

Elsie ducked down below the window, her heartbeat rushing like a fast moving stream. It wasn't until she was kneeling in slightly damp mulch that she realized the woman was an avatar. She'd had that shimmery quality around the edges.

Elsie didn't know whether that made things better or worse. An avatar would be hooked into the Galactic Knowledge Bank and was linked to every other room in the cottage. Depending on what action the avatar took, the whole household could be in an uproar.

When sirens didn't immediately go off and people didn't start pouring out of the building, Elsie found the courage to rise and walk around the corner of the house. A few seconds later, she peeked into the closest window.

Rows of jellach cribs greeted her, with some babies lying on their backs, some on their bellies, and others standing on their baby tiptoes, gripping the sides of their cribs for dear life. Jellach cribs had built-in sensors that made it possible for babies to lie on their stomachs without their faces being molded to their mattresses.

In the center of the room, Dar sat on the edge of a slick little chair that slid back and forth with a gentle motion. In her hands was a sunergy-powered guatar with eighteen strings for strumming. Its sound was pure, like water trickling over smooth, algae-covered rocks. And Dar was amazingly adept with her fingers. Elsie slumped to the ground. Now she could make out the tune, a sweet lullaby that every child on the planet had heard at one time or another. She leaned her head back against the smooth tevta wall and listened.

After a few minutes, Dar accompanied her strumming with song, and tears sprang to Elsie's eyes. In this moment, the girl was Shadara, singing with the most beautiful voice in ten galaxies and a thousand years.

Not a peep came from any of the children, unless one counted the intermittent clapping or the sighs of pleasure.

Elsie felt foolish. She'd imagined such dire things—that Dar was doing something unlawful, or dangerous, or at best slightly wrong—and here she was, taking care of the little clones, giving them a gift that she refused to share with any other living beings. It shook and humbled Elsie to see this softer side of Dar.

She listened for what might have been minutes but could have been hours, so mesmerizing was Dar's voice. Finally, there was silence. Elsie knew she'd intruded. Dar didn't want other people to be aware of her gift. She would be angry and upset if she knew Elsie had discovered her secret. But Elsie couldn't bring herself to run away. Instead, she slowly inched back up the wall to take another peek.

This time, Dar held one of the babies in her arms and gently rocked the little bundle. Her lips moved, but in such a quiet murmur that Elsie couldn't hear the words from this distance. After a few minutes of cuddling, Dar lowered her head and kissed the baby's nose, then settled him back into the crib and picked up the next one.

It was almost as if these infant clones had a mother.

Swiping at tears, Elsie pivoted away from the window and ran as fast as she could toward the main building. Preoccupied, she managed to barrel quite a few meters past Dr. Wei before she realized who she'd nearly run into. She whipped around and watched him march down the path, his black lab coat flapping with each long-legged stride. He hadn't paid her a bit of attention.

Attempting to catch her breath, Elsie furrowed her brow and stared at his receding back. She rubbed her eyes to remove the lingering tears.

Where was Dr. Wei going? His cottage was on the left set back from the path and partially hidden by a tall hedge. Dar had said the whole place was booby-trapped to discourage unwanted visitors. Elsie kicked at the gravel. He had seemed so purposeful, like he was on some sort of mission. Wasn't it her duty to follow him, just in case he was up to something? He was, after all, a suspect. She began to retrace her steps.

As she followed in his tracks, she was wracked with guilt. Hadn't she just spied on Dar and learned that she was innocent of wrongdoing? Now she was spying on the doctor. What if he, too, was innocent? Hadn't she learned her lesson?

But she couldn't shake the feeling that they needed to know what he was up to. If he was in cahoots with Instructor Legnarchi then he posed a threat.

With each crunch of the sparkling jewel-toned gravel, she shuddered. It didn't matter that Dr. Wei was a good fifty meters ahead. She'd been nervous following Dar because she knew how furious the girl would be if she found out; she was plain terrified following Dr. Wei. Anger didn't come close to the emotion she figured he'd feel if he found her snooping at his heels.

A couple of times she dived into the bushes for no particular reason except that some noise startled her. Then she had to crawl out to pick up Dr. Wei's trail with twigs and leaves stuck in her hair and her face bright pink.

The sky remained clear, a bright blue despite the rainfall planned for later in the evening. Only a few soft clouds scudded by, and about a thousand hover vehicles. Twilight birds chirped up a racket. The doctor's trail led her back the way she had come, and then further until he took a sharp right and disappeared behind the final cottage. She had to run to keep from losing him. She slowed at the last building and snuck a peek.

Dr. Wei continued to march down the gravel path toward a large open circle with a simple fountain centerpiece that Elsie immediately recognized from her neuro-session with the GKB—

the meditational circle. Ah-ha! If this wasn't evidence of his involvement, she didn't know what was. When he reached the spot, Dr. Wei settled onto a steelorq bench, where he contemplated the fountain intently. As usual, his definition of fashion was completely different from everyone else's. Who had even heard of black lab coats? And from her glimpse of his profile, she could tell he still had an awful lot of facial hair.

He just sat there staring at the marblon fountain, not noticing anyone or anything. What was he thinking? What was he doing? He almost looked as if he were going into some kind of meditational trance.

Using the old olive trees as cover, Elsie snuck as close as she dared. She was pretty sure her heart was about to explode. Crouching behind a tree, she hunkered down for a long spying session. Every few minutes, she checked her retro neon watch. After five minutes, she knew without a doubt that she was not cut out for any job that required surveillance. Forget about becoming a Cyborg officer or a galactic spy. She would die of boredom in half an hour. When one of her legs cramped, she sunk to the ground and stretched them out.

She was convinced that Dr. Wei hadn't moved a muscle since he'd sat down. Not even a twitch. There wasn't any actual proof that he was breathing.

It crossed her mind that this *was* a meditational circle. Didn't that imply that people came here to meditate? Was it possible that Dr. Wei was just performing a daily ritual?

What a yocto-brain she was! Once again she was spying on an innocent party.

Should she leave now? But what if she were wrong? She repositioned herself so that she stretched flat on her stomach with her chin resting on her hands. The ground was soft and slightly damp, because she was in the grove rather than on the gravel path. She was going to be a dirty, twiggy mess when she stood up.

After the fifteenth time she checked her watch—about forty-five minutes since they'd arrived—Dr. Wei moved. First, he twitched, and then he made some small stretching motions. After a couple of minutes of slow movements, the man stood up. Likewise, Elsie scrambled to her feet. She started to back away then turned and tore down the path. With Dr. Wei's long strides, he was bound to catch her.

She raced around the closest cottage, then dived behind some bushes. Though she was desperate to suck in large quantities of air, she kept her breathing as quiet as possible. As she heard him approach, she held her breath and prayed he'd miss her.

He strode past, and her shoulders sagged in relief. He would continue on his way home, and she would sneak back to her dorm room able to forget all about this narrow shave.

"What in blue blazes are you doing skulking over there? Whoever you are, come out here at once."

Dr. Wei's words caused her to jump with alarm.

"Come out, rapscallion, come out this minute, or I'll drag you out by your nasty little ear."

That had her shoving back through the bushes and onto the path.

One glance at Dr. Wei told her he was furious. Elsie looked down at her feet.

"I know you, don't I?" he barked.

"I don't know, sir."

"You were on that field trip yesterday."

"Yes, sir." She couldn't raise her head. Her whole body shook.

"What in galaxies were you doing hiding in the bushes?"

Was guilt written all over her? "I—I—that is, I," she gulped then spoke in a rush, "I was upset and hid because I heard someone coming and didn't want to be seen crying."

"Can't abide sniveling."

"No, sir."

"Shouldn't be sneaking around. You could startle someone. You deng near startled me."

"I'm sorry, sir."

Dr. Wei cleared his throat. "Aren't you supposed to be inside by now?"

"I think I'm cutting it close."

"Jam, then." Out of the corner of her eye, Elsie saw him gesturing for her to precede him down the path.

"Yes, sir." Her head bent, she rushed past him and pelted in the direction of the main building.

She had no idea how she made it back to her dorm room. It was as if one minute she stood in front of Dr. Wei watching her life flash before her eyes, and the next she was huddled on her bed, trembling from a weird mixture of fear and worry and guilt.

Worst of all was the guilt.

She'd been convinced that Dar was up to something, and nothing could have been farther from the truth. She'd suspected Dr. Wei of nefarious activities, and he'd proven innocent too.

With her knuckles, she wiped more tears off her face, then loudly sniffed. Flasers, what good was it being twelve years old if you made so many yocto-brained mistakes?

Ever since she'd been forced to come to this academy, her life had gone from bad to worse. Wasn't it about time for something good to happen?

She moaned. Not likely. They still had to get through tonight. Then there was her confession. She owed that much to Dar.

Not that she was going to do that tonight, not with so much at stake. They couldn't afford for Dar to be upset. Once the smuggling mess was behind them, she would reveal her bad behavior and swear to keep the girl's secret safe.

Elsie had a feeling Dar was going to be one angry clone.

CHAPTER 41
Everest's Dangerous Confrontation

Everest and Larry crowded Vlas while he made adjustments to PicoBoy.

"Will you get out of my face?" he snarled, which made them back off for a minute, until overcome by curiosity, they crept back.

Borneo was already familiar with PicoBoy, so he spent his time surfing the GKB looking for more lessons that would teach the little picobot useful skills.

Vlas talked to himself as he worked. "Hmm. Yes, that's it," he would say, and then chewing on his lower lip, he would make more modifications.

Vlas had already collected modules off the GKB that taught the little device to view and transmit from a variety of angles, and even one that allowed PicoBoy to transmit a hologram of his bird's eye view. Borneo had hacked into Identification Central within the GKB to retrieve Legnarchi's aura for PicoBoy to match. Now, he was fine-tuning how PicoBoy might use the info.

"PicoBoy," he murmured at the little flying bug in the palm of his hand, "I spy." The minuscule man-made creature chirped and jumped.

"I gave PicoBoy an upbeat personality so he would react with excitement to each new assignment."

"That's just dandy," Everest said grumpily. "I can't wait till PicoBoy chirps in front of the Instructor."

Vlas sneered. "Yocto-brain. PicoBoy knows when to keep quiet."

"He's wicked awesome," said Larry. "So, he's like a robot?"

"Yes, but we refer to picotechnology robots as picobots. Before tonight, he could execute approximately twenty-five thousand duties. We've just added about thirty to forty thousand more. His capacity is pretty much unlimited."

"What the heck is picotechnology?" Larry asked. "Everything's pico-this and pico-that—you know, like pico-brownies."

Vlas stared in amazement. "You don't know what picotechnology is?"

Everest reluctantly stepped into the conversation. "Deng, Vlas, the guy's from a thousand years ago. Pico technology is based on pico chips, which are really, really small. Before pico technology, there was nano technology, and before that, there was micro technology. The chips keep getting smaller and smaller. Course, nothing of any technological note happened during the Age of Darkness and Despair after the Vlemutz Wars. If anything, technology took a few giant steps backward."

Larry's eyes seemed to glaze over. "Well thanks for making everything crystal clear. If Pico stuff is so small, how come I can see the objects? Shouldn't they be invisible to the naked eye?"

"No," Vlas said. "There are all sorts of regulations about making things too small. The Vlemutz used pico technology in their weaponry—heck they used femto technology—and they nearly annihilated us. After that, all the planets banded together and made it a zetta offense to make something that small. There are exceptions, but they're really closely monitored." He patted his little man-made creature. "You're right, though. PicoBoy here is actually a bit large for pico technology because I don't have a full lab, but he's got a real pico processing unit and a pico memory card. I could have made him with a nano-chip, but I wanted to experiment a little."

Vlas turned to the other boys. "Anyone have ideas on how to sneak him into Legnarchi's office? When the instructor's on duty, he hangs in his office and plays hologames and pretty much relies on the Director's holograms to patrol the place. The man's not big on enforcing the academy's rules. Guess we know now that he's not big on any rules, even galactic ones. We'll just have to make up an excuse to visit him before curfew and leave PicoBoy behind as a spy. Then we can monitor him via JED when we go to the meditational circle with Dar and Elsie."

Larry nodded, his eyes bulging.

How much of their discussion did the boy actually understand? Despite the Age of Darkness and Despair, technology had still managed to evolve pretty drastically over the last thousand years. And Vlas was a real brainiac. Being more into sports than school hadn't stopped Everest from landing in the top ten percent of his class. Elsie had always been in the top five percent because she was such a fanatic about studying. But flasers, he and Elsie were going to have to bury themselves in study to even come close to competing with these clones, and there was nothing he hated more than studying.

Everest took a deep breath. Somehow, he had to contribute something to this mission or he'd never be able to face these guys. "I'll take PicoBoy in. I can talk to Legnarchi about my uniform; tell him I'm not sure I have the right size. Or ask him what the rules are for wearing exercise gear versus the regular uniform."

Vlas pursed his lips. "Yeah, that'll work. We'll wait here and watch Pico's transmissions. Come back as soon as you can."

"Doesn't this feel a little tame to you?" asked Larry. "I mean, watching from someone's room. Why can't we do some real spy stuff? You know, 007 James Bond action?"

"Huh?" said Vlas. "What are you talking about?"

Everest kind of thought he'd heard the name before, but he couldn't place it. Maybe he was a famous historical figure?

Larry clutched his throat and made a strangled noise. "Don't tell me the thirty-first century doesn't have James Bond. You're killing me."

"Don't worry, you'll be back in 2002 soon enough," Vlas returned.

"Funny, very funny." Humming a song Everest didn't recognize, Larry swept his arm out with his finger mimicking a flaser. He stopped suddenly when he noticed everyone staring at him as if he had five heads. Dropping his arm back to his side, he cleared his throat and said, "Why can't we stake out this Legnarchi guy ourselves?"

"No." Vlas spoke slowly as if to a small child. "That could get us caught outside our rooms after curfew, which at best would get us in trouble with Lester-Hauffer and at worst would tag us as the kids who saw Legnarchi, AKA Mr. Kisses, communicating with Mr. Snickers. Oh, and let's not forget that you would be caught outside your millennium. Hmm...detention for us, and who knows what extreme punishment for you?"

"Get a grip, man," Larry replied. "It was just a simple question. No need to jump all over me."

"The whole idea is moot anyway," Everest inserted. "Dar and Elsie need us with them tonight. I should go now." He held out his hand. "PicoBoy?"

"Yeah." Vlas transferred his creation. "Good luck."

"You the man," Larry added, and held up his fist.

Everest looked at Larry blankly until the boy reached out and tapped Everest's hand with his knuckles. He guessed that was Larry's way of offering encouragement.

Since it wasn't yet curfew, there were other kids in the hallways. He nodded as he passed people he'd met before. Near the common room, he ran into Jillian muttering to herself, most likely immersed in a new poem. She must have been zetta inspired by the literature class earlier today. If he hadn't been watching where he was going, they would have bumped into each other, because she was clearly oblivious to her surroundings. When red-haired Flanners joined him in the nanovator, Everest had to swallow several times before he could say "third floor."

"Instructor Tchakevska's avatar was pretty zeller today, eh?" Flanners asked, though it was hard to make out his words because his voice shook from the force of the nanovator. Old nanovators could be a real pain. They were at the third floor before Flanners could even finish the sentence.

Everest quickly stepped out, mumbling, "Yeah." He had a feeling Flanners wasn't speaking about the same avatar that Everest had confronted in Tchakevska's office. He'd missed the instructor's class, and no one had thought to fill him in on what had happened. He made a mental note to ask Elsie what had been so zeller about Tchakevska's other avatar.

All of a sudden, he thought he heard Tchakevska speaking nearby. She had a very stern voice. He paused and anxiously glanced around, but she was nowhere to be found. Then he heard Uncle Fredrick's voice.

"Really, instructor," his uncle said in his whiny nasal manner, "I don't know what you think I can do about the matter."

His heartbeat accelerating, Everest spun around, but the corridor was empty. The voices had to be coming from around the corner directly ahead. He crept as close as he could to the edge of the wall without revealing himself and held his breath while he listened.

"You are the hologram of the director of this facility," Tchakevska said, "and your primary function is security. If the director is not here, you must be his surrogate in all things. Someone has broken into my office and destroyed an extremely valuable collection. I demand that we interrogate all of the students tonight!"

Everest flinched. He was doomed. She would know the moment she saw him that he was the guilty party. It had to be written all over his face. She would turn the corner, take one look at him, and drag him off for his punishment. He wanted to run, but his skyboots were glued to the floor.

"My dear Instructor Tchakevska, please calm yourself. Let us go to the director's office and discuss this in private."

"There is nothing to discuss. I insist we not only interrogate the children, but we perform aurascans on every person on the premises tonight."

"I must protest," the hologram said. "Think of the cost to the academy. It would be astronomical."

"I don't care how much it costs! The monster that destroyed my property must be punished."

"I'm sorry, instructor, but we must wait until tomorrow morning when the director is back."

Silence reigned for several of Everest's booming heartbeats. He pressed hard against his chest, hoping to deaden the noise.

Around the corner there were menacing footsteps. "You will find the director now," Tchakevska said in a dangerously quiet voice, "inform him of the situation, and gain approval for the aurascans."

Everest cringed as if she were talking to him.

"I'm afraid the director left specific orders that he not be disturbed."

"These are extenuating circumstances."

"There is nothing I can do. I have my orders. Besides, the director did not tell me where he could be reached. My hands are tied."

"Is that your final word?"

"Ye—es."

"Very well, I will speak with the director tomorrow." Fury dripped from each of Tchakevska's syllables. "I will be forced to tell him how displeased I am with his hologram."

Everest was drenched in sweat, his palms clammy and wet. He couldn't seem to move. If the instructor turned the corner, he wouldn't escape.

He heard her footsteps. Was he imagining that they were receding?

"Oh," the footsteps paused, "one last thing. You'd better watch your step, FLH1. I have a few avatars who would be delighted to make your acquaintance. It could be...fun."

FLH1 made a funny sort of squeak at the veiled threat. "Excuse me, instructor."

Suddenly, the hologram rushed past Everest, who hugged the wall. Fortunately, FLH1 was preoccupied and missed him altogether. The hologram mumbled to himself as he raced by.

Tchakevska's footsteps continued to recede, as sharp and aggressive as her personality.

Everest shuddered. That had been way too close. What would he do if Tchakevska managed to hold her aurascans tomorrow? He didn't feel up to the visit with Legnarchi, but he had no choice. He took some deep breaths, wiped his wet palms on his exercise pants, thrust his shoulders back, and turned the corner.

When he arrived at Legnarchi's office, he hesitated, rubbing PicoBoy between his fingers. The man-made creature vibrated slightly in response. Everest cleared his throat. "Instructor Legnarchi, Everest Basker here."

There was no response.

What if the instructor wasn't in his room? He stood there indecisively, fidgeting from one foot to the other. Finally, he added, "Sir, I really need to speak to you."

Again there was no response. Just when Everest had given up and was turning away, the instructor said, "One moment please."

Another five minutes went by before the door erased, revealing the instructor on the other side. He wasn't the friendly, smiling man from yesterday morning, but he wasn't acting like a dangerous criminal either. He looked serious. Did he also look worried?

Everest shifted uncomfortably. Instructor Legnarchi was staring a little too intently.

"Uh—" He cleared his throat then cleared it again. "Uh—I had a question about the uniform."

"Hmm." Instructor Legnarchi just kept staring, making Everest zetta uncomfortable. After what felt like forever, the instructor stepped back and motioned him inside.

Uneasy, Everest moved further into the room. The instructor knew or suspected something. It was as if the guy were contemplating ways to dispose of him. Everest told himself he was being ridiculous. Legnarchi couldn't possibly know they were the ones who had heard his conversation with Mr. Snickers. Taking a deep breath, he told himself to keep his aura on.

"So, how are you settling in?" the instructor asked. Had he already forgotten that Everest had come with a particular question in mind?

"Uh, okay, I guess," Everest said. "It's different from what I'm used to."

"Yes, you have parents." Legnarchi spoke slowly, not at all the animated jovial man from yesterday morning. "I always wondered what it would be like to have parents. Do you miss them?"

"Yeah," he mumbled, suddenly painfully homesick.

"I suppose one benefit of not having parents is that you don't have to miss them when they're gone."

Everest managed to nod his head in agreement.

"I guess your parents miss you, too."

"Sure." Everest shrugged.

"It would be a terrible shame if something happened to you and they never saw you again."

Everest choked and felt his face heat up.

Instructor Legnarchi lunged forward to pound him on the back. "Would you like some water?"

"No, thank you." No way was he drinking any water from Legnarchi. For all he knew it was poisoned.

"You and your sister need to be careful while you're here—for your parents' sake. You need to play it safe and stay out of trouble."

"Yes sir, that's our plan." It was time for a quick exit, but Everest hadn't yet gotten PicoBoy in position. He unclenched his hand. The instructor's attention was so intensely fixated on Everest that there wasn't a simple way to sneak PicoBoy to a good spying location.

Trying for nonchalance, he eased his hands behind his back and began nudging the little picobot off his palm. With the slightest vibration to indicate his displeasure, the little guy took to the air. Everest hoped the techno-creature would know to land someplace discrete.

His duty done, Everest was ready to exit as quickly as possible. "Well, I guess I'll catch you later."

"You had a question," the instructor belatedly reminded him.

"Yeah, it was no big deal. I'll ask another student."

He backed up, feeling his way with his hands. The door had rearranged itself back to being solid, but as soon as he touched it, it disappeared. "Thanks."

The instructor stepped forward as if to follow Everest.

"No, no, don't worry about me," Everest said quickly. "I'll find my way out. I've got a lot of things to do before curfew. Better jam. I'll catch you tomorrow."

He forced himself to walk, not run, down the hallway toward the nanovator, though he felt Instructor Legnarchi's eyes boring into his back like flaser beams. Once inside the nanovator, he sagged against the wall and breathed a deep sigh of relief. "Top floor," he said weakly. Even the nanovator's excessive speed and turbulence didn't bother him as much as his already churning stomach did. No matter where he turned, he was in big trouble. The instructor's carefully veiled threats had sent a cold chill down his spine. Somehow, they had to bring Legnarchi to justice before he made his threats a reality.

And then there was Tchakevska. Who knew what she would do once she identified him as the culprit who had messed up her office and broken her glass box?

Flasers, things couldn't get any worse. But with a sinking feeling, he knew that they could.

CHAPTER 42
The Search

Elsie forgot about tagging Instructor Tchakevska with a tracking device. By the time she remembered, there was very little time left before the students had to be secured in their chambers for the night. Flasers, it was all too much, keeping track of Legnarchi, Dr. Wei, and Tchakevska, not to mention finding buried treasure without being caught by the bad guys.

The moment she remembered her task, she grabbed the tracking device and called, "Melista!"

The beautiful unicorn-woman shimmered to view. "Yes?"

"Tchakevska's office! Where is it?"

"My dear, calm yourself."

While Elsie fought to gain control over her ragged breathing, Melista tipped her horn and revealed the third floor with a strong beam spotlighting the instructor's office.

Elsie took a few seconds to memorize the location, then called, "Thanks, Melista, I'll be back," and bolted out of the room. She raced down the hall to Lelita's chamber, but the girl wasn't there.

"Deng!" Elsie said under breath, jamming to the nanovator. They should have coordinated. What if Lelita had already done the job? The shaky rocket ride to the third floor felt as if it took forever. She rushed down the hall then screeched to a halt in front of Tchakevska's office, panting like a mad cooligrar.

How was she going to pull this off?

A vague rumbling of voices came from the room.

"Uh," she said in a weak voice, "Elsie Basker requesting entry."

There was a dead moment, then the door shimmered to nothing, revealing a terrible mess. Furniture was overturned and all sorts of decorative boxes littered the floor.

"When I find those culprits, I'll wring their necks; I'll tear their hides off." Tchakevska angrily paced across the room. "I'll make them suffer." She moaned. "My beautiful things."

Elsie couldn't have moved if her life had depended on it. And given Tchakevska's ire, it was possible that her life did depend on her getting out of the office immediately.

Unfortunately, just as Elsie decided to make a quick exit, Tchakevska swung around to face her. "What do you want?"

Elsie tried to speak but no sound emerged.

Tchakevska sucked in her breath, and Elsie figured she was pretty deng close to being bludgeoned with an antique box.

"Whatever it is, you better be quick about it. I'm not in the mood for dawdling."

Elsie tried again. "Uh—"

"Stop stuttering!"

"I'm interested in more information on your avatar—Shlizarcl," Elsie babbled. She closed her eyes for just a second then purposefully stepped forward to close the gap between them.

"What kind of information?"

"Well, about the type of creature she is and where she comes from. I want to write my parents about her."

"She's an avatar. She comes from my brain. I invented her," Tchakevska said brusquely, though her tone had calmed ever so slightly.

"Wow, you invented her?" Elsie frowned. "Deng, I hoped Shomauloras existed." She'd grown up hearing about them. Her parents claimed to have known one. How come parents always fooled you with silly made-up tales? Not that whether Shomauloras existed had anything to do with the task a hand.

Remembering her purpose, Elsie took another step forward. Now she was within three meters of Tchakevska.

"I created Shlizarcl, not Shomauloras. Of course Shomauloras exist. Ms. Basker, you must fight this tendency of yours to leap to conclusions. Now, I'm terribly busy at the moment cleaning up after a couple of hoodlums." The instructor pivoted around and began to straighten up a small table in the middle of the room.

"Of course." Elsie stared at Tchakevska's back, her heart pounding so loudly she expected the woman to ask for the source of the racket.

She plunged forward. "Instructor, there's something on your back." As if swatting at a bug, she firmly swiped her hand down the woman's back, leaving behind the tracking device. When Tchakevska swirled around, she leaped backward. The woman's lips were a thin, straight, uncompromising line. "What do you think you are doing?"

"I'm sorry. There was a bug, a mosquito maybe or a fly of some sort." Elsie heard herself babbling again but couldn't seem to stop. There was a roaring in her ears. "I'll go now, you're so busy, sorry for taking up your time, love your boxes, see you soon—" She bumped into the solid door. It must have been set to require a formal request.

Tchakevska studied Elsie as if she were a new, particularly ugly humanoid species.

"What is the matter with this place?" Tchakevska fumed. "Vandals, mosquitoes, idiot holograms.... This is the second mosquito tonight. Lester-Hauffer has a lot to answer—" She brought her diatribe to a sudden halt as if she suddenly remembered the connection between Elsie and the director.

Elsie took the opportunity to whisper a request for the door to open. When it erased with a very slight whoosh, she tumbled into the hallway. After a self-conscious wave to Tchakevska, she flew back to her dorm room and collapsed on the jellach bed, her body the consistency of jellach itself.

An hour later, Elsie's heart had barely calmed when the door shimmered then disappeared to reveal Dar. She had expected the boys or Lelita to arrive first, but Dar had not only beaten the deadline, she had a few minutes to spare.

"Hey," Dar said.

"Hey," Elsie replied weakly.

As Dar strode into the room she linked her fingers and stretched her arms and shoulders. After a handful of jumping jacks, she flopped onto her bed. "What's up with you?" she asked. "Pre-game jitters?"

"Maybe," Elsie returned with a shrug. After the spying she had done earlier in the evening, she didn't know how to behave around Dar.

The girl sent her a long searching look. "Come on, what's got your aura in a twist?"

Elsie grasped for an excuse for her strange behavior. "Um, I just had a zetta bleck meeting with Tchakevska."

Dar settled more comfortably on her jellach mattress. "Really? Did you plant the tracker?"

"Yeah, I think so."

Dar moved over to her desk and picked up her JED. She fiddled with it for a few seconds. "Looks as if Lelita did, too. Both trackers are live and tracking the same thing. Excellent."

She set down the JED and flopped back onto her bed. With her hands cupped behind her head, Dar stared fixedly at the ceiling. "Psst, Melista!"

Immediately, the beautiful room avatar lounged in Dar's desk chair. She wore a diaphanous golden gown, and the horn on her forehead was wrapped in gold-tinted crystals that tinkled when she moved. Her wide, oversized golden eyes stared unblinkingly at Dar.

"Yes?" she asked melodically.

"Could you make a pretty night sky for us?"

After a silent moment during which Melista just contemplated Dar with her bottomless eyes, the ceiling swirled and waved. Then it was as if someone pulled a velvet curtain across it revealing a trillion twinkling diamond stars.

"Zeller," Elsie whispered. Her own avatar at home was more like an old-fashioned nanny than a magical creature. Could she modify her bedroom to be managed by a more interesting avatar? The thought brought on a new rush of guilt. How could she even think of replacing Mary? The avatar had taken wonderful care of her during her childhood.

"Thanks, Melista," Dar said, and Elsie quickly mumbled her own thanks.

Melista stretched slowly, like Pooker might on a hot summer day. "Your friends have arrived," she announced.

"Excellent." Dar grinned at Elsie, who managed a slight grimace in return.

"Go ahead and let them in," she told Melista.

The door erased to frame the whole gang on the other side: Lelita, Borneo, Vlas, Everest, and Larry.

"Excellent ceiling." Larry stared with wonder at the millions of twinkling stars.

"Melista's a master at ceiling art," Dar explained. "So, what's your status?"

Everest cleared his throat. Elsie wondered what had happened to him. He looked as shaken as she felt.

"PicoBoy has Legnarchi under surveillance, but before I made it to his office, I overheard Tchakevska fighting with Director Lester-Hauffer's hologram."

"And?"

"She's on a zetta rampage to find out who tore apart her office. She wants to do aurascans on every student at the academy."

"Yeah," Elsie said, "she's seriously mad. She's going to read Uncle Fredrick—I mean the director—the riot act, especially with the mosquito epidemic in the building."

She and Lelita exchanged glances and giggled.

"You used mosquitoes too!" Lelita cried.

"Yeah."

Dar shook her head. "Real smooth. Like we've ever had a mosquito in the building."

"It worked, didn't it?"

"Excuse me," Everest said, jabbing Elsie in the shoulder. "Can you all focus for just a minute? Tchakevska was talking aurascans! Thank the Light, FLH1 is making her wait until the director returns in the morning."

"Well, there's not much we can do about that," Dar said simply, "so we might as well put it out of our minds. Maybe if we finger her as part of a team of crooks, we'll discredit her enough to keep your uncle from approving the use of an auralizer. It's zetta expensive technology." She paced across the room, then pivoted to face Everest again. "Okay, Basker, what about Legnarchi? What happened during your visit?"

Everest shrugged. "I planted PicoBoy."

"Did you talk to Legnarchi?"

"Yeah." Everest ran his fingers through his hair, then blurted out, "I'm pretty sure he knows."

"Knows what?"

"Knows we're the ones who were in the history center. He was all over me—threatening, warning." Everest waved his hand. "Whatever."

Jeez, Everest's alien behavior was freaky. He never acted like this. After Elsie's encounters with Dr. Wei and Tchakevska, this was really adding to the tight feeling in her chest.

"Be more specific," Dar demanded.

Everest told them Legnarchi's exact words.

Elsie squeezed her eyes shut and wished for about the thousandth time that this whole big mess would go away.

Dar listened carefully. "Hmm. I think if he'd known for sure, he would have detained you." She turned to Vlas. "What's Legnarchi up to now?"

Vlas stepped forward, watching the JED in his hands. "He's poring over an old map—of the academy grounds!"

Dar let out a long, low whistle. "But he's still in his office?"

"Yes."

"And did you get confirmation that Gerard has gone for the night?"

"Yes, as far as I can tell," Vlas responded. "He's not in his office, and it's closed up for the night. I asked FLH1, and he said Gerard was gone. We're pretty safe."

Dar glanced down at her JED. "Tchakevska's still in her office. I think she's pacing." Two dots nearly on top of each other moved jerkily back and forth in the small square viewer.

"We better jam." Dar pursed her lips. "I take it you can watch Legnarchi and be mobile at the same time?"

"Sure," Vlas said, grinning.

"Then we'll all go down to the circle—that is, except Lelita, who will be in charge of the transport system, and Borneo, who will hang out near Dr. Wei's cottage to make sure of his activities."

"Are you sure it makes sense for me to be the one to do that?" Borneo asked.

"Absolutely."

"But he scares me," he admitted.

"We need you, Borneo."

Elsie knew how Borneo felt. She debated what to tell about her recent meeting with Dr. Wei. She was afraid to admit that she'd been wandering around in the garden. Dar might catch on that she'd been following her. On the other hand, Borneo had to be warned that the doctor was not a big fan of people skulking in the bushes.

While she struggled with her conscience, Larry asked, "What about me?"

"Yes, Larry, even you can come."

Larry let out a loud whoop.

Dar raised her eyebrows. "As long as you can keep quiet. In case you've forgotten, it's after curfew."

Larry grinned sheepishly and zipped his lips with his thumb and forefinger.

Dar continued. "Some of us will play lookout, and others will dig."

"Uh, Dar," Elsie said weakly. She nervously pushed her hair back from her face.

"Yes?"

"I ran into Dr. Wei in the garden this evening. Actually, I was caught spying on him."

Everyone gasped, and if anything, Borneo managed to look even more scared than he had a few moments before.

"Spill," Dar commanded, her eyes narrow slits.

"I had gone to visit Pooker," she said, not quite able to meet Dar's eyes. "I decided to walk around in the garden a little before going up to our room, and I saw Dr. Wei leaving his cottage. So I followed him." She paused and took a gulping breath.

"And?" Dar prodded.

"He went to the meditational circle."

Dar let out another low whistle. "Did he dig for anything?"

"No!" Elsie crossed her arms. "Weirdly enough, he just meditated."

"No kidding?" Dar grinned. "He's either really smart, or he's actually using the place for its original purpose. How'd he catch you?"

"I hid in the bushes, and he saw me as he passed."

"Does he know you were following him?"

"No! I told him I was hiding because I'd been crying and I didn't want anyone to know."

"Quick thinking," Dar said.

If she only knew, Elsie thought. Having Dar compliment her only added to her guilty feelings. "I just thought Borneo should know that Dr. Wei doesn't take kindly to spies."

"Believe me, that's common knowledge."

"I really don't think this is a good idea," Borneo said.

Dar rested her hand on his shoulder. "You'll be fine. Just stay out of sight. I'll give you my very best stunner. The one Everest used, in fact, so we know it works. You can communicate with me via the earpatches if he steps outside his house. Then we'll know to get out of the circle."

Dar turned to Lelita. "Have you narrowed down our search?"

Elsie couldn't believe it. Why hadn't Dar asked *her* to do more research?

"Um, I have, actually," Lelita started off hesitantly, tossing Elsie a nervous smile. "Elsie and I already found out that the circle of benches was built in 2603 after the last Vlemutz attack in this area. They're made from steelorq. I don't think even matter-movers work on steelorq. However, the area between the benches and the fountain has been virtually untouched over the millennium, and the grounds which surround the circle have always been some garden or other. The olive trees are remnants of an old orchard." She paused for breath then added, "The instructor could have hidden steelorq boxes all over the garden. If he went deep enough, there's no reason why they wouldn't have gone undetected for the requisite thousand years. He probably stockpiles a bunch of items in some kind of storage unit, then transfers them underground all at once." She paused, a quizzical look on her face. "The only thing that's weird is how he gets away with it. I mean, in 2002 it was a religious establishment. Wouldn't someone have seen him digging in the orchard?"

"He's got to be paying someone off," said Larry. "Probably the gardener. Money talks, you know. So how do we figure out where to dig?"

Vlas grinned. "No problem. I've got a portable object detector." He held up a small circular gadget about the size of a button.

"You expect me to believe that little thing's going to help us?" Larry asked.

"It turns different shades of pink whenever it detects any unnatural substance below. If there's a storage box underground, this baby'll turn bright fuchsia. It may take a while, but we'll find the spot."

"Pink!" Larry snorted. "Sissy color. How come it don't change different shades of green? Or brown?"

"What's wrong with pink?" Vlas asked. He looked to all of the kids to help him understand.

Dar sighed. "Back in the old days, men thought pink was a feminine color, so they didn't always like it."

"You're kidding!"

Larry shook his head. "Pink's for girls."

"Flasers, talk about the dark ages."

"We should begin searching at the marblon fountain, then fan out," Everest suggested.

"I agree," Dar said. "Let's get down there." She and Vlas handed around the two vials of earpatches. This time Dar was the one who wore two—one to communicate with Lelita, the other to communicate with Borneo, Elsie, and Larry. Because they didn't have enough for everyone, she asked Everest and Vlas to go patchless.

Once they had their earpatches in place, Dar picked up her sack and told Vlas to take Larry down first.

"Sure," Vlas said with his typically devilish grin. "Come on, Larry, let's scramble some atoms."

"Yeah, that's cool," the boy responded weakly as he braved the transport system in the closet.

Within minutes the gang was back down in Pooker's pen. Elsie took a moment to give the bobcat a hug and to receive a gravelly lick in return. She whispered to her pet that tonight they would sleep together again. Pooker looked wan and lonely in her tiny little cage, but she also seemed to be getting used to these visits.

"Still can't get over a pet bobcat," Larry said.

"Bobcats have been domesticated for over five hundred years," Everest said. "Truly, Pooker's harmless."

"Pooker? What kind of name is that for a bobcat? You got no respect. This is a powerful beast. It should be called Terminator or Claw." Larry made a face as if he were a lion roaring, but Pooker was too busy rolling in the dirt and enjoying Elsie's belly scratches to notice.

Elsie frowned at the suggestion, unable to imagine her baby being called some kind of hologame hero name. Pooker was the sweetest bobcat on Earth.

"Excuse me, but we have something a little more important to do than watch a bobcat play," Dar said acidly. "Light speed, Elsie, light speed! Vlas, what's Legnarchi's status?"

"He's still in his office poring over jellach documents."

"Good. Let's jam."

They quickly inserted their nighteyes drops, Everest helping Larry since it was his first time. Then they left Pooker's pen and followed the trail to the meditational circle. Elsie kept searching the shadows for bad guys about to pounce—especially Dr. Wei. She was jumpy and totally creeped out.

When they passed the doctor's little cottage, Dar turned to Borneo and handed him a stunner. "Okay, you know what to do."

"Yeah." The word ended on a squeak.

Dar patted him on the back. "Don't worry. He'll never know you're here. He won't leave his cottage. And even if he did, he'd never see you in the dark. Just go stand in the shadow of that big hedge." After one more shoulder pat, Dar led the rest of them onward toward the circle.

"There's going to be some planned rainfall later," Dar whispered. "Sometime around 2:00 A.M."

"Planned rainfall?" Larry whispered back.

"Yeah," Vlas said, "Every three days."

"You all just make it rain?" Larry asked incredulously.

"Sure, that way it doesn't rain during the day, and we have enough water for our needs," said Elsie.

"Cut the chittering," Dar hissed. "We're not at a party; we're on a secret mission."

Elsie just barely managed to refrain from reminding Dar that *she* was the one who had initiated the chittering.

Dar was busy checking Tchakevska's current position. "In the library," she murmured.

Vlas took the opportunity to check on Legnarchi, too. "No change in Legnarchi's office. Just maps and no-cals."

Elsie hoped that with the size of his belly, those no-cals would keep Legnarchi busy for a very long time.

CHAPTER 43
The Vlem Revealed

Despite the nighteyes drops, Everest still thought the meditational circle was zetta eerie in the dark. He'd never seen the spot during the day, so he had no idea what it looked like under bright sunlight. He smelled the roses and saw them dressed in gray, but he had the alien sensation that the arbor had more thorns than flowers.

He fought the constant urge to whip around and confront some unknown demon. Even innocent sounds like the steady chirp of crickets, the deep croak of a lone toad, and the gurgle and splash of the fountain took on a sinister note.

Dar squeezed her brightee so that a yellow glow illuminated the area. She clenched it between her teeth as she pulled out items from her sack. Vlas already had his object detector out and was crouching on his hands and knees next to the marblon fountain, sweeping the button back and forth, on the hunt for something solid and man-made.

When Dar caught Everest watching her, she yanked the brightee out of her mouth. "You and Elsie keep watch, okay? Grab stunners out of the bag. Larry, you can help me. I've brought some magnifiers, so we can check for signs that someone got here first—already dug holes, disturbed ground..."

"Cool," Larry replied and held out his hand.

Everest felt like kicking something…or someone. How come it was so easy for Dar to partner with Larry, and so hard for her to partner with him? There might as well be a ten-meter-high wall between them. It wasn't his fault he had parents, and just because Larry didn't have parents didn't make him a clone. Maybe it wasn't the clone thing, anyway. Mostly she was okay with Elsie.

Deng, what did he care if Dar kept her distance? Girls were so alien. Look at Elsie. Rubbing his nose with the back of his hand, he sought her out. She already stood at the edge of the circle, her back to the kids, her whole being focused on watching for bad guys. He crossed to the opposite side to do the same. He wasn't going to give her Darship the satisfaction of seeing him do a less than perfect job with his assigned task.

"Hey, Vlas," he called in a low voice, "do you want me to monitor Legnarchi while you search?"

Vlas raised his head from his work. "Yeah, good idea."

Everest loped over to where Vlas knelt and grabbed the JED. Legnarchi was still working his way through a pile of Blackholes and staring intently at maps.

He shook his head. Something didn't make sense. Why would Legnarchi be studying maps of this area? If he was the one who had buried the Hasty Sack toys, then wouldn't he know exactly where they were hidden?

After a stretch, he turned back to face the meditational circle. "Dar," he began, but at the same time, Vlas called excitedly, "Hey! I've found something!"

Even from the distance of some meters, Everest could see a hot pink glow between Vlas's fingers.

Dar and Larry immediately rushed to Vlas's side.

He could tell Elsie was desperate to join them, but she didn't budge from her post.

"Any guess how far down it is?" Dar asked.

"Can you beam it up or something?" Larry asked excitedly.

Dar laughed. "Not exactly, but we might be able to shift away some of the dirt."

"Uh, Dar," Everest tried again. He glanced down one more time at the JED that showed Legnarchi still glued to studying the maps.

"Yeah?" she responded absently as she rummaged in her sack. She pulled out a ten-centimeter-wide tube that looked a little like an ancient Chinese dragon once it was folded out to full size. It had jagged teeth on one end and was at least a meter in length.

Everest opened his mouth to continue, but Vlas got there first with an answer to Dar's original question. "I'd guess from how pink the color is that it's pretty close to the surface—maybe a meter or a meter and a half down at the most."

Dar gave the funny-looking tube a squeeze, then said, "Digger, dig. If you find a box, uncover it. If you go past three meters and don't find a box, return." She placed the man-made creature on the ground next to Vlas's pulsing bright pink button. Then she picked up the object detector and handed it back to Vlas.

"Step back," she said, moving a few meters away herself. Immediately, the odd-shaped tube began to churn the soil, first munching through moss, then dirt. From the tube, dirt shot straight into the air then arced slightly so that it landed to the left of the spot being dug. It was like a dirt geyser, and Larry, who stood too close, got a pile of dirt flung onto the top of his head. "Man!" He jumped back and everyone laughed.

But Everest couldn't shake his uneasy feeling. He crossed over to Dar. "There's something I have to run by you."

"What?" She spoke sharply, as if he were wasting her time.

For a moment, he almost powered down. It wasn't his

problem if she didn't listen. But what if they'd gotten the whole thing wrong? What if they were focused on the wrong person?

He shrugged uneasily. "I don't get it. Why would Legnarchi be researching ancient maps? It's almost as if he's looking for the treasure, too. But that doesn't make sense. If he's the one who buried the Hasty Sack toys, wouldn't he already know where to find them?"

"Maybe he's looking for new hiding places for the future?" Dar suggested.

Everest felt like a real suzo-shrimp. "Yeah, that makes sense."

Dar turned back to the volcanic churning of dirt and the ever-growing hole, and leaned over to peek inside. Some of the dirt rained on her. "I think I see something." She stared intently for a long moment, then reluctantly turned back to Everest. "You're right. It is odd," she admitted.

Suddenly she froze, listening intently. "Borneo, Borneo, slow down, calm down, keep your aura on. I can't understand you." She paused. "Dr. Wei's on his way here? Flasers! Do something.... Deng, I don't know.... Stun him."

Everest wished he could hear the other side of the conversation. Elsie and Larry were listening avidly. Elsie had gasped twice.

A few seconds later, Dar's eyes widened, and she swung around to the others. "He actually did it. He actually stunned him."

Vlas let out a cheer.

"Borneo's on his way here. We'd better put on some light speed." She checked her JED. "Tchakevska's back in her office. Vlas, are you positive Gerard left the compound?"

"No way to be positive."

Dar sighed and scanned the edge of the circle. "We'll just

hope for the best. At least we know where Tchakevska and Legnarchi are. If Dr. Wei's involved, it has to be a conspiracy. He didn't go on all the field trips." She pulled off her cap and jammed it on backward. "Digger, faster," she ordered, and the tube attacked the ground with even more ferocity. It made a funny sort of rumbling sound as it bit, chewed, and spit out the dirt.

"As soon as we pull up the box, we'll make a break for the transport system. We can open the treasure once we're safe and sound in my dorm room."

There was sudden silence in which Everest felt fear eating a hole in his belly as surely as the digger had been eating into the ground. Dar snapped around to check out the opening. Sure enough, a rectangular box a meter and a half long and at least two thirds of a meter deep was nestled in there. The digger slithered up to sit on the brink of the opening. Every few seconds it spit out small chunks of dirt.

Everest smelled the richer soil that usually remained underground, the soil that reeked of worms and old moisture.

"Vlas, hold my legs while I lower myself down to the box," Dar ordered. She was already leaning over into the hole and was digging her fingernails around the box's edges.

Everest crouched next to her, then went down on his belly so he could help Dar pry up the ice-cold box. By accident their fingers touched, and they both shied away as if they'd been burnt. *Bleck,* Everest thought. Their heads kept bumping, too.

All the while, Elsie anxiously hovered over them. Everest couldn't see her, but her emotions seemed to pulse from her. She was all churned up like the dirt that had gone flying.

At that moment, Borneo pelted into the circle. "I stunned him. I'll be expelled. He'll kill me."

Everest heard Elsie consoling him. The boy sounded as if he

319

were crying. Everest could relate. Stunning someone wasn't an experience he wanted to relive. Stunning Dr. Wei had to be zetta worse than stunning a strange kid from the twenty-first century.

He and Dar slowly worked the steelorq box up from its hiding place. It had lost its silver sheen and was a dark gray now. He'd never seen steelorq tarnish. Then again he'd never seen a container that was one thousand years old.

With a grunt, he heaved on his end, and Dar did likewise. The box popped loose. They dragged it out and shoved it to safety a half meter away from the edge of the hole.

Breathing heavily, Everest rolled onto his back and stared up at clouds that were readying themselves for the planned rain and jellach vehicles that were zooming and twirling toward unknown destinations.

"Time to jam," Dar whispered, already on her feet and holding one end of the box. "We'll jog to the transport system."

Everest forced himself upright and grabbed the other end of the treasure. Suddenly, a shape loomed on the far edge of the circle. Flasers, had Dr. Wei regained consciousness?

"Well, look what we have here," said a voice that Everest unfortunately recognized even though he couldn't yet make out the face. When the man strode forward a few more meters, though, he was revealed.

It was Instructor Gerard, smiling as pleasantly as ever and wielding a flaser in each hand.

CHAPTER 44
To The Rescue

"What an amazingly helpful crew you've been," Instructor Gerard said, wielding his bright, charming grin. "If you all would continue to be helpful and drop your stunners, no one will get hurt."

They dropped their stunners.

Elsie had trouble reconciling his cheerful face with the two deadly flaser weapons he held. A shiver ran down her back. Could this be real? Before they'd come to the academy, nothing even remotely dangerous had ever happened to them. Things like this just didn't happen in the Second Best Planet in the Galaxy.

Taking a shaky breath, she tore her gaze from the flasers and chanced a quick glance at her brother. Was he as calm as he seemed? No, she knew Everest like she knew herself. He was terrified, too. When she shifted her gaze to Dar, she was shocked by the girl's cocky expression. She even wore a slight smile. And Vlas's half grin was firmly in place. That kid wasn't afraid of anything. Larry didn't seem frightened either. Were they just really good actors?

She straightened her shoulders and glared at the vlem instructor. She could act bravely, too. Then she saw poor Borneo. He'd already been a mess after stunning Dr. Wei; now he looked as if someone could topple him with the smallest pinkie finger poke. He was even less prepared than she was for this type of danger.

Dar spoke as if she were sitting down to tea with Gerard rather than staring at him from the wrong side of the most diabolical of weapons. "Instructor Gerard, how delightful. We are so glad you could join us." She emphasized her words carefully. "We'd love for you to set down your flasers and stay awhile." Dar and Everest still held the heavy, oversized box between them.

That was when Elsie remembered their earpatches and Lelita on the other end. They were saved!

Then she frowned.

What was she thinking? Lelita was just a kid, and not even remotely the bravest one at the academy. What could she do? No B12 had a weapon to match a state-of-the-art flaser, let alone two.

"I can't tell you how pleased I am, Shadara, to catch *you* meddling in my business. Of all the clones in this drab little hell-hole for dupes, you are the one I will derive the most pleasure from punishing. Vlas is, of course, an added bonus."

Dar widened her eyes. "Surely you don't wish us harm?"

Instructor Gerard laughed.

Elsie tried to step forward, but her legs were too shaky. Instead, she cleared her throat and said, "So, you are Mr. Kisses."

The instructor looked at her out of the corner of his eye but kept his focus on Dar. "As you see. And you, Elsie Basker, are a foolish little girl who unfortunately knows too much for her own good. You and your brother have been busy-busy since you arrived at this school. Such a shame that you didn't concentrate on less dangerous activities."

"What are you going to do with us?" Everest asked.

"Ah. I'm quite pleased with my solution for dealing with pesky children who stick their noses in where they shouldn't. I'm delighted to inform you that I'll be sending you all back in time to fend for yourselves."

"Man, don't treat us like fools," Larry suddenly shouted. "You're going to kill us. At least have the guts to admit it."

For the first time, Instructor Gerard appeared to be caught off-guard. "And who might this be? You're not one of our students."

"I'm your worst nightmare." Larry said, puffing out his chest.

Now Elsie saw that the boy *was* afraid, with his hands clenched and his cheeks flushed, but he wasn't backing down from the instructor. She wished she were that courageous.

"Shadara," Instructor Gerard said in a clipped tone, "explain."

After a pause, Dar said, "He's a clone who's been living off-world. My sponsor sent him to check out the school. It's possible he will be attending soon."

Gerard's eyes narrowed. "That's ridiculous. I would know if we had any visiting clones."

"My sponsor wanted the visit kept hush-hush. Only the director is aware of it. Lawrence is a very special clone, with quite unique powers. He's been something of a project for my sponsor. I can't tell you how unhappy the man would be if anything were to happen to the boy—quite distraught, actually." Dar contemplated her fingernails then shot Gerard another look. "You do know my sponsor, Adriatic Mink, don't you?"

The instructor turned pasty-white, then cleared his throat a couple of times. Finally, he said, "Don't worry. When I inform him of your tragic disappearance, I'll be suitably grief-stricken. I'm afraid I won't be able to let him know about Lawrence's unexpected trip, since I won't be aware of his existence. I'm sure your sponsor will connect the dots. I'm afraid his little prodigy won't be attending the academy after all." As he spoke he regained his original confidence.

"*When* exactly are you going to send us back to?" Elsie asked.

Instructor Gerard's smile widened again to pure glee. "I'm going to send you back to 2575, smack-dab in the middle of the Vlemutz Wars. It's doubtful you'll survive the last twenty-four years of mayhem and destruction, but if you do, then I'm sure you'll have a bright future in the Age of Darkness and Despair. I do wish you all the best of luck in the past. Speaking of which, shall we move from here to the History Center?"

"What about Instructor Legnarchi?" Elsie asked.

"What about him? If tonight is anything like any other night, he's snoozing in his office after having devoured a steelorq box of no-cals. If Instructor Legnarchi is anything, he's predictable."

"But aren't you partners?"

Gerard's eyes widened. "You must be joking. Me and Legnarchi? That clone mistake? You insult me."

"Are you telling us that you and Instructor Legnarchi are not and never have been conspiring together?" Dar asked slowly.

Elsie realized the question was for Lelita's benefit.

"That man couldn't break the law to save his life. Besides, he's such a suzo-shrimp. Whatever gave you the idea that I would work with him?"

"He's got a Hasty Sack toy in his office, and he's in serious debt. You both disappeared for long periods of time in the twenty-first century. Besides, he's been on each and every one of your field trips. It all added up."

"To a big fat zero."

"So," Dar said, "Legnarchi is a *good* guy?"

"I have no idea if he's a 'good guy', as you so quaintly put it, but he's nothing to me."

Dar had a faraway look in her eyes. "Yes," she said, then said "Yes," a second time. She shook herself, then commented to Gerard. "I'm just so surprised, that's all."

Luckily, the instructor was so cocky he didn't seem to realize what was going on. Maybe his nighteyes drops were wearing off.

"And I find it equally surprising that you thought I'd partner with him." Gerard motioned with his flasers. "Now, all of you turn around and start marching. It's time for a little field trip."

"What about Instructor Tchakevska?" Elsie asked, ignoring his command. "Is she your partner?"

"Oh, please, that 'rule book' wouldn't steal a clump of dirt."

"I guess that leaves Dr. Wei as your accomplice," Dar boldly said.

"You're driving me crazy with your pesky guesses. Either shut down, or I'll flaser you."

Elsie and Dar shut down, but they also exchanged significant looks. Interesting that he hadn't given them a clear answer about Dr. Wei.

"Now," he pointed to Dar and Everest, "Since you are carrying my box of goodies, you can lead the way. The rest of you follow in one slow line. If anyone so much as trips, I'll turn them into permanent specks of dust. Have I made myself clear?"

All they could do was nod and move into formation.

After a moment of silence, Dar cleared her throat. "Isn't it a waste to send us back to another time so we can't turn you in? We're just a bunch of yocto-brained kids. No one ever listens to us, anyway."

"As you've been at pains to remind me, you have a very influential sponsor who does listen to you."

"Uh, our uncle will search for us for as long as it takes," Elsie said.

Gerard shrugged. "Since there won't be any breadcrumbs for him to follow, it will be an effort in futility. Besides, I sincerely doubt he's going to be as thorough as you imagine."

Surely by now, Lelita had alerted Instructor Legnarchi to what was going on. She had to understand that was what Dar had asked her to do. Elsie thought about what happened to people who were flasered, the way they melted into nothingness. In holopictures, people shrieked in pain as they disintegrated. And there was always the bleck smell of chemicals burning.

She didn't want to die that way. But going back in time to the Vlemutz Wars was in some ways an even more horrible option. Everyone knew the Vlemutz did gruesome things to the people they enslaved.

As they walked down the path to the History Center, the clouds grew darker and thicker and more ominous. Now all of the stars were obscured, and the jellach vehicles had taken on a gray hue. As the planned rainfall closed in on them, she could smell moisture in the air.

After a deep breath, she said to the instructor, "Aren't you worried about changing history? If you send us back, we could change the past, present, and future. What we do *then* could cause you to no longer exist in the here and now."

Instructor Gerard frowned. "If you are lucky enough to survive the Vlems, you won't have any currency, any identity. You'll be nothings in the middle of the worst Dark Age in the history of dark ages. There's no way you're going to alter anything, let alone the course of history."

"Nothings have been known to make a difference."

"I'm willing to take that risk. Those Vlemutz will be wild over fresh slavery candidates. You won't stand a chance. But if you'd rather, I can kill you now."

The first drop of rain splattered on Elsie as they passed Pooker's pen. Her bobcat stood as near as she could to the dancing lights without turning them black. Instead, they were a mustard shade in warning. A low growl came from deep within Pooker's throat.

The instructor swiveled his head to look at the bobcat. For a second he took one of his flaser weapons off its human targets and settled it on Pooker. "I despise that creature," he hissed. "It scratched me that first day. I should never have suggested a way for it to stay."

"Why did you?"

"You were making such a big deal. You weren't going to stay. Having two more B12s gave me two more Hasty Sack toys. More profit for me."

Elsie's mouth dropped open. If only Pooker could get close enough to scratch him again, or better yet, bite him.

Gerard regained control over his emotions, and his lips even formed into the semblance of a smile. "I think Pooker, here, would enjoy the tail-end of the twenty-sixth century. Besides, it would be cruel to separate such a monster from its loving owner."

With one of his flasers, he motioned Elsie nearer to the cage. "Bring it out, but be careful it behaves. One wrong move and your precious bobcat turns into a pile of dust."

Despite the fear that caused her limbs to tremble and her heart to skitter and skip, Elsie's overriding emotion was anger. The only monster here was Gerard. How could she have been so swayed by an oversized smile and a bucket of surface charm? Everest hadn't trusted him from the first. She should have listened to her brother.

Her steps slow, she moved over to the pen and pressed the blue button that disengaged a portion of the dancing lights.

"Pooker, come," she said, fighting back tears. Pooker was not an "it," and Gerard would regret it if he hurt even one patch of fur on her body. Pooker remained cautiously still.

"Hurry up," said the instructor.

Straightening her spine, Elsie held out her hand. "Pooker, come," she said with more command.

Slowly, the bobcat padded forward. When she was past the dancing light perimeter, Elsie clutched at the scruff of her neck.

"Light speed, folks." Gerard's flasers encouraged the kids to pick up their pace toward the History Center.

From her left ear, Elsie heard an almost inaudible whisper. "Legnarchi's on his way." Dar had spoken so quietly that Elsie almost thought she had imagined the girl's words.

What if Legnarchi wasn't strong enough to take on Gerard? Elsie worried her lower lip as she trudged toward the looming History Center. A light sprinkle of rain had begun, but soon it would come down in a steady downpour.

When they reached the door, Instructor Gerard paused and clearly said, "Disable security." As a trusted instructor and administrator of the facility, he had access to everything.

The door erased, and they filed in.

"Instructor, may we set down the box?" Dar asked.

"Yes," answered Gerard, "but do so slowly."

"Of course." She and Everest followed Gerard's directions and lowered the chest with caution. It still thudded when it landed on the floor.

Dar flexed her back as she eased herself upright and Everest rolled his head. They hadn't complained about the heavy box, but they were sweating from the effort of carrying it all the way from the meditational circle.

328

When they turned back to Instructor Gerard, he still wore the same brilliant smile, as if he were about to give them a wonderful gift rather than near certain death.

"What's to prevent us from using the time-travel vehicle to come right back home?" Dar asked.

My genius," Gerard replied. "I've been studying time travel for quite awhile, and I have a delightful little gadget that disables the machine as soon as it lands. Basically, it erases the machine's memory. Simple, but effective."

"Uh, that is zetta smart," Elsie said, doing her best to help stall the man. "How do you know it works?"

Gerard laughed. "Let's just say that I've managed to test it a couple of times in my colorful past. So far no one's come back. I figure it either means they are lost in the past somewhere, or the system self-destructed before they could land. All the same to me." He did a quick scan of the room and settled on an ancient hover vehicle. Motioning again, he said, "All of you, to the dark gray machine—over there next to the green hoverbus. Don't look so glum. Think of your trip back in time as a lovely adventure, one that will last you for the rest of your lives. Most likely quite short lives, but lives nonetheless. I promise to remember you fondly when I'm wallowing in my newfound riches."

With a flick of her head, Dar indicated that the rest of the B12s should follow her toward the vehicle. Elsie kept her hand tight on Pooker's neck. Now what? They had to think of something fast before they were jettisoned to Vlemutz annihilation.

Just then there was the slightest swishing sound of a door erasing itself.

When Gerard yelled, Elsie swung around and saw him blasting wildly with his flaser. A ragged hole gaped next to the now open doorway. No one was visible, either in the doorway or where the flaser had struck.

"Get him!" Dar yelled, and lunged forward. She plowed into Gerard, causing him to lose balance. One of his flasers went off again, burning another hole in the wall. The other toppled to the ground, and Elsie saw Everest dive for it.

She jumped into the fray, as did her bobcat. They all piled on top of Gerard. She heard him shout in pain and hoped Pooker had gotten in a good bite.

The man was surprisingly strong. He threw off Vlas, then Elsie, who landed on her rear a few yards away. Dar still had Gerard from behind by the throat, but he had managed to regain his feet and had her wrists caught in his right hand. Pooker sunk her teeth into one of his ankles, and Gerard screamed, but he didn't let go of Dar. In blind fury, he raised the flaser he still held in his left hand and targeted Everest, who was fumbling with the second flaser.

"Noooo!" screamed Elsie, leaping forward again.

Then Instructor Legnarchi was in the doorway, wielding a stunner. Dar threw herself off Gerard, and Legnarchi blasted him.

The vlem crashed unconscious to the ground.

Dar crouched over the motionless man and with a voice devoid of emotion, said, "I'd wager that your future will be quite different from what you've imagined. But we do promise to think of you as you wallow in your cyborg prison."

CHAPTER 45
Confessions

As the B12s raised their voices in spontaneous cheers, Everest heard Dar urge Larry to hide. Quick as a flaser beam, Larry dived inside an ancient carriage. Despite his relief at having been saved, Everest felt a spurt of frustration that he hadn't thought to warn Larry first. It zetta irked him that Dar was always one step ahead.

Everything happened in a blur. Instructor Legnarchi moved further into the room with Lelita. People were hugging, crying, laughing. Vlas slapped Everest hard on the back on his way to envelope Borneo in a bear hug.

It was as if Everest watched the scene from a distance, the beat of his heart slowly steadying. He no longer believed his life was threatened, but by the Light, it had been close. Elsie leapt at him and clutched him around the neck, and he scowled at her excessive display. She knew better than to hug him—bleck—but he guessed he'd better cut her some slack. After all, she had tried to save his life. As quickly as he could, he untangled himself from his sister's embrace.

He *was* happy, but it wasn't in him to show his emotions. Dar stood back as well, watching rather than participating in the celebration. She caught his glance and after a long look, slowly grinned. It was the first genuine smile he'd ever received from her.

Before he did anything else, Legnarchi crouched down next to Gerard and confiscated and pocketed the two flaser weapons. With a long, drawn-out sigh, he turned to face his audience. He seemed different from the warm and jovial Instructor Legnarchi with whom they were familiar. Under these dangerous and unusual circumstances, Legnarchi was suddenly self-assured, as if he'd dealt with such things before.

"You must have quite a story to tell," Legnarchi said, looking to Dar as the logical spokesperson. "You'd better start at the beginning, so I can figure out how much damage control is required."

"Who are you?" Everest asked, surprising even himself by the question.

Legnarchi laughed. "Just a man with a job to do, not unlike the instructor you thought me to be."

"If you're on our side, why did you threaten me earlier tonight?" Everest persisted, stepping forward, his eyes narrowed.

A small smile played at Legnarchi's lips. "I was trying to *warn* you, to scare you, if necessary, into desisting in your amateur meddling. I knew, you see, that you were the one who had searched my room earlier. But worse, I knew you had searched Instructor Gerard's room. Frankly, I was terrified for you."

"How could you know?"

"Simple, really. I, myself, was monitoring Gerard's office, and I watched a replay of your little break-in not ten minutes before you arrived at my chamber to ask me something you never got around to asking."

"Oh." Everest had a sinking feeling deep in his gut. What was Legnarchi going to do to him for his crime? Would he guess that Everest was responsible for Tchakevska's broken collectibles? Would he tell her?

"Can we sit down?" Dar asked, tapping her foot impatiently.

Legnarchi's smile widened. "Of course." He leaned his large frame against the nearest vehicle and motioned them to join him on the bench opposite.

Everest moved to the bench, his legs as wobbly as if he'd just played ten straight hours of skyball.

Once she took a seat, Dar leaned her elbows on her knees and proceeded to feed Legnarchi a tale that left out much of their own somewhat illegal activities. She started with their timed field trip then gave a fictional account of how they had come to overhear Gerard in the building that night. Instead of explaining about their unauthorized return to 2002, she told him that Elsie had lost her necklace in the dressing room. Because the pendant was so important to Elsie, Dar had agreed to bring her down that evening against school rules. She never explained why they hadn't asked for an instructor's help, nor did she explain how they had circumvented the academy's extensive security. She said nothing about Larry. She told Legnarchi about the research that morning that had provided the Hasty Sacks clue, and she explained what had led them to believe that Legnarchi was the smuggler, rather than Gerard.

At that, the man's laughter boomed out infectiously, and they all joined in, relief their predominant emotion.

"That Hasty Sack toy was a sample I took so I would know what to look for. I've been working with the cyborg police for months to capture this particular ring of smugglers."

"But what about all that VC you owe?" Elsie blurted out. Too late, she realized it was none of their business if he was in debt. She felt her face heat up.

Fortunately, he didn't seem offended by her question. "Just part of my cover," he said, still smiling. "There was some idea of me infiltrating the operation. Giving me a reason to need VC fast seemed like a good idea at the time. But you all brought things to a head much quicker than we could ever have anticipated."

A noise behind him brought the kids' attention to the door just as a powerful cyborg officer of law strode in.

"Wow!" Elsie breathed, temporarily forgetting her embarrassment as well as the many rules and laws they had broken.

Everest didn't blame her. Cyborg police were legendary—as revered as sports figures. To become one, you had to be the top in everything.

The woman was amazing, with her altered arms and legs and half of her brain revealed as an extremely sophisticated processor. She had no hair on her head, and with her height and width, she made them look puny.

She nodded to the children. "Cyborg Officer Lilituck at your service." She gave Gerard, who was still out cold, a cursory glance, then crossed over to the steelorq box. With a flick of her wrist, she popped it open despite its sturdy lock. Inside were neat rows of plastic toys in sealed plastic bags. "Excellent." She snapped the box shut and picked it up before addressing the B12s. She made the box seem as light as a feather, but Everest knew only too well how heavy it was.

"You found this?" she asked.

"Yes, officer," Dar responded.

"And this vlem," she pointed to Gerard, "admitted that it was his?"

"Yes, I recorded our conversation."

Gerard moaned and shifted slightly, his first movement since being stunned.

Lilituck shot Dar and then the rest of the group a look of approval. "Well done."

She then focused on Legnarchi. "Did you manage to link him to our other vlem friend?"

"Unfortunately, things came to a head before we could make that connection," Legnarchi admitted.

Everest wondered if they were talking about Dr. Wei or someone else entirely. He didn't much like the idea of a criminal still lurking at the academy.

"Pity." The cyborg's expression went from approval to disapproval in a blink of an eye—not that cyborgs ever actually blinked. "Our leader won't be pleased."

"I believe he will agree with my decision to put these children's lives first."

The cyborg lifted one shoulder slightly. "Perhaps. There's also a chance we can make this little birdy sing." With her free hand, she slung the still unconscious Gerard over her shoulder. Again, she made the physical exertion appear effortless. "I'll be back tomorrow to discuss this with Director Lester-Hauffer. Now that your cover is blown, you'll have to be reassigned."

"No doubt." Instructor Legnarchi looked sad at the thought. "I'll miss the teaching."

Everest felt a wave of sadness himself. Two days at the academy was hardly enough time to know someone, but Legnarchi was decent.

More noise ensued as the door erased to reveal Dr. Wei. "What in blazes is going on? Someone had the audacity to stun me, and that dastard is going to pay."

Legnarchi stepped forward. "I'm afraid we have a criminal in our midst. Instructor Gerard must have stunned you before threatening these poor children with death *and* with time travel to the Vlemutz time period. His actions are unconscionable."

Dr. Wei took in the cyborg officer, the inert Gerard, and the kids. His mouth twisted so that Everest had to wonder if it hurt.

335

"The man's a scoundrel."

Was Wei an amazing actor, or sincerely surprised by Instructor Gerard's criminal activities? Everest wasn't about to trust the doctor. Judging from the look Elsie tossed him, she felt the same way.

"Well," Dr. Wei said. "Since it appears you have everything under control, I'll go nurse my sore head." The man stomped off.

Officer Lilituck spoke to the ceiling. "Officer Gelarg, two to transport." She and Gerard shimmered slightly, then winked away.

Instructor Legnarchi took one long slow look at each of the children in the room, then said to no one in particular. "Perhaps you could tell your friend it's safe to come out now. His name is Larry?"

Six mouths hung open as they all stared at Legnarchi with various degrees of shock and horror.

The instructor smiled in a fashion that was equal parts calming and mischievous. "Remember, I saw Everest and Larry break into Gerard's office, and I'm not so blind that I can't see when someone dives into a carriage in front of me. I realize you gave me the abbreviated story of your adventures over the last couple of days." He shrugged. "You have your secrets, and I have mine. Since it appears I'm no longer going to be teaching at this facility, it is not my duty to take you to task. I'll leave you to sort out your stories, so that by tomorrow you've developed some consistency." He gave them all a slight bow and a wink. "It's been a very real pleasure."

With that, he pushed off from the vehicle he was leaning against, walked up to the door, watched it dissolve, and then strode into the rainy night.

CHAPTER 46
Cleaning Up Loose Ends

Since the following morning was Saturday, no one had to rise early for classes. This was a good thing, because none of the B12s who had participated in the adventures the night before were in any shape to crawl out of bed any time soon. They had stayed up late into the night talking over what had happened and agreeing on the story they would tell the director and the cyborg officer when they were questioned later today.

Despite her brush with danger and the threat of death, Elsie felt pretty content at the moment. Dar had decided that given everything else that had gone on, Elsie might as well have Pooker in her room. She had slept on her back with her bobcat's head on her belly while the jellach mattress gave her a very slow, relaxing massage. Pooker's familiar smell and stiff but cuddly fur made Elsie happy, and a flower garden scent added to her contentment. With her eyes closed, she let her thoughts drift.

In the light of day, it was hard to believe that all of last night's events had happened. They'd been threatened with banishment to the worst time in Earth's history, and they'd come close to being flasered to death. With their help, a dangerous criminal had been captured. They'd met a real cyborg officer, and they'd discovered an undercover agent in their midst.

How had so much happened in such a short amount of time? It felt as if she and her brother had lived at the academy for a lifetime, yet it was barely three days.

She squinted open her eyes. Dar's bed was empty, with the mlenler blanket tidily hidden. Elsie shot up to a sitting position and found Melista lounging in Dar's desk chair, her golden-eyed gaze intent.

"As the sun rises, so does Elsinor." Melista's voice was beautifully melodic. "How delightful that you have awakened."

"Where's Dar?"

"The dear girl was hungry, so she went in search of breakfast. She requested that I hang around so that you would not be concerned about her whereabouts."

"Thank you, Melista."

Because Dar wasn't there and avatars weren't capable of physical actions, Elsie couldn't return Pooker. Instead, she had a quick shower. When she returned to the dorm room, she found Dar jacked into her unregistered holoputer.

She had brought back a fruicey for Elsie.

After a few minutes, Dar halted the neuro activity, raised her head and smiled. "Ready to rearrange some bobcat butt?"

"Yeah." Elsie grinned back.

When Elsie returned from her little trip, she sucked on her playful straw and watched Dar, who was back on the holoputer. Finally, she had to ask, "What are you doing?"

At first it appeared that Dar hadn't heard her. She had to be deep in her holoputer zone. Then she lifted her head. "Trying to solve one last problem." She absently rubbed her ear.

"And that would be?"

"Finding some information in the GKB and feeding it some new data."

Elsie gasped. "You can't feed information into the GKB."

Dar refocused on her session and her neuro commands. "Sure I can," she mumbled. Then she lifted her head, her grin still in place. "I authorized myself."

Elsie groaned. "You are so in trouble."

"Only if I get caught. Anyway, this should do it." Her expression went blank, then Elsie and the room had her full attention, and it was apparent that she had jacked out of the session.

Dar rubbed her hands together. "Come on, we've got work to do."

Were their adventures ever going to end? Elsie had to run to keep up with Dar as she strode down the hallway toward the boys' dormitory.

The girl was on a mission.

It was no surprise when they landed outside of Everest's room, but Elsie still didn't know what Dar was up to. They announced themselves, and the door dissolved. Larry was involved in another crazy hologame, and Everest was shooting a skyball from his bed, making the lights flash and whistles toot. Vlas was already there mucking around with a portable virtual entertainment device.

"Okay, guys. There's one more thing we have to do."

"Haven't we done enough?" Everest asked.

Dar used her head to point to Larry. "We need to make him real in 3002."

Larry's resolution not to say bad words went by the wayside with that news, but it was obvious he was really happy. Elsie found that very confusing.

"Don't make me regret this," Dar said sternly, though her eyes sparkled with excitement.

"What about the rules?" Elsie asked. "What if we change history by doing this?"

"I did some extensive searching and couldn't find any mention of Larry Knight after April of 2002."

Larry looked glum. "I really hate to admit this, but back then, we didn't have the kind of galactic everything-you-ever-wanted-to-know-about-anything-or-everyone databases you have. There wouldn't be any mention of me whether I was there or not. I wasn't even attending school."

"I know, but get this: in May of 2002 a periodical called *The American Enquirer* ran a story that interviewed a guy named Gary Hefferson. This man swears that one Lawrence Tobias Knight was abducted by aliens in April. His story was corroborated by a security guard named Jack Gifford, who swears he was attacked by aliens who threatened him with laser guns and other even more horrific weapons of mass destruction."

"Deng, talk about blatant over-exaggeration!" Vlas inserted.

"Hey, Gary owned the arcade," Larry said. "He was the one who used to let me sleep there."

"And he knew you never came back. If we send you back now, we could screw up the previous millennium."

They all burst into laughter.

"Plus, I checked your aura from Folgar's aurascan against the database, and there were no matches. That means you haven't been reincarnated during the last thousand years, either."

"You mean we get to keep him?" Vlas asked with exaggerated excitement. "Zeller! I've always wanted a pet."

"Man," Larry said, his voice filled with disgust, "you better knock it off."

"Tsk, tsk, children. No time for squabbles. We have to sneak Larry out to the main gates, so he can arrive at eleven sharp. I sent a message to Director Lester-Hauffer letting him know about the imminent arrival of a new student."

"But Dar," Elsie said, "Why would my uncle believe he's legitimate?"

"I sent him the message from my sponsor, Adriatic Mink. No one questions him."

"Won't your sponsor figure it out?"

Dar shrugged. "He's a busy guy. He's never caught me using his identity before." She turned to Everest. "Aren't we lucky there's an extra bed just waiting to be filled in your room?"

Everest groaned. "Do I have to?"

"Man, this is going to be so *zeller*," Larry said, his expression suspiciously bland.

"Wow, Larry," Dar responded with a grin, "you're even beginning to sound like us."

"Hey, I'm one killer clone, aren't I?"

"Yes, *my man*, you are."

This time their plan went almost too smoothly. Once they rounded up Borneo and Lelita, they walked downstairs as a tight unit with Larry in the middle of the crowd. Since Larry was the shortest of the bunch—besides Lelita—they made it outside without drawing undue attention.

Pausing now and again and making a show of enjoying the garden, they strolled as a unit casually down the path that led to the front entrance.

During one of these moments while they all stared at a bobbing and twirling Lexlorio Dancer that was a particularly bright shade of blue, Dar quietly said, "Larry, you and I are going to walk straight up to the gate. Very confidently, you understand? When we get there, I'll use the matter-mover to make you an opening. Your job is to get outside as quickly as you can. Once you're there, you'll find a spot to hide, then wait till five minutes before eleven to introduce yourself at the gate. There will be a small communication unit to the far right of the entrance." She pulled a hot pink dot off her wrist and placed it on Larry's.

"This will let you know when it is five minutes to eleven. I've already set it."

Larry made a face. "Does it have to be hot pink?"

Dar made a face back. "Dot-clock, turn yourself—" she looked questioningly at Larry.

"Green," he responded.

"Dot-clock, turn yourself green."

The dot shifted through a rainbow of colors, first pink then red then orange and yellow, until it finally reached a rich green.

"Excellent," said Larry. He paused then asked, "Exactly how does this thing work?" He shook his wrist and the dot clung.

With a shrug, Dar said, "When it's five minutes to eleven, it'll turn hot then cold then hot then cold till you notice."

"How do I stop it?"

"Just tell it to stop. Make sure you call it by name. You know, 'dot-clock.'"

"Does it really tell time?" Larry couldn't take his eyes off the bright little dot.

"Sure—just ask it."

"Dot-clock, what time is it?"

The dot wiggled and stretched then popped till suddenly it had written out the time in fine lines—ten-forty-five.

"Dot-clock, be a dot," Dar commanded, and the time popped back to a green dot. "Larry, you better get moving. The director's expecting you, so he'll approve your entry."

"Piece of cake."

Elsie thought Larry looked a little nervous.

Dar shoved a JED at him. "Read this, it's got your bio on it. You come from a very impressive gene pool."

"Wicked zeller." He grinned.

"But you haven't quite reached your genius potential."

"Say what?"

"Look, Larry, it's going to take a lot of tutoring on our part to keep you from flunking out of the B12 program. So act humble for once in your life. This is no time to be displaying an attitude."

Getting Larry outside the academy compound was as easy as Dar had made it out to be. When they arrived at the edge of the facility, Dar and Larry split off from the group and casually sauntered toward the mirrored gates. As they walked off, Dar hissed to the rest of them to pretend they were just hanging together.

At the gate, Dar quickly put the matter-mover to work. Elsie was a little worried that the gate might be too thick, but within a few seconds, there was an opening. Dar gave them a thumbs-up as Larry dived through. She closed up the temporary hole, then with a quick look around, returned to the gang.

"That should do it. It won't be too long before we have a new clone on campus." She wiped her hands with satisfaction and pivoted around to lead them back to the main building.

"You are so busted," came a voice from the bushes to their left. A smirk pasted on his face, Kindu stepped into their path.

CHAPTER 47
A New Clone on Campus

Her lip curled, Dar said coldly, "I don't know what you're talking about."

Today Kindu wore what Elsie immediately recognized as binoc-glasses. It wasn't as if people wore corrective lenses in the thirty-first century.

"I saw that kid you just smuggled out of here." He tapped his lens. "I saw everything. I'm sure Director Lester-Hauffer will be quite interested in the fact that you were harboring a strange boy on campus. Where'd he come from? Where's he going?"

Dar's eyes shined with innocence. "I'm sorry, Kindu, but there must be something wrong with your magnifier." She spread her arms wide. "As you can see, there's no one here but us clones and a couple of ute-babies."

"*Shadara*, you won't get away with whatever you're up to. This time, I've caught you red-handed."

Dar considered the other members of her team. "Has anyone the slightest idea what being 'caught red-handed' means? I've never seen my hands go even the slightest shade of pink."

"Funny, *Shadara*. You won't be such an allen when you're facing the director—or worse, Instructor Sura."

Elsie was amazed that Dar was letting Kindu get away with calling her Shadara. She stepped forward. "Why don't you just leave Dar alone?"

"Ooh, Dar," He said in a high voice, wiggling his fingers. "The itty-bitty ute-baby's sticking up for you again." He sneered and let his voice return to normal. "You sure have sunk low."

"No one sticks up for me but *me*," Dar said through clenched teeth as she shot Elsie a furious look.

Elsie frowned back. What was her problem? The girl should be grateful for her support. She caught her brother rolling his eyes and felt marginally better. At least he was on her side.

Vlas stepped forward. "Go jump into a black hole, Kindu."

"I don't think so, clone-reject. I'll just hang out here to see if your little friend decides to show his ugly face again. I'm not sure who he is or why he was here, but don't worry, I'll figure it out."

"Sure you'll figure it out," Vlas muttered, "when the moon turns purple."

A slight noise from behind warned them that someone had entered the property. They all swung around. The gate had temporarily disappeared to reveal Larry on the other side, a big grin on his face.

He wasn't alone. Next to him stood a tall, slim man dressed in black. His skin was almost as dark as Larry's, and his short, trim hair pure white. He was quite handsome with a strong face. It was impossible to determine his age.

Who was he? Elsie wondered. He chatted easily with Larry, one hand resting on the boy's shoulder. He was the sort of person who gave his full attention to whoever he was speaking to. Elsie looked to Dar for guidance.

She'd never seen the girl show such honest shock. Dar's mouth gaped, and her green eyes were huge. She looked younger than Elsie had ever seen her look. For the first time since she had met Dar, the girl looked every bit her twelve years of age.

Then the man glanced their way, and his eyes settled on Dar. His smile broadened, exuding warmth and trustworthiness.

"Dar!" He strode forward with Larry practically skipping at his side.

"Sir," Dar croaked.

"Who is he?" Elsie hissed.

The man held out his hand as he reached Dar, and she shakily placed hers in his. His quick glance encompassed them all, and Elsie had a strange feeling that those extraordinarily bright blue eyes missed nothing. She sensed that he knew each and every one of their identities. And when his eyes focused on Kindu, they froze to ice. The boy took a faltering step backward under the man's penetrating gaze.

"You must be Kindu," he said, as if the boy were even less significant than a suzo-shrimp.

"Yeah, that's right." Regaining a portion of his bravado, Kindu planted his legs and crossed his arms.

After one long look, the man in black turned away and completely ignored the B14.

"Come now, Dar, you don't look that pleased to see me, and yet, I've brought you a delightful present." He motioned to Larry at his side. "See, I've brought you another friend, a clone who has never been to a traditional school before. You'll have to take him under your wing, maybe offer him some private tutoring."

Dar circled the elegant man slowly. "You brought this *clone* to enter him into the academy?"

He arched one brow and without blinking said, "Yes, I did."

Now Elsie gaped. Who was this man? And what was he up to? Vlas, Lelita and Borneo were all staring with matching looks of horror, and Everest's confusion was at least as evident as hers.

"Dar?" she said tentatively. As if coming out of a dream, Dar started, then swung to her.

"I don't know where my manners are." She faced her friends and her enemy. "Everyone, this is Adriatic Mink, my sponsor."

"Your sponsor?" Elsie and Everest responded at the exact same time, only Elsie's voice squeaked and Everest's croaked.

"Yes," Dar said slowly, "And—he's—brought—this—boy—to—live—at—the—academy."

"That's a lie!" Kindu yelled. "I saw that kid leave this property only a few minutes ago."

"You must be mistaken," Adriatic responded easily, though his eyes were cool.

"I saw him."

"Young man, do you question my word?"

Kindu suddenly looked unsure. Adriatic Mink was a very imposing figure. "I—that is—I mean to say—"

"You mean to say what?"

"I—ah—nothing." Kindu stepped backward. "I'll be going now."

"That would be wise," Adriatic advised.

Kindu took off at a run, no longer a self-assured fourteen-year-old who had made it his mission to harass Dar whenever possible, but rather a scared and troubled child.

Once he was out of earshot, Dar swung back to her sponsor. "How did you find out?"

He made tsking noises and shook his head. "For shame, Dar. You left a few of your GKB back doors wide open. Don't get me wrong, you did magnificently, but we're going to have to work on you covering your trail better in the future. Fortunately for you, I cleaned up after you."

"I don't understand," Dar said. "You're not angry?"

347

"Puzzled, perhaps, by what I've managed to piece together of the recent rather unusual series of events, but not angry. I anxiously await your story, but we can postpone that until after Mr. Knight here becomes a legitimate member of the academy."

"You don't think we're mucking up history, do you?" When had Dar ever sounded this uncertain?

"I admit that did cross my mind, so I did some of my own checking. It seems that Mr. Knight did indeed disappear in the twenty-first century, and his body was never discovered. I take it you also found out that his aura has never been reincarnated in all the intervening years. I think it is safe to assume that he is meant to stay in this time period."

Adriatic tipped his head in Larry's direction. "Are you ready to introduce yourself to the director?"

"Man, I am so ready."

"Excellent."

After that, everything was easy. When Director Lester-Hauffer and his staff met with Adriatic Mink and Larry, the director fawned all over Adriatic, as did most people. They quickly came to an agreement over Larry, and it was the director who suggested he join Everest, his own nephew, as roommate. At least, that was how Larry described the meeting later that day.

Larry had a great deal of fun describing the heated conversation between Adriatic Mink and Dr. Wei. The doctor had been beside himself because he had never heard of Larry, and he was, by his own account, the foremost expert on clones in the galaxy.

"It was so cool," Larry told them later. "Adriatic Mink made it sound all hush-hush and top secret. Man, you would have loved it. Dr. Wei was one annoyed dude."

Larry had also made a point of telling Dar about Sura slobbering all over Mink. "She made goo-goo eyes at him."

"You're making me sick."

"Telling you straight, that lady was all over him."

"Bleck!" they all cried in unison, then burst into laughter.

They never did hear the details of what passed between Officer Lilituck and Director Lester-Hauffer, but shortly thereafter, the Director held an impromptu holo-assembly so his hologram could express great sadness that Instructor Gerard would no longer be with them. Instructor Sura was assigned all of his duties along with her current load. For a woman who didn't seem to know how to smile, she had a very pleased expression on her face as she stood to the Director's right. Lester-Hauffer also indicated that Instructor Legnarchi would be resigning at the end of the term.

As Elsie and Everest left the assembly, Elsie felt a bit of a letdown. So much had happened in such a short time, and now they were back to normal with no more adventures. She should be feeling relieved—she'd been terrified for her life for most of the last three days—but instead, for some crazy reason, she felt a little sad. With all the activity, she'd had little time to be homesick, but now she wanted her parents back...and her home...and Zulu. She sighed. Thank the Light it was the weekend, so she could holocomm with Zulu. She wished she could tell her everything, but that was impossible. Besides, Zulu would never believe her.

"I'm going to visit Pooker," she told her brother.

He shrugged. Elsie could tell he felt as weird as she did.

"Okay," he said. They stopped in the corridor, and he looked around blankly. "I wonder where the skyball courts are." He gave her a half grin. "You'd think I'd know by now."

"Go ask someone. Maybe I'll catch you later on the courts."

"Zeller."

They parted, and Elsie weaved through crowds of students until she found her way outside. Scuffing her skyboots as she walked on the jewel-toned gravel, she made her way down the path to Pooker's pen.

As she veered to the left, her bobcat's cage came into view, and there, leaning against the rosewillow tree that faced Pooker's cage, was Dar. The girl stared at Pooker who basked in the sun and washed her back. Dar had changed into blue-silver sports gear, and as usual had her hair in a tight pony-tail and shoved up under her favorite cap.

"Hey," Elsie said.

"Hey." Dar glanced over briefly, then looked up at the perfect blue sky. "Do you ever wonder if we miss something by not having natural weather?"

Elsie shrugged. Having reached Dar's side, she joined her in contemplating the blue expanse, marred only by the constant ebb and flow of the quiet hover vehicles that bumped, twirled, stretched, and sped past. "I've never thought about it. Until I went on the timed field trip, I never really got it that weather happened differently in the past."

"I've heard that spring showers are amazing. The sun shines through the clouds and makes the moisture-drenched flowers sparkle. Sometimes, the rain is so light, it just mists you. It's supposed to smell wonderful. And what about rainbows? I've heard there's nothing more beautiful than a double rainbow."

It was weird having Dar speak so candidly.

Elsie searched the sky. "It would have been pretty blecky to have to do any real work in a downpour."

"Yeah, maybe." Dar laughed.

Elsie grinned. "I went to the mountains once for a ski trip, and they scheduled a planned snowfall during the day so we could play in the snow. It was great."

"I've never been anywhere but here." Dar grimaced slightly. "Unless you count my trips back in time."

Once again, Elsie was struck by how odd it must be to be a clone with no family—how lonely. And then she remembered Dar's role with the smaller kids on campus. Was she in some strange way their surrogate mother? Guilt reared its ugly head. She still owed the girl an apology.

"Uh, Dar," she shifted her weight from one foot to the other, "I've got something I have to tell you—confess, really."

Dar's eyes were as green as street moss, and they were unwavering. Elsie, on the other hand, wanted to look anywhere but at Dar.

"This is kind of difficult."

"Come on, Elsie, spill. I don't have all day." Dar pushed a drape of leaves away from her face and straightened so that she no longer leaned against the tree. Crossing her arms and raising an eyebrow, she waited for Elsie to continue. When Elsie still didn't say anything, Dar scowled intimidatingly, a more typical expression for her. "Deng, Elsie, just say it. You'll feel better once you have."

To hide the fact that her hands shook, Elsie clasped them tight. She took a deep breath. "I followed you last night when you went to that cottage."

Dar stiffened.

"I'm sorry," Elsie said quickly. "If I had known what you were doing, I never would have followed, but you were always late, and I didn't know why, and it seemed zetta suspicious." Deng, she was babbling like a total yocto-brain.

If only Dar would say something—anything.

Dar just stared, her expression growing grimmer by the second.

"I'm really sorry. It's not like I'm going to tell anyone. I promise."

At that Dar swung away so that her back was to Elsie. "Keep your aura on, ute-baby," she finally said. "It's no big deal."

But it was a big deal. Elsie felt as if she had ruined something precious. For a moment there, Dar had acted like a friend, had even shared her more personal thoughts. Now she might as well be living on another planet.

Then Dar turned back to Elsie with a smile firmly in place. "It's just a job. For a twelve-year-old, I make pretty good VC. Someday, I'll have enough to leave this dupe-dive."

For once, Elsie bit her tongue and stopped herself from more babbling. It wasn't a good idea to point out that what she'd witnessed had been much more than just a simple job. Instead, she changed the subject. "Why doesn't your sponsor ever take you on trips?"

"Adriatic Mink?" Dar laughed. "He's probably the most powerful man in our galaxy. He has no time for vacations with a pathetic dupe of a brainless fluff-girl." Her eyes flashed. "He's my sponsor, not my dad." She kicked at the ground. "Well, I've got things to do. I still have a research paper on Hasty Hawley's to finish." With a careless wave, she headed toward the compound. "See you later." She spoke brightly, as if she hadn't a care in the world.

Elsie felt terrible. More than anything, she wanted to stop Dar from being so down on herself, and on Shadara.

A heaviness weighed on her. Maybe she should have kept quiet. Had it really been necessary to make the big confession? She was such a blabbermouth. If only she were more like her brother. Why was it that he hardly talked at all and she never could shut down?

Dar suddenly stopped and swung back around. "Hey, Basker! With everything that's been happening, I forgot to remind you of something."

"What?" Elsie asked nervously.

"You still owe me for helping you with Pooker—not to mention all the other ways I've managed to save your sorry rear-end."

Elsie had to grin. It wasn't in Dar's nature to let her off the hook and Elsie was beginning to think that she wouldn't have it any other way. "Yeah, I owe you, and I'll pay up. Baskers always pay their debts." She'd heard her dad say that maybe a million times.

"You better believe you will."

CHAPTER 48
A Special Transmission

As Elsie went off to visit Pooker, Everest turned in the opposite direction to grab his favorite skyball, search out the skyball facility, and play until he was so wiped out he couldn't play anymore.

"Everest!"

His heart jumped and his body froze. It was Instructor Tchakevska.

He turned. "Hi."

"Good day to you." She was very imposing, with her impressive height and thin muscular build. "May I have a word with you in my office?"

He nodded, but his brain had gone fuzzy, and he couldn't even feel his tongue in his mouth.

"Come along," she said as she swept past him. As tall as he was for his age, he still had to jog to keep up.

When they reached her office, the door sensed her and rearranged its molecules to allow their entry. Everest hovered in the doorway, terrified to enter. What if he knocked over another one of her precious objects?

"Gingon, do join us," she called out.

Everest flinched as the monster he had encountered the day before revealed himself. Hunched over because the ceiling was too low for his impressive height, the giant stared at Everest with beady eyes. Each of his jagged dirty yellow teeth showed in a frightful grimace.

"Mr. Basker, meet Gingon, my office avatar. Gingon, this is Everest Basker, a new student at our academy."

Everest managed a half-hearted wave. Gingon continued to stare, but now he licked his lips as if he were hungry.

"Everest," said Instructor Tchakevska, "my giant has told me the most amazing tale."

"He has?"

"Yes, he has." She waved Everest inside. "Please sit down."

"I—" He searched the room for a safe spot, but everywhere he looked were those deng breakable objects. "I'd rather stand."

"Very well." She picked up a small jewel-encrusted pill box, studied it, then carefully replaced it on the table. "You may be aware that a couple of hoodlums broke into my office yesterday and demolished a number of my treasures." She paused again, but if his life had depended on it, he couldn't have uttered a single word. "My monster tells me you were one of the culprits."

Everest shook his head, or he tried to. In fact, he couldn't move a muscle. He fought to speak but nothing came out of his mouth. His body was frozen to the spot, incapable of any response to her accusation. After everything else they had gone through, was he going to be thrown out of the academy for this? What if the giant identified Larry? How would they explain his presence a full day ahead of his introduction to the director of the school? Flasers, they were sunk.

The instructor continued to hold his gaze, her expression pinched and frowning.

Everest tried to open his mouth again, but it still didn't follow his mental direction.

Then amazingly, impossibly, Tchakevska smiled. "I told Gingon that was a load of cooligrar dung."

Everest finally got enough use of his mouth for it to hang open.

"As if one of the director's own relatives would be party to such behavior! After learning about Instructor Gerard's shenanigans, it is my opinion that the person who messed up my office is none other than Gerard himself. I would not put it past him to have concocted some diabolical way to convince Gingon that a student—namely you—was involved." She crossed her arms and became quite stern again. "It's appalling that he tried to pin his heinous crime on you. Be that as it may, I expect you to hold your tongue on the matter. Instructor Gerard being a crook is a strict secret."

As if rumors hadn't already flown around the academy.

Everest nodded anyway. The last thing he wanted to do was to talk about any of the recent happenings.

Then the weirdest thing happened. Tchakevska grinned again as if she shared a joke with him, and even more alien, she burst into laughter. "You may go. Gingon, please treat Everest as a friend in the future. He is not the person you seek."

Gingon grunted, then bared his teeth, only this time it was in the semblance of a smile.

Mumbling 'goodbye,' Everest dashed out of the room. He pelted for the nanovator, sure that Instructor Tchakevska would change her mind.

As he waited for the nanovator to return from a trip up the tower, he contemplated what had just happened. It sure was odd the way Tchakevska had cornered him to tell him he *wasn't* the culprit. Why had she taken such pains to tell him she had decided to blame the whole thing on Gerard?

She had to know Everest was the person who had messed up her room, but for some reason she had let him off the hook.

It was so confusing. She was so confusing. Maybe she was more all right than he realized. Unless this was some kind of elaborate trick. It was too weird. He'd probably never figure it out.

The door to the nanovator dissolved, and he stepped over the threshold.

"Everest!"

Flasers, what now? He swung around, sticking his hand out to keep the nanovator door from going solid. One of his uncle's holograms rushed toward him.

"Yes?"

Because other students were pushing and shoving their way onto the nanovator, he stepped off and met the hologram in the corridor.

"Your uncle would like to speak to you," it said. "Your sister, too. FLH2 is tracking her down."

His hands jammed into his pockets, Everest contemplated the far wall, where the color mural had just turned neon yellow. In the twenty-first century, yellow represented caution. It seemed like an appropriate color under the circumstances. At the rate things were going, he'd never get around to playing skyball. "Okay," he finally said, and fell in behind FLH1 as the hologram moved in the direction of the director's office.

Not only was his uncle present, but Instructor Sura was there too. She had pasted a jovial expression on her face, but it made her look as if she were about to be sick.

Elsie was already there, and she didn't look good. He tried to make eye contact. What was the matter?

"Sit, sit," Uncle Fredrick said jovially. As usual, he smelled like rotten vegetables, and even though he smiled, his nose remained pinched, probably because he couldn't stand his own body odor. "I have something for you."

"You do?" they asked in unison as they plopped down and nervously waited for their uncle to continue.

"Yes." He held out a thin jellach journal. "From your parents—a transmission to the school's inter-galactic account. Unfortunately, it's too expensive to allow students to receive inter-galactic transmissions directly."

Everest nearly jumped out of his seat to grab the journal. He couldn't believe how desperate he was for that transmission. Their parents had only been gone from their lives for three days, but so much had happened, it might as well have been three lifetimes.

He stretched out his hand, but at the last minute Uncle Fredrick raised the journal just out of reach. "Strangely, the transmission doesn't indicate its place of origin. Did your parents tell you their final destination?"

That was when Elsie tried to grab the transmission, but their uncle just moved it higher. "Maybe their message tells us."

Their uncle cleared his throat. "I'm afraid it does not."

Instructor Sura quickly added, "That is, we doubt it does because your parents were quite secretive about where they were going."

Everest couldn't believe it. Both Uncle Fredrick and Instructor Sura had read their private message? He could tell Elsie was angry too. Her eyes were on fire, and her arms were crossed.

"We would appreciate it," she said, "if you would give us our comm. Now."

If anything, their uncle managed to pinch his nose even tighter. "Of course." He bypassed Elsie who stood in front of

Everest. "If you'll hold out your JED." In a heartbeat, the transfer was made.

Everest grabbed Elsie's arm to keep her from doing or saying something she might regret. Her face was bright red. If he knew his sister, she was really close to laying into their uncle and his assistant.

With Elsie fuming the whole way, they returned to the B12 recreation room and collapsed on a nanofiber couch in the corner. The room was deserted. Other B12s were probably using the school holoputers or taking advantage of their free day by playing skyball, as Everest had been trying to do all afternoon.

To make up for their uncle's rudeness, he handed the JED to Elsie, who quickly scanned it.

"Read it out loud," he said, then leaned his head back and closed his eyes.

Elsie cleared her throat. "Dear Elsie and Everest: We hope this message finds you happy and making friends at the academy. We know we've asked a lot from you. You cannot imagine what a relief it is for us to have left you in such a safe environment."

Despite their sour moods, they both snorted with laughter. Their mom would fall into a black hole if she knew the truth.

Once Elsie could contain her laughter, she continued reading. "Conditions here are primitive, but we are thrilled to be realizing a life-long dream with our research. We are ever mindful of how important our study is to humankind. We wish we could speak more plainly about what we are trying to accomplish. Please believe that we would never have left you if it hadn't been of vital importance. We live in an age of peace, but there are always threats to that serenity. Therefore, it must never be taken for granted. We must all use the gifts we were given for Earth's good. Someday, perhaps in some very small way through our research, Earth may attain status as the best planet in the *Universe*."

Elsie stopped reading for a second and absently rubbed the charm that was once again safely around her neck.

Everest could feel his matching charm warm against his chest. He still hated being forced to wear jewelry.

"Please let us know all about the excitement of new friends and new studies. It is our very dear hope that you will be able to reassure us with tales of the ordinary. Enjoy being children as long as you can and send us the details of your lives to ease our homesickness for you. Your uncle will transmit your messages to us. Stay out of trouble. Love, Mom and Dad."

Elsie and Everest looked at each other.

Finally Elsie said, "I guess we'd better not tell them about sneaking Pooker into my bedroom at night."

"Better not let them know about losing your necklace."

"Probably shouldn't mention our illegal time travel."

"Or Larry."

"Or about catching Instructor Gerard smuggling."

"Not to mention him trying to flaser us and nearly sending us back in time to the Vlemutz Wars."

"Is there anything we can tell them?" Elsie asked.

"I guess we could tell them about the time-travel field trip. That wasn't a secret."

"Yeah, that's good," she agreed. "We could tell them about our room avatars. They're pretty zeller."

"You're right."

"We could mention the food; it's not bad."

They sat down to write a response, doing their best to keep it excited and peaceful, safe and entertaining all at the same time.

"Dear Mom and Dad: We are so happy to hear from you. It sounds as if you are dealing with quite enough excitement for a whole galaxy of humanoids. You'll be glad to know that we are making friends and learning to coexist with our new dorm roommates. As you would expect, life here is very peaceful, and of course, very safe. You couldn't have picked a better place for us to stay while you are so far away. You won't believe it, but we got to go on a timed field trip. It was zetta zeller. We went back to this same area in 2002. We both have awesome avatars in our rooms. Everest's is kind of like a troll. His name is Folgar. Elsie's avatar is a unicorn-humanoid creature named Melista. The food here is great. Almost as good as home-cooked."

Elsie cocked her head. "Did we lay it on too thick?"

"I don't think so, but it's lucky we're bringing the letter to a close."

"Yeah...We love you tons and miss you all the time. Lots of love, Elsie and Everest."

"I'd end it Everest and Elsie."

"Ha, ha, ha!" Elsie sighed. "I wish we could tell Mom and Dad about everything that has happened."

"I wish they would come home."

"Yeah, me too." Elsie slid a sideways glance at Everest. "Only, it would feel strange. You know, to have them back and have to leave this place so soon."

Everest grimaced. "Yeah, we'd be zetta bored."

"Poor Mom and Dad. They have no idea what they've gotten us into."

"True, but the Baskers *can* and *will* handle anything." They both laughed.

EPILOGUE

Mr. Snickers Conspires with Captain Reeses

In another private conversation—a holocomm—there was less laughter and much more recrimination.

"Captain Reeses, you chose unwisely with Mr. Kisses," said Mr. Snickers, his voice disguised.

"I wholeheartedly agree." Reeses' voice was also masked. "Clearly, one must never delegate a truly important matter."

"As pleased as I am that you've turned this into a learning exercise, I'm afraid that does nothing to improve the disposition of my very unhappy clients. Is there anything you can do to boost their spirits?"

There was a slight pause.

"The box was confiscated by the cyborg police, and the academy is under surveillance at the moment."

"Pity."

"It is indeed."

Mr. Snickers clenched his fists, wishing he could at least have the satisfaction of wringing Captain Reeses' neck. Even more satisfying would have been to get his hands on one or all of those pesky children. He took a deep breath. Losing one's temper never solved anything. The key to success was to always have more than one venture in progress at any given time. If one scheme failed, the other would surely succeed.

"What about our other collaboration?" Mr. Snickers asked calmly. "Are you any closer to providing me with the information I require?"

Reeses hesitated again. "I'm afraid it has proven more difficult than I originally anticipated."

"You surprise me."

"It is harder than one might think."

"Perhaps you aren't trying hard enough," growled Mr. Snickers.

"I assure you, I am doing my utmost." Captain Reeses fought back a surge of fear.

"Very well. I will look forward to your next report. By then, I expect to have good news on at least one front."

"You can count on it."

With that, Mr. Snickers cut off the holocomm.

Leaning back, he drummed fingers against his throne chair.

Mr. Snickers had learned through experience that if you waited long enough, there was always an opportunity for payback.

CPSIA information can be obtained
at www.ICGtesting.com
Printed in the USA
FSOW02n1522161015
12259FS